# MURDER BY THE BADGE

RAYNE ROMO

Copyright 2018 Author Name



Paperback ISBN: 978-1-64184-929-6

ebook ISBN: 978-1-64184-930-2

• • • | • • •

JAKE LONG SAT on his horse, looking out over the vast expanse of the Oregon land spread out before him. He sighed, taking a deep breath of the fresh air. Jake hadn't felt this peaceful in a very long time. He didn't ever remember feeling this serene. Being a homicide detective wasn't exactly known for it's peace and quiet. He loved his job as a detective in the Los Angeles Police Department, but it took a toll on his life. Not only did Jake lose his wife Sara, to his job, he lost her to the very same serial killer he spent most of his career tracking down. She was murdered by her very own half brother, one that no one even knew about. Jake became so obsessed with catching the killer, and putting him away for life, Sara left him. Jake did get the killer eventually, but not until he had kidnapped Ann, Sara's sister, and Jenny, Jake and Sara's daughter. The killer held them hostage and drugged them. That was too close for comfort.

• • •

When they got married, Sara hadn't wanted Jake to become a cop, especially a homicide detective. Sara, along with her sister Ann, were raised by a father who was a detective. Sara knew all too well what happened when the job overshadowed family life. Her father, Joe, had an affair with his partner, Liz Rommel. He had a son with her, and was murdered by Liz's husband, Kurt. Their son, Billy, was the serial killer Jake sought for so many years. Billy not only killed Sara, but murdered seven other people.

● ● ●

Jake was happy that he retired from the homicide unit, but he knew he had to figure out what to do with his life from here on out. He couldn't live on his brother's ranch forever, even if Sam said it was fine with him.

Jake glanced over at the rider sitting quietly on the horse next to him. He had to smile. His daughter, Jenny, had grown into a beautiful young lady, despite her confusing childhood. Sara had given birth to Jenny without telling Jake about her. Jenny was told that her father had died, so she never knew him when she was young. They only found out about each other after Sara's death. Jenny was fifteen at that time. They had grown close in the past three years.

Jenny saw him smiling at her, and looked at him questionably. "What are you thinking about Dad? You are looking at me funny."

"I know, I'm just so proud of you, graduating with honors from high school, getting ready to move on with your education. You're a very gifted and talented girl. What are you going to do after college?"

"Well, I think you know the answer to that. You know I want to be in law enforcement, I just don't know what part of law enforcement yet. I was thinking either cold case, or maybe even just be a private investigator. With my abilities, I think I could really make a difference in the cold case unit. Do you think anyone would accept the fact that I can talk to dead people?"

Jake chose his words carefully. "Well, first and foremost, you will do great in any field you choose. I'm very proud that you want to follow in my footsteps, but you need to realize that any field of police work will be grueling. You know better than anyone what it does to a family, and what it does to you personally. As far as if people will accept your gift, you may want to think long and hard about making it known you even have it. I'm not saying you shouldn't use it, I know how much help it was to me in the serial killer case. You, and your mother of course, basically told me who the killer was, and I'll be forever grateful for that."

"I know people will be skeptical at first, but I can prove to them that it's real. I know what you're saying though, there are too many nonbelievers out there. That's why I'm leaning towards being a private investigator. I can be on my own and use my abilities whenever I want. I should say, whenever they come to me. I could also start up my agency right now. I don't have to wait until I graduate from college. Eighteen is the age in Oregon to be a private eye. If I do that, would you want to help me out Dad? I could be the brains and you could be the brawn."

Jake laughed, and nodded. "Maybe...I could help you out with the local police, too. I made some connections here when Sara got killed."

"Well, there, you just helped me make my decision. I'll take some classes in criminal law, and find someone who can teach me the ropes." Jenny grinned at her dad. "Which will be you, and I'll get my necessary training in Oregon to become a private investigator. I can take some classes while I work. With you there, I can kill two birds with one stone."

"Like I said, whatever you want to do, you should go for it, and I'll help in any way I can." Jake took one last look at his beautiful surroundings. "Well, I suppose we had better get back to the house before it gets too dark."

They turned toward home, and the horses wanted to run. The horses knew they were going to get brushed and fed when they returned to the ranch, and were wanting to get home. Jake looked at Jenny, smiled, and let his horse run. She spurred her horse on, and they galloped side by side, enjoying the wind in their faces. They slowed to a trot as they crested a hill, and Jake reined his horse in. He always enjoyed sitting here and looking over the ranch spread out below. Sam had added on five more buildings and another barn to hold the horses and tack.

The Long ranch was set up to help the families of fallen law enforcement and even some policemen who were injured in the line of duty. Sam took them in. Part of their therapy was taking care of the livestock, and learning different skills that helped them cope with their losses. They had weekly therapy sessions with a psychologist, and lived in the many outlying cabins surrounding the huge log home that Sam, Ann, Jake, and Jenny lived in. The Long Ranch was becoming very well known in the Portland area. It was starting to bring people in from the surrounding areas as well. Even as far away as Los Angeles. Jake had even worked with some of the men there.

Jake was very proud of his brother and his desire to help out people in need. Jake, Sam, and their older brother Tom were raised in a loving family with a father who was a police-man. They had a loving mother, who enjoyed being a cop's wife. Even when their father couldn't make it to the three boys' sporting events, their mom was always there. Not that their dad missed very many of his sons' various activities. Jake always knew that when he looked in the audience he would see his mom and dad standing or sitting in the same place, cheering loudly for him or Sam. His older brother Tom was the same way. All three boys were raised to respect the law. Two of them followed in their father's footsteps and became policemen. Sam had picked a different path, but he still helped out law enforcement people in need, so he still was involved in the field.

Speaking of Sam, Jake could see him pitching hay in the corral. There was no sign of Ann, but Jake figured she was nearby. The two of them were becoming pretty close. Jake was hoping Sam and Ann would overcome their shyness and admit that they were attracted to each other. He figured it was just a matter of time before that happened, and Jake was happy for them both. They both deserved happiness, and Ann had been through a lot. She was so young when her parents died. When she grew into a rebellious teenager, she got hooked up with the wrong crowd. Sara tried to get her on the straight and narrow, but when Ann moved to Portland, she got on drugs and was even homeless for a brief time. Jake was almost glad Sara came here and helped her sister out. The two sisters grew very close at the end. If it wasn't for Sam, Ann may have fallen back into her old habits when Sara was killed. She took it very hard, but she knew that she had to be strong, and Ann pulled through okay.

Every time Jake thought of Sara, it made him sad, he missed her so much. Granted, they hadn't seen each other much for fifteen years, but he still loved her. Jake found out after Sara's death that she still loved him too. She was finally going to share the fact that they had a daughter, when she was so brutally taken from this world. Jake just wished he would have tried harder to connect with Sara after she left him. That just goes to show that life is way too short to let stubbornness take over. He shook off the sadness and regret, as he and Jenny made their way down the hill to the corral and tack room.

Sam waved when they got closer. "Hey, you two. Did you have a nice ride?"

Jake stopped his horse and got off, helping Jenny dismount when she stopped beside him. Jenny walked the horses into the barn to start their rub down, while Jake stopped by his brother and grabbed a pitch fork.

"Yes, as usual. I can see why you love it here so much. It's breathtaking scenery, and these horses are so well behaved it's like you don't even have to do anything, they just go."

"I need them well trained because most of the people here are novice horseback riders and need a docile animal to ride. The kids love the ponies and they train hard to learn the ropes. The horses also get to know the various people here, because they feed and brush them daily. It's a win-win for the horse, and rider."

Jake nodded. "You've got quite the set up here, Sam. Have I told you how proud I am of you?"

Sam laughed and ducked his head. "Yes, you have, many times. Like I said, I have a lot of help from a lot of different people to make this ranch work. I absolutely love it here. The cattle drives are fun, and bring in extra income, too. Are you going to be ready to go on the next ride when the time comes?"

"Yes, I will. I hope you don't mind me hanging out here for a while longer. Jen is going to start her own private investigation agency. She wants to be a private eye. Do you believe that? I said I would help her out, so if I could stay out here that would be great."

"You're welcome to stay here as long as you want. Jenny is welcome too. For the record, I think she will make a kick ass private eye."

"I do too, Sam, but I'm still worried that she'll end up like me. I'll support her in any way I can. I just worry, that's all."

Sam put his arm on Jake's shoulder. "Welcome to fatherhood Jake. You will never stop worrying about her, no matter how old she gets."

Jake scoffed. "You sound like you know what you're talking about Sam. You would have been a great dad you know."

"Yeah, well, it wasn't meant to be I guess. I can be a dad to all of these kids at the ranch who need me."

"That you can Sam, that you can."

The two men finished their work in silence, pitching hay, and carrying buckets of oats to the various troughs for the horses to eat. The crickets were chirping as daylight waned, and a bright, full moon promised to brighten the night sky with its glow. By the time Jenny and the others got done brushing the horses, Jake was starting to get hungry.

"What's for supper tonight? I'm starving. All of this fresh air sure gives me an appetite."

"I wouldn't blame just the fresh air Jake, you've always had an appetite. We are going to barbecue steaks and Ann made a salad, homemade bread, and chocolate cake for dessert. I don't know where Ann learned to cook, but I like it."

"You need to marry that girl, Sam. Put a ring on her finger before someone else does."

Sam blushed, and Jake laughed, slapping him on the back. "Are you sure you're my brother? Neither Tom or I are as shy around girls as you are. But seriously, we aren't getting any younger you know, and Ann isn't going to hang around forever, waiting for you."

Sam just shook his head and changed the subject. "Come on, let's go see if the steaks are ready to go on the grill."

Jenny caught up to them after she got the horses bedded down. "I sure love it here at the ranch Uncle Sam. I loved Los Angeles, but I missed the animals and all of the sounds in the country. And that moon, just look at it!"

They paused at the deck and looked up at the full moon. It was a bright orange now, and you could barely see the stars because it was giving off so much light. Ann came out and joined them, and they just stood looking up at the sky. Finally, Ann broke the silence.

"As much as I would like to stand out here all night and stare at the moon, I'm hungry. The steaks have been marinating all day. They are ready to go on the grill, which is your job Sam. I've got everything else ready to go, so go get washed up now."

"Yes, ma'am! I'm on it." Sam didn't waste any more time, his stomach growling right on cue. They laughed, and the group headed in to get ready for supper. It was delicious, as usual. When they were done eating, Jake leaned back in his chair and patted his stomach.

"I think I've gained twenty pounds since I got here. You sure know how to cook Ann, I haven't had a bad meal yet. I'm going to have to start working out if I stay here much longer."

Sam smiled broadly at Ann when she blushed, and thanked Jake for the compliment. "She's the best, I don't know what I'd do without her here to tell you the truth."

Ann smiled at Sam, and Jake could see the love in her eyes. He couldn't believe Sam was too blind to notice it.

"Well, I thank both of you, but you need to stop with the compliments. It's going to go straight to my head. One thing you can do though, is help with dishes."

Sam and Jake nodded, picking up the dirty dishes and stacking them by the sink to go into the dishwasher. As Jenny helped Ann put them in, the two men grabbed a cup of coffee and headed for the deck. It was a nightly ritual, and they wouldn't trade it for the world. The huge wraparound deck gave them a great view of the night sky and the surrounding area. As the two men kicked back and put their feet on the railing of the deck, Sam looked at his brother. He couldn't help but ask him what he was thinking about.

Jake closed his eyes. "Nothing really, I'm mostly just thinking about my daughter, and how good she turned out after all of the turmoil in her life. Getting kidnapped by a madman, seeing him shot right before her eyes. It could have been so much worse. I'm just glad that part of our lives is over."

"I agree with you on that one. Ann is doing well too, after all that she went through. I'm so glad she didn't have any residual effects from the drugs Billy gave her. That was too close for comfort Jake." Sam rubbed his chin thoughtfully. "You know, you are right about one thing though."

"I'm right about a lot of things Sam, you need to be more specific."

Sam couldn't help but laugh at that comment. "What I mean is, you were right about life being too short to waste time. I don't think there is ever a *just right* time for love to enter a person's life. I do love Ann you know, and I think she loves me too. She does love me, don't you think?"

Jake burst out laughing. "Oh Sam, you're so dense sometimes I can't believe it! Of course she loves you, you can tell that by the way she looks at you. Open your eyes sometime and see for yourself, you dope."

"Yeah, I guess you're right there. Jake, I think I'm going to ask her to marry me." Sam paused for a moment. "I'm really nervous, what if she says no?"

Jake sat up straight in his chair, a more serious look on his face now. "Sam, she may say no, but I really don't think she will. I think she's been sticking around here, just waiting for you to ask. Besides, it wouldn't hurt to try. When are you going to do this?"

"No time like the present, I always say. I've had a ring for a couple of years now, just waiting for the right moment. I'm tired of waiting, I'm going to ask her tonight. Right now, as a matter of fact."

Sam jumped up. "I've gotta go Jake. See ya later." He rushed off, and Jake could hear him running up the stairs.

Jake whispered to himself as he entered the house. "It's about time brother, it's about time."

When Jake woke up the next day the sun was just starting to rise over the horizon, and the birds were singing. *It's going to be a great day.* Jake thought as he brushed his teeth and got ready to go help with chores. As he headed downstairs, he could hear voices in the kitchen. That was nothing new, the kitchen was the meeting place in this house. Everyone was gathered around the table, and he could see that Sam and Ann both had huge grins on their faces. Jake knew he didn't even have to ask, but he did anyway. "So, what's new?"

Sam grinned even broader, and looked over at Ann, who was nudging him with her elbow. "Ouch! Okay, okay. Well, we were waiting for you to come down before we announced it, but now that everyone is here…"

"Just spit it out Sam!" Jake and Jenny were in unison yelling at him.

"Okay. Ann and I are engaged!"

Jenny screamed, jumping up. She hugged Ann as they both jumped up and down. Jake walked over and hugged his brother, whispering in his ear. "I'm so happy for you Sam. Congratulations."

After the girls stopped jumping around, and Jake felt it was safe, he hugged Ann and congratulated her, too. Jake couldn't help but give her a little grief. "Are you sure you want to be stuck with my brother for the rest of your life?"

Ann laughed. "I'm sure Jake. I've been waiting a long time for him to wise up and ask me to marry him. I thought I might have to ask him for a while there."

Sam piped up when he heard her say that. "You should have, I *might* have said yes."

Ann punched him in the arm and giggled, looking down at her beautiful ring. Jenny rushed back over to her and grabbed her hand, oohing and aahing over her engagement ring. "It's so beautiful Ann, I'm so happy for you. Now we get to plan a wedding! When is it going to be? Soon, I hope, you two have wasted enough time."

"It is going to be soon, next month to be exact. I don't want to give her time to change her mind." Sam kissed Ann and they looked into each other's eyes. It reminded Jake how it was with Sara and him in the beginning.

Sam interrupted his thoughts, almost like he was reading Jake's mind. "Which reminds me. Jake, will you be my best man?"

Jake was a little choked up when he answered. "I would be honored Sam. I really am very happy for you both."

Now it was Ann's turn to interrupt. "Jenny, will you be my maid of honor?"

Jenny squealed, and everyone covered their ears. Running to Ann for another hug, she squealed again. "Of course Ann! I would be honored, and happy, to be your maid of honor!"

"Great! Thank you Jenny. We are going to have the wedding right here on the ranch. We love it here, and I have had the perfect place picked out for a long time now." She gave Sam a sidelong look.

Sam backed away with his hands up. "Okay, I got it, I waited too long to ask you to marry me. You don't need to keep reminding me. Now where is this perfect place? Don't I get a say in it?"

"Of course you do…well…maybe not." Ann laughed. "I want to get married down by the creek where that huge old oak tree is. It's not only the place where we always have our picnics, it's also where I go to get some peace and quiet. I just love it there, it's so beautiful. What do you think Sam?"

"It sounds perfect to me. Whatever you want. Well, we'll leave you two to make the plans, Jake and I need to get chores done. Some of the ranch hands are already out there." Sam kissed her again and as they headed out the door, he turned back. "I love you Ann, I always have. I hope you know that."

"I love you too, Sam, and yes, I have always known."

$$\bullet\bullet\bullet\ 2\ \bullet\bullet\bullet$$

ANN AND JENNY were enjoying their shopping trip in Portland. Ann had already found her wedding dress, and they were now shopping for Jenny's bridesmaid dress. Ann wanted rainbow colors for her wedding, so they were looking for a light yellow dress for Jen.

"I don't know about you, but I'm starving!" Ann patted her flat stomach. "Let's go grab a burger, all of this shopping is making me hungry."

"Yes, that sounds great! Shopping is hard work, and we need to conserve our energy." Jenny grabbed Ann's hand and they took off for the nearest burger joint.

After they ordered, they picked a table outside in the sun and waited for their food. Ann decided now was as good of a time as any to talk to Jen about her job choice. "Jenny, I've been meaning to talk to you about something. Are you sure you want to go into law enforcement? I know you were young when your mom died, but surely you remember the stories I've told you about how your dad's job ruined their marriage. Sara loved him, but she just couldn't take that life style. His obsession over his cases, his drinking, never being home. Don't you want a family some day? Children of your own? You need to think long and hard about this. Have you done that? I'm not trying to discourage you, I just want you to be sure, that's all."

Jenny knew what her aunt was saying, and she answered her truthfully. "Of course I remember everything you told me about what my mom went through Ann. It hasn't been that long since my mom died. I understand what you're saying, and I agree. I know I need to think about my decision, but as you know, this is something I've always wanted to do. It's in my blood. I do want a family some day. A husband, and children. I'm hoping I can do both. That's why I'm going with the private investigator route. I can make my own decisions on what cases I want to take. With Dad's help, I know I can make a go of it. It won't be as dangerous as regular police work, well, at least I don't think so."

Ann raised her eyebrows, and Jen threw her hands up. "Okay, okay, the job will have its dangers too. But that's okay, I can handle it. I can handle a job, and family, I know it. I'm not going to turn out like my mom and dad. I'll find a husband who can handle my job too, maybe even be a partner. I appreciate your worrying about me, but I'm sure this is what I want to do."

"Okay, I just wanted to make sure you understood the price of the job that's all. I think you can do anything you put your mind to Jen. We are so proud of the young woman you've become. Now, here come our burgers, no more talking."

The girls laughed, digging into their food. They polished off their burgers, and headed down the street to finish their shopping trip. It didn't take long to find Jen's dress, and shoes to match. Jenny was excited. "This is going to be the most beautiful wedding, Ann. I can't wait to see Sam's face when he sees you walking down the aisle in that dress. Getting married outside is so romantic, I hope the weather cooperates."

"I know it will, nothing is going to ruin our big day! I can hardly wait, only two more weeks and I'll be Mrs. Sam Long. I've waited so long for this. I'm so happy Jen. I have loved every moment of planning for this wedding. The food, the decorations, the dresses, everything. It's going to be a small wedding, but it'll be perfect, I just know it."

"I agree, are you going to write your own vows?"

"Of course, I only hope Sam can handle it. He's not the best with words. He may need some help. Oh, well, he'll figure something out. It could be interesting though. Well, we'd better get back to the ranch before the men think that we aren't going to feed them. That would be a disaster!"

Ann and Jenny walked back to the car arm in arm and Jenny looked up at her aunt before they got in. "Ann, I know this sounds weird, but can we go by the place where Mom died? I can't go all the way to Los Angeles very often to visit her grave, and this is as close as I can get to feeling close to her. I know it's just an empty lot now, but sometimes, I just like to go there and talk to her for a while, you know."

"I understand what you mean, and yes, we can go there now."

As they drove up to the empty lot where Sara lost her life, the mood turned solemn. The two women stepped out of the car and approached the area where a house once stood. Even though it had been almost three years, Jenny could still imagine the smell of the smoke in the air. Ann and her just stood in silence, and they both said a small prayer. Jenny couldn't help but feel the sadness that hung over the area. She sighed, and looked over at Ann, who was wiping away a tear. "Okay, enough sadness for this day. We are suppose to be celebrating a wedding. Besides, I still talk to Mom all the time, remember? She's going to be with us every step of your wedding. Now, I'm ready to get out of here."

Jenny took one last look as they drove away. Her mom was always with her, and always would be. This place is nothing but an empty lot, it was time to let it go.

By the time they got back to the Long Ranch, Ann and Jen had let the sadness go and were back to giggling and talking about all of the things they did that day. They snuck the wedding dress into the house so Sam couldn't see it. Ann went into the kitchen to check on the roast that she had put in the crock pot before they left. When she lifted the lid, the smell of the tender, seasoned roast beef wafted through the air. Sam entered the kitchen and took a whiff of the perfectly seasoned beef. "Oh boy, just the smell of that makes me hungry! I can hardly wait for supper."

He put his arms around Ann's waist and hugged her. "How was your day? Did you find a dress?"

Ann hugged Sam back, loving the feel of his arms around her. "I did, and no, you can't see it, so don't even ask."

"I wasn't going to ask to see it. I can wait until the wedding day. Besides, I know you will look beautiful in whatever you wear. Did you have a good day?"

"We certainly did. We got a lot done. These next two weeks are going to be busy, but I'm loving every minute of it. Have you contacted the minister and the band like I asked you to?"

"Of course. It's all set. Even the ranch hands are chipping in. They knew of a good band, who just so happens to have an opening that day. We are setting up a dance floor, complete with lights. What did you think, I was sitting here doing nothing?"

"No, I didn't think that, I guess I'm getting a bit anxious. I want everything to be perfect."

Sam hugged her again. "It will be perfect, no matter what, I promise. Now, get the rest of supper cooking. You're going to have a couple of hungry men coming here in just a few hours who need a hearty meal. Get going woman!"

Ann laughed. "Yes sir! I'll get right on it."

Sam was smiling when he walked out the door. His ranch foreman, Booker, was headed in his direction. "Hey Boss. I was just checking in with you to find out what you want done with the load of hay we have coming in tomorrow. Which pen do you want it in?"

"The west pen will be fine, Booker. By the way, have you seen Phil Carson lately? How is he doing? I know he is having trouble settling in. Is he doing okay? How about his family, his daughter Abby, and his wife Cara?" Phil was a police officer who had been shot in the line of duty. Him, along with his wife, Cara, and their daughter, Abby, lived in one of the cabins on the ranch.

Booker took off his cowboy hat and slapped it on his leg to get the dust off. "He's having a hard time, I'm afraid. His daughter and wife are adapting well, but he is having trouble accepting his handicap. I'm sure being a cop one day and in a wheelchair the next is hard to accept, but he's trying to stay strong for his family. I'm going to get him on old Red one of these days, if he feels up to it. That horse is one of a kind boss. He is so gentle with the handicapped people, it's like he knows that he needs to be extra careful. Pretty special horse, we need more like him."

"I'm working on that Booker. But, for now, he's all we've got for that type of rider. I think we need to concentrate on getting Phil on him and feeling some freedom. After the shooting took his ability to walk, he has been depressed and angry. I really think this will help him a lot. Let's get that done as soon as possible."

Just as they got done talking, a rambunctious ten year old girl came bounding towards them. You could tell who it was from quite a distance with her red hair gleaming in the sun. She had it in pig tails today, and she was grinning from ear to ear. "Mr. Sam, Mr. Booker. My mom told me I could try riding a horse today if it was okay with you! Can I? Can I please?"

Sam got down on one knee and grinned at Abby. "Whoa, slow down there little cowgirl. It's a little late today, but I'll talk to your mom and dad and find out what they want to do. If they say it's okay, then it's fine with me, but we had better wait for morning. Maybe your dad can ride with you, how about that?"

Abby frowned. "I don't think Daddy wants to ride horse Mr. Sam. He's always sad, and I heard him and Mommy yelling last night. I think he is mad at me, I heard my name when they were yelling at each other.”

“Oh, Abby, they aren’t mad at you. I think your dad just needs some time to get used to not being able to walk anymore, you know? I think we should go and talk to him right now, and see if he wants to try to get on Red in the morning, what do you think?”

“Yeah! I think he will want to. Let’s go ask him right now!” Abby turned around and starting running as fast as she could go.

Sam turned to Booker, setting up the time for the Carson’s ride. “Booker, on second thought, why don’t you get Buffy ready right now. I think there is time tonight to let Abby get started with her training.” Sam turned back to see Abby already half way to the cabin. He was going to get Phil on that horse tomorrow if it took him all day.

By the time Sam caught up to Abby, she was flinging open the door to their cabin. “Daddy, Mommy, Mr. Sam said I could ride Buffy if it was alright with you! Can I, please? Please say yes.”

Sam knocked, letting them know he was there. Phil and Cara were sitting at the table, they looked to be in a deep conversation. “I’m sorry if I’m interrupting anything, Phil, Cara. Abby just asked me about riding and I told her to check with you two. I think we’ll have to wait until tomorrow, but Booker is getting Buffy tied up and we can start the training process tonight. What do you think?”

Phil pushed his wheelchair away from the table and Abby jumped up on his lap. “Please Daddy? Mr. Sam said you could go with me, and we could both ride horses, doesn’t that sound fun Daddy?”

Phil Carson looked down at his daughter lovingly. “Well, I don’t know about me, but I think it would be okay if you ride little Buffy. But you have to stay in the corral, deal?” Phil looked over at Cara. “Sound okay honey?”

Cara smiled at her daughter. "Yes, that would be okay, as long as Sam or Booker is there with you, and you listen to everything he tells you, promise?"

Abby squealed. "I promise Mommy. Daddy will you come with us? If you don't want to ride, you can still watch me. I know I'll be the best rider ever, won't I Mr. Sam?"

"I bet you will be Abby, and Buffy will love you."

Abby jumped down off her dad's lap. "I have to go get my new boots on, and my cowboy hat of course."

While Abby went to get changed, Sam took the opportunity to talk to Phil a little bit. "So, Phil, are you sure you don't want to try out Big Red? He is gentle as can be, and is trained to handle people in your condition."

Sam could see Phil bristle at his words. "Well, people in *my condition* don't need anybody's charity, or some well trained horse to make us feel better. So, for now, I will just watch my daughter ride if you don't mind."

Sam was used to Phil's attitude by now, so he didn't take his words personally. "Listen, Phil, I'm sorry if I offended you, but don't you think it's time to lose that chip on your shoulder? Not only for your sake, but for your wife and daughter as well?"

Phil was a little taken aback, no one had talked to him like that before. "Well, how about we change places for a while and see if you still feel the same way! Now, if you'll excuse me I think I'll go help my daughter."

After Phil left the room, Cara sighed deeply and stood. "I'm sorry Sam, I just don't know if Phil will ever get back to his old self. He means well, it's just that he has a lot on his mind right now. More than just the shooting. Something is going on with him, but he won't talk to me about it. Maybe you could get him to open up."

"Well, I could try, but he won't do that until he's good and ready I'm afraid. I'm going to keep trying to get him on Red. I think that would help a lot. The sense of freedom you feel on a horse is unbelievable and amazing. Phil would love it, I just know it."

"Well, do what you have to do Sam. I'm behind you all the way. I'll do my part to encourage him."

Right then, Abby came skipping out of her bedroom, all dressed up in her cowgirl *duds,* as she called them. Phil was right behind her, looking as if the conversation between he and Sam had never happened. Abby ran up to Sam and grabbed him by the hand. "Let's go Mr. Sam, I'm all ready, and guess what? Daddy, said I could go fast on Buffy if you think I can. Can I go fast Mr. Sam?"

Sam grinned at the little girl. "Probably not today Abby. When you and Buffy get to know each other better, and you practice real hard, you can at least trot, okay?"

Abby frowned, then nodded. "I know I will be a good rider, and Buffy already loves me, I give her apples all the time with Mr. Booker. She loves them!"

Abby took off out the door, dragging Sam along with her. Phil followed, using the ramp Sam and Jake had built for his wheelchair to go down. Her giggles were infectious. Even Phil was grinning when they got to the corral, where Booker already had Buffy tied to the fence. Abby had been learning from Booker how to approach the little pony. She slowly walked up to the horse, her hand outstretched, with a small apple in it. The pony sniffed the apple for just a second, before nipping it out of Abby's palm. Abby giggled, and petted the soft nose of the little pony, easily becoming her best friend.

Sam glanced over at Phil, and caught him smiling at his young daughter's interaction with the pony. "Well, how about we get her saddled up, Abby? That is the first lesson in becoming a horseback rider. Are you ready to start learning the basics?"

"Yes, sir, Mr. Sam. I'm ready, let's go." She looked up at the sky. "It's not dark yet, can I ride Buffy for just a little while? Please?"

Sam looked at Phil. "I think that would be okay. Would you like to come along Phil? You could learn along with your daughter."

Phil thought about it for a minute. "I have no desire to ride a horse, Sam. They actually scare me a little. They are awfully big animals."

"Yes, they are, but they are also very smart. If you show respect and kindness to them, and learn how to control them, they will show you respect also. They are very well-trained animals. I wouldn't put you on one that I didn't trust. I'm not saying that there isn't a chance of something happening. There always is. The horse could shy from something, or sense something is wrong and balk. That's why you always have to be aware of your surroundings when you're on a horse. Right Abby?"

The little girl was listening intently to what Sam was saying. "Right, Mr. Sam." She turned to her dad. "I know you can do it Daddy. You are the best, and Red is so sweet. I know he will love you."

Phil almost looked as if he was going to give in, but shook his head at the last moment. He grabbed Abby by the hands. "I might try it later on honey, but for now, let's just get you going on Buffy okay?"

Abby frowned a little, but perked up when Buffy nuzzled her shoulder. She turned to see Booker carrying the small saddle towards them. "Okay Daddy. You can watch me and learn how I do it, then you can try, deal?"

"Deal, now let's get to it."

Abby turned to where Buffy was tied to the fence. She watched intently, as Booker showed her how to put on the saddle blanket, and pull the cinch tight so the saddle wouldn't fall off.

Sam sat with Phil while Abby got it on the first try. "She is very smart, and determined. You must be very proud of her. She's gonna do great."

"I am proud of her, she's about the only one who has taken my shooting in stride. She is young though. Life hasn't given her too many blows yet. I won't always be here to protect her, you know. Sam, promise me if anything ever happens to me, you'll continue to watch out for my wife and daughter."

Sam was shocked at his tone of voice. "Of course I will, but nothing is going to happen to you Phil. You're safe here on the ranch. You need to put what happened behind you and move on. It's not healthy to keep dwelling on things. The shooting was unavoidable, and it's part of the job. That man was hauling drugs back and forth from Mexico for a long time. You were doing your job when you encountered him on that road. It wasn't your fault Phil, you couldn't have known he had a gun hidden in his console. It was just a routine traffic stop up until that point. You managed to call for backup and get him arrested. You're a good cop, and a good man, remember that."

Phil bristled, giving Sam a long look. "I know it wasn't my fault, but that doesn't mean that I couldn't have prevented it from happening. I should have waited for back up, when his plate came back as a stolen car. I was cocky, and thought I could handle him alone. Well, I proved myself wrong there, didn't I?" With that, Phil turned, wheeling over closer to where he could watch Abby ride around the corral. "You're doing great honey, keep it up."

"Well, I guess that conversation is over." Sam whispered to himself. He made a note to talk to Jake and see if he could sneak in a conversation with Phil. Maybe if he talked to him cop to cop, Jake could get through to him better than he did.

The two men were silent now, as they watched Abby go round and round in the corral. Booker was always close by in case something happened. Sam looked toward the road leading into the ranch, when he noticed dust pluming up from a vehicle approaching. He got Booker's attention. "Someone is coming Booker, were you expecting anyone?"

"No, not today."

"Okay, I need to go see what's up. You okay here without me?"

"Yep, Abby here doesn't even need me. She's a natural, boss."

"I can see that. I think it's time to show Abby how to unsaddle her and get Buffy brushed and ready for her stall. It's close to suppertime."

He nodded at Phil, and walked towards the house, where a little red car was just pulling up. A woman stepped out, looking up at the house, just as Jake and Jenny were walking out the door. Jenny squealed and ran towards her.

"Dr. Nancy! I'm so glad to see you." Jen hugged her, and Jake grinned and hugged her too.

Sam approached them and smiled at the scene. He always thought Jake and Dr. Hall would make a nice couple, and Jenny loved her. She helped them both a lot when Sara was killed, and she also helped Jenny with her abilities. Dr. Hall was a great psychologist. Along with her main duties, she helps people with abilities like Jen's to cope with them better. They learn how to control the visions and voices that often plague the people who are born with this gift. She grew very close to Jenny and Jake, especially Jake, Sam thought. Sam was very happy to see her.

"Nancy, it's so good to see you. I'm glad you're here, but how on earth did you find the ranch so easily? You must have an inside source." He looked at Jake, who just shrugged. Jenny spoke up.

"Okay, I confess, it was me. I hope it's okay Sam. I invited Dr. Hall here for the wedding, but I also have an ulterior motive. I really need her help with understanding my gift, and she is the only one I trust. I figured I was killing two birds with one stone, so to speak."

Nancy laughed nervously. "I'm sorry, Sam. I thought you knew I was coming! I can always get a room in town if you don't have room for me here. I'm not sure what Jen was thinking, inviting me here without telling anyone." She glared at Jenny. "Thanks, Jen, for putting Sam and me in a tough situation."

Jenny blushed, and Sam couldn't help but let her squirm a little before answering. "It's fine Nancy. I would never allow you to stay anywhere else but here. We have plenty of room."

Jenny breathed a sigh of relief. "There, it's settled. No problem. Come on Dr. Hall, I'll show you to your room."

Jake stepped over to the car and opened the trunk. "We'll grab your bags Nancy. You go get settled in."

"Thank you Jake, and thank you, Sam for your hospitality. Where is the blushing bride to be?"

Now it was Sam's turn to blush. "She is inside, getting supper going. You're just in time. Ann is a great cook."

"I'm sure she is. Ann is a wonderful person, Sam. I'm so happy for you both. These next two weeks are going to be busy. I want to help out as much as I can."

"I'm sure she'll appreciate the help. Let's get you settled in before supper is ready."

The group walked into the house, laughing and joking. Ann came out of the kitchen and hugged Nancy. "I'm so glad you're here. I'm sorry I didn't come out to greet you, I was in the middle of getting supper ready. Which it is, by the way. Everyone get washed up. It's nothing fancy, but if you're hungry Nancy, come on down when you're ready."

"Actually, I am hungry, it's a long drive from Los Angeles." She glanced at Jen. "If you'll show me to my room, I'll change clothes and be right down."

Jake grabbed her luggage from Sam, and looked over at Jenny. "I'll handle this. Sam, you and Jen go and help your fiancé."

Sam grinned, and saluted. "Yes sir!"

Jake punched him in the arm and headed for the staircase. "After you, Dr. Hall."

"Why thank you, kind sir. By the way, you have a beautiful home here Sam and Ann. I'm going to love helping you with your wedding Ann. It's okay if I help, right? I've never even been a part of a wedding before, so I'm looking forward to this very much."

"Of course you can help. I am going to need all the help I can get. This is my only family, and we are already overwhelmed with it all. We pretty much have everything arranged, but I'll need help with the food and decorations for sure."

"Great! Well, I'll see you in a little bit then."

Nancy turned and started up the huge staircase. Jake was right behind her, and when they got to the top of the stairs, he directed her to a room just across the hall from Jen.

"This room will work great for you Nancy. Right across from Jen, and I'm just down the hall. You have a private bathroom, and can look straight out to the corrals and pastures. It's a beautiful view."

Nancy gasped when she walked into the room. It was painted a pale yellow and decorated with sunny portraits of sunflowers and yellow curtains. The bedspread was white, with yellow sunflowers on it. "This is beautiful Jake. I am going to love it here, I won't want to leave."

Jake stepped in and shut the door behind him. "Okay Nancy, spill. Why are you really here?"

••• 3 •••

NANCY LOOKED AT Jake innocently. "What do you mean? You heard Jen. She asked me to come and help her with her abilities, and be here for the wedding, that's all."

Jake sighed. "Listen, it's not that I'm not glad to see you, I really am, but I know my daughter. Now why are you really here?"

"Okay, fine. Jenny is worried about you. With the wedding coming up, and Sam and Ann finally getting together, she felt like you may need someone to talk to. I'm sure your thoughts have been with Sara, am I wrong?"

Jake ran his hands through his hair and let out a frustrated breath. "I am always thinking of Sara. Yes, Ann and Sam getting married has brought back some memories of my own wedding, but I'm fine. Sam and Ann deserve to be happy, and frankly, it's about time they got married." Jake frowned. "I hope I'm not the reason they waited so long."

Nancy sat down on the bed, and thought about what to say to Jake. "I don't think you are the reason they waited Jake. I think they needed some time to adjust after Sara's death too. Everyone was affected by her death, not just you. Ann lost a sister, Jen lost her mother, and Sam had to be strong for everyone. I think the timing is right, and you are all ready to move on. I'm not saying to forget Sara, you will never do that, but she would want you all to be happy."

Jake sat down by Nancy on the bed, and took her hands in his. "I agree with everything you're saying. This wedding will be a form of healing for all of us, and I, for one, am very happy for Ann and Sam. I have been feeling a little out of sorts lately, but I think it's more about not having a direction for my life yet. But now, Jen has asked me to help her out when she opens her private detective firm, and I'm going to do that. I have something to look forward to now. I appreciate Jenny worrying about me, but I'm fine, really I am. Now, let's get down there for supper. I'm starving."

"Sounds good Jake. I'm glad you're doing well, but just know, I'm here if you need me."

Jake nodded. He stood, reaching out his hand to help Nancy up. "Sounds good. I'll leave you to freshen up, and I'll meet you downstairs in a little bit then."

"Thanks Jake, I won't be long."

Supper was a jovial affair, with everyone laughing and joking around the big table. Nancy had to stifle a yawn, when they finally pushed away from the table, stomachs full. Ann noticed she was tired, and shooed her away when she offered to help with dishes. "You have had a long drive and I know you're tired. It's almost bed time anyway, you go rest. You can help with breakfast in the morning."

"I am a little tired now. I think I'll take you up on that. I'll see you all in the morning."

Everyone stood as Nancy left for her room. Sam turned to Jake, asking if he would come down to the barn and help him. Jake nodded and they headed out the door.

"Jake, I need to talk to you about something. You know Phil Carson, right?"

"Yeah, I know him. We've talked a little bit. He is pretty messed up over his disability."

"I know, that's why I want you to talk to him. Maybe you can relate more with his situation, being you were both police officers. I know it hasn't been all that long since the shooting, but he really needs to come out of this. Not only for his sake, but for his family. Do you think you could help out with him? Maybe he'll open up to you more than anyone else."

"It's worth a try I guess. I'm no psychiatrist, but I can relate to what he's going through. Blaming yourself, thinking you're not whole. I've seen it a lot, and not just with officers who are injured physically, but mentally too. Yes, I'll try to talk to him, but don't get your hopes up. He is still reeling from his injury. It'll take some time for him to get stronger. Mentally, and physically. He may not want to talk to me, but I'll give it a shot."

"That's all I can ask of you. We really need to try, and it's all I could come up with. I want to get him on Red, but he refuses. I know that would help him feel some freedom. Maybe you can persuade him to try, at least."

"Well, like I said, I'll give it my best shot." Jake looked toward the barn, where Abby was feeding Buffy another apple. "Isn't that his daughter with Buffy? She looks like she is a natural with Buffy. She seems to be adjusting pretty well."

"Yeah, she's young, and they bounce back much faster than we do from tragedy. But she did mention to me that her mom and dad were arguing last night, and she felt it was her fault. She's confused by it all, so I'm glad she has Buffy in her corner."

"That's too bad. One thing I know, if anything will help, riding Buffy, and helping with her care will."

Sam nodded, and the two men waved at Abby as they passed by the corral. Sam gave her a thumbs up, and Abby grinned, giving him a thumbs up back. The rest of the day was spent doing the evening chores, and arranging the bedding for the horses stalls.

The cattle were out to pasture, so Jake and Sam took the four wheelers out to check on them, before calling it a night.

Jake really did love these times spent with his brother. He only wished that Tom would contact them. Sam and Jake had tried to call him about the wedding, but were told that Tom was on a case. That was all they would tell them. Tom was in the FBI now, and Jake figured he was undercover somewhere. They only hoped and prayed he was safe. That's all they could do right now. Until Tom contacted them, their hands were tied.

• • •

The next two weeks went by so fast. Ann was getting nervous, as she waited in the Great Room in their huge log home. Her long, flowing, wedding dress, fitting snugly around her tiny waist. Jenny was by her side, dressed in her beautiful yellow bridesmaid dress. Nancy was flitting about, almost as nervous as Ann was. Ann took a deep breath, and tried to calm herself down, along with everyone else in the room.

"Okay you girls, we need to settle down. I'm about ready to throw up, and you two aren't making it any easier. Look outside, it's a beautiful day, the sun is shining, no rain in sight. We've been working hard, and everything is in place, let's enjoy this now."

Nancy took a deep breath. "I know Ann, but I was so honored that you asked me to be your personal attendant. I just want to make sure nothing goes wrong."

Ann gave her a hug. "You have done a great job Nancy, and I'm so happy you're here. We just need to take a deep breath now, and enjoy the moment, okay?"

So Nancy did just that. Taking a deep breath, she nodded to Ann. "Okay, I'm okay. What time is it? Is the minister here? Is Sam ready to go?"

Ann and Jen laughed. "Yes, like I said, everything is ready to go. In just under an hour, I will be Mrs. Sam Long. I can't believe it. I've waited so long for this day, and I want to thank you both for being by my side. It means a lot to me that you are here."

Jen saw that Ann was starting to tear up, so she stepped to her side and put her arm around her. "We wouldn't want to be anywhere else. Now what do say we go get this gig started?"

Jen suddenly felt a cool breeze and shivered a little. She looked around, startled to see a faint, white mist forming in the corner of the room. She knew what it was before it even formed all the way. Jen knew she was looking at her mom. Sara was here. She closed her eyes and tried to concentrate as hard as she could on the mist. In her mind, she could see her mom. Jen's grandparents were with Sara. They were all smiling, but Jen couldn't hear them say anything, all she could see were their mouths moving. She opened her eyes and turned to Ann.

"Mom is here Ann, along with Grandma and Grandpa. I told you they would be here." She turned to Dr. Hall. "My abilities are getting stronger. I could feel my mom here, and I saw her forming in front of me. I think if we just worked a little harder, I could see and hear them better. After the wedding, I want to get to work on that, but for now, let's get married."

Nancy was going to try and help Jenny, but she didn't know how yet. Jenny was hoping that she could could help strengthen her abilities, but Nancy wasn't sure if she even believed in them. Her personal side wanted to believe, but her professional side wasn't quite sure. Nancy could help Jenny cope with her abilities better. As far as strengthening her abilities, well, Jen was on her own there. In the meantime, Nancy would stay at the ranch, and help with the tenants that stayed here to heal from their traumatic experiences. For now though, she was going to enjoy this wedding.

It was a beautiful wedding, the sun was shining, and a gentle breeze rustled the leaves in the tree where Ann and Sam said their vows. The food was perfect, the music perfect, and Sam was so happy. He looked down at his beautiful wife while he held her close and smiled. "I don't know about you, but I can hardly wait to get out of here. I need some alone time with my wife."

Ann blushed, and smiled back at him. "There will be plenty of time for that later. Right now, I just want to enjoy every minute of this wonderful day. What do you say we dance, Mr. Long."

"Sure thing, Mrs. Long." Sam reached for her hand and Ann glided into his arms.

Suddenly, there was some commotion on the other side of the garden. Sam looked over at his brother, and Jake stood and took off at the sound of Jenny's squeal. Sam joined him after Ann encouraged him to go. He couldn't believe his eyes when he saw Jake and Jen hugging someone.

Sam ran over and joined the fray, shocked at who he saw in the middle of the crowd. "Tom! I can't believe you're here! How did you find out about the wedding? We couldn't get ahold of you. We tried, and your supervisor said you couldn't be reached! I'm so glad you made it, well, sort of made it." Sam hugged his brother, and Tom held him at arms length.

"Well, I got here as soon as I could, Sam. My assignment got resolved earlier than we thought it would, and I requested time off to come stay with you for awhile. Now, where is this beautiful, albeit somewhat crazy, woman who actually married you! I want to say hi to Ann, and warn her about your many bad habits!"

Sam punched him in the shoulder, standing back to look at his brother. Tom was tanned and lean, but Sam could see the bags under his eyes, and the strain around his mouth. He glanced at Jake and noticed that he saw the same thing. It had been years since they had seen their brother, but they had kept in touch by phone and computer. They knew his new job was very stressful, and working undercover wasn't for the faint of heart. Sam and Jake were just ready to ask Tom what his assignment had been, when Ann came over to see what the commotion was all about.

"Sam, what's going on?" When she saw Tom she gasped, and ran to him with her arms open. "Tom! Oh my gosh. I'm so happy to see you. How are you? You look like hell, come and get some food and drink. You need a drink, I can tell. Oh, where are my manners, maybe you need to rest first. I'll show you to a room, and you can clean up and rest before you come back down and party the night away with the rest of us."

Tom held up his hands. "Whoa, wait a minute you guys. Can I get a word in here? First of all, Ann, you are not going to leave your wedding party to make me comfortable. I can take care of myself. Second, just point me towards the house, and I'll find my own way."

Jen butted in just then. "Never mind, both of you! I will show Tom to a room, and you all will go back to the party. I won't accept any arguments from anyone, got it?" They all stood back and gave Jenny a wide path. Jake knew better than to argue with her over this.

"Okay, okay, you do that. We'll see you later Tom, it really is great to have you here with us. We'll bombard you with questions after you have rested a little while, but I hope you come back down and party a little."

"Oh, I will. I don't need much rest, kind of gotten used to it. I won't be long, I promise. Okay Jenny, let's go and leave the newlyweds to their dance."

As the two of them walked away, Jake and Sam looked at each other knowingly. They could tell that their brother was not himself. Jake knew what an undercover went through. You start to forget who you really are sometimes. You had to become someone else in order to catch the bad guys. The fact that Tom was here, showed them that he was deep undercover at one point, and needed to get away from it all. Either way, Jake was glad Tom was here. It will give him time to heal, and try to forget for a little while. Jake and Sam would do what they could to help.

Tom trudged up the stairs behind Jenny, trying to look happy and strong. He knew that his brothers could see right through it all. He knew it was just a matter of time before the questions started. That would have to wait though, he had a wedding dance to attend, and he wasn't going to miss another one. His job had kept him from Jake and Sara's wedding, and even Sara's funeral. He was tired, physically and mentally drained. Tom just needed a little R & R, and he hoped everyone would understand that and leave the questions out. He couldn't answer them anyway. Keeping secrets was part of the job. The more friends and family knew, the more danger they were in.

Jenny stopped in front of a door, and Tom almost ran into her. He was too engrossed in his thoughts. "Oh, sorry Jen. I was just thinking I guess, not paying attention."

"You're fine Uncle Tom. You know, you don't have to come back down if you don't want to. Everyone will understand."

Tom shook his head. "No, I'll be back down. I'm not missing another family get together."

"Okay, well, this is your room. I'll just leave you to it then. I'll see you in a little while." Jen hugged him and left the room without another word.

Tom set his duffle bag on the bed and looked around the room. The bed took up a lot of space. It was huge, and looked very inviting. He headed to the bathroom that was connected to his room. Looking in the mirror, he hardly recognized the face staring back at him.

"Wow, no wonder everyone looked so worried when they saw me. I look like hell." He proceeded to wash his face and grabbed his razor to remove the weeks of stubble growing on his face. Feeling much better when that was done, Tom grabbed a clean towel, and jumped in the shower. The hot water felt good, and not having to look over his shoulder at all times, felt even better. He didn't waste much time getting dressed. Tom wanted to get back down and renew his bond with his brothers, and get to know Ann and Jenny better. That was all he was going to think about right now. Not his past assignment, or his future one. Nothing but family for the next month. He could do this, no problem. With one last look in the mirror, Tom put on a happy face and headed into the fray.

Jake and Sam were waiting for him when he came back down, and Tom headed in their direction. He grabbed a drink on the way, plopping down at the table next to his brothers. "Wow, nice spread Sam. That room is fit for a king. I feel much better now that I showered and shaved."

"Thanks Tom. We love it here. It takes an army to keep it all going, and a lot of donations from people, but it is working out well."

Jake wasn't going to waste any time before asking his questions. "So, are you going to tell us what you've been up to the last few years, or are you going to keep us in the dark?"

Tom understood that they wanted to know what was going on in his life, but he also knew that he couldn't tell them everything. They knew it too, so Tom decided to tell them what he could, and leave it at that. "Well, as you know, I work for the FBI now. I became an agent about five years ago. It's a tough job, but it's very rewarding, and I love it. That's about it really."

"What do you mean, that's it?" Jake asked. "That's all you have to say about it? What about the undercover op you've been on? I know you can't go into details, but you could at least tell us if you were in danger, or if you still are."

"You know I can't tell you anything about that, Jake. Just suffice it to say, it's all good now. The bad guys are behind bars, and I'm not in danger. I wouldn't be here if I was. I would never bring danger to my family."

"I know that Tom, but we are all worried about you. Are you really okay?"

"Yes, I am now. Let's just enjoy the time we have together. No more questions, I've told you all I can, so just let it go, okay?"

Jake and Sam looked at each other and nodded. "Okay, no more questions." They raised their glasses for a toast.

Tom took over the older brother duties. "I would like to give a toast to the new bride and groom, Ann and Sam. May you have a long and happy life together. Even if you'll probably never be alone together, with all the company you have here."

They all laughed and toasted the couple. "Here, here."

The night went on, and everyone had a wonderful time. Even Phil Carson and his family joined in the merriment. Abby was dancing and laughing with the other children. It was a family affair, and Sam and Ann decided it was time to go. They said their goodbyes, and ran to the pickup, heading into Portland for a small getaway. Sam grabbed Ann's hand and they ducked their heads as everyone threw rice and wished them well. By the time they got into the pickup, Ann was breathless.

"Wow, what a day! That was the most wonderful wedding, Sam. Thank you for letting me do basically whatever I wanted to with the wedding plans. I absolutely loved every moment of it!"

Sam looked over at his wife. Her lovely face was glowing, and her smile was breathtaking. "I wanted you to have the time of your life planning this wedding. You could almost do that for a living if you wanted to. It was that good. It was perfect, and I love you. I only wish we had done it sooner."

"Listen, everything takes time. We were both healing from some very bad times in our lives. You were worried about Jake and Jen. And, well, I guess I've been trying to heal from everything in my life, basically. But that's all water under the bridge now. We're together, and I plan to stay that way for the rest of my life. You're never getting rid of me Mr. Long."

"Ditto, Mrs. Long. I promise to take you on a longer honeymoon later, but right now the honeymoon suite will have to do."

"It sounds perfect to me. Anywhere is perfect as long as I'm with you. Now hurry!"

They laughed, as Sam gunned his truck and headed down the road, leaving a plume of dust in his wake.

The party went on at the ranch without them, and everyone was having a good time. Jake looked over at his brother Tom, and smiled. "I really am glad you showed up Tom. At least I'll have help with the chores for the next week while Sam is gone."

Tom glared at his brother. "I figured you would think that. I don't know anything about horses or cows, or whatever they eat. You're on your own buddy."

"Hey! You think I knew anything about that when I came here? I can show you the ropes, and Booker is an old hand at this. You'll do fine. Besides, you need to earn your keep somehow. No sitting around here at the ranch. Even Nancy is pitching in with the cooking. I think you can handle it. You look like you're in pretty good shape for an old guy."

Tom threw his head back and laughed. Boy, it felt like it had been forever since he'd done that. He had to admit, it felt good. "I'll show you who's in better shape in the morning, for now though, I'm beat. Unless you need my help here, I think I'll hit the hay, and that's the extent of my ranch knowledge."

"No, you go to bed, we'll handle things down here." Jake stood when Tom got up from his chair. He gave him a slap on the back. "You'll be talking like a true rancher by the time you leave here. I guess we can rule out that you were a ranch hand while you were undercover. Listen, I understand why you can't share with us what you were up to, but you know you can talk to me if you need to. I know better than anyone the toll it takes on a person, and I can keep a secret too. We're all here for you."

"I know Jake, but I just don't want to talk about it, and I can't talk about it. I just want to put it behind me and move on, okay? Let's just leave it at that. So, good night for now. Tell Jenny and Nancy good night. Those two haven't quit dancing all night."

"Yeah, they're having fun, but it looks like the night is winding down. I'll see you in the morning then."

After Tom left, Jake went to find Nancy and Jen. They were over at the gift table, arranging the wedding gifts on a wagon, to be taken inside. "Hey, you two need some help here?"

Nancy looked up when Jake approached. "No, we've got this. You can help the other hands clear off the food table if you want. We're going to leave the rest of it until morning. I, for one, am beat. Too much revelry I'm afraid."

Jake laughed, when he looked over at Jenny dragging herself back to the gift table. "I see that. It's no wonder you two are tired, you never turned down a dance."

"Hm, I didn't know you had noticed Jake. I didn't see you trying to cut in."

"Yeah, I knew better. I was born with two left feet, I'm afraid. Besides, I didn't want Tom to sit alone, and he is even worse than I am on the dance floor."

"Yeah, I understand, maybe I can teach you some dance moves some day."

"Maybe, well, I'll see you in the morning. I'm going to help with the food, and then I'm going to bed. Good night, you two."

Jenny tiredly grabbed another gift and yawned. "Good night Dad. I'll see you tomorrow."

Jake glanced over to the side table when he finished up putting the food away. Phil Carson was sitting alone, gazing off into the distance. Jake walked over to talk to the man. "Hey, Phil, where is everyone else? I know it's late for little Abby, but what about Cara?"

Phil looked startled to see Jake. "Oh, they went to bed long ago. I've just been sitting here, watching the dancers, remembering when I could actually do that."

Jake noticed that Phil was slurring his words a little. "Yeah, well, I never have been able to dance. Do you need some help getting home? I could use the walk after sitting for so long."

"No, I don't need any help! For the last time, will you people just leave me alone?" Phil wheeled off towards the direction of his home. Jake shook his head and went to the main house. He made a vow to get through to that man if it was the last thing he ever did.

By the time Jake got into bed it was pretty late. He lay there thinking about the day, and how well the wedding went. He finally dozed off at about two a.m.

Six o'clock came early, and Jake had to admit, it was kind of hard getting himself out of bed. When he got down to the kitchen, Tom was already there. He had gotten the coffee going, and Jake could smell the aroma of the rich brew. "Mmmm…that smells great! Thanks for getting the coffee going."

Tom nodded between sips of his coffee. "No problem. I'm ready and willing to learn the ropes of this ranch life. Are you ready to show me? Or do you need some more beauty sleep?"

"I'm fine, just had a little trouble getting to sleep last night, that's all. I'll run circles around you any day of the week Tom!"

"Bring it on!"

When Nancy and Jen entered the kitchen, they overheard the two men baiting each other. Nancy laughed and looked over at Jen. "These two sound like they need a good breakfast, and some good old-fashioned farm and ranch work. What do you think Jen?"

"I think you're exactly right Dr. Hall. Let's get the eggs cooking before they square off and decide to arm wrestle or something."

Breakfast was a loud, and raucous affair. It sounded almost like the breakfast table at the Long home years ago. Tom could feel the stress of the job melting away already. He patted his stomach as he pushed away from the table. "That was delicious. I think we had better go work some of this off now Jake. This one time I'll let you be the teacher, and I'll be the student. Just don't get used to it."

"Let's get to it then. The other hands are already out there working, and there's a load of hay due in today sometime. I know Sam promised Abby Carson a ride today. Have you ever been on a horse, Tom?"

"When I was younger I used to ride at a stable near Las Vegas. I know my way around a horse. It's been awhile, but I will get the hang of it."

"Great, let's get to it then. I want to fill you in on one of the men here, Phil Carson. He was shot in the line of duty and is now in a wheelchair. Sam wanted me to try and get him on one of the horses that are trained to carry handicapped people. I'm going to do that today, I could use your help."

Tom listened intently, and nodded when Jake was done. "I'll try to help any way I can, but Jake, you know you can't force him to do something that he doesn't want to do."

"Yes, I know that, but we can at least try. Let's go then. We will see you ladies at lunch time."

"Bye Dad, see you Tom. Have fun out there."

Tom and Jake headed for the barn first. "We need to feed hay to the horses, and, lucky you, it's stall cleaning day! The tenants here pitch in and help, so it goes pretty fast. You know I wouldn't make you do it on your own."

Tom snorted. "Yeah right! I'm sure you wouldn't get any satisfaction at all by doing that. What are you going to be doing while I'm slaving away cleaning stalls?"

"I'm going to find Phil Carson and Abby. It's time Phil and I had a talk."

• • • *4* • • •

AFTER JAKE GOT his brother going on cleaning stalls, he went in search of Phil. Knocking on the door of his cabin, Jake waited patiently when he heard voices inside. The door opened, and little Abby answered the door. She was all dressed up in her boots and jeans, ready to go ride Buffy.

"Mr. Jake, are you going to take me riding today? Is Booker already over there? I'm all ready to go."

"Whoa! Hold up there little cowgirl. Is your dad here? I need to talk to him before we go."

"He's in the kitchen. He doesn't want to go with me today, I already asked. Come on in Mr. Jake."

Jake stepped into the small cabin, looking around at the clean and tidy home. He headed for the kitchen when Phil called him in. "Good morning Phil, how are you today?"

"Good as I can be, stuck in this wheelchair. Now, what can I do for you this morning?" Phil retorted.

"Well, I'll be straight forward with you Phil. Sam asked me to talk to you, and I said I would. So here I am. You can listen or not, but I am going to say my piece anyway." Jake sat down, getting eye to eye with Phil.

"Everyone here has some kind of disability, whether it be mental or physical. You are not the only one here that is hurting Phil. Think about your wife, your daughter, all of the others that are here. People cope with things in different ways, I know that. I also have seen a lot of bad things happen to good people. You need to buck up and be a man. Not only for yourself, but for your family. It sucks that this happened to you, and we all feel bad about it, but enough is enough. What do you think? Can you at least try to overcome this disability? Accept what has happened to you and move on? I just really think you can beat this Phil. If not, I don't know if there's anything more we can do here. I would hate to see Abby and Cara give up the friendships they have formed here at the ranch. Abby is thriving here. Cara still has a lot of sadness in her, but she seems to be coping. More than I can say for you."

Phil Carson bristled at Jake's comments. "You know what? You have no idea what I'm going through. I don't see you sitting here in this wheelchair!" He paused, thinking about what Jake had said. "But I do know what you mean about the other people here. A lot of them are worse off than I am."

At that moment, Cara and Abby came into the room. Abby was all dressed in her boots and jeans, ready to go. "Mr. Jake, are you going to take me riding now? Buffy is waiting for me, come on let's go!" The little girl grabbed Jake's hand and started pulling him towards the door.

"Hold on a second Abby. Your dad decided to come along this morning. Isn't that great?"

"He is? Yay! Daddy, I'm so excited. Are you going to ride too?" The little girl caught herself and stopped talking abruptly. She looked at her dad. "You don't have to if you don't want to."

Phil was starting to give his usual reply about what he thought about riding a horse, when he actually looked closely at his daughter's face. Jake could see the realization finally dawning on him. The realization that Abby was hurting just as much as he was. Phil glanced over at Cara, and was almost startled by the look of sadness on her face too. Phil looked like he finally realized how he had hurt his daughter and wife with his actions and words. He made a decision right then and there. He sat his daughter on his lap and wheeled to the door. "You know what? I think I will learn to ride Red so I can go with you on your adventures. I don't know if I will be as good as you, but I'll try. What do you say to that?"

Abby threw her arms around Phil's neck. "Oh Daddy, that would be so fun! You'll do great I just know it. Now let's go get started so we can leave the corral soon!"

Cara was startled by her husband's response but was relieved that he was actually going to try. She glanced at Jake with tears in her eyes, and silently mouthed a thank you. Jake nodded and left the house, feeling better about Phil Carson's recovery.

The trio approached the corrals to see that Booker was already waiting for them. He had the horses caught and tied to the hitching post. Phil looked nervous, and Abby walked over to Buffy with her treat in the palm of her hand. Buffy sniffed once, then nipped the treat out of her hand. Abby rubbed the pony's soft muzzle, giggling when Buffy snorted. "Come on Daddy, I have a treat for Red too. You can give it to him, he is very gentle."

Phil took a deep breath, reaching out his hand to Red. The horse sniffed his outstretched hand, and gently took the treat that Phil was offering him. Abby squealed, hugging her dad. "See Daddy, I knew he would like you."

Phil actually smiled, he hadn't even wanted to do that in a long time. "I hope he likes me honey. I think we are going to get along just fine. How about you teach me how to ride him?"

"I will Daddy, I'm a good teacher. Let's get Mr. Jake to saddle him for you and we'll go really slow in the corral."

Jake started saddling Red up while Abby saddled up Buffy. A special saddle is used for physically disabled people. Booker got the mounting ramp from the barn, and between the two men, got Phil mounted up without any problems. Abby rode beside her dad while Jake started out leading Red around the corral.

"Okay Phil, just let yourself move with the horse, this will strengthen your muscles. You're going to feel this later. You may be a little sore, so we aren't going to push it too far this first time. When your muscles get stronger, you can go a longer distance."

Phil nodded, and hung on to the saddle horn as Jake led Red slowly around the corral. "This actually feels pretty good. I must admit, I was terrified to get on this huge animal, but he seems very calm. I like the feeling of freedom I get up here."

"Red is very well trained Phil. He's pretty smart too. He knows that he needs to be extra careful with you. I think we should call it a day for now. It's almost lunch time anyway. We don't want to push it too much the first time."

"Sounds good to me, I think I can do this! What do you think, Jake?"

"I think you've got this. We'll take it slow. By the end of next week you should be able to leave the corral and go with Abby on a ride. I'll take you to a place that Jen and I like to go. It's absolutely beautiful. Now, let's get you down from this horse, and I'll show you how to groom him. We have a ramp set up over here. You can dismount on that and also us it to groom Red."

"Okay…Jake…I just want to say thank you for the pep talk. I really needed someone who actually understood to get me lined out. I know I've been hard to get along with, but there's more to it than you and the others know. I'm getting close to figuring it out, and when I do….well, let's just say, the shit is going to hit the fan. I know there is something bad going on, I just can't quite put my finger on it."

Jake looked at the man. "I understand completely. If anyone knows about things happening that shouldn't be, it's me. If you need anything from me, please let me know. I mean *anything*. Promise me you won't be doing anything dangerous. You have a wonderful wife and a beautiful little girl to go home to. Call me of you need any help." Jake noticed that Phil was sweating a little with the exertion of dismounting, so he let him off the hook with the grooming. "Why don't you take Abby home now. I'll groom and feed Red this time. From here on out though, it's your job to take care of your horse, okay?"

"I am a little tired. More so than I thought I would be. Thanks again Jake. I'll see you tomorrow."

The rest of the day was spent with Tom and Jake riding out to check the cows. Jake wanted to show Tom the rest of the ranch, so they rode the rest of the day. Jake was pleased with how the day went. Sam will be happy to hear about Phil's improving attitude. He will also be very happy with his brother Tom's accomplishments. Tom had pitched in right away, helping with the chores around the ranch.

By the time the two men got back from their ride, it was already getting dark outside. Jake and Tom led the horses into their stalls to bed them down for the night. Jake noticed that Tom was walking a little slowly. When he saw Tom rubbing his back end, he couldn't help but give him a bad time. "You a little sore Tom? I guess I pushed you a little hard for the first day."

"Well, I may be a little sore, but I'm fine. Good thing I'm in such great shape. You had to give me all of the animal poop duty, and I did it without complaint."

Jake laughed. "You never change do you? Always thinking you get the short end of the stick. That someone is trying to give you the bad jobs. I assure you, I only gave you the job of cleaning out stalls because it needed to be done. We all have done our share of shoveling shit."

"Right! Well, I did it. I hope you're satisfied. Is there more to do tonight?"

"It's already getting dark. Let's call it a night and go see what the girls have been up to while we have been slaving away down here."

Supper was waiting for the two men when they walked in the house. Jen and Nancy had been busy that's for sure. Jake and Tom were hungry after a hard days work. Jake took a deep breath of the savory smells that greeted him as he walked in the kitchen. "Wow, you two have outdone yourselves! This smells great!"

Nancy blushed, and Jen grinned at her dad. "Why thank you kind sir. Ann has taught us well."

Tom entered the room and greeted the two women the same way that Jake had. "Speaking of Ann. Has anyone heard anything from the newlyweds lately?"

Nancy nodded. "Yes, they are coming home Friday. They decided to come back early so Sam could be here to help prepare for the roundup and trail ride next weekend. I can hardly wait. I've never been on a real life cattle drive."

Tom was a little bit leery of that long of a ride. "Well, neither have I. I must say, I am excited about it though."

Jake nodded, and sat down at the table. "I am too. It's always an exciting time, but it is also a lot of work. I'm thinking about asking Abby, Phil, and Cara to go along on the wagon. We could bring Buffy along so Abby could ride her a little, and maybe Phil would be ready by then to ride Red a little bit too. I'm not going to push him too hard, but a little fresh air and a wagon ride wouldn't hurt him a bit."

Nancy agreed that Phil could use the outing. "I'll talk to him tomorrow about it and hopefully he'll agree with us. Now dig in, we slaved over a hot stove all day cooking, so enjoy."

After supper, the men helped with the cleanup, and headed for the porch for their customary drink and visit. Jake couldn't help but notice how Tom was already filling out and looking much more relaxed, after only one day of being on the ranch.

"How are you doing Tom? I must say, you look a lot better than you did when you got here. That's what the fresh air and hard work does for you. Just wait until you're here for a while, you'll be all beefed up. Especially with all of this good home cooking. Are you ready to talk about the case was that got you looking so stressed?”

Tom shook his head. “You know I can’t say anything about that. All I can tell you is, it’s an ongoing case that is taking it’s toll on a lot of agents, not just me. We arrested some of the guys, but there are still some out there. It’s bad, Jake, real bad. That’s all I can say.”

“So, you are basically still assigned to the same case? I thought it was over. That’s why you’re here, right?”

“My part is over, but the case itself isn’t. Not by a long shot, and I could get called back in at anytime. I really enjoyed my first day here, though. I can see why you guys love it here. It’s so peaceful. Well, I think I’ll turn in for the night. Good night Jake.”

“Night Tom. I’ll see you in the morning. It sounds like Sam will be home Friday, so you and I need to spend the rest of the week getting ready for the trail ride.”

It was the middle of the afternoon when Sam and Ann pulled into the drive. Ann grabbed her husband’s hand and squeezed. “You know, I loved being alone with you for a whole week, but I’m glad to be home too. I love this ranch.”

“I agree, I love it here too. I love everything about it, the smell of the hay, the horses, and the cows. Even the hard work it takes to keep a place this size going. I’m glad my brothers are here to help. Jen and Nancy too. Well, let’s go greet the family.”

After all the hugs and greetings, Sam excused himself to change into his work clothes. When he got down to the barn, Sam was shocked to see Phil mounting Red with the mounting ramp they had purchased. Sam stood back and watched the man struggle a little, but Phil managed to get on the horse unassisted this time. Red stood calmly while Phil settled himself into the special saddle.

Sam was grinning when he approached Phil. “Well, well. What have we here? I leave for a little while, and you are up on a horse looking like a pro already. How does it feel?”

Phil grinned back at Sam. "I'm doing great! Red is the best, and Jake said I could leave the corral a little bit. I'm a little nervous, but Jake is going with, and Abby and Buffy too. We aren't going far, but it's going to be a big step for me. How was your honeymoon?"

"Great, but I'm glad to be home. If you keep this up you can go on the trail ride next weekend. How would that be Phil?"

Phil nodded, and reached down to pet Red on the neck. "I will be ready by next weekend for some riding. Jake and Booker said I would mainly be on the wagon, but that will be fine with me. I just want to start moving ahead and dealing with my handicap the best I can. My family deserves it, and frankly, so do I."

"That's great to hear Phil. I am looking forward to the ride this year too. Well, I'll leave you to it then. If you need anything let us know okay?"

"Yep, I will. See you later then."

The rest of the day went by fast, with Sam getting back in the groove. By nightfall, the sounds of the ranch changed from horses snorting, cows milling about, and people working at their different jobs, to the frogs croaking and leaves rustling in the breeze. Sam, Jake, and Tom were sitting out on the porch when lights approached the house. The lights on the top of the car indicated the sheriff's vehicle. Tom slipped into the house without saying a word.

Jake and Sam stood as the sheriff stepped out and approached them. Sam spoke first. "Hello, sheriff, what are you doing out in my neck of the woods?"

"Hello Sam. I have something I need to talk to you about. Mind if I join you?"

Jake pulled up a chair for the sheriff. "No problem, have a seat. Would you like something to drink?"

"No, thank you. I just wanted to come out personally and let you know what has been happening around these parts lately. I don't know how well you know your neighbors, the

Browns. Their spread is about ten miles from here as the crow flies."

Sam nodded. "Yes, I know them. Has something happened? Are they alright?"

The sheriff took off his hat and ran his hands through his hair. "Well, we're not sure exactly what is going on. It may be nothing, but they found some tracks from a four wheeler around their property. It wasn't one of theirs, they hadn't been out in that area in awhile. Some fences were cut also. There were a lot of tracks. More than one vehicle driving around there. I went and checked it out and couldn't find anything else. My guess is some kids are looking for a party spot, but I wanted to let all of you know what is going on. Would you keep your eyes open and let me know if you see anything out of the ordinary?"

Jake, always the cop, spoke up. "I think we should go out and investigate a little. Do you have a drug problem around the area sheriff? Any labs in the area?"

The sheriff straightened his back and shook his head. "No, not that we know of. Listen, I know you are former law enforcement, but I don't want you running around investigating things on your own. Like I said, it's probably a group of kids blowing off steam before school starts. Nothing to worry about. You call us if you see anything, don't be handling it on your own, you hear?"

Sam stood with the sheriff, and shook his hand. "We'll let you know if we see or hear anything, but if need be, we'll handle it. We have our annual cattle drive and trail ride coming up. I don't want the safety of my employees and tenants to be compromised. Thank you for letting us know sheriff."

The sheriff shook Sam's hand and nodded. "Fine, just be on the lookout and keep me informed. Good night Sam… Jake." He glanced at Jake. "I know that you are a former detective, Jake. I'm the sheriff here, this county is my jurisdiction, you boys best remember that. Good night now."

After Sheriff Stills left, Tom appeared in the doorway. Jake looked at his brothers. "Well, what do you make of that? Anything to worry about Sam?"

Sam was a little worried, but he tried to keep it to himself. "I honestly don't know. This is such a remote area, I can't imagine kids coming all the way out here to party. I think the sheriff downplayed this a little bit. Tomorrow, we are riding out on the trail and looking around for anything odd. I'm not going to put people in danger this weekend. We may have to postpone the ride. Well, let's get some sleep, it sounds like we have some extra riding to do tomorrow."

They agreed, and made a time to get started in the morning before going to bed.

The sun was just rising over the horizon as the three brothers saddled up their horses, getting ready to follow the trail they were taking on the upcoming weekend. They had their food and packs ready to go. It would take them two days to ride the trail, so they needed a couple of pack horses to carry their tents and food. When Ann, Jen and Nancy heard about the sheriff's visit they had been worried, but agreed with the men that it needed to be checked out.

Jen approached her dad when he got his horse saddled. "Dad, I have a bad feeling all of a sudden. You know my visions are improving, as are my other abilities. I'm usually right about the feelings I get about things like this. Are you sure you three should go out on your own? Maybe you should call the sheriff. I can't put my finger on what it is I'm feeling, just that it's not good. I don't want anything happening to you guys."

Jake hugged his daughter. "I don't doubt your feelings at all Jen. If you say something is up, I believe you, but you are looking at three grown men. Two of which are in law enforcement. I think we'll be alright. We are armed, and we will watch each other's backs, I promise. We need to do this. If there is something going on we need to get to the bottom of it before the weekend."

"Okay, just be careful, and call if you see anything."

Jake hugged Jen again and noticed Phil Carson sitting near the corral. Phil was waving him over, so Jake walked to where he was sitting. "Good morning Phil. What are you doing up this early? You okay?"

"I'm fine, but what is up with you three? Kind of early for you to be taking off isn't it?"

Jake wondered how much information he should share with the man. Phil was a former police officer, so Jake thought maybe he should tell him what the sheriff said last night. "Boy, there is no getting anything over on you is there? Once a cop, always a cop, I guess. Okay…Sheriff Stills stopped by last night. I guess the neighbor found some strange tracks on his property along with a fence cut down. We are just going to ride the trail and see if everything is okay for the ride this weekend. Stills thought is was probably just some kids blowing off steam, but we want to make sure that's all. It's probably nothing."

"I will keep an eye on things around here while you're gone. I can still use a weapon, and I will if need be. My gut tells me Stills wouldn't have come all the way out here if he wasn't worried about it. I need to tell you something when you get back. I've been doing some digging, and have found a few things I would like to share with you. It's pretty interesting stuff. You were a cop in Los Angeles, right?"

"Yes, in homicide mostly. Why do you ask that?"

"I'll talk to you about it when you get back." Phil swung his chair around and wheeled away.

Tom and Sam walked up to Jake just as Phil was leaving. "What is he doing up this early? What did he have to say, Jake?"

Jake was confused. He told his brothers what Phil said about having something to tell them when they got back from checking out the trail. They all agreed that it was a strange thing for Phil to say. Sam turned to his horse and got on. "Well, obviously Phil is going to make us wait for whatever it is. We'd better get going if we're going to make this ride in two days." Tom and Jake mounted their horses. With Sam leading the way, the three of them waved at Jen, and headed out.

They rode along silently as the morning turned into afternoon, until Sam held up his arm to stop the other two. Dismounting, they looked around the area. There was a watering hole nearby for the horses, and some trees. Jake stretched his muscles, glad for the break. "Well, so far so good. Nothing looks out of place here. Should we grab some lunch before we keep on going to night camp?"

The other two nodded as they dismounted their horses as well. After loosening their saddles, they watered the horses. They tied the horses to some trees nearby, and grabbed their lunch from the packs. Tom was constantly looking around, surveying the area.

Jake could feel his unease. "What are you thinking Tom? You seem extra worried about this. What's up? I think it's time to spill about what you are really doing here. If it is bringing danger to our loved ones, we deserve to know."

Tom just looked at Jake and shook his head. "I'm not on duty right now Jake. I just don't like the fact that someone may be out here doing who knows what. I get the feeling it's some kind of drug thing. This is the perfect area for Meth labs or moving other drugs. It's pretty remote, and quite a ways from civilization. Even though we have cell service, it's pretty spotty. I just don't like it, that's all, and I am going to say it one more time. I can't talk to you about my case. Do you really think I would bring danger to my family? Now quit asking me about that."

"Okay, okay. I'll let it go, for now. But you have got to be straight with us, we are family. Family sticks together, I need to know you have my back Tom."

"I always will Jake, you too Sam. Always remember that."

Sam and Jake looked at each other and Sam shook his head slightly. That was the end of it….for now. "Well, I'm done eating and ready to head to night camp. How about you old cowpokes."

Tom threw an apple core at him as he got up and headed to his horse. "I'll show you who is old, you young punk."

The camaraderie between the three brothers was back after the stilted, and somewhat scarce, conversation earlier. As they reached night camp, everything looked calm and serene. They hadn't found any signs of intruders on the property. Not the human kind anyway. Just some coyote and deer scat, nothing unusual. As they rode up to the camp where they were spending the night, they scared some deer that were watering in the dam. It was a good sign, the animals wouldn't be hanging around if there was danger nearby. The three men dismounted and turned the horses into the makeshift corral. Sam stretched his back and noticed Tom and Jake doing the same.

"Looks like we need to ride more often. We are all getting older I guess, some of us more than others."

Jake and Tom glared at Sam, but couldn't help but laugh. Tom couldn't let Sam's comment go without a smart retort. "We like to call it more experienced, right Jake?"

"That's right Tom. Sam has always needed to grow up a little. Hopefully Ann will help him with that. Now let's get some shuteye so we can get back home tomorrow. I can see that the tracks that were found were an isolated thing. There doesn't seem to be any dangers out here."

The morning was beautiful, with the orange and yellow colors of the sunrise glowing in the distance. Jake, Tom, and Sam already had their camp cleaned up and were saddling their horses. It was only about four hours from home, so they would be there for some of the morning chores.

They rode in silence, enjoying the early morning sounds and sights. "This is really a beautiful area." Tom said as he looked around. "I could definitely get used to this Sam."

"Well, you know you're welcome here anytime Tom. You could retire from the FBI and stay here. There's plenty to do around the ranch to keep us all busy, and I would like to expand a little. Just something to think about."

Tom laughed a little. "Well, it is tempting that's for sure. I'll keep it in mind, but for now, I need to keep doing what I've been doing. There's too many bad guys around to quit now. You might find this surprising, but the bad guys are even around here."

Sam and Jake looked at him in surprise. "Does that mean you *are* doing some investigating in this area?"

"No comment!" Tom spurred his horse and galloped off. Sam and Jake did the same, and nothing more was said.

They returned home from their ride at ten a.m. The ranch was already bustling with activity. Abby was on her pony, riding around the ranch. She had shown herself to be an accomplished horseback rider, and had been granted permission from her parents, and Sam, to ride outside the corral. Phil and Cara were watching her from the porch of their cabin. Sam walked over to talk to them when he got done with his horse.

"Well, she is coming along well. She should be able to go on the trail ride this weekend. Buffy will keep up great, we don't move too fast." He looked at Phil. "How about you? Are you going to go along?"

Phil shook his head. "I don't think I'm ready for that, Cara is going on the wagon to keep an eye out on Abby."

Sam didn't try to change his mind on his decision. "Sounds good. This week will go fast, we have a lot of preparations to make before we go. I'll see you all later." He turned back when he remembered what Phil had said before they left. "Oh, what was it that you wanted to talk to me about Phil?"

"Oh, it turns out is was nothing important. I'll talk to you when you get back from the roundup."

Sam nodded, heading for the house. More than ready to get the last two days of dirt and grime off his body. But first, he was going to say hello to his wife.

Sam was right, the week flew by. He hadn't seen much of Phil. He wondered what the man had wanted to talk to him about. It was going to have to wait though, this was a busy time.

There was excitement in the air on the day of the trail ride. Everyone was bustling around, getting the chuck wagon ready to go and saddling horses. It was an eclectic group of people this year. Two ex police officers, one had been injured in the line of duty, the other had post traumatic stress disorder from witnessing his partner getting killed. There were two wives of police officers who were killed, one was riding on the wagon, and one had a horse. Then there was little Abby, and her mother Cara. Sam, Jake, Booker, and Tom brought up the rear. It was quite a sight to see. Ann, along with Nancy, were in the wagon in the lead, that carried supplies and first aid if needed. Jenny was on her horse, riding alongside the lead wagon.

They were heading to the west pasture to bring the rest of the cows home, closer to the homestead for the winter. There were only about a hundred head left to bring home, the rest had already been brought to the winter pasture. Sam always left these cows for the trail ride, so some of the people could enjoy the life of a cowboy, even if only for a few days. It was an enjoyable time for everyone.

Phil had decided to stay home, opting for enjoying the quiet of the ranch with only a skeleton crew there. He was a little distant this week. Sam figured he had something on his mind, but when he asked Cara, she didn't know what it was. She thought it was probably the visitor he had earlier in the week. One of his former coworkers from the Portland Police Department had come out to the ranch to see Phil. Cara said Phil was distant and seemed a little off when he left. He wouldn't talk about it. Basically telling her it wasn't any of her business, and leaving in a huff.

Sam brought this up to his brothers as they rode along. "I can't figure Phil out. One minute he's doing pretty good, and the next, he's going back to how he was. I hope for his family's sake, he comes to terms with everything that has happened in his life. I can only imagine how hard it must be for him. I think I'll make a point to find out who came to see him, and why. Cara didn't know who it was, just that it was a policeman from Portland. He must have pushed Phil's buttons, and got him upset about something."

Jake looked thoughtful, and he agreed with Sam. "Yes, I think just seeing another policeman when you can't be on the job anymore must be tough. He may have said something to Phil about work, and that got under his skin. Who knows? I do think that we should lay off him for awhile though. What he has gone through is devastating to him. We need to remember that. It's hard for us to realize just what he's going through."

Nothing more was said on the subject, and Jake trotted up to where Jenny was riding. Tom stayed in the rear, and Sam took the lead, guiding the trail riders to their destination.

The crew set up night camp in the same area as the men had earlier in the week. As the chuck wagon got set up for cooking the evening meal, the men tended to the horses. By the time they were done, supper was almost ready. Phil had arrived on the ATV, and seemed okay to Sam. As Sam watched Phil sitting with his wife and daughter, laughing and talking, he remembered what Jake had said. He had to agree with Jake on that. They should lay off of Phil for awhile. Sam headed for his wife, who was preparing the meal with Nancy and Jen.

"How's it going here? Do you need any help?"

Ann glanced up from her preparations. "I don't think so, it's almost ready. Jake and Tom are over setting up the tents, and getting the camp fire ready for tonight. I'll let you know when the food is ready, now shoo!"

Sam backed away with his hands in the air. "Fine, I'll go, but remember, you have a lot of hungry cowpokes to feed."

Ann nodded to Sam and he thought he'd better go before he got himself in trouble.

The meal was delicious, as usual, and Jake told the women they had outdone themselves. Nancy blushed, and Ann thanked Jake. "We couldn't have done it alone. Thanks to everyone who helped, it went smoothly. Now, you men can help with the cleanup, and we can sit around the campfire for a little while. I brought the makings for s'mores. I thought that would taste good, and the young ones like them."

"So do the older ones." Sam joked as he approached. "I, for one, love them. Let's get this cleaned up. The fire is started and it's ready to go."

The campfire was roaring and people were sitting around it on some of the straw bales that were brought along on one of the wagons. It was a beautiful night, stars shining in the sky, and no wind. One of the cowpokes had brought along his guitar. They started singing some campfire songs, just enjoying the evening. Phil had gone back to the ranch with one of the hands, and little Abby was trying hard to stay awake. Cara stood, and stretched. "Well, I know a little girl who is tired, and ready for bed, so good night everyone. I'll see you all bright and early tomorrow morning."

Good nights were said all around, and the party started dispersing after that. The campfire was doused, and everything was quiet. The only sounds were the crickets chirping and the occasional whinny of the horses as they munched on the hay.

Tomorrow, they would reach their destination, and the roundup would begin. Then, the crew would start the cattle drive back to the ranch. This night camp would be their stop tomorrow night, so in the morning, the men were going to prepare the corral for the cattle and horses to stay. Sam fell asleep as soon as his head hit the pillow. The fresh air and exercise always made for a good night's sleep.

The next day went without incident, and soon the group was heading back to where they had set up camp. The cattle that Sam had left behind for this ride were pretty easy to push to their destination. Most of them had done this before, and knew the way.

The chuck wagon had headed back early, so they could get things prepared. Abby insisted on staying behind and pushing the cattle with Buffy. Cara agreed, only if she promised to stay by Jen, and not wander off anywhere on her own. The little girl was holding up quite well, and so was Buffy. *Abby was born for this life.* Sam thought, as he rode along. *She is such a sweet little girl, I hope her dad realizes how lucky he is."*

Before they knew it, they could see the camp looming in the distance. It was a good thing, because the cattle were getting tired and restless, needing a break from the round up. The cattle roundup and ride back to the ranch usually went without incident. The older cows usually knew where to go and led the younger ones along. The only thing the horse riders did was keep the cattle moving and chase the occasional stray that would wander off on its own.

Sam could smell the food that was being prepared by the women in the chuck wagon. Tonight was the big meal. BBQ beef with all kinds of salads, fresh buns, and corn on the cob. Sam's stomach growled on cue. He was more than ready to get off this horse and settle down for a good meal.

The older cattle did their job well. They could smell the water, and headed straight for the dam. It didn't take long for the cowboys and girls to get the cattle into the makeshift corral. They didn't have far to go tomorrow to get them back to the ranch. Sam wondered if Phil Carson was coming out to night camp like he said he was going to. He looked around, but didn't see the side-by-side anywhere. Sam thought he would have been there by now. He approached Ann and grabbed her around the waist for a kiss. She blushed. "Sam, not here! There's too many people around."

Sam loved her shyness. "So what? I love my wife, and everyone knows that. By the way, have you heard anything from Phil? Is he coming tonight?"

"Cara has been trying to call him, but no answer. She said he has been wrapped up in something, and she's worried Sam. He has all kinds of files and papers he has been going over every night. She shared the fact rather reluctantly. I think it's been going on for a while now. He is getting more and more distant with her and Abby."

Sam frowned. "Hmm, I'll call one of the ranch hands and have them go check on him. He's probably just trying to figure out his future for himself and his family. I'll call after we eat. Everyone is starving, and it smells delicious."

"Well, everything is ready to eat, we set up a table and some straw bales for everyone to sit on. Let's eat."

It was a hungry and jovial crowd, everyone was talking and laughing. Sam sat by his brothers and told them the story Ann told him about Phil. They were not overly concerned, knowing what Phil had been going through. They did agree that Sam should have someone check on him just in case.

After the meal, Sam walked to the side and used his cell phone to call the ranch. He got a hold of one of the hands and asked him to check on Phil. When Sam got that done, he hunted down Booker, and they decided that he would ride back early in the morning to prepare the ranch for the arrival of the herd of cattle. When his phone rang later in the evening, Sam recognized the number as that of the hand he had talked to earlier.

"Long here. Yes, Don, did you check on Phil? Is he okay?"

"Yes boss. He said he hadn't charged his cell phone so that is why he hasn't been answering. He seemed very distracted though, and had no desire to go out to night camp. Phil did look a little haggard, and he had papers strewn all over, but other than that he seemed fine."

"Okay, I will let Cara know. Thanks Don. I'll see you tomorrow."

Sam hung up, and went to find Cara. She was glad that Sam had gotten a hold of someone. "Oh, thank you. I'm so relieved. I must admit, I was very worried."

"He'll be fine Cara, I think it was good for him to spend some time alone. He is probable trying to figure out where to go from here. He loves you and Abby, he'll figure something out." He glanced over at Abby, she could barely keep her eyes open. "Looks like someone is tired. I'll leave you to get her settled in, good night."

"Good night, Sam. I'll see you in the morning."

● ● ●

At the ranch, Phil was pouring over all of the papers he had gathered and printed out from the internet. There were more that he had written by hand. His friend from the police department had brought out all kinds of papers that he had smuggled out of the building. "I'm getting closer to figuring this out, I just know it! Any day now, I am taking them all down. All I need is one more thing, and I've got them! Then I can do what needs to be done! I'm tired of this. So tired."

● ● ●

Phil thought he heard a noise outside the window that faced the barn. He wheeled over and looked outside. *Nothing there, you're being paranoid now Carson.*

Phil's cell phone rang. He recognized the number. He sighed, and answered on the third ring. "What is it? Why are you calling me now? I told you, I don't know anything for certain yet. I'll see you tomorrow, and I'll let you know what I have so far." He hung up before he could even reply.

Phil yawned, and looked at his watch. It was midnight, past time for him to be in bed. His wife and daughter were going to be back at noon tomorrow, and he had plans for when they got back. Phil shut off the lights and headed to bed.

# ••• 5 •••

THERE WAS AN eerie silence outside when Phil heard the shrill ring of his alarm clock. Dawn was just starting to break, the sun glowing orange in the distant sky. He gathered up all of the copies he had made, grabbed his gun, and headed out the door. Today was the day, he was resigned to whatever was going to happen. The other papers were safely tucked away, he had what he needed. No one was going to find the duplicates he had made.

Phil wheeled his way down the ramp, and slowly made his way to the barn. The horses were quiet, no ranch hands were working yet. Perfect. He saw movement out of the corner of his eye. They were here. Whatever happened, this was ending today. Phil couldn't help but think of his young daughter, and his wife Cara. This was for the best, he couldn't go on this way. Nothing was going to happen to him, he trusted these guys. By the time he got to the barn, the sun was rising even more. He had to hurry, the hands would be here soon.

When Phil entered the barn, he could hear the horses snorting. They were ready for their morning exercise and feeding. He jumped when he heard a voice.

"About time you got here Carson. Now what do have for us, we don't have all day."

Phil took a deep breath, and handed over the brown envelope he had meticulously put together. The man slid out the papers and looked them over. "Hmph. This isn't bad Carson, you've gone to a lot of work here. Too bad you trusted the wrong people with your info."

Phil was stunned. "What? No way! You can't be....."

At that moment one man stepped forward and disarmed Phil, grabbing his chair, pushing it toward the center of the room. Someone else stepped out of the shadows. Phil was helpless now.

"I should have known you had something to do with this. What are you going to do to me?"

"I promise it won't hurt too bad Carson. You won't even know what hit you."

The man grinned, as Phil's gun was pressed to the side of his head. Phil tried to resist, but he just wasn't strong enough. The man forced Phil to use his own hand to pull the trigger. The horses were spooked by the noise, jumping and whinnying loudly.

"Come on, we got what we wanted, let's get out of here. Our work here is done."

Don awoke to the sounds of the horses snorting and whinnying in their stalls. "What the heck is going on down there? The riders aren't suppose to be back for a couple of hours yet." He quickly got dressed, hurrying to the barn to see what was going on. When he opened the door, he immediately smelled the tinny scent of blood and the distinct odor of recent gunfire. Turning on the lights, he saw Phil Carson slumped in his wheelchair. He ran to the man, knowing it was probably already too late. He saw the gun lying on the ground next to Phil's right hand. "Oh no, please be okay, please be okay." Don slowly reached out and touched his hand to Phil's neck, hoping for a pulse. There was none, it was too late. Don quickly ran for the house and called the police. It seems Phil didn't want to live any more, but that was for the police to decide. Right now, he needed to send someone out to tell Sam and the others what had happened.

The wagons and riders were almost back to the ranch when Sam noticed a four wheeler coming out to meet them. The cattle were startled and it took a little bit to get them settled down when the four wheeler got closer. "Whoever that is, they better have a good excuse for riling up our cattle. They know better than that." Sam recognized one of his hands, Matt, and rode out to meet him before they scattered the cattle all over the countryside.

"Whoa there, slow down partner. You know better than to ride out towards these cattle so fast. What's going on?"

"Boss! You have to come quick! Phil Carson has shot himself in the head. I saw it with my own eyes! The police are on their way. It's awful boss, just awful."

Sam was stunned. "Wait, just slow down a minute. What exactly happened? Are you sure about this?"

Matt took a deep breath. "Okay. Don got up to do the morning chores, and noticed the horses were spooked about something. When he got to the barn, he found Phil sitting in his chair with a hole in his head. The gun was lying there, it was horrible Sam! Don called the police, they are probably there by now."

Sam heard other horses galloping up to where they were at. It was Jake and Tom. He quickly filled them in on what had transpired at the ranch. The three men looked at each other and then glanced at the approaching wagon carrying Cara Carson, and little Abby riding close by. "Damn!" Jake exclaimed. "What should we do about his family? They can't see him like that."

Sam took charge. "Jake, you and Tom slow down the caravan. I'll ride ahead and see what's going on. I am going to make sure those two don't see him like that. Let Ann know what is going on. We'll break the news to Cara first. She doesn't need to be surprised by all of the police cars in the yard. Let's go. Matt, you go back and see if the police are there. Tell them that we will be there in an hour, and I'd just as soon the body be gone by then. I know they have a job to do, just let them know we have his wife and daughter with us and will be there soon."

Jake and Tom trotted their horses back to the wagon. Ann could tell something was wrong the minute she saw them. "What's going on? Where is Sam going?"

Cara was equally curious, but she had a bad feeling about this. "Is it Phil? Did something happen to him? I couldn't get him on the phone yesterday, what has happened?"

Jake pulled his horse up next to the wagon. "Cara, I really hate to tell you this, but something has happened to Phil. We need to get back to the ranch right away. Ann, take the wagon directly back to the ranch. I will get Abby, she needs to go with you. I'll lead Buffy home."

Cara was really starting to panic now. "I'm not going anywhere until you tell me what happened. Is Phil okay? Was there some kind of accident?"

Jake was reluctant to say, but he felt Cara deserved to know, so he told her as gently as he could. "Damn, I thought I left all of this behind me. Okay, Cara…I'm afraid Phil is dead. I am not saying anything more, we don't know the facts anyway. The police are there, and Sam will find out the details. Right now, you need to go and be with your daughter, and husband. I'm so sorry."

Cara was sobbing uncontrollably now. Ann was in shock, but she quickly took control, and comforted Cara. Little Abby, seeing the wagon was stopped, was now riding towards them. Cara composed herself the best she could when she saw her daughter. She had to be strong for her, that's all there was to it. Abby reached the wagon just as Cara got herself under control.

"Mommy, why are you stopping? Are we done with the ride already? Mommy, have you been crying? What's wrong?" Abby jumped down off her horse and ran to her mom.

Cara stepped down from the wagon and hugged her daughter. "Honey, something has happened back at the ranch and we need to get there as fast as we can. You need to come with Ann and me on the wagon, and Jake is going to bring Buffy, okay? I need you to be a big girl now and don't argue with me on this. We need to go right now, okay?"

Abby could tell that her mom was serious. She didn't argue, just handed the reins to Jake, and went with her. "Mister Jake, you take care of Buffy for me okay? I know she likes you, so it'll be alright." She gave Buffy a hug then. "I'll see you when you get home Buffy, now you be good for mister Jake you hear?"

After the wagon left, Jake turned to Tom, leading the little pony along. "Well, let's get to it then. This is the worst of the worst. I have been to many suicides. It's not pretty, I hope Cara doesn't have to see it."

"I agree, let's go let the other people know what's going on. They should be able to handle the cattle from here on out. I think we are needed at the ranch."

Jake nodded, and the two men solemnly hurried back to the ranch. That wanted to get there before the wagon. This wasn't the end of the ride they thought it would be.

When Sam got back to the ranch, the first thing he saw were the police cars everywhere, and the crime scene tape at the door of the barn. He headed there and handed his horse off to Don. "Tell me what happened Don. What are the police saying? Was it a suicide?"

"They aren't telling me anything Boss. From what it looked like to me, I would say that Phil shot himself. The gun was lying beside him on the ground. That's all I know."

Sam nodded, handing the reins to Don. "Would you take care of my horse? I need to talk to whoever is in charge here."

At that moment a detective walked up to Sam. "That would be me, sir. Detective John Groves. Who might you be?"

Sam shook the man's hand. "I am Sam Long, I own this ranch. Could you tell me what you've found so far? I knew Phil quite well, he is a tenant at my ranch."

"Mr. Long, I'm not in the business of sharing details with friends or ranch owners. All I can say is we have a deceased male in the barn. Were you here when this happened?"

Sam bristled at the man's response. "No, we were out on a roundup. Mr.Carson's wife and daughter were with us. They are on their way here right now. I would hope that you would remove the body by then?"

"The coroner has just arrived. He is taking the body to the morgue now to perform an autopsy. I need to speak to the deceased's wife as soon as she arrives. Make sure you bring her to me right away."

"I will do that sir, but you need to realize that she will be devastated by this. The couple have a ten-year old daughter, I will expect you to be a little more understanding with them, understood?"

The detective nodded, and turned away, obviously done speaking with Sam. Sam didn't much like the man, but knew the detective had a job to do, and so did he. Sam heard horses approaching the ranch, and turned to see Ann and Cara in the wagon, coming towards him. Nancy was riding alongside the wagon. He was surprised to see Abby with her mother in the wagon. Sam grabbed the horses reins when they approached. Cara jumped down and started running towards the barn. Sam grabbed her around the waist.

" Believe me, you don't want to go in there Cara." He glanced toward Abby. "Does Abby know what's happened?"

Cara just looked at him blankly, she was in shock. Sam waved Ann and Nancy over. "Honey, will you take Cara and Abby to the house, please? The detective wants to talk to Cara, but that is going to have to wait. She needs time to deal with what has happened. I won't allow her and Abby to be harassed by him right now, he isn't a nice guy." He whispered in Ann's ear. "Listen, someone needs to tell Abby about her dad before she hears it from someone else. Can you do that?"

Ann nodded, and grabbed Cara and Abby by the hand. With Nancy's help they would handle this. "Come on, let's get them away from here."

Cara just stared at the barn, where right at that time, the coroner was taking out the body of her husband. Abby was looking at it too. She didn't understand what was happening, thankfully. Sam watched as the women made their way to the house. He turned back to the barn and shook off the bad feeling he had about this suicide. It was going to be devastating for everyone involved. Sam slowly walked toward the coroner and detective Groves.

"What's your take on this Dr. French? Was it a suicide?"

The coroner turned to Sam. "It's good to see you again Sam. I'm sorry it's under these circumstances. To answer your question, it appears to be a suicide. There was one gunshot wound to the right side of the head, and the gun was lying on the ground beside the body. I won't know for sure until the complete autopsy, but he did have gunshot residue on his right hand. I'll let the police know when I've completed the autopsy."

Detective Groves spoke up then. "Yes, you do that Doctor. Now, Mr. Long, was that the wife you were talking to? I told you I needed to talk to her right away."

"Yes, that was Cara Carson. She is in shock, and is in no shape to talk to you right now. I'm afraid that is going to have to wait detective."

Detective Groves looked like he was going to argue with Sam over that, when they heard horses approaching. Sam turned to see Jake and Booker riding in. He waved them over to where he was standing with the detective. He needed his brothers right now. "Jake, Booker, I'd like you to meet Detective Groves. He is with the homicide unit in Portland. Detective Groves, this is my brother Jake and my foreman, Booker."

The detective barely gave Booker the time of day, addressing Jake first. "Yes, I've heard of you Long. Former homicide right? I'm assuming you'll stay out of my way here, I don't need some former law enforcement thinking they need to stick their nose where it doesn't belong."

Jake wasn't surprised by Grove's attitude, he took it in stride. "I don't plan on getting in your way detective, but I'll certainly try to help if I can. Why don't you fill us in on what happened here?"

That satisfied the detective and he softened a bit. "We got a body of a white male, presumably Phil Carson. I need the wife to verify that, but Sam here won't let me talk to her. He has a gunshot wound to the head. Looks pretty cut and dried that it's a suicide. Carson was a troubled cop. Always was, as I recall. After the shooting that took his ability to walk, it only got worse. We are conducting a complete investigation, but everything is pointing to suicide. Now, could you please let me talk to Mrs. Carson? I need to at least show her a picture of the body and get positive identification of the victim."

Jake and Sam shook their heads simultaneously. "That isn't going to happen right now. We can look at the body and make an ID ourselves."

Groves let out a breath and nodded, handing Jake the picture of the body. "Well, that will have to do for now, but I need to talk to the wife eventually. You know that Long."

Jake nodded, and showed the picture to Sam. "That is Phil Carson."

Jake quickly handed the photo back to the detective. "Yes, we know you need to talk to her. Just give her some time to come to terms with her husband's death."

"I can give her a couple of days at the most, then I'm coming back out here if you don't bring her to me. You know better than anyone, Jake. Until it's deemed a suicide, I need to rule out homicide myself. Now if you'll excuse me, I'll go do my job."

Jake let out a low whistle. "Wow, someone got up on the wrong side of the bed this morning. Let's go into the house and let him do his job then. There's nothing we can do here, and Cara needs us."

Sam looked around as they walked to the house. "Where is Jenny and Tom? Why didn't they come in with you?"

"I'm not sure. Tom was adamant that he needed to stay with the cattle, and Jenny wanted to stay with him. Tom wanted me to call him after all the police left, for some reason. I don't know for sure, but I think it may have something to do with his job as an undercover. He has been getting a lot of phone calls lately. I think he'll be leaving us soon. You know, Jen told me a while ago, that she was having some bad feelings about this cattle drive. I guess we know why now, don't we? I wish I would have listened to her. Jen has been working hard on honing her abilities. I think she has been making some good progress. It will come in handy when she goes into her private eye business."

"I agree Jake. She starts school next week right? I'm glad she decided to take her courses online. Especially now. Abby has grown attached to Jen. She's going to need a lot of people around her. So will Cara."

"Yeah. She decided to get her investigator license right away so she could go straight to work. She can take her courses online in the meantime. It worked out well for her."

When the men reached the house they could hear talking in the great room, so they walked that way. Cara and Abby were clinging to each other on the couch, and Ann was crouched in front of them, holding on to their hands. Nancy was sitting beside Cara, her arm around her and Abby. They all looked up when Jake and Sam entered the room.

Sam cleared his throat. "Well, everyone out there is getting ready to leave. I'm afraid the police need to talk to you Cara. I told them to wait a few days, so you don't need to talk to them today."

Cara looked up with tears in her eyes. "Thanks Sam. I just can't believe this is happening. Phil was doing so much better. He was even working with Red, trying to get his life back. I don't believe it! Something else must have happened. There has to be more to it than what they are saying. Phil wouldn't shoot himself, I know that. We need to find out what really happened."

Abby sobbed loudly, and Cara stopped talking abruptly. She put her arms around her daughter. "Come on Abby, let's go home and get you to bed."

Ann stood up and spoke to Cara. "Why don't you stay here tonight Cara? There is plenty of room, and I think that Abby would sleep better, what do you say?"

Cara nodded, she really didn't want to go back to their house anyway. All of the memories would be too much for Abby, and her.

As the women walked away, Sam got on his cell phone and called Tom. "The police are all gone now, you can quit hiding out there. Jake and I will be out to help you finish herding the cattle into the yard."

Tom scoffed. "I wasn't hiding. Someone needed to stay with the cows, and Jenny and I volunteered, that's all. How are things in there?"

"Not good. It looks like Phil committed suicide. He shot himself in the barn. Cara and Abby are understandably upset, they are staying here tonight. Nancy is helping them deal with Phil's death the best she can. I'm sure glad she is here. Well, we'll take off right now, you're not too far out are you?"

"No, we're holding the cattle about a mile out. We'll keep pushing them in. See you in a bit."

Sam hung up, grabbing his hat and striding towards the door. "Let's go get the cattle in Jake. Then we'll deal with what happened here. I have a feeling this is going to be a long week."

By the time all of the cattle were in the corrals surrounding the ranch waiting for them to be sorted out for the various winter pastures, it was getting dark. The men were tired and solemn, knowing what had happened here earlier. The horses seemed to know what had happened too. They didn't want to go into the barn. They could sense something was wrong. Most of them balked and sniffed the air, smelling the scent of death and blood in the air. Sam decided to leave them outside, some of the barn was still roped off with the crime scene tape anyway. He didn't blame the horses for their reluctance to go into the barn. He didn't much want to either.

After calming the horses, and bedding them down in the corral, Jake, Tom, and Sam trudged to the house. Ann, Jen, and Nancy were waiting for them in the kitchen. The men washed up and headed to the kitchen. Sam hugged Ann, and just held her for awhile, breathing in deeply. "This has been one hell of a day, hasn't it? I don't want to let you go. How are Cara and Abby doing?"

Ann held Sam tightly. She knew how he felt, life can be so short and unpredictable. She felt like she didn't want to let him go either. "After you left, Cara took Abby to one of the spare rooms. I doubt they'll get much sleep tonight. I borrowed them some night clothes so they didn't have to go to their house at all. Nancy was a big help, with her training as a psychologist. I couldn't have done it without her." She finally let Sam go. "You must be starving, I'll fix you something to eat."

Sam reluctantly let her go, turning to the others in the room. "Yeah, we better eat something, but just a sandwich is good enough. Don't go to much trouble. I know you're tired too."

As the group sat and ate their sandwiches, Jake spoke up and said what everyone was thinking, but never wanted to come out and say. "Well, we have to talk about what happened at some point." He looked at Sam, and then at Tom. "What do you two think? Did Phil kill himself, or was there someone else involved? I know he had a lot on his mind lately, kept saying that he was on to something. Could that have gotten him into some kind of trouble?"

Tom put his sandwich down, and took a swig of his beer. "I think we have to let the police do their work, and not get in their way. If they say it is a suicide, then that is what it is. Sam, when was the detective coming back out?"

"Tomorrow. The coroner had pretty much made up his mind about Phil's death, so had detective Groves. I have a feeling the doctor will pronounce it a suicide tomorrow sometime, and the police will come out and close the case. I guess we just have to wait and see."

"Well, I'll go out and help the hands get the cows sorted early, and we'll start hauling them out to pasture. You two need to be here when the police come back. Do me a favor will you? Don't mention to the police that I'm here. I would rather stay incognito, that's how I have to be for this job."

"We figured as much, nothing will be said. I'll let you know when everything is done, and Jake and I will help with the cattle the rest of the day. Well, I for one am beat, this has been one hell of a day. My wife and I are going to bed. Good night all."

The group rose and headed to their rooms, still pretty quiet after the events of the day. It didn't take long for silence to envelop the house. In most of the rooms anyway.

Jenny was tossing and turning in her bed, having a hard time getting her mind to shut down. She kept seeing Phil, sitting in his wheelchair, smiling at his daughter. Then, all of a sudden, he was in the barn, with half of his head missing. Blood running down his body, and pooling on the floor. Jen jumped up, hearing a noise in the corner of her bedroom. It was Sara, her mom, she was sure of it. Sara always showed up when Jen needed her. It was like she knew that Jen needed help, and her mom was there.

Jen rubbed her eyes. "Mom, I knew you would come. What is going on? Do you know what happened to Phil Carson?

Please, tell me. Let me know so I can help soothe Cara and Abby's pain."

Sara stood there staring at Jen and smiled. Jenny finally could hear her mother clearly. "*Jenny, my darling, you will soon find out for yourself what happened. I can't tell you because I don't know the whole story yet. I will help as much as I can. I know that this goes deeper than anyone can imagine. You need to follow your dream, and everything will come together. There is one thing you need to know Jenny. Someone will be coming to you besides me, and you need to keep an open mind, okay? It will be a shock at first, but I promise that it will be okay. They will help you with this case. Just promise me you'll be careful, and keep your dad by your side. That's all I can say right now. I only have so much time left. I love you darling.*"

Jenny was a little confused by what her mom said. What did she mean by all of that? Who is going to help with a case, and what case exactly? She needed to talk to her dad right away in the morning. Jenny yawned, and fell into a deep, dreamless sleep after her mom left her. She had a goal, and that was to be the best private investigator that she could be. She wanted to help people the only way she knew how, through her abilities. She knew with her dad by her side, and with Sara's help, she could do some good in the world. She just hoped that people would understand how she solved her cases. Well, her dad was right on one thing, she needed to keep that to herself, for now.

The morning was bright and sunny, no sign of the devastation that had happened the night before. Cara looked a little better, but had bags under her eyes from no sleep. Abby was understandably quiet and solemn, not even asking to go feed Buffy her apple. When the phone rang, everyone jumped, and Sam answered. Everyone knew who it was just by listening to Sam's end of the conversation. "Yes, detective. Already? I understand. I will let everyone know. I'll see you in an hour."

When Sam turned to the family standing around the table, he addressed Cara. "Cara, that was detective Groves.

He is on his way out here to talk to you, but he wanted me to let you know that the autopsy is already over. It's like they thought, Phil shot himself. The doctor has pronounced his death a suicide. I'm so sorry."

Cara held back a sob. "Thank you Sam. Thank all of you for everything you have done for us. All of us, even Phil. He really did appreciate everything, even if he didn't show it. Well, I guess I had better get ready for the detective to get here." She sobbed loudly. "I have a funeral to plan."

Ann and Nancy stepped forward. " You're not alone Cara. We will help you however we can. You know that you are welcome to stay here on the ranch as long as you want to. It would be good for Abby to be around familiar things. I know there will be bad memories too. We'll all go along with your decision."

Cara nodded. "I don't know what I'll do, but thank you for that. I can't really think straight right now. I'll just have to keep putting one foot in front of the other. If you will excuse me, I'll go get ready now."

The detective's interview was pretty cut and dried. He said all the right things. The chief was with him and offered a traditional police funeral for Phil, even if it was a suicide. Cara agreed, and the funeral was set for four days later.

● ● ●

Cara and Abby were numb, going through the motions of the funeral, and reception afterwards. There was a good turnout, all of Phil's colleagues were there, along with Cara's. Everyone gave their condolences, and Cara was beginning to see that Phil had a lot of friends in the police force. She had to admit, it was nice to see them all there, especially since neither one of them had any family left. Then it was over, and Cara and Abby stood by Phil's grave, saying their own goodbyes. Cara felt as if someone was watching her, she turned to look, but no one was there. She shrugged, shivering a little. Cara took

Abby's hand, leading the little girl away from her father and on to their life without him.

Cara had decided to leave the ranch, there was just too many bad memories for her, and Abby. She needed to start fresh. It didn't take long to clean out their cabin, there really wasn't much there. Just some clothing, a few boxes that Phil had been storing old papers in, and a box that he called, "*his own personal hell.*" Whatever that meant. All she knew was that she was going to have to wait awhile before she could bring herself to go through all of his things. Sighing, she picked up the boxes and left her past behind.

● ● ●

The Long ranch seemed to be clearing out fast. First Cara and Abby left, then Tom took off on a new case that he refused to say anything about. Sam, Ann, and Jake were sitting on the huge porch after supper one night, having a nightcap and talking about the events that had happened that summer. Jake held out his glass.

"I would like to make a toast to the people who aren't here right now. To the safety of our brother Tom, and to Jenny, who is following her dream. Also, to Phil, may he Rest In Peace. To Cara and Abby, may they find peace also, and to the three of us."

Sam lifted his glass. "Well said Jake. I'm sure glad Cara said that Abby could come and visit the ranch whenever she wants to. I sure miss that little girl's laugh. Last I heard they were doing okay."

••• 6 •••

TIME FLEW BY, and before Jen knew it, she was opening her own private investigation office. Jen knew that she was a little young, but with her dad's help, she could do this. She may be young, but she was more than ready for this.

She hadn't heard much from Sara. Her mom had told her some strange things the last time she saw her. Jen had been so busy with school, she hadn't thought much about it. Is her mom gone for good? She shook her head. She had gone for some time without seeing and talking to Sara before. This was no different. Jenny knew her mom was around, she could feel it.

She couldn't believe she was actually doing it. She was at the top of the class in her criminal classes. That was no surprise, seeing as how she grew up with a detective as a father. She thought back to the days when she talked for hours with her dad, telling him that she wanted to be just like him someday. Little did she know then, that she would take a different path, albeit somewhat the same. Using her abilities, she hoped that she could help people just the same.

As she looked around her tiny office, she smiled. *I can't believe this day is finally here. All of my hard work is going to pay off, I know it. With dad's help, and whoever else I can connect with, I'm going to make it.*

She smiled, and set her nameplate on her small, worn out desk. *Nothing fancy, but it's all mine.* Jen turned when she heard a noise at the door. Jake, Sam, and Ann were standing there with a huge plant in their hands. Jen squealed and ran to them, hugging them one by one. "Thank you so much! My first office warming gift. You guys are the best."

Jake cleared his throat. "Hey, I don't see my name on the door, what's up with that?"

"If your name was on there, it would probably chase people away. I think that's the opposite of what Jen is trying to do here, Jake." Sam piped up, smacking his brother on the arm.

Jake glared at Sam and Ann stepped between them. "Alright you two, Jenny is the one who worked hard to get her license to open her business, not you. Besides, you're only the hired help Jake."

Jake and Sam both laughed at that, and Jenny hugged Ann. "Thanks Ann, I needed the back up there. Now all I need is to advertise my services, and get people coming in. I need to make a name for myself if I'm going to get this to work."

"You'll do great Jen. Just be patient, and everything will be great. Now, what do you say we go to lunch? I'm starving!"

"That's the best thing you've said all day Jake. You're buying!" Sam turned and headed out the door before Jake could even answer.

Jen locked her office door, and rubbed her hand over the lettering on the door. "Jenny Long, Private Investigator. I still can't believe it!" She turned and went arm in arm with her family to the nearby restaurant.

● ● ●

Cara Carson was exhausted. She had just worked a double shift at the restaurant where she was waiting tables. Now, she had to go to her cleaning job at the office building next door to her apartment. The past year had been hard, for her, and for Abby. Her eleven year old daughter, Abby, was asleep at the neighbor's apartment. It seemed as though Cara was spending less and less time with Abby. She sighed, looking around the small apartment. All she did was work and come home to an empty apartment. She really needed to get a better job so she could spend more time with Abby. She just didn't know how she was going to do that.

Cara stopped in the middle of her bedroom, looking at the sparse interior. Her gaze fell on the box that she had brought from the ranch. It seemed like ages ago that she was dragging Abby away from the ranch. She really needed to go through Phil's things and throw them away, but it wasn't going to happen tonight. It seemed like she always had some excuse. Cara dragged herself away from the unopened box, and got ready for her other job. She yawned, and gazed longingly at her bed. She had the weekend off and she was taking Abby to the ranch to spend some quality time with her during the summer break. She could hardly wait. Ann was so kind to invite them for the weekend. Abby was so looking forward to it.

"Well, one thing at a time. I'll deal with this box when I get home. For now, I have a job to do." Cara sighed. She left the silent apartment, locking the door as she walked out, unaware of the eyes that watched her from the darkness.

• • •

The weekend was here before she knew it, and Abby was bubbling with excitement. Cara had to admit, she was excited too. It had been awhile since they had been back to the ranch. She didn't know how she was going to handle it. Let alone her young daughter. Too many memories I guess. They weren't all bad ones. She was glad they were going back, she couldn't wait to see her friends. She needed the fresh air and open spaces, and Abby wanted to see Buffy. Even though the little pony was getting older, Abby still rode her. She loved that pony, and Buffy loved her. Sam had purchased more horses, and Abby was excited to try them out. Cara needed to get away from this dingy apartment too. There was something not right, but she couldn't put her finger on it. Cara was going to talk to Sam and Jake about it, but she already knew what they were going to say. Come back to the ranch. But she just wasn't ready for that yet. She did have something to talk to Ann about though, and she knew what the answer was going to be. Cara smiled when Abby ran into the room with her overnight bag, smiling from ear to ear.

"Let's go mom, I'm ready. Can we go now please?"

"Yes, I'm ready to go now. I just talked to Ann and she is waiting for us. I can't wait to get there, how about you?"

"I can't wait either. It seems like it's been forever since I have seen Jenny, and Sam and Ann. Jake too, but I know that Buffy will be happy to see me. Mom, are you okay? You seem worried about something."

"I'm fine sweetie, just a little tired. Let's go have some fun this weekend."

They laughed and sang songs with the radio all the way to the ranch. It was only an hour drive, and Cara relaxed a little.

When they pulled into the drive, Ann came out to greet them. "I'm so happy to see you two. How have you been?"

"We've been good." Cara gave Ann a hug, and Abby gave her a high five as she ran by, talking the whole time.

"Hi Ann. Where is Jenny? I can't wait to see her. Is she with the horses? Mom, can I go down to the barn and see the new horses?"

Ann smiled at Abby. "Yes, Jenny is down at the barn. If it's alright with your mom you can go down there."

Abby glanced at her mom, already turning to run down that way. "Can I Mom?"

"Yes you can, but don't get in the way, and be careful okay?"

"I will, thanks mom."

The women laughed, and Ann helped Cara with their overnight bags. "I wish you were here to stay Cara. I love having Nancy and Jen here, but some days I feel like I'm outnumbered."

"Well, maybe some day, but right now I'm where I need to be. I do have something I want to talk to you and Sam about while Abby is at the barn. Jake too, but first you two. Is Sam around?"

"Yes, he's in the house doing some dreaded book work. I'll get him when we get you settled. This sounds serious, is everything okay?"

"Yes, everything is fine. But, I need to ask you something, and I don't want Abby to overhear what I have to ask. Can we go to Sam's office right now?"

Ann was a little surprised at Cara's impatience, but she agreed. Sam looked up from the paperwork he was looking over when he heard them talking. He stood when they entered the room. "Hello Cara. I'm sorry I didn't come out to greet you, but I'm a little overwhelmed here. I'm happy for the distraction though."

"Hello Sam, it's so nice to see you. I'm sorry for disrupting your bookwork, but this is kind of urgent. I really need to ask you and Ann something, and I don't want Abby to hear me. Please, sit down."

Sam frowned, and looked at Ann for an answer. She shrugged and shook her head.

After they were seated, Cara decided to just come out and ask what she came here to ask them. No beating around the bush. "Okay, I don't know for sure how to say this so I'm just going to ask you. Please, feel free to say no, and take your time answering." She took a deep breath. "As you both know, neither Phil nor I have any family left. I have thought long and hard about this, and I want to ask you a huge favor. If something happens to me, heaven forbid, but if something should happen…will you two raise Abby? I will put it in my will if you agree, and you can adopt her if she wants you to. Well…what do you say?"

Sam and Ann were in shock. Neither one of them spoke for a couple of minutes, they just stared at Cara in disbelief. Cara asked again. "I know it must come as a surprise to you that I ask this, but I need to know Abby will be taken care of in my absence. Please, just think about it okay?"

Sam finally found his voice. "Cara, I think I can speak for both of us when I say that we would gladly take Abby in. But is something going on we should know about? You're not sick are you? Are you okay?"

"No, no, I'm not sick. I just need to know that she will be okay if something happens. We all know how fragile life is. Anything could happen at anytime."

Ann stood and hugged Cara. "Of course. We would love to have Abby with us. We already love her, so it wouldn't be any hardship to take her in. You can rest easy there, but let's hope nothing happens to make that possible."

Cara let out the breath she had been holding. "Thank you both so much. You don't know how much this means to me. Of course, we'll keep this conversation to ourselves for now, okay?"

Ann and Sam nodded in unison. "Okay, enough seriousness. Now that we have that out of the way, let's start a fun weekend."

"Sounds good. There is one other thing, but I need Jake here to talk to you about that. Then we can start the weekend."

The women walked arm in arm out the study door. Sam stared at them with a frown on his face. He wondered what the real reason was for Cara's sudden question about Abby's welfare if something should happen to her. He had a feeling something more was going on than Cara was saying.

It was an enjoyable weekend, with Abby riding horse everyday, and Cara getting some much needed rest and relaxation. She loved it that she could walk outside without looking over her shoulder constantly. She shared with Ann and Sam and Jake and Jenny, her feelings of being watched, and they agreed that she needed to take extra precautions. "I still think it's all in my head. Ever since Phil's suicide, I have been feeling paranoid. It's been long enough, I need to let it go. I need to go through his things when I get home, and get rid of some of that paperwork. I think I will call his precinct, and see if they want some of those boxes. They are marked police business anyway. I'd have to say that Phil was doing some work for them. Either way, I need to get rid of those boxes and move on. I'm never going to forget my husband, but he's gone. I think it would be in Abby's best interest to go on with our lives."

Ann nodded. "I have to agree with you on that one Cara. You can go on with your lives without forgetting your husband. It looks as though Abby is doing well. Do you want me to come in and go through those boxes with you?"

"No, thanks though, I can handle it. It's something that I need to do alone. I hate to ask, but would you mind keeping Abby for me for a couple of weeks? Could I bring her out this next weekend? I would rather she wasn't there when I start throwing things away that belonged to her dad."

"Of course, you can bring Abby out anytime you need to. Just give us a call, and we can come in and get her too. Jenny is there every day getting her office set up, she could bring Abby out here too."

"Thank you Ann. I am going to do that sometime soon."

The weekend at the ranch went by way too fast, and before Cara knew it she was back at work. She vowed to go through those boxes the following week. She was going to have Abby stay at the ranch, and she was spending the whole week doing that. She was dreading it. She had called Jen, and she was going to come and pick up Abby and take her to the ranch on Friday.

After Jenny left with Abby, Cara dug in. Most of the boxes were Phil's old clothes, his police badge, and some papers from his desk at the police station. She put his badge and the papers into a different box, one she had been saving for Abby. The other box was scheduled to go to his precinct. She had already made a call, and the captain said he would send someone by to pick it up. Cara was meeting Jen for lunch, and she wanted to see her office, and spend some time with her. She opened the last box, lifting out some of the papers that were marked "Police business." Cara was getting ready to put the papers in the box that the captain was picking up, when something fell out of the stack of papers. Cara picked it up and noticed that her name was written on it. It was Phil's handwriting. She slowly opened the letter.

*Dear Cara,*

*If you're finding this letter, something has happened and I must not be around to tell you this in person. Cara, if I am dead, know that I love you and Abby very much, and I would never do anything to take me away from you. If I'm dead, someone killed me. I would not leave you two alone unless someone took me from you. Get this box of papers to someone who would be able to prove that. Jake Long was a good cop, I would trust him with my life. You can too. Remember, I love you and Abby, I always will.*

*All my love, Phil*

Cara had tears streaming down her face. She was sobbing uncontrollably, glad that Abby wasn't here to see her this way. What did this mean? Should she take it seriously? What was Phil's intentions with this? Did he write it just to confuse her? She didn't know, but she was going to talk to Jen about it at lunch. Cara wiped the tears from her face, freshened her makeup, and went to meet Jen.

Jenny was at the restaurant waiting when Cara arrived. She waved at Cara, and hugged her tightly, looking at her with concern in her eyes. "Are you alright? You look a little pale. What's going on?"

Cara knew that she wasn't going to be able to keep this from Jen, she didn't want to anyway. She might as well get it over with. Grabbing the letter out of her purse, she silently handed it off to Jen. No words were needed. Jenny frowned, and read the letter slowly. She looked up at Cara when she was done, the shock showing on her face. "Do you believe what he wrote in this letter? He didn't kill himself? What do you think, Cara?"

"I don't know what to think. I have often thought about his suicide. I could never figure out why he would do it. I mean, it's obvious, I suppose. Phil was sad and angry most of the time, but I honestly thought he was coming out of it. He seemed happier toward the end, like he had a mission or something. I went through most of the papers in the last box and didn't find anything interesting. There is still more to go through, but none of it made any sense to me. Just some notes on different cases, and some policemen's names. Nobody I knew. I'm waiting for someone from the police department to come and pick it up. I can't make heads or tails of it anyway. But Jen, promise me you'll look into this. If Phil didn't kill himself, then what happened? This is all giving me a huge headache."

"If you want me to, my dad and I can look into it. It could be our first official case, pro bono, of course."

"I hate to do that to you, but as you know, I'm barely scraping by. It's your decision whether or not to do this Jen."

"Well, clients aren't exactly beating down my door." Jen laughed. "I'll talk to Dad tomorrow, and show him this letter. I'm sure he'll agree that it does need looking into. Now, let's enjoy our lunch. No more talk of work."

The lunch date was enjoyable. Cara felt a little more relaxed, and was glad that she shared her feelings with Jenny. She knew she could count on her and Jake to find out what happened to Phil. She was confused by all of this. Was it true? Or was Phil just trying to cover for him taking his own life. Maybe he thought if he blamed someone else for his death, it would change the stigma of suicide. Cara recalled some of the conversations between Phil and her about just that topic. He basically said that any cop who commits suicide shouldn't have been in law enforcement anyway. It was a legacy that he said he would never leave his family to deal with. But that was before he ended up in a wheelchair. His growing depression was taking over his personality, but he was fighting it, and overcoming it. So she thought.

Cara walked into the empty apartment. The darkness and silence were all that greeted her, along with the boxes and papers scattered about. She sighed, and started putting them back in the box marked for the police to pick up. She had been through some of the papers that Phil had been working on. None of them made much sense to her, there was too much police jargon for her to understand. She had to smile, Phil always wanted her to get more involved in his job. To hang out with him and his cronies, along with their wives. She just couldn't do it. She had a daughter to raise, and was too busy to go out with his friends. It was a sore spot between the two of them, but they worked it out. Anyway, she was glad that she at least tried to go through all of Phil's things. She never would have found that letter if she hadn't. Cara shook her head. *Did Phil kill himself? What did he mean when he said that someone killed him? Who on earth would want to kill her husband?* She was more confused than ever, but Cara was glad she involved Jenny and Jake. They would get to the bottom of this, she was sure of it.

After packing up the boxes and taping them shut, Cara sighed, and moved them closer to the door. It was sad, really, to see all of Phil's life summed up in three boxes. Someone's life, all wrapped up into boxes, ready to be taken to their perspective places. Cara glanced at the clock on the wall, it was already ten o'clock, and she hadn't eaten since lunch with Jenny earlier in the day. Her stomach growled on cue. Opening her refrigerator door, she grabbed an apple, and some cheese, along with the milk. This was going to have to do for now.

She was going to the grocery store as soon as Abby got home tomorrow, the cupboards and fridge were getting bare.

She had talked to Abby earlier, and she was having a blast at the ranch. Cara figured that Abby could stay there all the time if she would let her. Cara shrugged. "Oh well, that's not going to happen. I have to work to keep food on the table, and I'm not driving back and forth from the ranch. Abby understands that I'm doing the best I can here. She will just have to be happy with her visits to the ranch."

Abby was staying with Sam and Ann next week too, because Cara was working for a friend of hers at the diner downtown. With that, and her job cleaning the office, she was going to be exhausted.

The next day, Cara was getting ready for Abby to come home for the weekend, when she heard a knock at her door. Peeking out of the peephole in the door, she saw a policeman who she didn't recognize standing outside. Cara opened her door. "Can I help you?"

The officer took his hat off and nodded to Cara. "Ma'am? I am officer Blake from the fifth precinct. The one that your husband worked for. I was sent over to pick up a box that you called about?"

Cara opened her door wider. "Oh yes, please come in. I did call about that. I just didn't know what to do with it. It has some papers that looked to me like something Phil was working on for the police. There were a lot of words that I didn't understand. I didn't know that he was working on anything for the station, but you can make that decision when you look at the papers. The box is right in here."

Cara led him to the hallway, where she had put the box with the papers, along with the two boxes with Phil's clothing in it. "It's just this one box. Do you need my help carrying it?"

"No, thank you Ma'am, I can get it. I just want to say that I am very sorry for your loss. I didn't know your husband personally, but I have heard nothing but good things about him."

"Thank you for that. Phil was a good man, and a good cop."

Officer Blake picked up the box easily, and headed out the door. "Well, I'll get these things to my Captain. He wanted me to take them directly to him, so I will get them out of your way, Mrs. Carson."

"Thanks for coming over to pick this up. Tell Captain Keller hello for me would you?"

Officer Blake nodded, and carried the box to his car. *Well.* Cara thought. *I guess there's one box down and two to go, but they're going to have to wait. I have to go and pick up my daughter at Jenny's office.*

Cara locked the door behind her, and headed downtown to Jenny's office. She was just heading towards the door to the office, when she heard Abby's voice. "Mom, we're over here. Jenny took me to the park for a little bit while we waited for you."

Cara turned toward the sound of her daughter's voice. "I'm so sorry I'm late getting here, but something came up, and I got sidetracked. Were you a good girl at Sam and Ann's?"

Abby rolled her eyes at her mom. "Mom, I am always good, you know that. I'm eleven years old now, practically a teenager. I know how to behave."

Cara looked at Jen, trying to hold back a laugh. "I'm sure you do, but that isn't going to stop me from asking, making sure you were good. You will always be my little girl, no matter how old you get. Now scoot to the car over there, I have something I want to ask Jen."

Abby took off at a run for the car, and Cara turned to Jen. "I'm so sorry I was late. An officer came by and picked up the box of papers that Phil was working on, and I lost track of time."

"It's fine. Abby is certainly no problem to have around. It's surprising how well she has adjusted to Phil's death. I could tell that she was uncomfortable going into the barn at first, but she overcame her fears. She had a great time with Buffy and the other horses. She's a natural ranch hand."

"I'm so glad she got to spend more time there. I'm sure she will be driving me nuts this weekend, getting ready to stay there another whole week. I certainly do appreciate it. My neighbors are going on vacation, and I will be working all the time. I am very glad that I won't have to worry about Abby. It's one less thing on my mind. By the way, did you get a chance to talk to Jake about our conversation the other day?"

"Yes, and after looking at the letter from Phil, he agreed that we should look further into Phil's death. Although, that letter could have been written a long time ago, before his accident. I don't want you to get your hopes up that Phil didn't shoot himself Cara. Everything points to that. When Dad gets here today we're going to get started on it. We're starting with interviewing Phil's captain, and getting more details on the shooting that left him paralyzed. We have an appointment this afternoon. I'll let you know what we find out."

Cara let out a breath. "He never talked to me much about the shooting. The only thing that Phil would say about it is that it involved drugs. The man that shot him got sent to prison, and was killed there." Cara rubbed her sore neck. "Thank you again. I don't think I could sleep at night without knowing the truth. Whatever you find out, I will accept it. I just need to know for sure. Thank you too, for giving Abby a ride in. You guys are a Godsend."

Jen hugged Cara tightly. "You and Abby are family to us Cara, always remember that. Anytime you need anything, just call, okay? Now, go spend time with your daughter before you have to start working double time."

"I will, I'll see you on Monday then. I'll have Abby here by three o'clock okay? I have to clean the office at five."

"Sounds good, I'll see you then. I should have some information then. I'll let you know what we find out."

Cara nodded, and headed to her car, where Abby waited. "Okay, missy, we have to get some groceries, then we are starting our girls weekend. How does that sound?"

"Great mom! Can I pick out a movie for tonight?"

"Sure can! Let's go!"

Abby and Cara had a great time over the weekend. Walking in the park, binge watching their favorite movies, and eating whatever and whenever they wanted. Cara didn't want it to end. But by Monday morning, Abby was too excited about going to the ranch for a whole week, she already forgot about the fun they had. Cara had to laugh at her. "I wish I could bounce back from things as fast as she does." She told Jen when she dropped her off. "That girl ran circles around this old woman this weekend."

Jen laughed along with her, looking over at Abby, already waiting in her car. "She does have some energy, that's for sure. By the way, we had our meeting with Captain Keller, and it went as I expected. He didn't want to tell us anything. He kept saying that Phil's shooting was not anything other than a drugged out man who panicked when he got stopped by the police. The captain assured us that the man had been trafficking drugs, and when Phil pulled him over, he shot him. The man was killed in prison, conveniently, and couldn't answer any questions for himself. He said that an investigation was done internally, and everything was found to be just a routine traffic stop gone bad. Nothing more, nothing less. I was sure glad that my dad was there with me. It was very frustrating. The captain didn't want to tell some young girl anything at all. I'm afraid I may have my work cut out for me to make a name for myself in this field. The police kind of frown on private detectives, especially young females. Oh well, I am going to do this, and do it well. They are just going to have to get over the fact that I'm young. Anyway, that's all he would say about that. We may have to go over his head to get any of the paperwork from the internal investigation, he just wasn't going to cooperate."

"Well, just do what you can Jenny. Maybe after looking over whatever those papers that Phil was working on are all about, he'll be more cooperative. Well, I had better get to work. Let me know if Abby gets to be too much, I could figure something out."

"She won't be a problem, Cara. You just take care of yourself, and try not to overdo it."

After giving the reluctant eleven year old a kiss and hug, Cara went on her way. *Let the fun begin*. She thought, as she dug for the keys to her car.

Cara was exhausted by the time she got done cleaning the office that night. She dragged herself into the apartment, taking her shoes off at the door. Her stomach rumbled, and Cara realized that she hadn't eaten all day. After dropping Abby off with Jen, she went straight to the diner, and then to the office. She sighed. "Well, I guess I had better eat something, I don't need to get sick with everything going on this week." Cara opened her fridge and looked around for something to eat. All she could find was a jug of milk and a few eggs. "Good grief, that girl eats me out of house and home. I definitely need to get some groceries again before she comes home." She opted for a bowl of cereal, there was always cereal in the house. Yawning, Cara poured the milk over the cereal in the bowl. She curled up her nose a little at the bitter tasting milk. "Even the milk is getting sour. Oh well, it's not too bad, besides, that's all I have to eat." So Cara forced down the bowl of cereal, and dumped the rest of the milk down the sink. After rinsing out the box the milk was in so it didn't stink up the whole kitchen, she threw it in the garbage. Sighing again at the sight of the full trash bag, Cara pulled it out of the trash can and carried it out to the larger bin in the alleyway. When she opened the lid, she turned quickly, after hearing a noise toward the back of the alley. Cara let out a little scream. When she turned, a black cat ran out from the corner of the building, hissing at her as he ran by. Cara laughed to herself. She had to tell herself to calm down, it was just a cat. But she couldn't keep the ominous feeling that had been plaguing her for a while now at bay. She shrugged, and headed back to her apartment. Suddenly feeling dizzy, Cara opted for a quick shower instead of her usual bath.

Cara was confused. What on earth could be making her feel ill so suddenly? She doubled over in pain as she leaned over the toilet to vomit. She was sweating profusely, and very dizzy. Her head was pounding, she couldn't figure out what was going on. As she shook violently, and doubled over in pain, she managed to make her way to the bed. *What is happening? It must be food poisoning. I'll be fine.* She felt so tired, she was asleep before her head hit the pillow.

••• *7* •••

THE SMOKE WAS billowing out of the apartment build-ing. All you could hear was sirens, and the sounds of people milling about. Some were the residents, and some were just curious onlookers. There was always a contained amount of chaos around a fire. The police had to keep people away from the area, and the firefighters were busy trying to contain the fire, and get people out of harms way. There weren't a lot of residents in the old building, so it didn't take long to get everyone out. The fire was contained fairly quickly, but the building was a total loss.

The fire chief, Tod Beckham, approached the onlookers. "Does anyone know who the apartment manager is? Please come forward if you do, we need to talk to you."

A tall man came forward at the chiefs request. "I am the manager here. My name is Rod Tolley. How can I help chief?"

"Mister Tolley, can you verify that everyone got out of the building? Is everyone accounted for?"

Rod looked around. "I think so. We have fire alarms in each hallway and apartment. As soon as they went off, every-one evacuated. I hate to admit it, but I'm not sure about everyone. Some people work nights, and aren't always home. I wish I could be of more help."

The chief looked the man up and down. He looked genuinely upset over the fire. "Okay, Mr. Tolley, we will take it from here. You need to go over to the paramedics and get checked out for smoke inhalation, along with the rest of the residents. I'll let you know if we need you."

Coughing, Rod ambled over to where the other residents were getting checked out by the paramedics on the scene. Chief Gary Thompson turned to the nearest fireman, Pat. "Okay, as soon as it's safe, I need you to go in and check each apartment for bodies. Apparently the manager doesn't keep a very close eye on his residents. God help us, I hope he's right, and everyone made it out okay. I'll get the fire inspector out to help find out just what started this fire."

The fireman nodded, and along with the other men, entered the building. Going from apartment to apartment, room to room, the building was cleared. That is, until they got to apartment 4B.

The firemen entered the apartment, noting the children's belongings scattered about. Everything was pretty much destroyed from the fire. "Dear God, please don't let there be a child in here." He trudged through the remnants of the foam that was used to quell the fire. He breathed a sigh of relief when all of the rooms were cleared. Until they got to the master bedroom. The fireman could just make out the silhouette of a body lying on the burned bed. He rushed over to the body. The fireman grimaced, and turned to his partner. "Got a body!" He yelled to his partner.

When his partner entered the room, he walked over and glanced down at the body. "Oh man. Looks like they just never woke up. Call the coroner, get him here pronto."

Pat got on his radio and let the chief know that they had found a body in apartment 4B. The chief took off his hat and wiped his brow. "Any more?"

"No." Pat replied. "All clear in the other apartments."

"Okay, the coroner is on his way." Tod turned his gaze back to the onlookers and spotted Rod Tolley. Waving him over, he looked hard at the man. "Mr. Tolley, I need to ask you a question. "Who lives in apartment 4B?"

Rod rubbed his chin. "I'm not sure, but I think it's Cara Carson, and her daughter, Abby. Oh my God! Please tell me they aren't dead." He turned, and waved over another woman standing by the crowd. "Sally, do you know if Cara is here? I know that she works nights, was she home last night?" He looked at the chief. "I'm sorry, this is Sally, she lives on the fourth floor, not far from Cara and Abby."

Sally looked startled. "You know, I haven't seen Cara since the fire, but the last time I talked to her, she was going to take Abby to the Long Ranch for the week. She had to work double shifts all week. I know she was home though, because I saw her go into her apartment around ten." She sucked in a breath. "Oh no, she never got out, did she? I knew I should have knocked on her door when I ran out, but the alarm was blaring so I thought she would hear it!" She started sobbing uncontrollably, and the chief called over a paramedic.

"Okay, thank you both, I'll let you know what we find out. Please, don't leave town until we figure out what happened here." At that, he turned and headed over to where the coroner was just pulling up. "Doc French, we have a body on the fourth floor. She was burned, but looks like she basically died from smoke inhalation. I'll take you up myself."

The doctor nodded and sighed. "Why can't the bodies ever be on the first floor? I'm too old for all of those stairs. Well, let's go then." Grabbing his kit from the van, he turned and followed the chief towards the building. "Are you sure it's safe to go in there?"

"I wouldn't take you in if it hadn't been cleared, Doc. You'll be fine."

Doctor French trudged along behind Chief Thompson. "When my assistant arrives he can bring up the body bag. I want to look over the scene first. Was this fire an accident? What exactly happened here?"

"We don't know that yet. The fire inspector will be going over the scene, trying to figure that out. He will let us know what he finds out. Watch your step Doc."

When the two men got to apartment 4B, the door creaked eerily as they opened it. The stench of smoke and burnt flesh greeted them, along with the eerie silence. The two men grimaced as they walked through the door. The fireman who found the body waved them to the master bedroom. "Over here sir, hey Doc."

Doctor French nodded to him, and entered the room. He and the chief had to turn away for a moment, it wasn't a pretty sight. Even the seasoned professionals were struck by the sight of the burned body lying on the bed. All business, Doc checked over the body, letting out a low whistle. "This was a hot area. The body is burned, but I can tell it is a female. I will be able to tell you what exactly killed her when I get her to the office. Until then, you do your job and I'll do mine." One thing about the coroner, he never pulled any punches. The chief was used to him by now.

"Right, well, let us know the minute you find out cause of death." Chief Thompson turned at the sound of the coroner's assistant coming up to the door. "I'll just leave you to it then." He couldn't get out of there fast enough.

When the chief got back outside, he let out a long sigh. Taking out his cell phone, he called the homicide detectives, just in case. He had a bad feeling about this. This was going to be a long day.

Back at the coroners office, Doc French was just finishing up his autopsy when the chief called him. "I have positively identified the body as that of Cara Carson. I managed to lift a print from her, and it matched a print we had on file for her. She was fingerprinted when she applied for an office cleaning job. She had smoke in her lungs, so cause of death was asphyxiation from smoke inhalation. There was nothing suspicious found so far. I sent her blood samples to toxicology for testing, but we won't know for a few days if she was taking any drugs or anything like that."

"Okay, thanks Doc. I appreciate you hurrying on the autopsy, I know you're busy. I'll let the detectives know so they can call next of kin." He hung up the phone, glad that he didn't have to notify her daughter that her mom was dead. He quickly dialed the police and told them what the coroner had said. They would take care of the death notification. The chief told them what Rod Tolley had said about Abby being out at the Long Ranch. The Long Ranch was well known to the police because of the work they did with former and current law enforcement. The policeman took the report in to his captain. He sighed, and picked up his phone to call Sam Long. He hated this part of his job the most.

Ann Long was just starting to get supper going, when the phone rang. She quickly wiped the flour off of her hands and ran to answer it. "Yes, Long Ranch, Ann Long speaking."

The captain cleared his throat. "Yes, this is Captain Dan Blank of the Portland police department. I understand that Abby Carson is out at the ranch, is that correct?"

Ann frowned. "Yes, that's correct, is something wrong captain? Has something happened?" Sam and Jake had just entered the room when Ann was asking these questions. They looked at her with puzzled expressions. Ann shrugged. "Captain, I am going to put you on speaker phone, my husband and brother-in-law just entered the room."

"Okay, but make sure the little girl isn't in the room, I'm afraid it's not good news."

Ann gasped. "She isn't in the house at the moment. Hang on while I put you on speaker. Okay, go ahead."

The captain cleared his throat again. "I am sorry to tell you this, but there is no other next of kin listed. Mrs. Cara Carson died in a fire last night. It appears that she died of smoke inhalation. I'm so sorry."

Ann nearly dropped the towel that she had been using to wipe her hands. She sat down on the chair next to her. "Oh my gosh! No! Are you sure it's her?"

Sam spoke next. "What did you say your name was? Are you aware that Cara's husband killed himself a little over a year ago? What precinct are you from?"

"I am Captain Dan Blank. I work at the third precinct, and no, I wasn't aware of the suicide, Mr. Long. I'll check into that, thank you for telling me. Cara had been fingerprinted for her job at the office she cleaned. She was positively identified from those fingerprints. Her toxicology report isn't back yet, and she had smoke in her lungs. That's all we know right now. Are you keeping the little girl for now? We'll try to track down some next of kin. If we can't find any, I'm afraid the girl will have to go to family services for now."

Ann gathered herself together long enough to talk. "Abby is staying with us. If you look at Cara's will you'll find out that we are her only relatives. Cara already asked us if we would keep Abby if anything happened to her. Abby isn't going anywhere!"

Sam laid his hand on Ann's shoulder. "I'm sorry captain, but what my wife said is true. You will find that out when you reach Cara's lawyer."

"Well, that's interesting, thanks for letting me know Mr. Long. I'll call the lawyer next, but there will be a lot of paperwork and legal mumbo jumbo to go through before you can take custody. It will be up to the courts in the end. I'll leave the girl where she is for now, but if the courts decide she needs to be somewhere else, I'll see to it that happens. Goodbye Mr. Long."

Everyone was very quiet when Jen brought Abby into the house later. It had been decided that they would tell Abby about her mother after supper. Abby talked to Cara every night on the phone, so the news couldn't wait much longer. It was a solemn supper, but the adults tried to be normal, not wanting to break it to Abby until after they ate. The little girl babbled on about her ride with Jen, and how she couldn't wait to tell her mom about it later. Sam and Ann looked at each other, and nodded to Abby. "That sounds fun Abby. I'm really glad you enjoyed your ride." Ann looked over at Nancy, who had a knowing look on her face. She was so glad Nancy was there. They were all going to need her help with this.

After dishes were all done and everything cleaned up, Sam, Ann, Jake, Jenny, and Nancy, called Abby into the room. The eleven year old girl looked confused when she noticed all of the adults in the room. "What's going on? I was just going to call my mom."

Ann put her arm around Abby. "Abby, could you come in here and sit down please? We have something to tell you." The little girl did as she was told, getting more worried now. Sam stood and walked over to where she was sitting.

"Sweetie, I'm afraid we have some very bad news to tell you. There was a fire last night at the apartment building where you live. Your mom didn't make it out, honey. She's gone."

Abby screamed. "No! That's not true! I just talked to her last night, she was fine. You're wrong! You're wrong!" She broke down and cried, doubling over in pain. "That can't be true. Not my mom too, not my mom."

Ann and Jen hugged Abby tightly. "We're so sorry Abby, but I'm afraid it's true. Your mom was still in her bed honey. She didn't feel any pain, Abby. She just fell asleep."

Abby looked up at them, confusion in her young eyes. "This can't be happening again. It just can't! No! I won't believe it, I won't!" She jumped up and left the room, running for the door. Jake looked at Jen, and she got up and followed Abby outside.

Jen found the little girl just where she thought she would be. With the horses. Abby was stroking Buffy's mane and talking softly to her as Jen approached. Abby looked up at her with tear-stained eyes. "Is it true Jen? Is my mom really gone?"

Jenny sat by the little girl and started petting Buffy. "I'm afraid so, Abby. I'm so sorry, but you will always have a place here at the ranch. You'll never be alone, do you understand? Never! We will always be your family, all of us. You can stay here as long as you want to. We'll be with you all the way through this, I promise. Will you be okay?"

Abby just looked at Jen and shook her head. "I don't know Jen, I really don't. What will happen to me? I don't have a mom or dad now. What'll I do?" She burst into tears.

Jen held the little girl tightly. "Remember what I said, you can stay here for as long as you want. We'll always be there for you, all of us. We will make sure you're taken care of Abby. It's what family is all about."

The two girls sat like that for a long time. Jenny held Abby until her tears subsided. They just sat in silence, listening to the outdoor noises. There were coyotes howling in the distant hills. The cows were mooing, calling to their babies. It was so peaceful, the rest of the world not knowing the pain one little girl was going through at this very moment. The loss of her father and mother within one year. Just how much could one little girl take? How was she going to get through this?

••• 8 •••

THE NEXT WEEK was a blur to the Long's and little Abby Carson. They were preparing for Cara's funeral, which was being held the next day. Abby was so quiet, it was worrying Sam and Ann. Ann tried to talk to Abby about everything that was happening. Cara's lawyer had called, and it was confirmed that Sam and Ann were asked by Cara to be Abby's caretakers if anything happened to her. There was still a lot of paperwork to do, but it seemed Cara's will was pretty much all that was needed. They were not going to push Abby right now, she needed to deal with her mom's death in her own way. Ann and Sam had decided that they were just going to be there for her every step of the way, and Abby knew that. They just needed to get her through the next couple of days, and then they were going to take it one day at a time after that.

The day of the funeral was bright and sunny. It just seemed wrong for it to be such a beautiful day, when you had to bury a loved one. To say goodbye forever to someone who loved you unconditionally, and you loved unconditionally. It just didn't seem right. Abby walked silently alongside Jen, sticking close to her side the whole day. When they got out to the cemetery, Abby couldn't control herself when they started to lower the casket into the newly dug grave right beside her dad. She cried, and threw herself on the casket, not wanting to let her mom go. Everyone just let her cry, she needed to get it out. Abby had been way too silent since her mom's death. She needed to let it out and start healing, if that was at all possible.

After Abby's outburst, they left the cemetery. They promised to come back whenever she wanted to visit with her mom and dad. This promise was the only way they could get her to leave. She fell into silence again. It worried Sam that she wasn't talking. He knew from experience, that she needed to talk about her feelings, not hold them in. He only hoped that she would come out of it and talk to Nancy Hall if she couldn't talk to them. Their life had just changed dramatically. They were now parents of an eleven year old girl. A troubled girl at that, but Sam knew that in her heart, Abby was a good girl and would be fine in time. He hoped that he and Ann were up to the task of raising a daughter. He panicked a little as they pulled into the ranch. *Oh my God! We are parents now! I don't know if I can do it!* Glancing at Ann, he settled down a little. She must have been reading his mind, because she smiled and nodded. She always seemed to know what he was thinking. He nodded back, and the small group of people headed for the ranch house.

Nancy excused herself to go and change, and Jake did the same. Sam and Ann stuck close to Abby. They weren't sure what to do next. Should they talk to her now about what her mom had wanted? Did she already know? Maybe Cara had already told her. They didn't know what to do. Abby looked up at them, and it broke their hearts when the little girl sucked in a shaky breath, and started telling them about the discussion that she and her mom had a while ago. "Listen, I know that my mom asked you two to keep me if something happened to her. We talked about it. I just didn't think it would happen, that's all. I just want you to know that I'll be fine with whatever you decide to do. You don't have to keep me if you don't want to. I can go to social services or whatever that is called. I'll be okay, I promise. I love you both, but I'll understand if you don't want me." She held back another sob, trying to stay strong.

Ann burst into tears, hardly able to form a sentence. She knelt down to look Abby in the eye. "Listen, we were so happy when your mom asked us to be your guardians. We really didn't think it would happen either, but now that it has, we really want you to stay with us. Forever, if you want to. Do you want that Abby?"

Abby thought for a minute, and answered Ann honestly. "I do want that, but you gotta know that no one is going to take my mom's place. I will always love her, and my dad. Nothing is going to change that. I just don't know how I'm going to get over this. I need some time."

Sam couldn't get over how grown up little Abby sounded. She had been through a lot for such a young girl. "We are not going to push you into anything you don't want to do. We just want you to know that you're not alone, not by a long shot. You have a place here with us for as long as you want it. We know that we can't take your parent's place, and we aren't going to try. We loved them too. We love you too Abby, a lot, always remember that."

With that, the three of them hugged and cried some more. Jenny left the room, and headed to her own. Everyone had a lot of work cut out for them. It wasn't going to be an easy transition, but she knew that they were all up for the challenge.

It was only a couple days after the funeral when the captain came out to the ranch. He had the rest of the autopsy results. Jenny took Abby down to the horses so the adults could talk privately. The captain pulled out some paperwork, and read from it. "Well, it looks as though Cara Carson died of smoke inhalation, like we thought. There was something that I thought was odd in the toxicology report. There was a trace of cyanide in Cara's system." Captain Blank held up his hand. "Now hold on." He said, when Sam started to stand up. "Listen, I talked to the coroner, and some other doctors. They all told me that is common when a person dies in a fire. Often times, smoke inhalation is a source for cyanide. The doctors assured me that was the case with Cara. There was no suspicious circumstances in the fire either. It was caused from faulty wiring. The building was very old, and not very well taken care of, I'm afraid. You could sue, but there isn't much to gain. The owners of the building don't have anything. I wanted to come out and tell you in person that the case is officially closed. You all can move on with your lives. Again, I'm sorry for your loss."

Sam stood when the captain stood to leave. The men shook hands. "Thank you for letting us know captain. We'll tell Abby when she comes in. I'll walk you out."

When Abby heard about the cause of the fire she broke down crying. "That old building was always having problems. Mom always said that she wanted out of there, but it never happened." She choked out the words. "What now? Have you heard from the lawyer? I want to know what will happen to me now. I'll never forget my mom or my dad, but I know I have to move forward with my life. Are you going to keep me here?"

Ann thought that Abby looked so small and frail, even when she was trying to be so strong and grown up. "Of course we want you to stay here. We are going in next week to our court date. The judge will have the papers to sign, and then it will be official, you will stay with us."

Abby held back a sob, and hugged Ann tightly. Sam too. She thought to herself that she was lucky to have them in her life right now. Even though she missed her mom, this family would play even more of a pivotal role in her life now. She was very lucky. Well, as lucky as she could be anyway. A kid with no mom, and no dad either. She still couldn't believe this was happening to her. Why did her mom not wake up when the fire alarms went off? I guess she'll never know the answer to that. She had nothing. Not any pictures of her mom, no extra clothes. Even her favorite blanket that her mom had lovingly made her. All of it was gone. Lost in a senseless fire. She felt alone, even when she had a new family now. It was going to be hard, very hard, to adjust to all of this. Abby sighed, and looked at Ann. "Ann, I hate to ask you this, but I have no clothes or anything left from the apartment. Could you take me shopping tomorrow to find something to wear? All I have is what I came out here with. I'll work on the ranch to pay you back, I promise."

Ann smiled sadly. "Abby, remember, you can ask us anything. Yes, I will take you shopping. I'll get Jenny and Nancy to go with us. Are you sure that you feel up to it? You can tell me your sizes and we can pick some things up. You can stay here if you want to. We are your family now, you don't need to worry about anything. Not working to pay us back, nothing. What's ours is now yours okay? Promise me you'll always remember that."

Abby nodded and yawned. "Okay, I promise, but I need to go with you. My mom wouldn't want me moping around here." She yawned again. "Well, it's been a very long day, and I'm tired. I think I'll go to my room now." She paused, and shook her head. "That sounded weird, 'my room'. Well, good night."

Ann and Sam just stared after Abby as she walked from the room. Ann wiped a tear from her eye. "Well, we may have our work cut out for us, but she is a very special little girl Sam. I couldn't feel more proud of her."

"I agree. I still can't believe we are parents. I never thought I would be a dad to anyone. Do you think she will ever look at us as any more than caregivers? I kind of hope so."

"I think in time she may feel differently. I would like to adopt her, but I'm not going to push it. She needs time to adapt to all that has happened to her. Sam, do you think that Cara knew that something was going to happen to her? Why did she decide to ask us to take care of Abby so soon before she died? I have a bad feeling about all of it."

Sam shook his head. "I don't know Ann. She may have just been thinking about what would happen to Abby, and wanted to cover her bases. I know she felt that someone was following her. Maybe that was why, I just don't know. Do you think we should look further into her death? Did the cops miss something? I doubt it. They seemed pretty certain of her cause of death and the cause of the fire. I think it was a clear-cut accident. Nothing seemed suspicious to the authorities."

"I know, and I agree with you. I just don't feel right, that's all. I think it's just everything that has happened in the past year, along with Jenny's visions. Or visits, I guess I should say, with her mom. I have trouble understanding what Sara meant by what she said about someone else coming around to help her. She was so cryptic about everything. I guess maybe I'm just being paranoid. Anyway, I'm tired too. Let's go to bed, everyone else already has."

When Sam and Ann walked by Abby's room, they could hear her crying softly. They decided to let her be. She needed this time alone.

Abby wasn't the only one crying softly though. Jen couldn't help it, she was so sad. She knew what Abby was going through. After all, Jen lost her mother basically in the same way that Abby just did. Jen was so glad she had her dad though. Abby didn't even have that. All of them were going to have to step up and fill a gap in the young girl's life. Jen fell asleep, thinking about Abby, her own mother, and their deaths. Half way through the night Jen woke up, hearing voices in the corner of her room. She opened her eyes, to find her mom and about three other people standing there, silently staring at her. They seemed to start arguing about something. Jen shook off the sleepiness, and waited patiently for one of them to talk. It was as if they didn't even want to acknowledge her presence. She couldn't quite make out who was with her mom, but one was definitely another woman. Could it be Cara, coming back so soon? She could only wait and see what they had to say, if they were going to talk to her at all. Suddenly, Sara looked over and seemed startled that Jen was actually awake.

*I'm so sorry we woke you honey. I told them to be quiet. We just wanted to check on you, and see how Abby was doing, that's all. We are very worried about your safety, all of you. Will you be okay?*

"Of course we'll be okay, and so will Abby. Mom, who is with you? Is this who I'm suppose to talk to, who is it?"

*Honey, you don't need to worry about it right now. Cara is here, along with Phil. It was hard for them to come to you like this, but they didn't want to bother Abby. I told them that you would let us know how she is doing. We won't stay long, I just wanted to check in on you, that's all. There is one more thing we need to tell you. Phil is adamant that you go to the cabin where they used to live. There is something there, something important. He says to look under the floor. I don't know what that means, but it's important.*

Jen could barely hear Sara. She was fading away a little bit at a time. "I can't hear you Mom. What did you say? Mom, I'm so happy to see you, I thought you weren't coming back. Please don't leave me again, I don't think I could stand it. Promise me you'll always be here for me to talk to. You can tell Phil and Cara that we will watch over Abby, and protect her with our lives."

*Jenny, I can't promise you that I'll always be here. It's beyond my control I'm afraid. I will always watch over you, one way or another. You may not see me, but I will be there, I can promise you that.*

With that comment, Sara faded away, along with Phil and Cara, if that is who it was with her. Jenny lay back down and promptly fell back asleep, feeling better after seeing her mother. She slept soundly until her alarm went off bright and early the next morning. Stretching, she did her morning ritual and headed downstairs to the kitchen. Ann was already there, cooking as usual. Jen hugged her. "Do you ever get tired of cooking every day for all of us? You should let someone else do it once in awhile. Take a break."

"Good morning. No, I love cooking, you know that. It's my job anyway, and no one takes over my kitchen." Ann chuckled.

Jen put her hands up and backed off. "Okay, Okay. I get the point. I don't think I could eat my own cooking anyway. Well, I need to get to the office early so I'm just going to grab a piece of toast and be on my way. Would you tell dad that I'll call him if I need him? I have some paperwork to catch up on so I don't think I'll be in the field today. It's not like people are banging down my door anyway. I'll probably close up the Phil Carson case now."

"They will, don't worry. As soon as you get a couple of cases under your belt, the word will get around how great you are. You will be so busy, you won't have time for any of us anymore."

"Well, I'll always have time for you guys. You can't get rid of me that easily." Jen quipped as she grabbed her toast, and headed out the door.

As she pulled up to the office building where her office was located, she had to let out a sigh. So much had happened in their lives. Was it always going to be this way? One thing after another? She hoped not, this family needed some healing now. Jenny hoped that things would calm down for awhile. She parked her car, and headed up to her small office. When Jenny entered her office, she noticed that something was wrong. Someone had been in her office. There were papers strewn about, and her desk drawers were pulled out. She could tell someone had gone through the filing cabinet. She called the police first, and then her dad.

"Dad, someone broke into the office last night. I called the police, but would you come in please? I may need you here."

Jake was shocked. "Are you okay? Why would someone break in there? What do you think they were looking for?"

"I have no idea. We haven't even had a real case yet. I don't understand what anyone would want in here. Will you come in?"

"Of course, I'm on my way."

After hanging up with Jake, Jenny looked around a little more closely. Nothing was missing. There really wasn't much to take, she was only just getting started. Jen was in such deep thought, she was startled when the police showed up. After showing them her credentials, Jen told them what had happened. They found some fingerprints, so they took hers so they could rule her prints out, and left. The police said there had been break-ins around the area lately. There were other offices in the building that kids broke into looking for anything and everything they could get ahold of to sell for drugs. That was probably what it was in this situation too. They would let her know what they found. That was it, they were gone when Jake arrived.

"Have the police been here? They are already done?"

"Yes, they didn't have much to say I'm afraid. Just that kids have been breaking into buildings around the area looking for valuables. They think that is what happened here. They found a few fingerprints, but more than likely they're mine or yours. That was it. They left. I guess I can clean up the mess now."

"They're probably right. Is anything missing? Have you gone over your files?"

"There isn't much here. The only files I had were what we had found about Phil Carson. Those files are in the safe. They never got in there. Besides, there isn't anything in there anyway. The letter from Phil to Cara is in the safe though. I had better check that it's still there."

Jen opened the safe and found the letter, along with the other notes on the case. "I guess we can close up this case now, huh?"

"I suppose. I still think we should follow up on some things though. We can let it go for now."

Just as Jenny and Jake were getting things cleaned up, there was a knock on the door. Jenny looked up to see a woman standing tentatively at the door.

"May I help you?"

The woman cleared her throat. "Yes, are you Jenny Long, the Private Detective?"

"Yes, I'm sorry, come in please. Please excuse the mess, I'm afraid someone broke in here last night, nothing was taken. Probably some kids having some fun on our dime. This is my dad, Jake. Have a seat. How can we help you?"

"Well, I'm not sure that you can, but I have to know the truth. My father was a policeman for thirty five years. He killed himself about ten years ago, right after he retired. I know that's a long time ago, but I just need to know what really happened. My mother recently passed away. She didn't want me to delve into his death, but now that she is gone…. well, you know."

"I understand. I'm sorry for your loss, Miss….?"

"Oh, where are my manners. I am Julie Grant. My dad's name was Griffin, everyone called him Grif. He worked for the Portland Police department for many years until his death. Anyway, he killed himself shortly after he retired. Needless to say, my mom was devastated. She was never the same after that day. She started drinking heavily, and basically my brother and I were left on our own. Oh, look at me, going on and on. What I'm here for is this. I don't think my dad committed suicide, and I need someone to look into it. Would you be interested in taking the case? I know you are just starting out, that's why I'm coming to you. I need someone who will be unbiased. Nothing to do with the police department. I don't trust anyone, Miss Long. Not anyone. Not the retired police, and definitely not the current ones. My dad would never take his own life. I don't know what was going on, but I need to find out for sure. My brother and I need to move on. What do you think? Will you take the case?"

Jake and Jen listened closely to what Julie Grant had to say. Jake was frowning when Jen looked over at him. "Ahem, Miss Grant, can I call you Julie?" Julie nodded. "Julie, it's true that we are just getting started here. But I need to tell you, my dad here, Jake Long, is a retired detective from Los Angeles.

If you don't want any ties to the police, then we may not be the private detectives you want on your dad's case. I think you should maybe think about that for a couple of days, and if you still want us we will be happy to help, if we can. Why don't you take a few days and let us know what you decide?"

"I appreciate your honesty, Miss Long. I will do that, but I don't think it will make any difference. As long as Mr. Long wasn't with the Portland police, it should be okay. I will talk to you in a few days then."

She stood to leave. Jake had to ask her one thing. "Miss Grant, may I ask what precinct your dad was with? I may get started on some research, in case you want us to take the case."

"Yes, he was with the fifth precinct. He started out as a patrol cop, and ended up in the drug enforcement division. Feel free to research it, it is a matter of public record. I'll show myself out. Thanks again."

When Julie Grant left, Jen looked at her dad. "What are you thinking dad? Why did you ask her about her dad if we may not even have the case?"

"Just a feeling. Did you get that he worked in the fifth precinct? Same as Phil Carson. Is that a coincidence? Maybe, but it just gives me a bad feeling, that's all. Call it cop's intuition. We could work on Grant's case while we are at a standstill on Phil's."

"Well, that's why I have you around, I guess. I agree that we could work on both cases. I wonder if she'll be back."

Jake nodded. "I have a feeling that she will. Call it a cop's intuition." Jenny chimed in with her dad on the cop's intuition and they laughed together.

"I'm so glad you're here Dad." Jen said as she hugged him.

"So am I, now let's get to work on cleaning up this mess." The two of them worked all afternoon on rearranging the office, and doing a little computer work. Jake stood, stretching his back. "It's already almost quitting time. I'm going to call Ann and see if we should pick up a pizza for supper. Ann has been busy with Abby, and I think she deserves a break from cooking, what do you think?"

"I think it's a great idea. I just said that to her this morning. Good luck talking her into it."

Jake picked up the phone to call Ann, and Jen started shutting the computers down. She could hear him arguing with Ann, and had to smile. When Jake hung up, he called the nearest pizza joint, and ordered the pizza to go. After he ordered, he looked over at Jen. She couldn't help it, she was still smiling. "Well, how did that go? Evidently you won that argument, since you ordered the pizza."

"Wow! Ann takes her job seriously. I didn't think she was going to give in. I don't think that she would have if Abby wouldn't have helped me out. I won't lie, I called Abby first. I'm not above using a little help where I can get it."

They laughed, and Jenny agreed. "Boy, I just keep learning more and more from you dad. Let me just write that one down so I don't forget."

"Well, keep watching me Jen. You never know what you could learn. I've been around the block a time or two. Now, let's get out of here. We can finish this in the morning."

"Sounds good, we just need to replace the lock on the door, and we can take off."

Jake decided he was going to leave his car at the office, and rode home with Jen. They picked up the pizza and suffered through the wonderful smells coming from the back seat all the way home. They could barely wait until they got in the house to dig in.

Ann was standing in the kitchen with her arms crossed when they walked in. Sam was standing behind her, smirking. Jake looked at Ann innocently. "What?"

"Don't think I don't know what you're up to Jake Long! Using a little girl to get your way! That's stooping pretty low, even for you."

"I don't know what you're talking about. I just asked Abby if she wanted pizza for supper, and what kind she would want if you say it's okay. That's all. Nothing else to it. Anyway, I'm starving. We've been smelling this all the way home. Can we eat please?"

Abby came into the kitchen right then. "Yay! Pizza! My mom and I had a pizza night every week. We would eat out in the living room, and watch TV. It was so fun. Can we do that Ann? Please?"

Jake noticed Ann softening while she listened to Abby. He could tell that she loved the little girl. Abby had her wrapped around her finger already. "Of course we can Abby. Let's warm up the pizza a little bit and go get some blankets to sit on. It'll be just like having a picnic." She still glared at Jake as she walked by, but he could tell she was okay with the pizza thing.

The next week went fast, It was almost time for Abby to start school. She was still having trouble adjusting to life without her mom or dad, but she was doing okay. Buffy and the other horses helped a lot.

When it came time for her to go to school, Abby was a little apprehensive about what the other kids would say to her. Ann sat her down the morning of her first day of fourth grade. "Abby, are you sure you're ready for this? I'm sure we could work something out to start a little later. I could call the principal and tell her what has happened. Maybe they could send out work for you to do out here at the ranch?"

Abby shook her head. "No Ann. I need to do this. Mom would have wanted me to live my life. I am a little worried about my friends though. Do you think that they will treat me differently now? I don't want them to. What should I do?"

"You should talk to them first. Tell them how you feel, so they can share their feelings with you too. Kids can be mean, but if someone says something you feel uncomfortable with, just try to ignore it. If you need my help, I will be there in a flash. Your teachers are aware of what you have been through, go to them if you need to."

Abby stood and straightened her spine. "I will. I think they will be fine though. I will talk to them right away, get it over with."

They hugged, and Jenny walked through the door. "Are you ready for the big day Abby?" Jen drove into Portland every day, so Abby would ride in with her and come home with her after school.

"I'm ready Jen."

Everything went well at school, and the family was getting into a routine. Abby was settling in. Sam and Ann weren't going to bring up any ideas of adoption to Abby. She needed to heal, and didn't need any more pressure put on her.

Jenny and Jake were given the okay to look into Griffin Grant's case. So far, they hadn't gotten very far on the case. Julie, Grif's daughter, was wanting some closure. Jen could understand that, but Jake and her just couldn't find anything substantial that screamed murder. Jenny found it odd though, that the fifth precinct was being so difficult in handing over Grif's case files. They had to go over the captain's head just to get into the cold case room, and then, only one small box of Griffin Grant's cases were shown to them. Nothing substantial was found in the box they were shown. Granted, it had been over thirty years since Grif was a cop, and it was ten years since he committed suicide. It was very frustrating. They were going back to the precinct today. Jake was nothing if not persistent.

"Dad, I just don't think this is going to do us any good. The last time we were here, the captain wouldn't give us anything. Why are we coming back here?"

"Jenny, this is what detective work is all about. You can't give up so easily. You keep coming back until you find something. Do you want to give up?"

"No, it's just that, well, I think everything is pointing to suicide. Maybe we should tell our client that and move on."

"Well, one last look in the cold case room, and I'll be satisfied, deal?"

"Deal."

They got the same reception as they did before when they entered the building. Cold shoulders from everyone. They weren't making any long time friends here that's for sure. Jake didn't care about that, as long as they got the job done right.

Jake and Jen followed the officer, who, somewhat reluctantly, took them into the dark, cold room that held all of the boxes labeled cold case. Some of these boxes were from police suicides. Why they were kept in the cold case room is anybody's guess. Some of them were kept here because the families just didn't want the belongings of their dead family members for one reason or the other. It was sad, really. "Listen, we are just trying to do a job, just like you. Just show us one more time, and we'll get out of your hair."

The officer didn't reply, just shrugged. Jenny looked at her dad and grimaced. They were led to a small box, the very same one that Jake and Jen had gone through before. The only one that the captain allowed them to look at. "We have already gone through this box, officer. Are you sure there are no more in this room? Nothing at all?"

Jen looked around the room. She wandered as she looked, trying to figure out how to close this case and move on. She stopped dead in her tracks when she suddenly heard some scraping sounds coming from above her head. Some dust fell on her head, and she looked up. One box on the highest shelf was moving ever so slightly. Every time she moved, the box would move.

Suddenly she knew. Someone was trying to tell her something. She cleared her throat. "Um, officer Thompson. What is in the boxes on the highest shelves?"

Thompson looked up. "I'm not sure. Probably the older cases go higher up. No one looks at them anymore. Most of the time, we get rid of the older boxes, but some of them get overlooked. Why?"

"I was wondering what was in this box right here?" She pointed at the box above her head. "Could I take a look at it please?"

Officer Thompson grabbed a ladder and set it in front of her. "Knock yourself out Miss Long." He shuffled away, and Jen grabbed the ladder. Jake rushed over and climbed the ladder in front of her. "Let me get it Jen." When the officer was out of ear shot, Jake whispered. "What's going on Jenny? Why this box?"

She just shook her head. "I'll tell you later. For now, just get this box down for me."

"No problem, boy, is it dusty up here." He blew off the dust on the top of the box as he handed it off to Jen. "Let's get it opened up and see what's inside."

The outside of the box was labeled 'John Doe.'

"Jen, this guy wasn't even identified. I don't know what good it's going to do us to go through it. Whatever it was that brought you to this particular box, I wouldn't get my hopes up if I were you."

Jen grabbed the box and set it on the nearest table. "I know dad, but something tells me we should go through it anyway. Just humor me okay?"

They opened the box and noticed that there were only a few files in it. "Doesn't look like much to go on. Just a few files, and looks like some photos. Must be photos of a crime scene, or they wouldn't be in here. Let's take a look." Jake spread out three photos on the table. The first one was a picture of a street corner. There was no markings with the name of the corner on it, which was unusual. The second picture was of a car. It looked like it had been rammed into. The driver's side door was bashed in, but there were no other signs of what happened to the car. The third picture was some tire tracks on the ground in the intersection. That was it for the photos.

Jake opened up one of the files. He read out loud so Jen could hear. "Looks like the date was 1977. It says here, that our John Doe, who has never been identified, was traveling west on Pine Street. A car traveling through the intersection at a high rate of speed side-swiped him, killing him instantly.

He didn't have any ID on him. The police investigated for awhile, ten years to be exact, until the case went cold. Wait a minute. It says here the cop who investigated the case, was none other than Grif Grant. Our dead cop." Jake let out a low whistle. "Now this is getting interesting. Maybe this has something to do with our guy's suicide."

Jenny grabbed the other files, getting excited now. "Wow, now that *is* interesting. Why wouldn't they try harder to ID this guy? We have a dead young man, says here he was only seventeen years old. A hit and run, with no evidence taken except for a few pictures of the scene? Dad, something smells rotten here. I can feel it in my bones, and someone wanted me to see this. I'll tell you all about it later." Turning to officer Thompson, she asked him one question. "Do you think we could take this box with us? It may have some things we need for the case we are working on."

Thompson let out a laugh. "You know better than to even ask, never mind, I guess you don't know." He turned to Jake, pointing at him. "*You* know better than to ask. I don't know why you would want that old box, but no, it doesn't leave this room. My captain would kill me himself if I did that. What's so interesting in it anyway?" He walked toward the files they had lain out.

Jen quickly grabbed them up. "Nothing really, just some old case files and photos. We will just put them back." She glanced at her dad. He took the cue, and steered the conversation away from the box of evidence.

"Thompson, would you show me where they keep the old files on retired police officers who have died in the line of duty? I have a feeling it may be pertinent to our case." He grabbed the man's shoulder, steering him away from Jen.

Thompson turned his head, eyeing Jenny. "You'll put those items back?"

She nodded. "Sure thing. I've got this, I'll be in there in a second."

While Jake distracted Thompson, Jenny took out her cell phone and started snapping pictures as fast as she could. She only got two pictures of the photos in the table, when another policeman came in and she had to stop. *"Damn!"* She whispered. Jenny quickly put the rest of the files back in the box. Leaving it there, she joined up with her dad and officer Thompson. She glanced at him and shook her head, letting him know that she had gotten all she could.

Jake nodded. "Well, we had better leave you be for now officer Thompson. I think we got what we came here for. Thanks for your help." Jake let his sarcastic tone come through with that statement, letting him know how he felt.

They practically ran out the door. Jake looked over at Jen when they closed the doors to their car. "Okay, what the hell was that all about? That old box had nothing in it worth looking at. How did you know it contained something about Grif Grant? Why were you so adamant about opening it?"

"I don't know dad. When I walked by the box, I could have sworn I saw it move a little. Wait, I know I did. Dust was falling on my head when I walked by. Something, or someone, was trying to tell me to look in that box. I know it. Just go with it okay? You know how my abilities work. Sometimes it doesn't make much sense, but I know someone was telling me to look in there. I didn't get many pictures, just a few of the photos that were there. None of the files I'm afraid. I really want to get back in there and look around some more. Who knows what we would find if we could take our time and go through them alone. Besides, we did find out that Grif Grant was the first on the scene of that accident. That means something, right?"

"Well, short of breaking in there, which is not going to happen, we may have trouble getting back in. I do agree with you that it's interesting that Grant was first on the scene. We don't have much to go on. We have to work with what we've got. Which is basically nothing. I think we need to call Julie Grant and set up a meeting. Let her know that her dad more than likely committed suicide. Maybe she knows something about this accident."

Jenny let out a breath. "Maybe he did, but I still am curious about that other box. Okay, I'll let it go for now. Let's get back to the office and call Julie, but I'm not giving up on this. If Julie says that her dad mentioned this accident at all, we are looking further into it.

Jake laughed. "I didn't think you would give up, honey. We just have to figure out a different way to get in that cold case room. We need to be able to spend some time alone in there."

••• 9 •••

JULIE GRANT WAS disappointed, to say the least, when they met with her later that day. She didn't know anything about a hit and run accident. She wrote out a check nonetheless, paying them for their work thus far. Julie sighed when she handed it over to Jen. "Look, I'll go with what you said, but I still don't think my dad killed himself. Isn't there anything else we can do?"

Jake picked his words carefully. "I'm afraid not, we looked over all of the evidence they had, which wasn't much. They don't keep the evidence after so long. It has been ten years since your dad's death. Look, I know this is hard, but don't you think you should just let it go? Your mom is gone now, will bringing up all of this help you or your brother? Really? I think it may just bring up more bad memories. Let me give you a little advice. As a former homicide detective, I have worked with a lot of grieving families. You really need to let this go Julie. For your sake as well as your brother's."

Julie sat back in her chair with her chin up. "I know, but I just can't. If you won't look into this more, I am going to find someone who will. It's just that the stigma of a suicide sticks with the whole family. All of our lives, all we ever knew was my dad's dedication to the police force. Then he kills himself only ten years after retiring? It just doesn't make sense to me. Mom couldn't let it go, and I don't know if we will be able to either. Thank you two for listening to me, I do appreciate it. If anything else comes up promise me you'll let me know okay?"

Jenny hugged her. "Okay, listen, we'll keep looking into this for you if you want us to. One thing we are not, is quitters. We'll keep trying."

Jenny and Jake sat back in their chairs after Julie Grant left the office. Jenny let out another long sigh. It seemed she had been doing a lot of that lately. "Well, this has turned out to be a frustrating first case. Our first paying case that is. Phil's case was frustrating too, just not quite as old. What do we do now dad?"

"Well, we go through what we have. We need to keep trying to get back into that box in the cold case room, that's what. There has to be more evidence than what we saw. This is where you learn patience, and determination my dear. Every good investigator's mantra."

"Well, I know we have tons of both, determination and patience. So where do we start?" Jenny pulled her chair closer to her desk and Jake did the same.

"Let me see those photos you took of the scene of the crash. Did you get any of the files on your camera?"

"No, but I did get the pictures of the car after the hit and run." Jen brought the pictures up on her phone. Sliding through the pictures, she commented on the second one. "It's definitely a Honda, looks like it's black, newer model. What do you see?"

Jake perused the pictures. "Not much more than that, I'm afraid. We don't have much to go on. But we can do a computer search on the accident itself and see if there were any articles on it. Maybe we will luck out and a witness will pop up. If we could interview them, they may be more apt to talk to us rather than the police."

"That's a great idea. Let's get started."

After searching the computer for hours, they finally came upon one little article in the newspaper. The headline read. HIT AND RUN KILLS YOUNG MAN. It was a very short article. The only reference to any witnesses was one man who said he heard a crash in the early morning hours. He made the 9-1-1 call. Jake pointed to the line that had the man's name. Art Lee. "Ha, that's it. First thing tomorrow morning, we go find Mr. Lee. That's where we start. Are you sure that you want to get into this? No one asked us to take this old case. There is just a slight reference to Grif Grant."

"I know, but I just have a feeling that this ties into Griffin Grant's case. He was the policeman that investigated the case. Then he kills himself? Just sounds fishy to me, that's all."

"I do have to agree with you on that one. Okay, but I have to warn you, this isn't going to be easy. It's been ten years since Mr. Grant died, and the accident was more than thirty years before that. This witness may not even be alive. Forty years is a long time. I'm surprised that cold case box was still in there."

"I am aware of the pitfalls of this case dad. But tomorrow I am getting another look at those case files. Whether the police want me to or not. It seems to me, the police are trying to get in our way on this case, and I want to know why."

Jake and Jenny were thinking about this case on the drive home, Abby was spending the night with a friend, so it was just the two of them. Both of them thinking of Grif Grant, and the John Doe. What exactly was their connection beside the fact that Grant did the investigating on the accident? Was there any more of a connection? What would they find out tomorrow? Jenny rubbed her eyes. "Well, I for one, am very tired. We probably missed supper. I hope there's some pizza left, I'm starving."

"Me too, we should have grabbed something in town I guess. Oh well, we'll figure something out. Knowing Ann, she left something in the fridge for us."

By the time they pulled into the ranch, it was dark. The moon was barely a sliver, and the stars were shining bright.

Jen and Jake took a minute to stare up at the sky. "Nothing beats the view here. I swear, I could stand out here all night." Jen grabbed her dad's arm, and they just stood there, breathing in the fresh air.

"Me too, but I am hungry, let's go in and see what Ann has for us to eat. Then, I'm going to bed."

The two walked arm in arm to the house. It was pretty quiet. Everyone was already asleep. Sure enough, Ann had a plate fixed for each on them. Jenny grabbed both plates out of the fridge, and put them in the microwave to warm up. "Ann is the best. This looks yummy."

They dug into their plates filled with mashed potatoes and gravy, steak, and corn. Jake sat back, rubbing his stomach when they were done. "I swear, I am going to gain weight if she keeps cooking like that. Especially if I keep sitting at a desk instead of doing physical work."

"Well, I suggest you do both dad. I hear you though. I may have to get a gym membership. Well, I'm going to bed. I'll see you in the morning."

Jenny dragged herself upstairs, thinking about the cases they looked at today. She couldn't figure out why the cops were making it so difficult for them to look at the files they needed. Yawning, she tried to shut her mind off for the night. *I need to sleep, tomorrow is another day.* She fell into a deep sleep.

Jen awoke to a noise. She groaned. *Not tonight! I need to sleep.* But she knew that when the dead decided to grace her with their presence, they did it on their own time. She had no control over that. Jen opened her eyes to see a figure of a man standing beside her bed. *Okay, this is new. Who could this be?* She rubbed her eyes, and asked that question. "Who are you? What do you need?"

The figure just stood there, staring down at her. It was a little creepy, even if she was used to seeing dead people. Her mom though, was nowhere to be seen. "Are you with my mom? Please, tell me your name. What can I help you with?"

His lips weren't moving, but Jen could hear him. *You are on the right track, Jenny. I'm so glad that you listened to me when I moved that box. I couldn't come to you then, but I'm here now. Believe in your abilities Jenny. They won't lead you astray. Keep looking into the accident, and it will all come together. I can't tell you who I am yet, I don't know if I ever will. You may not want to listen to me if I do. Just know that things are not as they seem.* The man faded away.

"Well, that helped a lot." She whispered, as she lay back down. "He Just added more mystery to this case." She grabbed her journal, and wrote down what he had told her. She read her last entry, the one where her mother told her someone else would be coming to her. "Okay Mom, I'll try to keep an open mind. Besides, we are going to need all the help we can get with this."

Jenny slept soundly through the night after that. It always happened that way. Her restless sleep almost always led to her seeing someone. It was getting to be a pattern. One that she knew quite well by now. Things were about to get interesting now.

When Jen woke up the next morning, she could hardly wait to tell her dad what she saw. Everyone was in the kitchen when she walked in. She didn't waste any time telling them all. "Okay, you're not going to believe this, but some guy came to me last night. It wasn't Mom. She had said someone else was coming, and she was right. I sure hope that doesn't mean I won't see her anymore. Anyway, he said he was the one who moved the box in the evidence room. He said he was glad that I listened, and that we need to look into that accident some more."

Sam and Ann just looked at Jake with a confused expression. He filled them in on what happened yesterday at the police station. They both agreed that it was weird that no identity was made on the young man that died forty years ago. "Then, ten years ago Grif Grant killed himself. I don't believe that is all a coincidence. There have been a lot of suicides in that precinct. I talked to my old captain, Tony, and it seems that Los Angeles has had it's share too. I can't quite put my finger on it yet, but something just doesn't seem right. Ever since Cara came to us about Phil's death, I haven't been able to stop thinking about it all. I know suicides are not uncommon among police officers, but it just seems like a lot. I think we've just scratched the surface. I'm worried about what we may find when we start digging deeper."

Sam agreed. "I think you definitely need to look into all of this. We have had many cops out here at the ranch who have been very depressed, and they have come out of it with a lot of therapy. With the help of a lot of people, they can be helped. That's why we do what we do. You need to figure this out Jake. The sooner the better."

After listening to what Sam and Ann had to say, Jenny was even more determined to get back into that room and check out that box of evidence, along with the others that may *come forward*. "Let's get to work dad. We are going to the cold case room right away this morning, and they are going to let us in there. We have a right to see that evidence, and besides that, we could help them solve some of those cases. What's the big deal?"

"I agree, they should be more helpful." Jake looked over at Ann. "We'll bring Abby home with us at four-o'clock when school gets out. Do you need anything in town?"

Ann shrugged. "Well, I think we need some milk, and maybe cereal. I'm not used to feeding people just cereal for breakfast, but that's what Abby likes, so that is what she gets."

"We can pick some up. She can pick out her favorite. Abby seems to be fitting in around here. She is missing her mom, but I think she'll be okay."

"Yes, she is a very smart and mature girl for her age. She had to grow up fast, I'm afraid. But she's a tough one. She has been through a lot. We're giving her some space right now, but we may as well tell you now. Sam and I are wanting to adopt Abby. She needs a stable family, and it's what Cara wanted. We just don't quite know how to bring it up to her."

Jenny hugged Ann. "You know what? I think she would take it in stride, just like she has everything else. I think she would be happy if you two adopted her. Just ask her, and let her make the decision. She'll make the right one, I'm sure of it."

Sam laughed. "When did you get so wise, little girl? I still see you as the little spitfire who followed me around, talking a mile a minute. Now look at you, all grown up."

Jenny actually blushed at that comment. "Yeah, look at me now. Look at you two, finally married and now parents. It's funny how things happen. Sometimes bad things happen for a reason, I guess. It just doesn't seem like it at the time."

Jake cleared his throat. "Well, I hate to break up this deep conversation, but we had better get going Jen."

They headed down the road, still thinking about all that was said earlier. Jenny was deep in thought, when she noticed something out of the corner of her eye. She looked in the side mirror. "Dad, do you see that car behind us? How long have they been there? It seems like it's coming up pretty fast."

"I've been watching it for awhile now. It's been following us for five miles or so. Looks to be a dark sedan. That's about all I can tell from here. I'm going to slow down, and see if they slow down too. I don't know why anyone would be following us. Maybe we're just being paranoid. Keep your eyes on the car, I'm going to slow down a little."

Jake slowed down to about fifty miles per hour, and sure enough, the car slowed down too. Jenny kept watching, hoping to catch a glimpse of a license plate, or the person driving. "I don't see a plate in front. Could be just dirty from the gravel road. Maybe we should make a quick turn and see what they do."

Jake nodded. Coming up on a turn off, he maneuvered the pickup around the curve. Turning sharply, he careened down the road, his car skidding on the road. The sedan kept going down the road towards Portland, not slowing at all.

"Well, maybe we weren't being followed after all. I guess if we were, they didn't want to give themselves away too much by following us onto this road."

"Either way, I think we need to be more diligent. Remember when Cara said that she kept feeling like someone was following her? Then all of a sudden she is dead? There sure has been some strange things happening. Let's get back on the road, I'm even more anxious now to get a look at that box with the accident evidence in it."

Jake and Jen pulled up to the fifth precinct at nine o'clock. When they entered the building, they headed straight to the captain's office. Knocking on the door, Jake noticed that the captain looked a little haggard. "Sorry to bother you Captain Keller, but we need to talk to you about something if you have a minute?"

Keller let out a loud breath, acting like it was going above and beyond the call of duty to talk to them. "I suppose, but I don't have long. Come in, have a seat."

"We won't keep you long. I'll get right to the point. We are investigating a couple of cases that led us to your cold case room. We found some evidence that we need to look at again. We would like to make some copies of the papers and photos inside. Officer Thompson didn't want to cooperate the other day, so we are here to ask you for your permission to reopen the case. Who knows? We may help you close some of these cold cases. What do you say? Do you want our help, or not?"

"I will be honest with you two. I don't have much time for private eyes, even former detectives turned private eyes. You guys run loosely with the laws. More or less follow your own rules. But, if you want to look at something again, go ahead. Take pictures, but leave the evidence where it is, got it?"

Jake stood, reaching out his hand to shake the other man's. "Got it. Thanks captain, we appreciate your cooperation."

The captain just nodded, and sent them on their way. They had a different escort this time. He didn't look any happier than his predecessor did. Armed with their camera, Jake and Jen headed straight for the evidence box on the hit and run accident. When they walked up to the shelf, all that was there was the dust. No box. Jake turned to the officer. "What happened to the box that was sitting on this shelf? Did it get taken to a different room? Where is it? Captain Keller said we could have access to whatever we needed in here, and we need that box. The John Doe hit and run from 1977."

The officer shrugged. "Don't ask me. I was just told to bring you in here, I don't know anything about any box. Feel free to look around, maybe it just got misplaced."

"Oh, we will. Thanks for your help." Jake added sarcastically.

Jenny and Jake searched the room all morning to no avail. As they left the police station, they stood on the steps for a minute, taking it all in. Jen was frustrated. "What do you suppose that was all about? One day it's there, and the next day it's gone? I for one, don't buy it. What do you think is going on here dad?"

"I don't know Jenny, but we're going to figure it out." Jake turned to walk to the pickup. He glanced up, noticing a piece of paper stuck on the windshield. "Wait a minute, what's this?" He reached up and grabbed the paper, looking around for anyone that could have put it there. Jake opened the paper carefully, trying not to touch much of it. It read:

"Leave this case alone or you will be sorry! Just forget whatever anyone has told you about anything involving the hit and run. LEAVE IT ALONE!!"

Jake was even more determined now. He and Jen were not going to stop until they figured all of this out. There was something going on, and Jake was afraid that no one was going to be left unscathed after it all was said and done. It was time for them to go and find Art Lee. They needed to talk to someone who was there at the time of the accident. Hopefully Mr. Lee was still alive after all of these years. They went back to the office to find Mr. Lee's address on the computer. They needed to find out where he lived, and if he was even alive. If they could talk to him, maybe someone else would come forward with more information. It was the only shot they had of identifying John Doe, and finding out just what he had to do with Grif's death, and maybe even Phil and Cara's. This was getting more complicated by the minute. Jake was rubbing the back of his neck. "This computer stuff isn't for me. I need to be out walking the streets. We have his address now, what do you say we go talk to Mr. Lee?"

Jen jotted down the address, and the two of them had a renewed determination in their case. If they could talk to Mr. Lee, they could find out a lot more about the accident than they could with the few things in the evidence box anyway. Jen hoped their luck would hold out, and Art Lee was alive, and still living in the same place he was forty years ago.

Jake pulled up to the address of Art Lee that they had found on the computer. The lawn was well kept, and the old house was painted a beige color, with a dark brown door. He looked at Jen. "I don't think we should get our hopes up here. I doubt Mr. Lee is still living here. Let's keep our fingers crossed."

Knocking on the door, Jake and Jen stood back as they heard a shuffling inside the house. The door opened a crack, and a man peeked out. "Yes? Can I help you?"

Jake stepped forward. "Yes, Mr. Lee?"

The man nodded. "Yes, that's me. Who might you be young man?"

"Mr. Lee, my name is Jake Long, and this my daughter, Jenny. We are investigating the hit and run accident that happened here forty years ago. I understand that you called 9-1-1 and reported the accident? Would you mind talking with us about that?"

The door opened wider, and Jen could see that the old man was leaning heavily on his walker. He squinted at them over his glasses that were resting on his nose. "I already told the police everything I know about that. That was a long time ago, but I still remember it like it was yesterday. Well, don't just stand there, come in!"

Jake and Jen stepped into the man's house and looked around. There were pictures covering every inch of the walls, and on all of the end tables. Jenny stopped to look at the pictures on her way into the living room. She stopped in front of a picture of a group of kids standing around him while he sat in a chair. "Are these your grandchildren Mr. Lee? What a beautiful bunch of kids."

"Yes, they are my grandchildren, and I agree they are a good looking bunch. Thank you Miss Long."

"Please, call me Jen. Do your children and grandchildren live close to you?"

"No, they are scattered around the country, but they visit as often as they can. Now, what can I do for you two?"

Jake spoke as he sat down on the couch. He sank into the cloth covered sofa. "Well, why don't you start at the beginning, Mr. Lee. Just tell us what you remember from the day of the accident."

Mr. Lee cleared his throat. "Well, like I said, I told the policeman all of this. I think his name was Grifton, or something like that. Anyway, I heard a loud noise outside, squealing of tires I would say. Then, I heard a loud crash. I knew right away what it was. I looked out my window, and there were two cars sitting in the street, smoke coming out of the hood of the one. There was a pickup truck sitting beside the car. The car was a Honda, I do believe. Anyway, the truck was sitting there idling, like nothing was wrong. A man got out of the truck and walked over to the driver's side of the Honda. He looked in the window, and then drove away. I didn't get a license plate number or anything like that. I do know that it was a Ford pickup, red in color. I couldn't see the man who got out of the truck. That's about it. Does that help you at all?"

Jake nodded. "Yes, as a matter of fact it does. It is a lot more than we knew yesterday."

"Why are you looking into this accident after so many years?"

Jake nodded to Jen and she answered. "Well, to tell you the truth, we are looking into the death of the policeman that you spoke to, Grif Grant. This accident came up in our investigation. We're just gathering all of the information we can on Mr. Grant's cases." They stood to leave. "Thank you Mr. Lee, you were a great help."

The old man nodded. "Well, it was good to have company. Gets a little lonely sitting here in this big old house by myself. I'm sorry I couldn't get a license number. I should have been more observant I guess."

"No sir, don't be sorry. You helped a lot, really." Jake and Jen turned to leave. "We'll let ourselves out. Thanks again."

They headed for the door, when Mr. Lee stopped them. "You know, I just thought of something that I didn't tell the other officer. That car that got hit? I know they lived in the area. I had seen that car drive by my house almost every day. There was a young man driving it. I can't recall his name, but I know he lived around here. A couple houses away maybe. I saw the pickup that was sitting there too. I didn't see who was driving it though. I can't believe I didn't remember that before, but I haven't forgotten that accident. Man, I wish I would have told the police that before. Oh well, I'm sure that they have figured that out by now anyway. Well, I had better let you get out of here. I'm sure you don't want to sit and talk to some lonely old man."

Jake and Jen just looked at each other, shocked at the man's words. Their John Doe might just get a name after all of these years. Now they had something to sink their teeth into. "You have helped a lot Mr. Lee. I'm so glad that you told us about this. We will let you know what we find out about the accident. In the meantime, you enjoy those grandchildren of yours."

When Jake and Jen got into the pickup, they just sat there for a minute. They looked around, trying to imagine the car sitting in the street, with a pickup idling beside it. Jake looked over at Jen. "Are you seeing something? Something the rest of us can't see?"

Jen smiled, and shook her head. "I wish I could say yes, but sadly, no such luck. I was just thinking that we could actually identify the victim of this hit and run after all of these years. All we have to do is go back to the records of who lived around here at that time, and then who owned a black Honda. I'm excited, I think we may solve our first case Dad."

"Whoa! Hold on a minute. Don't be jumping the gun Jen. This kind of information is great and all, but this happened a long time ago. I don't know how far back the records go, but we will certainly investigate it. You never know, we could get lucky. Maybe even have some visitors tell us something?"

Jen laughed. "Maybe, who knows. It would be nice to have some help from beyond the grave for this one. Maybe even the victim himself, or Grif. I have a feeling he knew too much. That may be why he was killed, *if* he was killed at all. This is getting very complicated. I love it though. I can certainly see why you loved your job so much. It's very exciting, and gratifying, when you find new clues."

"It can be exciting, and it definitely is gratifying. But you have to remember the cost. I hope you're ready for that."

Jen didn't reply to his comment. She couldn't wait to find out who this victim was so they could figure out what really happened to Griffin. It was going to have to wait until tomorrow, though. A certain little girl was waiting for them to pick her up at school. They rode in silence all the way to pick up Abby, each of them thinking about Grif Grant, and the accident. Jake was thinking about how his little girl was going to handle the pressures of the job, even the pressures that private investigators face. Jen was thinking about the poor boy who lost his life in a hit and run accident. The person who had gotten away with it for all of these years. Were they still alive? Were they hiding somewhere? In plain sight maybe? Time will tell.

### • • • 10 • • •

THE NEXT DAY, Jen could hardly wait to get on her computer at work. They needed to find those records as soon as possible. She only hoped that there still were records of that neighborhood from forty years ago. She was frustrated by the time she got done searching. Jen couldn't find anything. When Jake asked how it was going, she rubbed the back of her neck. "I can't find anything on my computer, nothing goes back that far."

"Okay, don't get discouraged. I think that we need to go to City Hall, and see if they have the records for back then. Sometimes they keep them on microfilm if it's not on the computer."

Jen sighed. "I knew I had you around for a reason. Let's go."

Jake had to laugh. He just couldn't help but reply with a touch of sarcasm in his voice. "Wait a minute. I thought I was the brawn of this duo, not the brains." They laughed together as they headed for City Hall.

After hours of searching through different documents, Jake and Jen struck pay dirt. They found the street where the accident happened, and, sure enough, there was a list of names. They looked for Mr. Art Lee first. There he was. Now, to look for anyone living close to him on that same street. At least living on that street. Art seemed convinced that the victim of the accident lived near him. It was their only lead, so they needed to follow up on it. Art had forgotten about it when Griffin interviewed him forty years ago. Jen was just happy he remembered it now. "Okay, what are we looking for exactly? Just the names of his neighbors? Or everyone on that street?"

Jake looked up from the computer. "We start by looking at everyone on that street. Then we will cross check that with DMV records to find out what everyone drove at that time. If we find someone who drove a black Honda, we are golden. Here, you take half, and I'll take this half."

It seemed like hours had gone by, when Jen squealed with delight. Everyone looked up from what they were doing, startled by the noise. "Sorry." Jen tried to hold back her excitement. "Dad, I think I've got it. There is a Jerod Sims listed as the owner of a black Honda. He lived three houses down from Art Lee. Do you think this could actually be him? After all of these years, we have identified the John Doe? Why didn't the police run the plates from the car forty years ago? It should have been easy enough for them to identify Jerod Sims as the owner of the black Honda. There had to have been a registration in the car, even his drivers license. It is very confusing to me that Sims was listed as a John Doe. I wish that Grif Grant were here to answer some of our questions. What now, do we go to the police with our information?"

"Let's not jump to conclusions. If Grant didn't investigate the crash properly, there has to be a reason. First, we need to make sure that the body is that of Jerod Sims. We need to check that out first. Let's go to the address listed and talk to the people who live there. Maybe we will luck out and they are related somehow."

Jake and Jen headed back to the scene of the hit and run. They found the house listed as the home of Jerod Sims.

Ringing the doorbell, they stepped back when a woman answered the door. "Yes? May I help you?"

"Ma'am, my name is Jake Long, this is my daughter Jenny. Do you mind if we ask you a couple of questions?"

The woman looked them up and down. "I guess so. What questions? What is this about?"

"We are investigating the hit and run accident that happened on this street about forty years ago. I realize you may not have been living here then, but do you know who was? Do you know the history of the residents of this house?"

The young woman pondered the question for a moment. "No, I don't know anything about the history of this house. I only moved in a couple of years ago. I don't know who owned it that far back. Maybe the people that I'm renting it from would know more.I can give you the name of the person that I am renting it from."

Jenny was a bit deflated. "Would you mind if we came in?" They entered the house. It had been very well kept. Neat and tidy. Jenny looked around. "Do you know anyone by the name of Sims? We have information that someone lived here by the name of Jerod Sims."

"No, I don't know anyone by that name, sorry. You know, I did find some old photos when I was doing some cleaning downstairs. I meant to give them to the owners of the house, but I haven't gotten around to it yet. Would you like to see them?"

"Yes, please." Jenny looked over at her dad when the woman came out of the kitchen with the photos in her hand. It was all she could do not to yank them out of her hands. "Thank you Ma'am."

"Please, call me Sam, everyone does."

Jenny nodded. "Okay, thank you, Sam." Jenny and Jake looked over the photos when she handed them over. One of the photos was of particular interest. It was a picture of a young man standing proudly by a black Honda. It looked new, and he was grinning from ear to ear. This was him, Jen just knew it. This was their John Doe. They just identified the victim of the hit and run from so many years ago.

"Sam, would you mind if we took this photo? We need to show it to the police right away. It's very important."

"Sure, go ahead." She handed them all over to Jake and Jen.

"Thank you Sam. You have been a great help."

Walking to the pickup, Jake noticed that Jen was unusually quiet. "What's wrong? Why so quiet?"

"Nothing's wrong. It's just that…well, do you want to hand this over to the police? I have a bad feeling about it all. Why wasn't this followed up on when the accident happened? Dad, what do you think is really going on here? Something just doesn't feel right."

"Well, I will agree with you on one thing. It does seem odd that the police gave up so easily on this case. I mean, why didn't they follow up on this? We will go with your gut on this one. I think we should hang on to these pictures for awhile. Let's do some more investigating on Jerod Sims."

Jenny felt better when her dad agreed with her. She let out a sigh, and jumped in the truck. She was more than ready for some good old fashioned detective work. She was going to figure out why Jerod Sims was killed, which is what it looked like to her. Then, she was going to figure out the connection with Grif Grant. His death was looking more and more like a homicide too. His family was right.

This was getting complicated. Jenny felt that it was probably going to get more complicated as time went on. "Dad, if the police didn't look into this more, there had to be a reason for it. After all of these years, do you really think we can find that reason?"

"I'm not sure yet, but we're going to try. This could get a bit hairy if the police were in the wrong here. Are you ready for this? Do you want to get involved in this? We could just hand the evidence over to the police and let them handle it." He glanced at Jen as he talked. She was already shaking her head.

"No way! We are going to figure this out. Julie Grant, and the rest of the Grant family deserve to know the truth. So does Jerod Sims' family."

Jake nodded. "Okay, I agree. Let's go look at the rest of Grant's cases. Maybe something will come up in his old cases that will tell us why he was killed. We will have to go back to the police station. Let's just tell them we are following up on a case, and tell them we need to close it. His daughter, Julie, wants us to close it once and for all. We'll act like we are convinced it was a suicide."

"Sounds good to me." Jen looked at her watch. "It's probably going to have to wait until tomorrow though. It's already four o'clock. We need to go pick up Abby and head home. I guess we leave it for another day."

After picking up Abby, the trio headed down the road towards the ranch. Jake and Jen weren't getting a word in the conversation. Abby was chattering on about her day at school. "You know what? Today in school Hanna threw up! It was so gross! The teacher had to call her mom to come and get her. I almost threw up with her! Then, after that we had a fire drill. I always listen very carefully to the teachers, after what happened to mom. Jenny? Do you think what happened to mom is going to happen to me too? I mean, my dad dies first, then my mom. Alex Young said that I'm probably cursed. He made fun of me because I don't have a mom or dad."

Jen heard the sadness in the little girl's voice. "You know what Abby? You are not cursed. You're actually blessed. Look at where you live. Look at all of the people who love you. You have us, and Sam and Ann. We all love you very much. So does Nancy, and Tom. Buffy loves you to the moon and back. Should I go on?"

Abby shook her head. "I get it, but I wish I had someone to call mom and dad. Do you think it would be weird if I called Sam and Ann mom and dad?"

"Not at all. I know they would love it if you would do that."

The little girl nodded, and the rest of the ride home was pretty quiet.

Ann had supper almost ready when they arrived. Abby hugged Ann, and ran upstairs to change. Jen and Jake filled everyone in on what they had found out that day. Jen was excited to get to work the next day and find out just what was going on. She was convinced that Jerod Sims was the John Doe. It all fit together perfectly with what Mr. Lee had told them, and Jerod owned the same kind of car that was in the accident. Now, all they had to do was find out who ran into him, and why they took off from the scene.

While they were at the supper table, Abby was busy telling everyone about her day. Not caring that they were all trying to eat as she told all about her friend vomiting. Jen looked over at Sam. He was busy trying to hold back a laugh, when he noticed Ann's face turning green. Sam thought he had better step in. "Um, Abby, maybe you should wait a little while before telling us anymore of those kinds of stories, your mom is looking a little green." Everyone stopped what they were doing, and looked at Sam with a startled look on their faces. Sam looked dumbfounded. "What?"

Abby was smiling broadly. "Sam, you just called Ann my mom! That is so cool! Do you really think of her like that?" She turned to Ann. "Can I call you mom too?"

Ann choked back a sob. "Of course you can Abby. In fact, I would love it if you would. Sam would love for you to call him dad too if you want."

Abby squealed. "I do want that. Just so you know, I think it's cool that you want me to do that. I will always love my mom, and my dad. But now I have you guys." She jumped up and hugged them both. "Now, can I go out and see Buffy? I need to give her an apple."

"Go for it." Sam said. After Abby left, he turned to the rest of the family. "Well, that girl is something else isn't she. She is only eleven years old, it's only been a year since her mom died.

Look at how she has handled it all. I'm very impressed with how grown up she is. Too grown up probably."

Ann stood. "Well, I for one, am happy that she has handled the pain in her life this well. She has all of you to thank for that. Now, who is helping with the dishes tonight?"

Nancy stood and raised her hand. "It's my turn. You go outside and sit down. Enjoy the sunset, you deserve it."

"I second that motion." Jen said as she started clearing the table. "I'll help Nancy, you go and relax."

Chairs squeaked as they were pushed back from the table. "I think I'll do just that. Sam, Jake, will you join me?"

The men nodded, and followed Ann out to the huge deck. Getting comfortable, everyone was pretty quiet, just enjoying the evening air. The silence was broken by the sound of a car coming up the lane. Jake stood as the sheriff's patrol vehicle approached the house.

The old man got out of his car and shuffled his way to the deck where everyone was standing now. Jake stepped forward when the overweight man finally made it to the house. "What brings you out this way Sheriff?"

The sheriff took off his cap and wiped the imaginary sweat from his bald head. "Evening folks. I came to talk to you Jake, as a matter of fact. Can you go and get your daughter please? This involves her also."

Jen opened the door and stepped out. "I heard your car pull in. What can I help you with Sheriff?"

The sheriff looked around. "Could we go somewhere we could talk in private?"

Jake was just starting to protest, when Sam spoke up. "We'll just head down to see how Abby is doing. Excuse us."

After they left, Jake couldn't help but be a bit sarcastic when he turned back to the sheriff. "Okay, you have our undivided attention. What do you need?"

The sheriff cleared his throat, uncomfortable now. "Sorry about that. I Just didn't think I should talk in front of them. Anyway, I understand you two have been poking around the hit and run case from forty years ago. I also found out that you think that you have figured out who the victim in the accident was. You do realize that by holding back that information, you are withholding evidence in a police investigation? What exactly is your business with this accident anyway? You will tell me right now what you know, or I will arrest you both!"

Jake was a little taken aback at his attitude. "Well, first of all, since when is this an ongoing investigation? As far as we knew, it was a closed case. Our client asked us to look into something for her, and we stumbled upon a connection to this case, that's all. And we are not at liberty to say why we're investigating this, or who our client is. That is privileged information, and we don't really have to tell you what we found. I'll say it again, this case was closed by the police long ago." Jake decided that he didn't like the sheriff's attitude at all. He was done sharing information with them.

"Listen, I'm here because the commissioner asked me to come. I don't even know what this is all about. I'm not trying to step on any toes. I know you PI's have your own way of doing things. I'm not sure what the big deal is about this case, but I was told to come here and find out what you know. That's all."

Jake bristled at his comment. "Well, you can tell the commissioner that we really haven't found out much about this hit and run. I don't know where he is getting his information, but if we find out anything we will let him know. Good night, sheriff."

The sheriff stood a little straighter, and looked like he wanted to say more, but decided against it. He turned and walked back to his car, stopping before he got in. He turned back to Jake. "I don't know what is going on here, but I would watch my back if I were you. Just a little warning. Take it or leave it."

Jake nodded, and turned for the door to the house, ending the conversation. After the sheriff left, Jake and Jenny went in the house and found Sam, Ann, and Nancy sitting on the huge, leather couch. They had taken Abby through the back door and up to her room so she didn't see the police here. They were waiting for an explanation. Jake couldn't tell them much. "Listen, we can't say much about this case. You already know what we are investigating. Most of it is privileged information, but I can tell you that this is getting very interesting. It could get messy before it's all over. We need to figure out why the police are so up in the air about this investigation." Shaking his head, Jake yawned. "I'm going to bed. That's all I can say for now."

Sam stood. "Listen, I understand that you can't say much, but you know we have your back, no matter what. If you need our help, just ask."

Jake hugged his brother. "I will, thanks Sam, and good night."

"Good night Jake. Sleep tight."

Jenny yawned. "I am going to do the same. Good night everyone." She laid in bed for a little while, looking at the pictures she took of the folder that went missing in the police files. There just wasn't much there to see. You could plainly see the car, and it definitely looked like Jerod Sims' car. No license plate was visible, but there was a pair of black and white die hanging from the rear view mirror. She looked a little closer, zooming in on something stuck on the back window. It was a parking sticker for a local college. This could be big. If they could find a relative of Jerod's, they could show them the pictures of the car in the hit and run. If the relatives had some more pictures of his car, they may be able to match the sticker on his car to the sticker on the car in the accident. She put her phone away, feeling very optimistic about this case. Everything was pointing toward Jerod Sims being the victim of the hit and run. Jenny yawned again. After setting her alarm on her phone, she fell into a restless sleep.

Jenny felt a cold breeze blowing over her. She shivered and pulled the blankets up over her shoulders. The cold persisted. She opened her eyes to see a white shape floating above her.

Jen blinked, startled by the shape. She hadn't ever seen anything quite like this. She had to admit, it scared her a little.
Usually, the people that came to her were in more of a human
looking form. She had never had this happen. She decided to
try and communicate with it the best she could, which was
basically talking to it. "Um, hello. Who are you? Are you here
to try and talk to me? I can't see you very well. Can you show
yourself better?"

The shape just hovered over her, not changing form or
trying to communicate in any way.

"Okay, listen, you're scaring me a little. I need to be able
to hear you if you need my help. I can't help you if I can't hear
or see you. What do you need from me?"

The shape just hovered there for a little while longer and
then just disappeared into the night. Leaving just as fast as
it appeared. The shape whooshed over the top of her dresser.
She jumped when her lamp suddenly came on and her cell
phone blinked to life. Jenny picked up her phone, looking at
the screen. The pictures of the accident came up on the screen,
along with a message forming right before her eyes. *Keep looking for the answers here. You will find out that this is important
in more than one murder. Don't stop. Drugs are involved. Keep
looking into Phil Carson's death.* That was all it said.

"Well, that was an interesting form of communication.
This keeps getting more and more interesting."

• • • ǁ • • •

THE NEXT MORNING, Jenny relayed the message that had mysteriously appeared, then disappeared, from her cell phone. "It's a good thing I write everything down in my journal, or I may have forgotten something. That is what the message said, word for word. What do you think Dad?"

"Well, we need to listen to your visions. They have never let us down before. I'm not sure about the drug thing, but we definitely will look into that too. Maybe we should connect with the DEA and see if any drug rings were in the area at the time of the accident. That would be a start. Let me make a few phone calls when we get into the office. I know a few people in the drug enforcement agency."

They finished their breakfast, listening to Abby talk about what she was going to be doing in school that day. They were taking a field trip to the museum, and she was so excited. Ann was one of the chaperones so Jake and Jen didn't have to take Abby to school. Abby was more excited about Ann being with her than anything else.

Jake and Jen left before them, wanting to get into the office early to connect with the DEA. Jenny could never get over the feeling she got when they approached her office.

Her name on the door was so exciting to her. She just felt proud. Of herself, and of the rest of her family. They had been through a lot, and had come through it together. The family had grown closer because of the hardships they had faced. She loved them all. Her musings were disrupted by Jake waving his hand in front of her face. "Hello! Earth to Jenny. Evidently, I've been talking to myself for the past few minutes. Did you hear anything I said?"

"Sorry Dad. I was just thinking. So…you were saying?"

Jake laughed. "Never mind. I'll take care of it."

He grabbed his cell phone and started scrolling through his contacts. Jake pushed the number and waited for an answer. "Yes, this is agent Lawry. How can I help you?"

"Jeez, Lawry. Have you deleted my contact already? I though we would be BFF's forever." Jake asked.

Gary Lawry laughed. "I know who this is Long. I'm just trying to ignore you, that's all. Whenever you call, it seems like the shit hits the fan. I don't know if I want to get involved with any of your schemes."

"Yeah, well, that's your job Gary, so just grin and bear it. Anyway, you wouldn't have answered if you didn't want to hear my voice. It's been awhile buddy!"

"Yes, it has. Good to hear from you Jake. I think. Now what can I help you with? I'm sure you didn't call me just to catch up."

"Yeah, you're right. I need some help with a case I'm working on."

"Are you still in homicide? I thought you hung up your shield?"

"I did. I'm working with my daughter. She opened her own Private Detective office here in Portland. I'm helping her out, and we have a doozy of a case we're working on here. It's an old case, forty years old to be exact. It may involve drugs, and I thought of you right away when I heard that. This case could go back even farther than that. You being so old, I thought you could help me."

Gary laughed, but got serious when he answered Jake back. "Okay, I'm not that old Long. What do you need from me?"

"Can we meet? I would rather talk to you in person. Can we come over to the DEA division sometime this morning?"

"Well, let me drop everything and see if I can see you." Gary answered sarcastically. "Good grief! Okay, come on over around ten, and I'll see if I can fit you into my busy schedule. I got a new partner a while back, so I'll see if he can help us out."

After hanging up, Jake relayed to Jen what Gary had said. "We have an hour until we meet with him. What do you want to do until then?"

"I want to blow up this picture of Jerod Sims' car, and figure out for sure what that sticker says. This is our best clue so far. If we can find a relative, and show them the sticker, we can positively identify Jerod as the victim here. We need to look into the missing persons from that year also. Maybe someone reported him missing and we can find a relative that way. Let's head back to the library, and go through the old microfilm. We can head to the DEA office after that."

Jake was impressed. "Wow, you're getting good at this Jenny. Have I told you how proud of you I am? I am, you know. Very proud."

Jenny blushed a little. "Thanks Dad. Let's go, enough messing around."

When they got to the library, they headed straight for the area where the microfilm was stored. The woman working there was very helpful. She showed them the area that held all of the film from the old newspapers for the year 1977. Jenny couldn't get over how many missing person reports there were for that year. "Good grief! How many people went missing in 1977 anyway? Are you having any luck?"

Jake rubbed his eyes. "Not yet, you?"

"No. Wait a minute! Here it is. The article says that Jerod Sims went missing on June 10, 1977. Dad, the accident was on the eighth of June. That fits. I can't figure this out. Why didn't the police do this forty years ago? Anyway, it says here that he was a student at Portland State University, a freshman. How much do you want to bet that the sticker on the car in the accident is a parking sticker from Portland State University?"

"I wouldn't make that bet. I'm sure that it is. What does the article say about relatives? Who does is it list as the reporting party?"

"Says here, it was his sister. Mary Sims. She lived at the address that we found for Jerod. They were living together. Wow, if we can find her, and show her the pictures that Samantha gave us, she could tell us when they were taken. Here is her current address. I just remembered that Sam was going to tell us who is was that rented her the house. It would have saved us a lot of time and energy if we would have gotten that information."

"Well, I think we got a little too excited over those photos and just forgot. She did say that she didn't know who owned the house. I guess we messed up there. We should have asked her who she rented from. Live and learn I guess. Our appointment with Gary Lawry is soon. We'll go over to this address after we meet with him."

They gathered up all of their printouts, and headed for the pickup with a renewed sense of purpose. They had blown up a picture of the sticker, and had it, along with the picture of the die hanging from the rear view mirror. All they needed was to meet with Mary Sims, and have her positively ID the car, and the sticker, along with the die, and they had their man. John Doe would be identified. Jen was excited, things were moving along with the hit and run case. They just had to figure out a connection with Grif Grant, other than the fact that he handled the accident itself. Now they were on a roll.

After grabbing a coffee, Jake and Jen headed to the DEA with a certain amount of trepidation. They didn't know quite what they were going to ask Gary Lawry. Jake glanced over at Jen as he drove. " Okay, What is our plan here? We can't very well tell Lawry about your visitor last night. How should we handle this?"

"Yeah, I've been thinking about that. I guess be as up front as we can, without saying why we came up with the idea that drugs may have been involved in the accident. Just feel him out, I guess. So how do you know him?"

"I've worked with him on different cases here and there. He's a good guy. I know I can trust him."

"Well, it's always good to know somebody in the DEA that's for sure. Here we are. Here goes nothing. Let's keep our fingers crossed that it will turn into something."

They entered a huge brick building, the doors sliding open as they approached. A uniformed officer stood guard at the door. Jenny wasn't armed, so she waited for Jake to relinquish his weapon at the gate, and they emptied their pockets. They took turns walking through the metal detectors after letting the officer know who they were here to see. One of the officers showed them to the elevator, where he gave them directions to Lawry's office. They entered the elevator, and headed for the fourth floor. A tall, gray-haired man was waiting for them when they stepped out of the elevator.

He grabbed Jake's hand and shook it. "Long! It's been a while. So good to see you again."

Jake smiled and shook the man's hand. "Good to see you too, Gary. You haven't changed a bit."

Gary threw his head back and let out a laugh. "You know you don't need to flatter me Jake. I have always been here to help you. Now come on in and tell me what you need this time."

Gary's office was filled with various awards. Pictures of what looked to be his children and grandchildren lined the walls. Jenny and Jake sat on the over stuffed chairs in front of his desk. "Well, to tell you the truth, we're not sure what we need. I'll tell you what we know, and you can take it from there. There was a hit and run accident forty years ago that took the life of a young man around eighteen years old. He was never identified. After some good old fashioned detective work, we came across a name that we think fits with the car that was driven by the John Doe." Jake brought out the pictures of the car. "Everything matches, right down to the die hanging from the mirror. We haven't talked to his family members yet, but we are fairly certain that this young man is Jerod Sims, from Portland. He was living with his sister, so we're hoping that she is still around the area."

Gary interrupted Jake with a frown. "So what exactly does this have to do with the DEA?"

"I was getting to that. We have reason to believe that drugs may have been involved with the accident. I was hoping that you could look back in your records and check for any drug activity in the area at that time. Maybe some gangs, or anything, really."

"I see. Well, that shouldn't be too hard to figure out. Everything got downloaded into computers. Let's hope the records from forty years ago got downloaded as well. If there was any gang activity or drug activity, we'll have it in there. I think I'll get the new guy to take a look, he is better at these computers than I am." Gary picked up his phone and punched a number. "Dan, could you come in here, please?" It only took a minute for a man to walk into the office. He had a mustache, and a goatee, and looked like his hair hadn't been cut for some time. It was a dark brown color and his bangs were hanging in his eyes. Jake glanced at the man, thinking that he didn't know how he was going to be able to see anything with that hair hanging down. Jen flinched a little beside him, and he looked at her questionably. She had a strange look on her face, and was staring at the man who just entered the office. Gary stood. "Jake, this is Dan Crowley, my new partner. Dan, this is Jake Long, an old friend."

Jake stood to shake Dan's hand and looked closer at his face. He stammered a little with his words. Standing right in front of him was his brother, Tom. He opened his mouth to speak, and Tom shook his head slightly. Jake caught his subtle movement. He regained his composure, and glanced at Jenny and smiled. "Nice to meet you, Dan. This is my daughter, Jenny Long. We're from the Long Agency, a Private Detective Agency here in Portland."

Jenny stood and shook his hand. "Nice to meet you…*Dan.*"

*Tom,* or *Dan,* smiled, and shook their hands. "Nice to meet you too." He glanced at his partner. "What can I do for you all?" He asked, with a slight accent.

"Dan here, is from Texas. We brought him in about a month or so ago to help out with a case. We're between cases right now, so he should be able to help us out with this case."

"Sure thing boss! I'm a whiz at helping people out. What's up?"

"I need you to look in the computer around 1977 and see if there is a record of any drug activity in the Portland area involving college age students." He looked at Jake. "Where exactly did this accident happen?"

"Pine Street. I would like to know if there were any drugs being sold around that area too, if at all possible."

Gary nodded. "We can do that. Right Dan?"

"No problem, I'll get right on it. It won't take long to find that out. Just give me a minute."

Dan left to another office, and got to work. Jake stood to leave. "Could you give Dan my cell phone number and have him call me when he finds anything out? I want to go and see if Mary Sims is still around. We have her address. We want to show her the pictures and see if she recognizes the car. If she does, then I'm sure that it's Jerod Sims. We'll probably have to get some DNA to know for sure. I wonder if she will want to exhume the body to find out for sure? Anyway, that'll be up to her. Thanks for your help, Gary. I appreciate it. Let me know if I can do anything for you."

"I will Long. You owe me more than one, you know."

Jake laughed, and headed out the door. "I probably do Lawry. Just don't make it too tough for me to pay you back, my resources are limited now."

Gary slapped Jake on the back. "No problem Jake. If I need anything, I'll certainly let you know."

Jake glanced in the adjoining office as he left. Tom looked up and quickly looked back down. Jake opted for not saying anything more. He certainly didn't want to blow his brother's cover.

Hopping into the pickup, Jenny let out a breath. "Okay, that was awkward. Wow! Uncle Tom is undercover with the DEA! That's incredible. Did he say anything to you or Sam about this?"

"No, nothing. I knew he couldn't tell us what he was up to, but a hint would have been nice. He's lucky we didn't blow his cover. I wonder what is going on in the DEA that the FBI would put him in there? That's very interesting. Well, he certainly isn't going to tell us the reason. So, let's go find Mary Sims."

After driving around the area for awhile, they found the address of Mary Sims by using their GPS. It was a miracle that she still lived there. She was sixty-five years old now, according to the research they found. Her husband had been dead for five years, no children. It appeared that she lived alone. Knocking on the door, Jake and Jen waited for Mary to answer. The door opened a crack. "Who are you? What do you want?"

"Hello ma'am. My name is Jake Long, and this is my daughter Jenny. We are Private Investigators, could we come in and talk to you?"

"Cops? What do you want with me? I don't know anything!"

Jenny stepped forward. "Not cops ma'am, Private Investigators. We just want to talk to you about your brother's disappearance in 1977. Do you remember anything about that?"

The door opened wider. "Of course I do! He's my brother, I remember everything about it. Why wouldn't I? I'm not that old! Come in, I guess. What do you know about Jerod?"

They walked into a small foyer, with a few pictures on the wall. Not many memories were in this bare home. It looked like she kept the place neat and tidy, not much clutter. Mary showed them to the couch. "Have a seat. Now, what do you want to know? Have you found him? It's been forty years and the cops haven't even tried to find my brother. They have been useless. What do you want to know?"

Jake brought up the pictures of the car and the parking sticker. "We don't know much Mary, may I call you Mary?" Nodding, Mary moved forward in her chair.

"What have you got there?"

"We have a picture of a hit and run accident that happened just down the street from whee you used to live. Do you remember that? It happened around the time Jerod went missing."

Mary scratched her head. "I vaguely remember that. My husband and I were gone at the time of the accident, but the neighbors were all up in the air about it. I didn't associate much with the neighbors. I do know someone died. Wait a minute. You think that was Jerod? Why wouldn't the cops put two and two together and question me? They never even came to my house. I would have been able to tell them if it was Jerod or not. So inept, I always said they weren't interested in finding out what had really happened to my brother."

"Mary, we have a picture of the car that was in the accident. It is a bit graphic, but we wondered if you could look at it and tell us if it's Jerod's car. Would you mind doing that?"

"Of course I will. If it will help find my brother, I will do anything. Show me the damn picture." When Jake brought up the picture, Mary gasped. "That's his car! That's my brother's car!"

Jake held up his hand. "Hold on a minute Mary. We have something else to show you." He brought up the pictures of the sticker, and the die hanging on the mirror. Mary started tearing up. She sobbed a little. "I'm sure of it. That's my brother's car. He was a freshman at Portland University. That's the parking sticker he had in his back window, and those stupid die look just like the ones he had. That's it, that's his car."

She looked up with tears in her eyes. "Where did you get these pictures? Why is this coming up now, after all of these years? Not that I'm not grateful mind you. I want to know why the police didn't know that this was Jerod. So inept. Nothing was ever said to our family about the car, or anything else. Where did you get this? Tell me!"

"We were looking into a different case and this came up on our radar. Mary, Jerod's body is buried in a cemetery especially for John Does. Would you want to exhume the body, and prove once and for all that it's Jerod? We could use DNA if it's still available, or use dental records to identify him. We would need DNA from you to compare it to. Would you do that if we can arrange it? It may be hard to do, but I know a good lawyer who would handle it."

"Of course I would! I want Jerod buried in the family plot, not in some nondescript grave somewhere. He was a good boy, he deserves that."

"Okay, we are going to get right on that. I have one more question Mary. You may not like what I'm going to ask you, but all I ask is for you to be honest with us. Can you do that?"

Mary nodded. "It's the least I can do, after all, you found my brother. What do want to ask me?"

"Mary, did Jerod do drugs? Anything at all that you know of? I know back in the seventies, drugs were pretty loosely used. Did Jerod do that?"

Mary sighed. "I'm afraid so. I tried everything to get him to stop, but the kids he hung out with were not good influences. I'm afraid that's why the cops gave up so long ago. They just figured that he was some drug addicted kid, lost on the streets. Jerod was a good kid, he just didn't have much hope, with mom and dad dying when he was so young. My father was not a nice man either. I did the best I could, but I had troubles of my own."

"We understand, Mary. I'm sure you did the best you could. We'll leave you alone now, but you need to understand that we don't know for sure that the body buried in the unmarked grave is Jerod. I'll call the lawyer right away and get him to get the paperwork going to exhume the body. Then we'll know for sure. I hope it is Jerod, Mary. I hope we can help you find your brother."

Mary stood slowly. "I hope so too Mr. Long, I hope so too. Please, let me know what I need to do. I'll do anything, pay anything to find out for sure."

"I don't want you to worry about it, Mary. If it turns out to be Jerod, someone has a lot of explaining to do. We had better get to work on this. Mary, you've been a lot of help, thank you."

No, thank you, Mr. Long. This could be the closure we've been waiting for all of these years."

Jake frowned. We? Is there someone else involved in this?"

Mary stammered a little, but regained her composure quickly. "N-no it's just me. I guess what I meant was, my family needs this. Both the ones deceased, and me. That's what I meant."

"Sure. Well, okay, we'll stay in touch Mary."

When Jake and Jen got in the pickup, Jake pulled out his cell phone. He dialed the lawyer, and got him working on the exhumation. He didn't think it would be a problem, since it was a John Doe. Jake hung up the phone. "Well, the lawyer said it will probably take a couple of weeks before we can get to the body, and a week or so after that until the DNA tests come back. He said that he would try and get the tests expedited so we can find out sooner. I think we should do a little more research on Jerod Sims while we wait. Just who were his friends back then? What did he do with his time? That sort of thing."

Jenny nodded. "Sounds good to me. Where do we start?"

"Well, how about the college? Let's go there and ask some questions. Maybe some of the professors are still there."

They were very surprised to find that two professors from forty years ago were still employed at the university. Jake and Jen were led to the office of one of the men. Doctor Jim Shultz. He looked to be about seventy-five years old, with gray hair, and bright blue eyes. He looked as sharp as anyone else there, looking Jake and Jen up and down. "Please, come in. What can I do for you folks?"

Jake introduced themselves, and came right to the point. "Dr. Shultz, we're looking into a case that involves a student from this college from 1977. We would like to run some names by you, and see if you remember this student."

"Oh my! That's a long time ago, but I will try to help, if I can."

"Thanks, we appreciate your help. The student in question was Jerod Sims. We were wondering if you remember him at all. We were hoping you could tell us who Jerod hung out with back then. Any friends he had, things like that."

The old man rubbed his chin. "Hmm. I don't recall the name right off hand. Maybe if I saw a picture of him. Let me look in the yearbooks and see if I can find him." He turned to his shelf, filled to the rim with books of all kinds. After running his hands over a few of the books, Dr. Shultz reached up and grabbed a book off the shelf, seeming to know right where it was at. "Awe, here it is. I go through these every now and then. I like looking at my younger face, I guess." He laughed, more to himself than anything. "Anyway, what did you say this boy's name was?"

"Jerod Sims, sir, he would have been in the freshman class at the time."

He turned the pages one by one. It seemed to take hours, before he finally found what he was looking for. "Here it is. 1977, freshman class. Let's see, Sands, Scott, SIMS! Found it." He squinted at the picture, frowning. "Awe yes, I do remember this boy. He seemed to drop out after his freshman year. Never showed back up after the end of the year as I recall. His sister, I believe, came around asking about him. I remember, because the boy was very popular. Ran with an elite crowd. I believe his best friend's name was Grant. They were inseparable, yes Jim Grant. That was his name."

"Are you sure about that sir? Grant?"

"Yes, I'm sure. Grant was a cop's son, as I recall. Cocky, arrogant. Sims clung to him, wanting to be part of the in crowd. I think Grant was a year older than Sims. Yes, there he is. Jim Grant." He pointed to a picture on the page of the yearbook.

Jake looked closer at the page. "Do you mind if we take a picture of both of these boys? We may need them for identification purposes."

"No problem, take all the pictures you want."

Jake snapped a few pictures, and they excused themselves and left the office. Jen let out a breath. "Wow! Dad, do you think the Jim Grant that was friends with Jerod Sims, is Grif Grant's son?"

"I'm not sure, but I think it's time we find out. Julie Grant needs to come back into the office with her brother. We need to ask him a couple of questions, and find out if he knew Jerod Sims." Jen called Julie Grant and set up the appointment for ten o'clock the next day. She agreed to bring her brother along.

"This is getting even more interesting now. I can hardly wait for tomorrow. I wonder if Jim Grant will put together a few more pieces of this puzzle." Jen said.

"Well, we'll find out tomorrow." Jake's phone rang. A number he didn't know showed up on the screen. He frowned, and answered. "Long here."

"Long. This is Dan Crowley, from the DEA. I just wanted to check in and let you know what I found out about Jerod Sims." Jake raised his eyebrows, and looked at Jen. "Hang on Dan, let me put you on speaker." He pushed the speaker button, and Dan filled them in on what he had found.

"Well, Jerod Sims wasn't on the DEA's radar at all. He was a fairly good kid from what I could find out. No gang affiliations or anything like that. You have to remember, in the seventies, the drugs were fairly easy to obtain for these kids. You just had to know who to talk to. More than likely, Sims just got his drugs from a friend or family member. I'll keep looking, but that's all I know, for now."

"Okay, thanks for calling, Dan. Could I get your phone number? In case I have anymore questions?"

"Umm. Okay, sure. Just call this number if you need to talk to me about *business*." Tom made sure that Jake understood that there was to be no communication between them other than business. He couldn't afford to have his cover blown. Jake understood that without Tom telling him.

"Yes, I understand. Thank you Dan, we'll be touch."

Jake hung up. "Well, Tom made it perfectly clear that we weren't to try and get a hold of him. How dumb does he think we are anyway? We could have blown his cover earlier, and we didn't. Good grief! Anyway, sounds like our boy Jerod, was pretty much squeaky clean. He did dabble in drugs though. Let's call it a night and go home. Tomorrow, I aim to find out what the relationship was between Jim Grant and Jerod Sims, if there was one."

••• 12 •••

THE NEXT DAY, Jake and Jen were sitting in the office, catching up on some paperwork. Julie Grant, along with her brother, Jim, knocked on the office door, and came in. Jake looked up from what he was doing. "Come in. I'm sorry for the mess. I guess I got caught up in what I was doing, and lost track of time." He stood and reached out his hand to the man standing next to Julie. "Hello, my name is Jake Long." Jake called to Jenny, and she came over to greet them. "This is my daughter, and boss, Jenny Long."

Jenny smiled. She reached out to shake hands with Jim Grant. Not waiting for Julie to introduce them, she took Jim by surprise. "It's good to see you again Julie. Hello, you must be Jim, it's so nice to meet you." Jenny took a chance, letting him know that she figured his name was Jim Grant. The very same Jim Grant that was best friends with Jerod Sims. She and Jake had decided to wait and see how the man reacted when they mentioned Jerod Sims.

Jim Grant looked at them both with a wary eye, but shook hands with them nonetheless. "Yes, nice to meet you two. Why are we here? From what I understand, you closed my father's case already. I never wanted Julie to dig into this anyway. I already told her that Dad had killed himself. She should have just left it alone like I told her to."

Julie cringed, glaring at her brother. "I apologize for my brother's behavior. He is a bit spoiled, I'm afraid. My father doted on him a bit too much."

Jake looked the man over carefully. He didn't like what he saw, and Jake always followed his gut instinct on these things. If his gut told him that something wasn't right, it usually wasn't. "No problem. We asked you here, because we actually uncovered some new evidence that includes your father's cases as a police officer. Nothing is definitive yet, but we just wanted to let you in on what is happening. We were following up on some leads, and we found a case involving a hit and run from forty years ago. Your dad was the lead investigator on this case. To make a long story short, we found some evidence of a cover up involving the people in this case. It was a John Doe that was killed." Jake watched Grant carefully. "We may have identified the boy. We think his name was Jerod Sims, but we don't know for sure yet. Witnesses have come forward to identify a truck that fled the scene. What we need from you, is this. Did your dad leave anything behind concerning a hit and run? Any paperwork? A notebook? Anything?"

Jenny noticed that Jim was squirming a little in his chair. He looked a little uncomfortable, and more so as Jake continued his story. Julie was the one who spoke. "He may have left something. To tell you the truth, I haven't been through all of the boxes he left behind. It's just too much." She glanced at Jim. "Have you seen anything like that?"

Jim cleared his throat. "Um, no. I don't know what you're talking about."

Jake watched Jim carefully, hoping he would slip up and tell them the truth. That didn't happen. The guy was smart, too smart. "Okay, well. Would you mind if we take a look at his things? We won't disturb anything personal. We're just looking for anything concerning this accident."

Julie started to nod, agreeing to let them look, when Jim spoke up, standing as he spoke. "No! You won't be going through my dad's things, and that's final. He didn't leave any information about this accident." That was all Jim had to say. He turned, and left abruptly.

After Jim stormed out of the office, Julie nervously turned to follow him out. "I'm sorry, I'll talk to him about this. I don't really know why he's so touchy about all of this. I'm afraid Dad's death hit him very hard. I'll be in touch."

Jake let out a whistle after they left. "Wow, that guy was wound up tighter than a clock. He wasn't going to give anything up about his relationship with Jerod Sims that's for sure. Well, there really is nothing we can do now until we get the okay to exhume the body, and find out if our John Doe is really Jerod Sims."

Jenny agreed. "That's true. Dad, I've been thinking about something, and I want you to hear me out okay? What if Grif didn't kill himself? This all seems to connect with Phil Carson's death too. Supposedly, he shot himself. Supposedly Grif shot himself. You saw all of the boxes of cop suicides when we were in the police station. I know that most of them are suicides, that happens a lot with former and current policemen. I just think it's odd that Julie is convinced that her dad didn't kill himself, and Cara was wondering about Phil too. My friend that appears in the night told me that Phil's death needed to be looked into further too. Phil wrote a note saying that he wouldn't kill himself. I really think that we should look further into Phil's death while we wait for the lawyers to hash out our exhumation."

"You know, I think you're right Jen. Cara's death was questionable too. Let's get this figured out. The police aren't going to like us digging into their business. I have a feeling that we're going to meet with some resistance along the way."

"I agree, but I feel like it's a necessity. Something just isn't right about all of this. We need to start connecting some dots."

"Well, let's start with Phil's shooting when he was on the job. It seemed pretty straightforward, but maybe if we figure out exactly why he got shot in the first place, other things will start falling into place. I guess we have to make a trip back to the fifth precinct."

Jenny grimaced. "Yeah, what fun that will be."

They headed straight for the fifth precinct's Captain. Jake knew that he would have to go straight to him to get any paperwork that involved Phil's shooting. Captain Keller looked up from the paperwork he had scattered in front of him. He sighed, and rubbed his eyes. "You two again. You're like a couple of bad pennies, always showing up. What is it this time?"

Jake decided to get right to the point. "Well, hello to you too, Captain. What we need, is to see the reports on Phil Carson's on the job shooting. I'm presuming it's all public record now? As long as we are doing that, we want to see all of Grif Grant's case files. We think their suicides are connected somehow, and we aren't going to stop until we figure it out. You may as well cooperate. You don't want lawyers involved do you?"

Captain Keller bristled at Jake's tone. "Now hold on here. You can't come in here demanding to see things like that. I would suggest that you change your tone of voice, Long. Haven't you ever heard the saying, you can catch more flies with honey than vinegar? You should try that sometime."

"I apologize, but this is all getting frustrating, and you seem to be blocking us at every turn."

"I can hand over all of the public files on Phil's shooting. Grant's personal things, and his private belongings, have been handed over to his family."

"Well, we would like to go over everything again, and find out if there was any forensic evidence from the hit and run accident from 1977. I understand that Grif Grant was the lead on that case. If any was kept, we could find out what happened, and maybe even who did it. The last time we were here, the box of evidence had mysteriously disappeared. Has it been found by chance?"

"Let me check on that." Keller picked up his phone and pushed a number. "Yes, I have two Gumshoes in my office asking about Grant's old file on the hit and run, and Phil Carson's shooting. I want the evidence brought to my office." He hung up, and looked over his glasses at Jake and Jen. "They will bring up what they have. That's about all I can do from here. You can look over the evidence in the interview room. Now get out of my office."

Jake nodded. "Great, thanks for your help Captain."

Jen and Jake stood outside the door waiting for the evidence to be brought up. Jake whispered under his breath to Jenny. "Well, if I only knew that bringing up lawyers would work, I would have done it long ago."

"No kidding. I wonder what we are going to end up getting for evidence. If there was any DNA, or blood evidence from the accident, it's probably too degraded to do us any good now anyway. But any little bit will help."

"Yes, it will. Here it comes now. Let's dig in."

The officer plopped the boxes down on the table, and glared at them as he left. Jake just glared back at him. "Such hostility around here. I don't remember there being a dislike for private eyes in my office in Los Angeles."

"I think they just don't like us digging into their mistakes, that's all. Whatever, if we find they screwed up on this, they will really dislike us."

Just as they opened the boxes, and started digging out what little evidence was there, Jake's phone rang. It was the lawyer he had hired to get the body exhumed. "Long here." He answered.

"Long, this is Tim, from the lawyers office. I have some good news. The judge okayed the exhumation of the John Doe. We have to wait for all of the paperwork to go through, but it should happen sometime next week. Do you want to be there?"

"No, that's okay, I just need to see if we can get any DNA off of the body. Or dental impressions, so we can identify him by dental work. The coroner can handle that. This is great! Thank you, Tim. Please get back to me when the body reaches the coroner's office. I'll handle it from there. Thanks again."

After hanging up, he filled Jenny in on what was said. She grinned. "This is turning out to be a pretty good day Dad. Let's see if our luck holds here."

They looked over the things that were in the Grant box first. It wasn't a surprise that the photos were gone, but Jenny found something interesting. It was a part of a car's blinker. Just a small piece of glass. Everything else was just the files that they had already seen. But this tiny piece of lens may be the evidence they needed to find the person who killed this young man. If they could identify the vehicle, that would be one step closer to the identification of the killer. Jen was excited.

Next, they turned to Phil's shooting. There really wasn't much there either. Jen frowned. "It just seems odd that his fellow police officers wouldn't look into this more. The shooting did happen on the job. I suppose because the shooter was killed, the case was closed."

"Probably, but who was this guy? All it says here is his name, Julio Garcia. He was from Los Angeles, which is especially interesting to me. I can check with my contacts there, and find out more about this guy. Well, we have gotten a lot done today. Let's go and see if we can take this lens with us. We need to find out the make and model of this vehicle. It will bring us one step closer to finding the driver. I don't know if all of this connects to Phil's death, but I aim to find out."

"I agree. Let's talk to the captain about what we found. He seemed to be in a good mood, let's hope he still is." Jen said sarcastically.

Sure enough, they lucked out, the captain let them take the lens cover, only after signing their names on several different pieces of paper. Jake and Jen took the piece of the blinker straight to a nearby car dealership. Luckily, the mechanic on duty, was an old truck enthusiast. After looking at the piece from the turn signal, he knew right away that it definitely was from an old Ford pickup truck. "See those numbers that are on this lens cover?" He took a magnifying glass, and showed Jake and Jen. "They couldn't have seen this number unless they knew where to look. I'll take this number, and punch it into my computer. I should get a make and model of the pickup that this lens came off in no time. Do you want to wait?"

"Yes, we sure do. Go for it." Jake could hardly contain his excitement. When he looked over at his daughter, he noticed that she was feeling the same way. Grinning, he gave her a fist bump. "This is it Jen. I can feel it in my bones. We are one step closer to solving this case. Then, we can focus on Phil's case."

While they waited for the news on the vehicle involved in the hit and run, Jake called Tom, or *Dan,* he should say. "Dan, this is Jake Long, from the Long Agency. I was wondering if you could run a name for me? It is involving a police officer shooting. Phil Carson was the cop. He was making a routine traffic stop, and the guy just stepped out from his car, and shot him. The perp died in prison. His name was Julio Garcia, from the Los Angeles area. Could you check and see if anything pops up on the DEA radar? There were drugs found in his car. Four kilo's of cocaine to be exact."

"Yes, I can check it out. I'll call you when I find out anything. I think we should meet to discuss it. Would noon tomorrow work? At Lori's restaurant? A lunch meeting?"

"Sounds good to me. We'll be there."

The mechanic came back just as Jake hung up the phone. "I found it! Gotta love computers. The number on the shard of glass matched up with a 1970 Ford F-150. That's all I could find out, no information on an owner or anything. The color was red though. There was a paint chip on the back of the lens cover. I guess you could look up all of the owners of a red F-150 for those dates. It may take awhile though. Well, good luck, I hope that helps you."

"It does help, thank you very much."

Jake filled Jenny in on what was said on the phone call with Tom. Heading back to the office, they pulled into a fast food joint for a burger. "We have some work to do on this pickup. The licensing division keeps pretty good records on the vehicles they license. Hopefully we can find out who the owner of this Ford was. First thing we do, is get to a computer in the court house, and check that out. Then, we can narrow it down more by comparing the address on file, with the addresses on the street the accident happened on. I have a feeling the perp lived in the area. That isn't a well traveled street. Why else would he be on that street? What was he doing there? We are getting closer now."

"Yeah, we are. I'm very excited about this turn of events. We need to pick up Abby now, let's leave this go until tomorrow. Maybe by then, we'll have our DNA sample too. This case is just about solved. That makes me feel pretty good. Our second case, and we nailed it. I really want to solve Phil's case too, for Abby and Cara's sake. Abby deserves to know the truth. I can't stop thinking about that letter from Phil. If he didn't commit suicide, then what exactly happened? I think when we talk to Tom tomorrow, we are going to find out a lot more about that. Wow, my mind is spinning with all of the information we found today. It's interesting how things just start falling into place. This is so cool! I love it!"

"Me too, but don't go jumping to conclusions. We have a lot of work to do yet. Even if we figure out who rammed into Jerod Sims, we need to figure out why it wasn't solved forty years ago. This could go deep into the police force. I agree with one thing. It's time to call it a day."

On the drive home, Jake and Jen were listening to Abby talk about her day. The young girl was handling everything that happened to her so well. They couldn't believe how resilient she was. If only more people could be like that. Jake's phone rang, and everything went quiet, for the time being. It was Tom a.k.a Dan. Jake was kind of shocked that he would be talking to him again so soon. "Hello, Dan. To what do I owe the pleasure?"

"Long, I got the info you wanted already. My bosses want me to get them to you right away. If you are free tonight could you meet me?"

"Actually, I'm on my way home already. Would you want to come out to the ranch? It's only about an hour drive. I could give you directions."

"Sure, I could do that. I can get the ranch up on GPS. I'll see you around eight o'clock, if that works for you."

"That'll be fine. I'll see you then."

Jake finished his call just as they pulled into the driveway. He shared what Tom had said with Jen. "We need to let the others in on Tom's undercover op before he gets out here. I don't know if he can talk freely or not. We'll let him decide on that."

"I agree Dad. I'm sure Sam and Ann, and the others, will handle it well." Jen turned to Abby. She was listening intently to what was being said. "Abby, if you see Uncle Tom you need to pretend that you don't know him, do you understand? Remember when we told you about his job?"

Abby rolled her eyes. "I know Jenny. I'm not a little kid anymore you know."

Jake and Jen couldn't help but chuckle at her pre-teen attitude. "I know that. I just wanted to make sure."

Abby crossed her arms over her chest, and nodded. She knew the rules, she was a cop's daughter, after all.

Jake pulled the truck up to the deck. Sam was down at the barn pitching hay to the horses, so Jake dropped the girls off, and headed that way. He grabbed a pitch fork, and joined his brother. He needed to tell Sam about Tom's undercover job.

"Hey, Sam, there's something I need to tell you. It's not a big deal, but you and Ann need to be aware. Jenny and I went into the DEA offices in Portland the other day. To our huge surprise, our brother Tom walked into the office of Jim Lawry. He is working undercover there at the DEA. I was shocked, but Jen and I held our surprise, and kept our cool. He didn't want us to spread the word too much, so I didn't tell you all before. He is coming out here tonight to bring us some information we had asked for. I don't know if he can be open with us or not, so we need to keep his real identity a secret. I know you all know that, but I wanted to tell you ahead of time."

Sam pitched a little more hay before he answered. "So, that's where he ended up. I wondered why he came here in the first place. I knew it wasn't just because of my wedding. He is so involved in his work, I figured there was an ulterior motive. I'll talk to Ann and Nancy, and let them know. It'll be fine. I hope that he knows he can trust us."

"I'm sure he does. We'll have to wait and see what happens tonight. I think he'll be able to open up and be himself unless someone is with him. It should be late enough that the hands will all be hunkered down for the night, so we shouldn't have to worry about that." The two men worked in silence then, pitching the hay. The ranch work always calmed Jake. He couldn't believe how much he loved it here. After growing up and living in the city most of his life, the country life was growing on him. The silence was a little hard to get used to, but he loved it. He wouldn't want to be anywhere else.

Supper was a raucous affair, as usual. The eclectic group of people sitting around the table talking and laughing. Jenny loved listening to everyone talk. It was good to hear laughter at the ranch again. There had been too much sadness for them. They all were ready for some good times.

She was one of the lucky ones. Jenny had a great family to fall back on when she lost her mom. Abby did too. They were her family now, and she knew that. Abby was growing into a lovely young lady. She was smart, funny, and popular in school. Her parents would have been very proud of her, that's for sure. If Jenny sees them again, she is going to tell them that. Her visions have been very sporadic lately. She hadn't had much happen since the white mist appeared above her head. As of right now, all Jenny could do is wait for the apparitions to come to her on their own. She was just going to have to be patient and wait for them to appear.

Jen was deep in thought, when she realized that the room was quiet, and everyone was looking at her. "What? What's going on?" She looked from one person to the next, looking for the answer to her question.

They all burst out laughing. Ann got up and hugged her. "You were so deep in thought, you missed one of Sam's stupid jokes, that's all. Nothing major. You probably know them all by heart anyway, his jokes never change."

Sam gave Ann a glare. It was shared with a smile, which defeated the purpose of the glare itself. "You love my jokes and you know it. You just won't admit it."

With the table cleared, and the dishes done, the men were sitting out on the deck. It was a ritual that they did almost every night. They just relaxed in the lawn chairs, enjoying the quiet around them. They soon noticed a car driving up the lane. The dogs barked loudly, alerting them, just in case they didn't see the vehicle approaching. Sam silenced them with a command.

Tom pulled up to the house. When he got out of his car, he had to stop and look around at the sprawling ranch. He really did enjoy his time here with his brothers, even though it was short. He knew that his brothers were not going to be happy with him about the purpose of his visit, but that couldn't be helped. Tom looked at Jake and Sam, standing now, waiting for him to approach.

He always thought that the three of them looked alike, but they really didn't. Which helped him out in his chosen profession. No one could know that they were related, there was too much danger involved in his job. He changed his looks often, as the job entailed. Tom would grow a beard for one op, grow his hair long, even shave his head if need be.

This particular op, he had a mustache and goatee. Tom had the same lanky frame as his brothers, there was no hiding that, but he knew that is where the resemblance to his brothers ended. Both Sam and Jake were dark haired and dark skinned, where he was blonde with blue eyes. He had dyed his hair for the undercover op that he was currently on, so it was dark brown right now. Tom looked like his mother, and they looked like their dad, it was as simple as that.

Tom grinned as he approached. "It's okay, we can be ourselves, I'm alone." They did their usual hugs, and Tom grabbed a beer. "Man, I really do miss this place. It's beautiful out here."

Jake and Sam weren't going to let him off that easy, though. Jake took a swig of his iced tea. "You know, you could have trusted us with this job of yours. We know how important it is to keep your secret. You really took Jen and I off guard when we saw you at the DEA."

"I know, but after all of these years of keeping secrets, I guess it's just ingrained in me to not tell anyone, even you."

Sam knew what his brother meant, and so did Jake. "Well, we know now, so the gig is up. How long do you think you'll be around? I know you can't just come out here for no reason, but if you need anything you will let us know."

"Sure thing, it's good to know you're there for me. But, the reason I'm here is this." He addressed Jake. "Your boy Julio was on the DEA's radar. It took me awhile to get his info, but it turns out he was involved with a drug cartel that has been around for a long time. The DEA has been after them for years, but they always seem to keep just under the radar. The DEA has been gathering evidence on them for many years. They figure that this cartel, the CS group, has been around since 1978. I know, some coincidence, right? I don't know about you but I don't believe in coincidence. I can't quite put my finger on it, but the hit and run accident, the fact that Julio would rather kill a cop than get arrested, and all of the so called suicides in the past years, seem odd to me. That's why I'm here, the FBI is tired of this group being able to cover their tracks so well. They wanted me deep undercover. I've just started my investigation, but so far, most of the DEA look clean. You need to be careful though, Jake. I wouldn't trust anyone. They shoot first, and ask questions later. Keep your eyes open."

"I will. Thanks for letting me know this. We're going to keep digging into this hit and run, and Phil's death. If Grif Grant and Phil Carson were murdered, the families deserve their pensions, and life insurance. They deserve to know the truth, and we aren't going to stop until we give it to them. Just how much do you know about this cartel? Who is running the show?"

"That's just it. We have no idea. There are so many people involved in it, no one stands out as the boss. He, or she, has kept their nose clean all of these years. They are smart, and the people around them are very loyal. They would rather die than give up any names. It takes a lot to keep a cartel going all of these years, and not even give up a name. It goes pretty deep that's for sure. I'll keep working my end, and you need to keep me informed also. It's a good thing that you came to Lawry instead of anyone else. That way, we have an excuse to keep in touch."

"That's true, and we will do that." Jake glanced at Sam. "I haven't filled you in on our cases, but I will. If there is a drug cartel involved, you need to keep the ranch safe. These people will stop at nothing to get away with their crimes. The whole family could be in danger."

Sam knew the ropes. He has been around law enforcement his whole life. "I realize the danger involved. I can handle things here, don't worry about the family. You two just watch your backs, and be safe. If you're poking around in drug cartel business, anything could happen. Jake, you watch out for Jen. She's been through enough."

"No worries there. She's my daughter, I'll keep her safe."

They all stood. As Tom walked to his car, he turned back to his brothers. "It really is great to see you again. After this is all over, maybe we can spend more time together. I'm about ready to hang this job up. To tell you the truth, I've been working this case for a long time. It seems to be coming to a head now. I hope we can figure this out so everyone is safe. We need to get these drugs off the street. Jake, there is one more thing. This goes all the way down the coast. From Los Angeles all the way to Seattle. You may want to check with your contacts in LA, see if they will keep their ears to the ground there."

"I will do that. I do know that my old partner would like this information. I haven't talked to him in awhile, it'll be nice catching up."

After Tom left, Sam and Jake sat awhile longer. They weren't talking much, just taking in all that was said tonight. The horses were milling about in the barn and corrals, the cows were grazing in the pasture, and all was so serene. Sam stood. "Well, it sounds like our peace and quiet is soon over. This family just can't help but get in the middle of danger. It's in our blood I guess. Well, I'm tired. I'm sure Ann is wanting to know what is going on here. I'm not going to keep anything from her Jake. They deserve to know what's going on."

"I agree with you on that, Sam. I'll fill Nancy and Jen in too. I don't think Abby needs to know the whole story. She's tough, but she's been through enough."

They went to their separate areas of the huge house, thinking about the upcoming days, and weeks, maybe even months. The family was going to have to be on their toes for this one. No one knew what the outcome was going to be, they were going to have to take it day by day.

••• 13 •••

IT WAS CLOSE to Christmas by the time the courts decided that they could exhume John Doe's body. The weather was cold, but the ground was good enough to bring up the coffin. It still will take days before they find out for sure if the body was Jerod Sims. Jake and Jen still had some investigating to do on Phil Carson, and Grif Grant, while they waited. They hadn't heard anything else from Tom, which wasn't unusual. Things had been moving along slowly. There was no connection with Jerod Sims to any drug cartels that they knew of. Jim Grant was a person of interest in the case. Jake was convinced that he was involved somehow, but he wasn't cooperating at all. That just made Jake more suspicious.

Looking into the cartel that called themselves CS Group was going nowhere. Jenny was getting frustrated. "Dad, this is driving me crazy! I can't handle this waiting. Let's call the coroner and see if he knows anything about the body yet."

"You can call him if you want, but I don't think he'll know anything yet. It takes time for the DNA results. I asked him to look into dental records too, maybe he got something from them."

Jenny literally ran for the phone. "I am going to try anyway. We really need to know if the body is Jerod Sims. Things will snowball from there, I just know it. Besides, it's been three days!"

Jake laughed to himself when she grabbed the phone and dialed as fast as she could. He could hear her side of the conversation. "Yes, Doctor. I understand. But Doctor, could you please hurry with this? Someone's life has been on hold for a long time because of this. Not only that, but the poor man lying on your slab right now hasn't been identified for forty years. Okay, we'll call back."

Jenny let out a loud sigh when she hung up. She looked at Jake sheepishly. "Okay, you were right. But…I did get him to rush the results. We should know by the end of the day." She stuck her tongue out. "So there."

Jake shook his head. "Well, you used the old Long charm on him, that's why he said he would rush it."

"That's right. What should we do in the meantime?"

"I talked to Tony last week and filled him in on the Cartel. He has heard of them. Tony said that they were in business even when I was in homicide there. I guess I just never paid attention to the narcotic division's business. I was a little tied up in homicide, and catching a serial killer. Anyway, he thinks that the CS group goes back even longer than we think. It worries me, if they have gotten away with their illegal activities that long, they are good. Damn good."

"Yes, and little old us, a rookie, and an *older* cop, are going to bring them down."

"I certainly hope so. We're going to try anyway. Except, who is this older cop you're talking about?" They laughed together. "Seriously though, I think we need to go way back into the early seventies, even before the accident. We should research all of the suicides, and other killings, of policemen and women. I have Tony doing that in Los Angeles. We need to do that here also. Back to the police station we go. Captain Keller will be so happy to see us."

"Sure, he will. He'll greet us with open arms. Especially when he finds out why we're there."

Jake and Jen received the same cold shoulders and glares that they usually got when they walked into the station. They ignored them all, heading straight for the captain's office. He was expecting them, judging by the scowl on his face. "What do you two want now?"

"Well, hello to you too." Jake got straight to the reason they were there. "We need to look into all of the suicides, shootings, and any police internal investigations in the past fifty years. Where would we go to get that information?"

"Wow! You're not asking for much, are you? Persistent too. Like I said before, you know you can't see any files on internal investigations, and the suicides are public record. Go to the library. Good day."

Jake turned and started out the door, turning back before he left. "You know, your cooperation will be duly noted in our files Captain. Thanks so much." Jake nodded to Jenny, indicating that they leave. They weren't going to gain any more information here. "Wow, these people are growing more uncooperative every day. It only makes me more suspicious, how about you?"

"I totally agree. Something isn't right here, and we are going to find out what. With, or without their cooperation. In the first place, I can't believe that they didn't work harder to identify John Doe's body. It sounds like they didn't even look into his driver's license or registration. Let's get to the library. Maybe the articles on the accident will tell us more. At least the people there are willing to help us out."

After looking for about an hour on the library's computer files, along with microfilm, Jenny found several articles on police suicides. There were several shootings too, but most of them were justified. "I just don't know Dad. There is a lot of suicides, but that's not uncommon. How do we separate the suspicious ones from the explained suicides?"

Jake had been reading over the articles on the accident. He stopped what he was doing, and rubbed his eyes. "That's a good question. I guess we just have to interview family members of the victims and see what they have to say. I hate to dredge up the past for them, but I think it's necessary. This isn't going to be fun. Make some copies of all of the names, and we'll track them down." He looked back at the pages he had printed out. "Whoa, wait a minute. I just found out why they didn't identify the John Doe through regular means. I don't know how we missed this before. It says here, there was no ID found on the body. No registration, and no plates. Everything was removed from the car. Even the VIN number was filed down. That's interesting. Whoever got there first, must have taken those things to keep the police from finding out who it was. They probably figured that it would most certainly lead back to them. Now I am sure that if we identify the John Doe, we will find out who ran into him. I also think that we'll find who covered it up." Jake rubbed his eyes again. "Let's get out of here. We have what we need. We had a good day Jen."

With the copies in hand, they headed back to the office to finish up the day. They had the addresses of the families of the fallen policemen that were still around the Portland area. A lot of them had died or moved away, but there were a handful still in the area. Jake and Jen contacted some of them and they agreed to meet with them after the holidays. For now though, their work day was ending. It was time to pick up Abby and go home. Abby was starting her Christmas vacation, and she was excited to be able to stay home and ride her horse. That was her life basically, when she wasn't in school. She loved it that way. Abby has always loved the animals on the ranch, and enjoyed helping with their care. That's how she had grown up. Most of her life was spent on the ranch.

When Jen and Jake picked her up, she was her usual bubbly self. Full of excitement for the upcoming Christmas holiday. She held up her gift from the secret Santa at school. It was a mixture of colored pencils, markers, and a book to color in. She liked art projects, and was excited to start coloring the pictures. "Look! All of the pictures are of animals. Horses, cows, even chickens! Whoever got me this knew exactly what I would like. This is awesome!"

Jenny loved Abby like she was her own little sister. She couldn't help but get into the spirit with her. "That's great Abby. Maybe this weekend we can go riding, just like we used to. I miss the time spent on a horse. I've been so busy I haven't been able to ride like I used to. What do you say?"

"Yes!" Abby squealed. "I miss that too. I've been having to go by myself all the time, unless one of the kids on the ranch want to go. There aren't that many around anymore. I want to go with you Jen. You're the best! You know all of the fun places to ride around the ranch. When can we go?"

Jen laughed, getting caught up in the young girl's excitement. "I can't go until the weekend, but you get practiced up. We may end up going for a camp out or something, depending on the weather. We'll see what your mom and dad say. I mean, Sam and Ann, sorry."

Abby looked thoughtful. "It's okay if you call them my mom and dad. I kind of feel the same way about them. I don't know about you, but I think this is going to be the best Christmas ever!" Abby got quiet then. She finally softly whispered to herself. "I'm sorry Mom and Dad. I didn't mean that it would be the best Christmas. I miss you both so much. I love you."

They pulled into the ranch shortly after that, and Abby jumped out and ran straight for the barn. Jake shook his head and glanced at Jen. "That girl just never ceases to amaze me. I can't remember ever being that young and carefree."

"She is an amazing kid. I love her like a sister. We could all learn a thing or two from her attitude. I think we have become a little too serious about life. I know that all of the things that have happened over the years have made us that way." Jen sighed. "I really miss Mom a lot. I wish she were here in person, not just in spirit, but I'll take what I can get. Her appearances have been few and far between. I only hope that she sticks around. I need her here Dad."

Jake put his arm around Jen. "I know honey, but you said yourself that she mentioned that she may be replaced by someone else for this case. I think she'll be back though. I'm sure of it. She won't leave you again if she has a choice."

"I know, it's just that her being there in spirit has kept me going all of these years. I can't believe it's been a few years since she died. It seems like yesterday to me. So much has happened."

"Me too, Jen, and I basically didn't get to see her for fifteen years before that. I wish that things could have been different. Jen, you know that I would have been there if I would have known about you, right? I don't blame Sara for not telling me, but if I would've known that I had a daughter, I would like to think that things would have been different."

Jen hugged him tightly. "I know Dad. I don't hold any hard feelings about that. I totally understand that what you were doing was important. I wish that Mom would've stuck it out with you. She did what she thought was best I suppose."

"Yes, she did. You know the story about her past. She and Ann had a tough childhood, and she blamed the job. Joe was caught up in his detective work, just like I was. It was just too hard on her. Besides, Ann needed her, and Sara had to be there for her, too. I don't blame her a bit for leaving me. She gave me fair warning many times. I just wouldn't, or couldn't listen, I guess." Jake shook his head again. "Well, they always say that things happen for a reason. It's made us stronger, I guess. Look at us now, working together. I think your mom would have been proud of both of us. If she wasn't, I don't think she would be helping us right now, do you?"

"You know, you're right Dad. She keeps on helping in the only way that she knows how. She has even gathered other people to help out. She was, and is, an amazing person."

"Yes, she is. All anyone needs to do is just look at you to know that."

They walked arm in arm to the house, feeling serene and happy. They didn't realize that the can of worms they were about to open was going to spit out more than they bargained for. Making not only their lives miserable, but other lives as well.

### ••• 14 •••

THE CHRISTMAS HOLIDAY went by without a hitch. It was fun watching Abby open all of her presents. She loved every one of them. They all overindulged in food and merriment. Even Nancy was joining them in the games that Abby talked them into playing. Jake sat back, watching all of his family having fun. After his talk with Jen, he realized just how much he missed the company of a woman. Sam seemed to think that Nancy was in love with him. Jake wasn't so sure of that, but he did have feelings for her. He felt a little guilty still, but it had been a long time since he had any kind of relationship with a woman. He missed the warmth and camaraderie of having a spouse, or even just a significant other, to talk to.

Jake's musings were interrupted by Abby grabbing his hand and dragging him over to join the others. She plopped him down beside Nancy. It was like she had been reading his mind. He had been thinking about Nancy for awhile now. Good thoughts.

Nancy smiled at him and he smiled back. Jake decided then and there, that he wanted this woman. He just wondered if she actually felt the same way. He was going to find out tonight, before he and Jen got busy with their case again. This time, Jake was going to do it right. Nancy was going to come before his job. He had waited long enough for this moment to come.

When the games were over, and Jen had taken Abby to bed, Jake invited Nancy out to the deck for a nightcap. She agreed. Jake mixed her a drink, and grabbed an iced tea for himself. He knew what alcohol did to him, and he had been sober for awhile now. Nothing was going to change that. He could have used the liquid courage, though. He felt like a teenager, asking a girl to go with him to the school dance. They sat down on the huge padded chairs surrounding the fire pit. "It's a little chilly tonight." Jake grabbed the blanket and covered Nancy's shoulders. "Would you like me to start a fire?"

"That would be great. I love sitting by the fire."

Jake rushed to grab firewood, taking his time. Some would call it stalling, I suppose, but he needed to gather his thoughts together. Jake didn't want to screw this up, like he had his previous relationships. He had to find the right words. Even though Jake and Nancy had known each other for a few years now, Jake felt like he actually didn't know her at all. It was time to change that, if Nancy was willing. He was going to take a shot at it. All she could do was say no, right?

Jake filled the pit with dry kindling, and got a blaze going in no time. Nancy was quiet, just enjoying the time she spent with Jake. She knew that he was feeling uncomfortable about something. Nancy knew Jake well enough to know that he had something on his mind. She could hope that it was her that he was thinking about, but she wasn't going to hold her breath on that one. She had been very patient, waiting for Jake to come to his senses, but she was growing tired of waiting. Nancy had already decided that she was going back to Los Angeles after the New Year. She couldn't hang around here forever, waiting for Jake to figure out what he wanted. Sam and Ann had been more than welcoming to her, even letting her use her Psychology degree to help out the people on the ranch. That definitely kept her from being bored, and she loved helping people. That's why she became a Psychologist in the first place, and she knew cops well. That's what she did in Los Angeles, helping out the police officers and detectives who needed her. She has helped a lot of people over the years. It was time she got back to her work.

Jake nervously wiped his hands down the leg of his jeans. Nancy had to smile. He was a gorgeous man. Tall, with a full head of hair, just graying at the temples. His brown hair and dark brown eyes, were the stuff of her dreams, he just didn't know it. She smiled at him, feeling sad that this may be one of the last times they sat out here like this. Jake brought her out of her thoughts with an odd question.

"Nancy, I don't really know how to ask you this, so bear with me okay?"

She sat up straighter in her chair. Where was he going with this? "Sure, you know you can ask me anything Jake. What's wrong? I couldn't help but notice that you had something on your mind. Is it the case you're working? Do you need my help?"

"No, no, it's not the case. We're coming along pretty good with that. This is more personal." Jake cleared his throat. "Good grief, I feel like a teenager."

Nancy laughed. "What are you talking about Jake? Just spit it out. What are trying to say?"

"Okay, I'm just going to come on out and ask you something. Nancy, how do you feel about me. I mean, really feel?"

"What do you mean? I like you Jake. You and I have been through a lot together. I feel like we know each other pretty well. We are good friends, aren't we?"

"Yes, we are good friends, but I guess what I'm really trying to say is this. I want to be more than friends with you. I have been thinking a lot about this, about us. I think it's time that we took our relationship to a different level. Maybe we could go to dinner sometime? Am I making any sense?"

"Of course you are Jake. But let me try to understand a little better. Are you saying that you think you and I should start dating? I just want to be clear before I blurt out something stupid here. You want to have a relationship with me?"

"Yes. I think we are close as friends, but I want more than that. I just need to know how you feel. What do you say?"

Nancy squealed like a little girl, and jumped up. Grabbing Jake by the hand, she pulled him into a kiss. After coming up for a breath, she looked him in the eyes. "Does that answer your question Jake? If you need me to spell it out, it means y.e.s. I have loved you for a long time Jake. I was just getting tired of waiting for you to realize it. If you don't mind my asking, what changed your mind?"

Jake was still reeling from the kiss they shared. He shook the cobwebs out of his brain before answering. "To tell you the truth, Jen kind of helped with that. A few days ago, we had a long talk about Sara. How much we both miss her. How things could have been different if I hadn't been so caught up with my job, and drinking too much. That case cost me a lot Nancy. My wife, the first fifteen years of my child's life. I just think it's time I get back into life. I have been too dense to really realize how I feel about you. It took my daughter looking me in the eye and saying that Sara was gone, and not coming back, for me to admit that I have feelings for you. I love you, Nancy. I still need to take it slow, but I promise that you will be the most important thing in my life, next to my daughter. I won't make the same mistakes I did before."

"It's okay Jake, we all make mistakes. Don't beat yourself up over it. I was just as guilty for not coming forward with my feelings. I just wanted you to be sure, that's all. Are you Jake? Are you sure that you are ready for this? Are you sure that Jen is ready?" Answering her with another kiss, Jake took her hand and led her into the house and up the staircase.

When the household woke up the next day, everyone was busy getting ready for their day. When Jake and Nancy walked into the kitchen holding hands, Sam just looked at them and smiled. Ann was a little more taken aback, and Jen hugged them both. "It's about time you two wised up and admitted your feelings for each other. I, for one, am very happy for you both."

Nancy looked relieved. "Thanks Jen, you don't know how much that means to us. I must admit, I was a little nervous to tell you guys. I'm so happy. I really do love your dad. Very much."

Sam slapped his brother on the back. "Way to go Jake. It's about time. Maybe you won't be so grouchy all the time now."

Jake elbowed him. "I'm not the grouchy one around here. Nancy and I just decided that we were both ready to start a new life together. No wedding plans are in the near future. We are going to take it slow."

"Take it slow! I would have to say that you have already done that. I mean, how long have you known each other, like eighteen years? Give or take? You have already taken it slow."

Jen decided it was her turn to put in her two bits. "Sam is right, Dad. Mom has been gone for three years now, you can move on. I am eighteen, almost nineteen, I can handle it, I promise. You and Mom were apart for a long time Dad. You deserve to be happy."

Jake hugged his daughter. "I know that, but we have decided to start slow. Go out on a few dates, you know. Now, enough about that. We have a big day ahead, you and I. Let's get started."

Jen got more serious now. "Yes, we do. Today we are going to be asking some tough questions. It's going to be a rough day. On more than one person. Let's go get started." They got in the pickup and took off. "Okay, first on the list is John Kellog. He is the son of Bob Kellog, killed himself in 1985. Eight years after the hit and run. He knew Grif Grant, worked in the same precinct."

They pulled up to the address that John Kellog had given them. He was expecting them. The door opened before they got up the steps. Jake shook his hand, introducing Jen. John seemed cordial enough, but also wary of his two visitors. "Come in, sit down. Would you like some coffee?"

"No, thank you Mr. Kellog. Look, I know this is hard. Dredging up the past always is. But this is important to a case we are working. Would you mind telling us a little about your dad?"

John sighed. "Right to the point huh? Okay then. Well, Dad was a man's man. Tough, no nonsense kind of a guy. He was a good cop. Loved his job, more than he loved me I'm afraid. It was okay, I admired him a lot. Wanted to be just like him when I grew up. I guess every son does. Anyway, when he retired, things went downhill. Mom died, and that was hard on us all. It didn't take long for him to spiral downhill even faster. I guess he couldn't handle the pressure anymore, and he shot himself in the garage. No note, nothing telling me or my brother goodbye. My brother couldn't handle his death, and he killed himself two years after that. Anything else you want to know?"

"I'm so sorry, John. I do have one more question. Was it a proven fact that he killed himself? Was his death investigated?"

John was shocked at the question. "I never really thought about it as anything other than a suicide. He was alone in the garage. It was investigated, and they said he had gun residue, or whatever you call it, on his hands. He had handled the gun. It was a suicide, no question."

"Okay, well, thank you for your time John. Again, we are so sorry for the loss of your loved ones. We will leave you alone now. Thanks again."

Getting in the pickup, Jen picked up the papers they had printed out. She crossed off the name of Bob Kellog. "Sounds like it was pretty cut and dried suicide to me. I think we can cross him off the list of potential homicides."

"I agree. Who is next on the list?"

"Leslie Brown. Her dad was a patrol cop. Died while he was still employed with the Fifth precinct. This one sounds more promising to me. He died by his own hand, it says, in

1980. I want to know if he was friends with Grif Grant. His daughter should be able to tell us that."

They drove to the address of Leslie Brown. She was a little more forthcoming than Kellog was. She graciously invited them into her home. "Please, come in. It's been a long time since I had any company. Please forgive the mess."

Jen looked around the tidy house. "I don't see a mess, Mrs. Brown. You have a lovely home."

"Why, thank you missy. My husband and I have lived here for twenty years. We love it here. Now, what do you want to know about my dad's death? He died while he was still employed on the police force, nearly forty years ago. They say he messed up on a case, and couldn't handle the pain. He was so devoted to his job, and quite a perfectionist. My mom suffered from that devotion to the police force. So did I. He took his own life. What more is there to it?"

"Did your mom say anything about his colleagues? A man named Grif Grant by chance?"

Leslie rubbed her chin, contemplating the question. "I was pretty young then, but that is an unusual name. I don't remember hearing it before. I'm afraid I haven't been much help, have I?"

Jake stood. "You did fine, Leslie. We're sorry we had to bring up that painful time of your life."

Jen let out a breath when they got back on the road to the next name on the list. "Well, this has been a bust so far. What do you think? We only have three more names of people that have family still around from that time. What are the odds of us lucking out and finding one that is a more suspicious death? Or one that knew Grif? I don't think the odds are with us."

Jake agreed with Jen on that one. "Yeah, I don't think we are going to find out much with this lead. But we have to try."

They were disappointed when they got done talking to the relatives Jen had found in their research. No one was questioning their relative's deaths. They were all legitimate suicides as far as the families knew. This lead was a bust. It had been a long, and tiring day. Stressful, is more like it. Jake and Jen made their way back to the office. Jake was tired, and frustrated, along with his daughter. Jake broke the silence in the pickup. "Well, where do we go from here? Back to the drawing board, I guess."

"I guess so. We need to go back to Grant's death. Interview his son again. I think he knows more than what he is saying."

"I agree. I'll call Julie and set up the meeting. Nancy and I are going to dinner tonight. She is meeting me here, so can you take my truck home?"

Jen grinned. "Of course I can. I can drive you know. Pretty good at it actually. This reminds me of when you got me my first car in Los Angeles. Remember how nervous you were? More nervous than me, really."

"I do remember that. It wasn't that long ago. I'm not that senile, and I wasn't nervous…well….maybe a little." They laughed together.

Jake's phone rang. He showed Jen the name that came up on the screen…Dan. "Yes, Dan, this is Jake Long."

"Long, I wanted to get in touch with you. I found something out about Jerod Sims. He was a low level drug user. He didn't sell any, but he did use. His connection was a kid named..wait for it…Jim Grant. Son of none other than Grif Grant. Some coincidence isn't it? Jerod Sims' best friend was his dealer. Guess what Jim Grant drove? A red truck. Didn't you say that a truck was seen in the vicinity of the hit and run?"

Jake leaned back in his seat. "Wow! Yes, a witness saw a truck there. We didn't find anything when we looked into the truck that left that piece of turning signal at the scene. I don't know how we can prove it was Jim Grant, but I personally think we just found our driver who killed Jerod. Hang on Dan, I am getting a call from the coroner."

Jake pushed a button on his phone, putting Dan on hold. "Yes Doctor, have you found something from the DNA?"

"I have, as a matter of fact. Your John Doe is definitely Jerod Sims. The dental records prove it. I just talked to his sister. She is coming in to pick up the remains and bury them in their family plot. Good job you two. It's always good putting a name to a body after so many years."

"Thank you, Doctor." Jake hung up from him and got his brother back on the phone. "That was the coroner, he identified the John Doe as Jerod Sims. This case just went from cold to steaming hot. Our next step is to talk to Jim Grant, and find out what he was doing on the day that Jerod died. I would bet money that he doesn't have an alibi."

"Good going you two. I'll keep up the work on my side. You let me know what you find out from Grant."

Jake gave his daughter a high-five, and quickly dialed Julie Grant, putting the phone on speaker so that Jen could hear what was said. "Julie, would it be possible for you to come back in with your brother tomorrow? We have a few more questions for him."

"I guess so. I haven't seen Jim since the day we met at your office. I'm afraid we're not close. I'll try to get ahold of him. See you tomorrow then."

"Well, what do you think?" Jake looked over at Jen. "Will he show up?"

"I think so, he seemed pretty confident that we didn't know anything. If he killed Jerod, it was probably an accident. I wonder why he took off? Seems odd, but he probably had drugs on him at the time." Jen stretched. "Well, hopefully we'll find out tomorrow when they come in. Right now, I want to go home, and you have a hot date to get ready for. Now go!" She pushed him out of the pickup.

Jake caught himself before he fell on his butt. He scowled at Jenny. "Hey, take it easy on this old man. I'm not as spry as I used to be you know."

"Oh, I think you'll be okay. Now go! Get ready for your hot date." Jenny looked up as a car pulled alongside them. "Here she is now, and you're not ready."

"I'm as ready as I'll ever be darlin'. But on a more serious note, you be careful going home. Remember, we have been stirring the pot on these cases we're investigating, and we've been followed before. Just keep your eyes open okay?"

"I'll be fine. I learned how to drive in Los Angeles remember? I learned from the best, which is you. Don't worry about me, I'll be fine. You go have a good time." Jen waved at Nancy, put the pickup in gear, and took off.

Jake watched his daughter drive off, feeling a little nostalgic. He turned to Nancy. "I remember when she came into my life. I know it hasn't been that long, but I love her more than life itself. I can't help but worry about her, you know." He shook his head. "I only wish I could have been there for her when she was younger. Sara did a wonderful job with her, but it isn't fair that I wasn't there for her, for them."

Nancy leaned over and kissed him on the cheek. "I know Jake, but there is nothing you can do about it now. You are there for her now, and you were there for her in her teenage years. That counts for a lot, and she understands why you weren't there before that. I know that Jen resented you at first, but she got over that pretty fast. I really think that Ann helped with that. Jenny is a great girl, Jake. You and Sara did good."

"I know. She is pretty great isn't she? Anyway, where do you want to go eat? You name the place, I'm starving."

Nancy laughed. "It doesn't matter to me, but a good steak would taste great right now. Let's go to the steakhouse and chow down."

Their dinner was fantastic. Jake found himself relaxing and having a good time with Nancy. She understood him better than anyone else did. They were great friends, and now their relationship was growing into something else entirely. Jake was okay with that. They laughed and talked for a long time, finally realizing that all of the other customers had left the restaurant. Jake reached over and grabbed Nancy's hand. "Looks like we are the only ones left. I guess that's our cue. We had better take off too, before they kick us out of here."

Nancy looked around the restaurant, blushing a little. "Wow, I was so into our conversation, that I didn't even notice that everyone left." She stood up when Jake pulled her chair back for her. "Jake, I had a wonderful time. I'm really glad you came to your senses where we are concerned."

"So am I Nancy, so am I." Jake held back a yawn. "Oh, I'm sorry. Guess it's been a long day."

"No need to apologize. It's late, I'm ready to go home. I guess I'll be driving?"

"If you want to. I am a little tired, but I could do it."

"No, I'll do it. I don't mind. It's not a bad drive."

Jake did fall asleep on the way home. The drive went smoothly, and Nancy shook him awake when they pulled into the drive. He apologized again. "Oh boy, I'm so sorry. I really didn't mean to fall asleep."

"Don't worry about it. You go up to bed, and promise me you'll get some sleep. I have some paperwork to do on a patient, then I am going to bed too." She put her arms around Jake and kissed him deeply. "Listen, I had a great time tonight. I really did. Let's do it again soon okay?"

Jake kissed her back. "I did too. I can't wait for the next time." He yawned again. "Good night."

Jake was asleep before his head hit the pillow. Someone else wasn't sleeping quite as well though. Jenny was tossing and turning in her bed. She kept hearing different voices in her head. They were all talking at once. It was a jumble of voices, none of it making sense. Jen sat up in bed. "Okay, listen! Whoever you all are, you need to talk to me one at a time. I can't understand a word you're saying. If you need me to help you, please, just talk to me one at a time." She rubbed her eyes and got out of bed. Heading for the bathroom, Jenny almost tripped over something in the middle of the floor. It was her journal. "Good grief! How did this get over here?" She picked up the book, noticing that it was opened to her last entry. Jen read it out loud.

"Tonight, my mom came to me. I know it was her. She spoke of someone else coming to me to help with this case. Someone who I may not be willing to talk to. I don't know what she means by that. I would accept help from anyone right now. Mom told me that this person was from her past. Someone who changed her life forever. I still don't know who she is talking about. No one has appeared to me lately. I guess they are taking a break, or giving me a break. Whichever it is, I don't mind. It gets confusing when they don't appear clearly to me. Sometimes, it is too much."

Jen put the journal back in her drawer where it belonged, shivering a little. She lay in bed with her eyes wide open, wondering who it was that was trying to communicate with her this time. She was unaware of the dim figure in the corner of her room. Watching, waiting for the right moment. The man just hovered in the corner, staring at Jen. *Soon, I will come to you, Jenny. I only hope that you can keep an open mind when I do. Your father, on the other hand, definitely will not be so open minded. When I do appear, things will start clearing up, I hope.*

Jenny shivered again. Pulling the covers tighter around her, she fell into a restless sleep. Memories of her mom surrounding her in the darkness.

••• 15 •••

JAKE WOKE THE next morning, excited to get to work on finding Jim Grant, and getting him to come clean. Jake was positive that Jim was the driver of the truck that hit and killed Jerod Sims. He was sure of it. If they could get him to fess up to it, the district attorney might just let him off with a shorter sentence. Jim had to realize that he can't run from his past forever. Sooner or later, everything was going to catch up to you, no matter how hard, or how far, you try to run.

Jake followed the sounds to the kitchen. It was like this every morning. Everyone talking at once, each one trying to out do the other with their stories. He shook his head as he entered the kitchen. "You guys never change. I can't even hear myself think. But I wouldn't change it for the world."

Jenny handed him a cup of coffee. "Good morning Dad. Did you sleep well? How was your date last night?"

Jake looked over at Nancy, who, unbelievably, was blushing. "It was great, but I'm sure you all have heard all about it already. Am I right?"

"Maybe, but we wanted to hear it from you. I'm glad you had a good time. Now, are you ready to get to work?"

"More than ready. I want to put an end to this case so we can get back on Phil Carson's case. I have a feeling that we are going to close that one for good too. But, first things first. We need to get in touch with Julie and see if she tracked her brother down. Let's get to the office, and we'll call her from there."

Grabbing a piece of toast, Jen followed her dad out the door. She was giddy with excitement. "Dad, is this always how it feels when you crack a case? I can see why you love it. The excitement of tracking down the perp, getting him or her to justice, it's very cool. I love it already, and it's just my first case. I'm going to really love my job. I'm so happy you're here with me. It just wouldn't be the same without you here. I love you, Dad."

"I love you too, Jen. I'm really happy that I can help. Tom helped too. He kind of brought the case to a head with his information on Jim Grant. I don't know how he found it out so fast, but I'm glad he did. I still don't know for sure what he is doing undercover in the DEA. We probably will never know. I hope he's careful, and I hope that we didn't screw anything up by going there. I had no idea that he was working there."

"He'll be fine, and we didn't give anything away. He has been doing undercover work for a long time. Tom knows what he's doing Dad. I wouldn't worry about him."

"You're right Jen. Tom knows what he's doing. I'm not that worried about him I guess. I hope that Jim Grant does the right thing."

Jake and Jen walked up the stairs to their office. To their surprise, Julie Grant was standing at the door. Even more surprising, Jim was standing next to her. He hung his head. "Listen, you two. I just want to apologize for my actions the other day. As you well know, I have been carrying this guilt around for many years. My sister has convinced me that it's time to come clean." Jim put his arm around Julie's shoulder. "My sister knew absolutely nothing abut this, by the way.

She is totally innocent in this. I'm glad that she got this ball rolling. I am more than ready to go to the police and get this load off my shoulders. I only hope that they understand that it really was just an accident. If Jerod just wouldn't have been on the corner that day…..Anyway, I guess I'll save my story for the DA."

Jake had to shake Jim's hand. "Listen, I'm glad that you have decided to come clean. You can tell the District Attorney the whole story about the accident. I think when he hears it all, you'll probably get a lighter sentence. There may be some jail time, are you prepared for that?"

"Yes, I know. I deserve it. Back then, being a young college student, there just wasn't any money, you know. My dad was a cop, and you know what that's like. I was young and stupid, just trying to get by. I got caught up with the wrong people, and so did Jerod."

Jake nodded. "I understand, well, should we head on over to the DA's office right now? He is expecting us. I took the liberty of calling him yesterday when we found out about all of this. I guess I hoped that you would do the right thing, Jim."

"I'm ready to get this off my chest. Let's go right now. Is it okay if my sister comes with us? I have learned to rely on her a lot lately. That is, if she wants to come with. Julie?"

Julie was a little flabbergasted by what was being said, but she loved her brother. "Of course I'll be there. I love you, Jim. You're my brother, and I'll stand by you through thick and thin. That's what family is for. I just don't understand all of this, that's all. How did no one know about this? How did you get by with this all of these years? You know, never mind, I guess I'll find out all of the details when you make your statement to the District Attorney." She turned and headed out the door.

Jim shrugged, and turned to follow her. "Well, I guess that is my cue to leave. Let's get this over with."

The DA was expecting them, like Jake said. Jim was very nervous. His sister, Julie was quiet, and looked as if she was sending her brother to the gallows.

Jenny pulled her aside. "Listen, Julie, whatever happens here today, your brother is going to need you to be strong. From all of my years as the daughter of a cop, there's one thing I know, most of them are fair and just." She glanced at the office, where the men were gathering, getting ready to be seated. "Of course, I don't know as much about lawyers." They laughed a little, and Julie took a deep breath, preparing for the worst.

"I know this needs to end, but I'm scared for Jim. He is a genuinely good person Jenny. He's done nothing but help people. I guess I understand a little better why he wanted to help the people involved with drugs now. He really is a good person. I hope the DA takes that into consideration."

"I'm sure he will, Julie. It's not just up to him though. The judge will have the final say, but we can always hope for the best, and the District Attorney will suggest a sentence. Let's go get this part over with. Then we can take it from there, on step at a time." They turned to enter the office. "Julie, if you ever need anything from us, my dad and I will be happy to help. Remember that, okay?"

"I may take you up on that."

The DA had his notebook and tape recorder out when they got into the office. "I understand that you want to make a statement Mr. Grant. Jake here, has filled me in on most of the case. You understand that what you say here today is considered an official statement. You have to talk to the police also, but what I say will go a long way with the judge. I will decide what the charge will be after you tell me your side of the story. Now, let's get started." He pushed the buttons to record Jim's statement.

"Well, I'm going to start at the beginning, this may take awhile. I hope you kept a large portion of your morning open. Anyway, here goes nothing. Jerod Sims and I were good friends, best friends, really. We did everything together, including drugs. It all started with uppers, just trying to get through finals, you know. We were kids, everyone was doing it. Then it kind of spiraled from there. We started needing downers to finally get to sleep at night. Jerod was getting deeper and deeper into all sorts of drugs. Speed, cocaine, even heroin. We were spending a lot of money on the drugs. Money that we didn't really have. Like I said, we were starving college kids. He was the one that came up with the idea of selling the drugs. I was the son of a cop, you have to remember. I knew my dad would eventually find out about the drugs. I could never keep anything hidden from him. I knew he would find out what I was doing. At first, I said no to Jerod. No to the drug thing, and no to selling drugs. I know that everyone thought that I was the one selling to Jerod, but that wasn't true. He was the main dealer, I just kind of went along with it. The money was great, and Jerod had all of the drugs he needed. It was getting pretty bad. Then one day, my dad called me out on it. He had figured it out. Dad was a great cop, but he was my dad. He told me that if I turned in the whole drug ring at the college, he could talk to the DA and get me a reduced sentence. I couldn't, and wouldn't, be a snitch. I told my dad as much. We got into a huge fight about it. I left the house angry and confused. I didn't know what he would do with the information that I gave him. I got into my truck, and roared off in a huff. I was so angry with my dad, and Jerod. The whole world actually. Well, as I was speeding down the street a couple blocks from my house, Jerod was sitting in his car at the corner where he always sold his drugs. I was so blind with rage, I just wasn't paying attention to the stop sign. Or the car sitting there. I missed the sign, and plowed right into the car. I didn't know it was Jerod at first, I swear. It was an accident, that's all."

The DA listened intently. He let Jim finish his story before he started asking his questions. "Okay, so you're admitting to killing Jerod Sims. I understand that it was an accident Jim, but what I don't understand is this. Why didn't you come forward right away? Forty years is a long time. Would you have come clean if Jake and Jenny here wouldn't have figured this out? It was your own sister that got this ball rolling. You still didn't come forward. Why is that? How is it that this was covered up all of these years? Explain that to us Jim."

Jim hung is head, and shifted in his chair. "Listen, I told you the truth about the accident, isn't that good enough? Why do you need to know all of that other stuff. I don't see the relevance."

"Oh, but it is relevant to this case. I need to know if anyone else helped you cover this up. Some punk college kid couldn't have done this on his own. You need to tell us everything in order for this case to come to a complete close. I can't help you if I don't know the whole story."

Julie squeezed his hand. "Jim, you need to tell the whole truth here. It can't be all that bad. This happened forty years ago. Most of the people involved are probably either in jail or dead by now. Tell them everything, please. For me, for Dad."

Jim looked at his sister. "Well, if I tell you everything, you may not feel the same way, Julie. I honestly don't even know how to say this, but…okay, here goes nothing. The whole story, I won't leave anything out."

The group settled in for Jim's story. "Okay, this is what happened. After the accident, I was so scared. I knew that it was Jerod that I had hit. I ran over to him and saw right away that he was dead. I was a terrified kid, you have to understand that. Anyway, I got in my truck and headed back home. I told my dad what had happened. He told me to stay put, that he would take care of everything. All I know is, when he got back home hours later, he said that everything was taken care of. That I didn't need to worry about anything. All I had to do was keep my mouth shut." Jim glanced over at his sister when he continued his story. "Julie, I just did what Dad told me to do. I didn't know exactly what he had done until I saw on the news that there was nothing left in the car to identify the body. No witnesses, nothing. I didn't really know what Dad had done. I just kept my mouth shut like he told me to. Minded my P's and Q's, you know. Everything was pretty much forgotten until Dad killed himself. I guess he couldn't stand the guilt anymore. He went against every bit of his character to keep me safe. He really was a good cop. That was the only time he covered up anything, as far as I know. He did it for me, Julie. I was young, I didn't understand the consequences of my actions at the time. For years, nothing more was said. Everything just went on as usual. Dad struggled in his job, that's for sure. I could tell that his dishonesty with this accident was wearing on him. Every day, he would look at me with disappointment in his eyes. I don't think he ever really got over it." Jim bent over, holding his head in his hands. "That's why he killed himself, Julie. It was all my fault." The last two words were choked out. They could barely understand him.

Julie was stunned by the information she had just heard. She just sat there, trying to hold in the tears. When Jim broke down completely, she finally came out of it. Julie put her arms around her brother. "Jim, I don't know what to say to you right now. That accident changed a lot of lives. I just don't understand why Dad felt like he had to cover it up. Him of all people, Mister straight and narrow. Growing up, he was our hero, you know. He raised us to be honest, upstanding people. Why did he do it Jim? Why?"

"I don't know exactly what he was thinking. I suppose because drugs were involved. He didn't want his only son's name dragged through the mud like that. He also didn't want his name being said in the same sentence as a drug user. Even though we were only small time operators. We were just selling enough to keep ourselves in supply. Just stupid kids, that's all. If I had known what chain of events would unfold because of my stupidity, I would've never let him cover it up, you know? But, I didn't know, and I just let it go. When Dad killed himself, I just figured it would all end with that. I could go on like nothing had ever happened. That is, until you got this going again. I don't blame you. I guess it was just a matter of time before it finally came out. I'm kind of glad it did." Jim looked up at the District Attorney. "That's all of it. The whole story. What happens now?"

The District Attorney stood and waved to the policeman standing outside the door. "We have to arrest you for killing Jerod Sims. You will be charged with manslaughter, and for hindering an investigation. Officer, take him away."

Jim stood, and hugged his sister one more time. "I'll be okay Julie. I'm relieved that this is out in the open now. I hope our dad can Rest In Peace." He went with the officer, and Julie just stared after him.

"I'm happy that it's all over too. I almost wish that they would have told me about all of this. I honestly don't know if I would have been silent all of these years though. In a way, I'm sorry that I got all of this going. But, I'm also glad that I did. Does that make any sense?"

Jen hugged her. "Yes, it does make sense, Julie. You didn't know what coming to us would uncover, but you have to know that you also helped another family. Jerod Sims' sister got to bring her brother home. After all of these years, the family of Jerod Sims, can have a place to go and visit their brother. I understand that Ms. Sims is his only living relative, but at least she now knows what happened to her brother. You did that Julie, and so did Jim. You both can start to heal now, and so can Jerod's sister."

Julie nodded. "You know what? You're right. We should feel good about this. I only hope that the judge will give Jim a break. He really has suffered a lot from all of this. Well, I had better go and find Jim a good lawyer. Thank you for all of your hard work."

Julie walked out of the office, and Jake and Jen followed. Jake put the key in the ignition of his pickup, but hesitated in starting it. "Well, there's one case closed. How do you feel about it all?"

"I feel good Dad. Even if it was a sad story, I think everyone deserved the truth. I meant what I said to Julie Grant, the truth needed to come out. I just can't believe that Griffin

Grant would risk his job, and his life, for that matter. If he wouldn't have covered for his son, things certainly would have been different. It never ceases to amaze me the things that people do. What now? What do we do now?"

Jake grinned. "We go celebrate. Then, we get going again on Phil Carson's death. Something is fishy there, I just can't put my finger on what it is. Oh well, it'll be our job to figure out what that is."

Jen agreed with her dad on that one. "Yes, I think we should look into his death a little more. Even though Cara is gone now, Abby deserves to know the truth. Even if it turns out that he did commit suicide. That all can wait until tomorrow though. I have some tests that I have to take tonight, and I really need to study. This Grant case kind of got me behind. Let's grab some food and head home."

● ● ●

He was pacing back and forth in his office. Gripping his cell phone tightly in his hand. Cursing under his breath, the man pushed redial, waiting for an answer on the other end of the line. The phone rang and rang, with no answer. He threw his phone across the room. "Dammit! If you don't answer your phone, I'm going to track you down myself. Believe me, you don't want that to happen!"

He rubbed his hands down his face, red with fury. Walking to his window, trying to calm himself a little, he looked out. "How could this have happened? I told that idiot to lay low for awhile, and everything would blow over. Then he goes and turns himself in? This all started with that idiot dad of his knocking himself off. I knew that old man was a weak link in this operation. I should have handled him and his son long ago. My revenge was sweet the way it worked out, but they had pretty much lost their usefulness long ago. I told his handlers that he was losing it. Now they won't even take my call! I'll deal with them when I find them. Right now, we have other pressing matters to take care of. I will not lose every-thing I have worked so hard for. Those damn PI's better take my warnings to heart and step down, or I'll have to take care of them too."

Breathing deeply, he picked up his phone off the floor, and dialed the number again. This time, there was an answer.

"Yeah?" His voice was shaky with fear. "Listen, boss, I'm sorry. I really didn't know that Grant was going to do that. I had just talked to him. We had a plan to get him out of the country. Everything was going great until his sister called him. He just kind of lost it after that. I'll take care of him. He won't do any talking, I promise. What do you want me to do?"

He took a deep breath before talking. "First of all. When I call, you answer, got it? Second, you had better take care of this situation. You give him our ultimatum, and make sure he follows it. If not, I will take care of you, understand?" He hung up before the man replied.

● ● ●

Jim Grant was pacing back and forth in his cell. *What the hell was I thinking? I can't do this. I'm as good as dead. Julie too, prob-ably. What the hell am I going to do now? I can't believe I didn't get rid of that damn box!* Jim had called his lawyer. He needed to rescind his confession right away. Maybe by doing so, he would gain the forgiveness of the boss. After all, there really was no real evidence of him being the one who ran into Jerod. He had something on the boss anyway. Jim was the only one who knew that Jerod was not alone in the car at the time of the accident. Jim had told the kid to take off. It was his only leverage, and he was going to use it. If the boss wanted him to keep quiet, he would pay up. Jim could break his long held drug operation up with just a few well placed words.

Jim admitted to himself that his idea could back fire. The boss wasn't anyone to be trifled with. A lot of men have tried over the years, and failed. But Jim figured this was his only chance. He was going to take it. For his sister's sake as well as his own. He had to try.

Jim heard the clanging of the cell doors. Someone was coming. Jim was shaking as he watched the guard leading someone towards his cell. He only hoped it was who he was expecting, and not someone he didn't want to see. He held his breath as they approached. Jim let out the breath he was holding, when he saw his lawyer with the guard. *Thank God! Okay, let's get this ball rolling.*

$$\bullet\ \bullet\ \bullet\ 16\ \bullet\ \bullet\ \bullet$$

HE LAUGHED HEARTILY when the lawyer that he had hired came back with Jim's demands. He couldn't believe the gall of the man. Here he was, prepared to help him, and Grant thought that he could blackmail him? Better men than him have tried. "Well, this changes things." He waved the lawyer off, and the man scurried out the door as fast as he could. The boss grabbed his cell phone, one of many, and made a call. "I have a job for you. You owe me, and I'm calling in the chips. Get over here, right now." That was all that needed to be said right now. The boss knew that his orders would be obeyed. He was feared, and for good reason.

When the man he had summoned got to the boss's door, his hands shook. Ted paused, as the boss's right hand man led him to his office. Ted was sure that this wasn't going to be good, but he needed to stay on the good side of the boss. If there was such a thing as a good side to him. Ted took a deep breath when the Goliath of a man knocked once, and opened the door for him when the boss spoke.

"Come in Teddy. Don't just stand there like an idiot." His smile was not welcoming.

Teddy entered the office. It was decorated quite nicely, in contrast to the rest of the building. "I came as soon as I could boss. What do you need from me?"

"Sit down Teddy. Take a load off. Relax, this is nothing that you haven't done for me before. That's why I called you. I know that I can count on you to be discreet. My name is not to brought up at all, understand?"

"Sure boss. I understand, now what is it you need me to do?"

"I need someone taken care of. The only problem is, the guy is in jail. I know that you have connections. Can you get someone in there to take care of him? His name is Jim Grant. I need him gone, and I need an example made of him. I need it to look like a suicide, like before. No one can know that it was murder. You've done this before, I expect it will be a piece of cake."

"Sure thing boss. I can do it. I know a lot of people willing to kill for drugs. That will be the payment right? Just like always?"

"Whatever it takes, just get it done, and get it done now. I want this done before Grant talks anymore. Luckily, he has only spoken to the lawyer I sent in. The idiot should have known that I was behind getting him a lawyer so fast. He screwed up there. Should have kept his trap shut. Now go, and do what you're told. I never forget when someone crosses me, do you hear?"

"No problem boss. I'll get right on it. I have just the right person in mind. But sir, with all due respect. Do you think it's wise to get rid of Grant? I mean, killing someone in jail is tricky, to say the least. We may be biting off more than we can chew. With Long on our trail, it may just make him more suspicious. I know for a fact that Jake Long is a tenacious detective. Once he grabs on to something, he doesn't let go."

The boss sat back in his chair, trying to control his temper. "You just do as you're told. Let me worry about Jake Long and that brat of his. Now leave, before I change my mind about letting you out of this office in one piece!"

After Ted scurried out of his office, the boss gazed out the window. He thought about all of the events that had taken place to bring him to this point. His life had been forever changed after that accident. No more carefree kid. His dad had doted on his oldest son, Jerod. Grooming him to take over the family business. But that all ended when Jim Grant ran that stop sign.

Their father didn't need a blemish on his record like his son selling drugs on some street corner. His dad had helped cover up the accident. Along with the cop that had been the unlucky one to draw the short straw and get called out to it. It was the beginning of a very long and prosperous career for him after his brother died. Dad would be proud of what he had managed to accomplish. He had taken his father's legacy and expanded it like his father couldn't do.

It wasn't easy keeping control of all of the people under him, but he did it. Fear was a great contributor in this. As long as his underlings feared him, he would keep control. That's why he needed to take care of Jim Grant. No one turned on him like that, no one. Especially someone who he had under his thumb all of these years.

He thought for a moment about what Ted had said about pushing his luck. Could he be right? Was he getting too cocky? He shook off the thought, an evil smile coming to his face when he thought about the lesson that will be learned after Jim was taken care of. It was all worth it in the end. After all, it has worked for all of these years, why stop now?

Jim Grant paced in his cell, waiting for his lawyer to come back. He needed to know if the boss accepted his terms. Jim knew how the boss would react to his confession. He wasn't going to like it one bit. Jim had to admit, he was scared. He wasn't safe anywhere, not even in jail. He knew that better than anyone, but he did trust his lawyer. That was the only person he did trust, besides his sister. Jim wasn't talking to anyone but him.

He heard the guard coming down the narrow hallway. Jim lay down on his cot, trying not to draw attention to himself. He looked up when the guard paused in front of his cell. Jim could hear the key turning in the lock. It was an eerie sound. The echo seemed deafening. Jim sat up. "What do you want? I already had lunch, I am just waiting for my lawyer to get here. I'm not talking to anyone. I don't need anything."

Jim was worried now. The guard kept turning the key, looking around as he entered the cell. There was no one else in this cell block. Jim was the only one. Jim knew that they had planned it that way. He feared that something was going to happen. He just didn't think it would be this soon. He hadn't even talked to anyone yet about the things that he did for the CS Group. Jim backed up against the wall. "Listen, I promise I won't say anything to anyone. Just leave me alone, okay? He can trust me! Have I ever let him down before?"

The guard just grinned, not saying a word. Jim knew that this was it. He had played out his last hand. The only person that he thought about as the huge guard took out the thick rope, was his sister. She was the only one who would miss him.

The guard made one phone call when he finished his job. The man answered after just one ring. "It's done." That was all that was said before they hung up.

The next morning, when the day shift took over at the jail, they found Jim Grant hanging in his cell. The sheets were taken off his bed, and used as a makeshift noose. Nothing was found in his cell. No suicide note, or anything else for that matter.

His body was taken down, and sent to the medical examiner. It was his job to call next of kin.

Julie was surprised to hear her phone ringing this early in the morning. She answered with a frown. "Yes, Julie Grant here. Can I help you?"

"Miss Grant. This is Doctor French from the medical examiner's office. I am calling to inform you of your brother's death. He hanged himself in his cell last night. I am sorry, Miss Grant. Jim was found this morning when the guards did their daily cell checks."

Julie sat down on her couch, her head in her hands. "No! That can't be true. Jim was just getting ready to turn his life around. He was going to tell the whole truth about that fateful day when he accidentally killed Jerod Sims. He wouldn't kill himself, not now. I don't believe it. Not one little bit! Are you sure doctor?"

"Yes, I'm sure. Everything points to suicide. He used the sheets off of his bed to make a noose. Your brother was found hanging in his cell. I'm sorry, Miss Grant, but it was a suicide. No question about it. I'm sorry for your loss."

Julie hung up the phone. She was in a state of shock. "This can't be happening again. Not Jim too!" She hung her head and cried, pulling up a blanket and wrapping herself tightly with it. Julie not only was crying for the loss of her brother, but she was feeling the loss of her father and mother too. She was alone now, no family left. She didn't know what to do.

When Julie cried herself to sleep that night, she thought about her family. She never believed that her dad had killed himself, but the Long's proved that he did. Actually, her brother had pretty much convinced her that he had. After covering up for Jim all of those years, Grif Grant couldn't handle the guilt anymore.

The Long's were good people, and Julie intended to get to the bottom of her brother's death too. She hoped that the Long's would help her again. Julie was going to call them right away in the morning. Julie was going to take the box of her father's notes over to them. She couldn't make heads nor tails of them, but with Jake Long being in law enforcement, maybe he could.

When Jake and Jenny got to work, they were just gathering up what little bit of evidence they had on Phil Carson.

They had the newspaper article on his shooting, and on the death of the inmate that had shot Phil. They also had the note that Phil had written to Cara, denouncing his suicide. They had the information that Tom had given them on the CS Group. Jake planned on getting to the bottom of this. He was going to put an end to this drug cartel once and for all. From what they had gathered, this cartel had been carrying on basically without any repercussions, for many years. Jake didn't know how they did it, but he was going to find out.

The phone rang in the office. Jen answered. Jake glanced over at her. He could only listen to her side of the conversation. She was frowning. "Julie, slow down. What are you saying? Yes? Okay, come over right now. We'll be waiting. Julie, I'm so sorry."

When Jen hung up she looked worried. Jake walked over to stand in front of her. "Jen, you're white as a sheet. What's going on?"

"Dad. Jim Grant killed himself. He was found hanging in his cell yesterday. They said that he used his bed sheets to hang himself. I can't believe it. Julie is beside herself. She, of course, doesn't believe he did it. Why would he? I really don't think that he was going to spend much time in jail for the accident do you?"

Jake was shocked. "Oh no! That's just awful. Poor Julie. She has been through so much. I really couldn't say what Jim would have had for jail time. It was up to the judge, but I can't imagine he would have spent too much time in jail. I can't believe he would kill himself. I'm sure the judge would have had to give him some jail time, but probably not that long. Did Julie say exactly what happened?"

"She is coming over here. She wants to talk to us about it. I'm not sure what she wants us to do, but I guess we'll find out soon enough. She did say that she had found a box in the garage. It was labeled with Jim's initials. She didn't know what that meant, and she hoped that we could figure it out. I think it may be some more information on the hit and run. Maybe even this CS Group. I guess we'll find out. In the meantime, let's go over what we do know about Phil Carson. I want to get to the bottom of his death." She looked thoughtful for a moment. "Dad, all of this has something to do with drugs. From the hit and run accident, to Grif's suicide, and now to Jim's death. Even Phil's shooting.

We need to tell Tom about all of this. The only problem is, we don't know that much. Only that this CS Group is involved somehow. I have a feeling that Jim's death is tied in with this group too. We are getting closer to the truth. We just need one bit of information that could catapult this investigation into overdrive. I am not giving up on this."

Jake was so proud of his daughter. She was still so young, but she had the police spirit in her. Just like he did, and his father before him. Her Grandfather too. It was in her blood. "I know, and quitting isn't an option. No matter what, we are going to put a stop to this drug ring. We just need to figure out who the main man is. We start at the bottom, and work our way up." Jake picked up his phone. "You know, I think I know just where to start. With the DEA. I just happen to know someone there."

Jen nodded, and waited for Jake to call his brother. "Dan, this is Jake Long, from the Long Agency. Good morning. I was wondering if you could come over to the office, we may have a new development in this CS Group investigation. I know that you are investigating on your end too. Maybe we should get together and compare notes."

"Sure thing Jake. I'll be over later this afternoon."

Julie Grant arrived shortly after they talked to Tom. She was carrying a small box when she entered the office. Jen stood and hugged the woman. "I'm so sorry Julie." Jen took the box out of Julie's arms. She pulled out a chair. "Here, have a seat."

Jake rounded the table and reached down to hug Julie also. "Julie, we are so sorry for your loss. What can we do for you?"

Julie wiped the tears from her eyes. "I just don't think that Jim would kill himself. I know I sound like a broken record here, but why would he do it? He already told the DA his story. All he was waiting for was his lawyer so he could put it all in writing. I talked to him three days ago. Jim was upbeat, and he told me that he felt so much better after unloading his burden. Jim couldn't wait to tell the whole story. Which I guess means that he hadn't told us everything? I'm so confused." She glanced at the box. "I found this in the garage a week ago. It slipped my mind because of all that has happened, but I thought of it when I talked to Jim the other day. I mentioned it to him, and he got very upset. He told me to get rid of it, but I just couldn't. When I looked into the box, there was some notes from my dad. I was hoping that you could make some sense of it. I'm afraid I don't know all of the police jargon. Jake, would you look at it? With your police background, I think you will know more than me."

Jake nodded. "Sure, I can look at it. You did the right thing Julie. Bringing this here."

Julie stood. "I know. I want to know what really happened, and I trust you two. You're about the only people I do trust right now. If you'll excuse me, I have to get over to the medical examiner's office now. They want me to take care of Jim's remains. I know that he wanted to be cremated, so that's what I'll do I guess. Please, call me when you find out anything at all."

Jake and Jen showed Julie to the door. "We certainly will. Julie, we want you to know that you're not alone. Let us know when Jim's service is. We want to be there."

"Thank you both so much. It's good to know that someone will be there with me. I know I haven't known you for very long, but I feel like I can count on you."

"Yes, you can. We'll be in touch Julie."

When Julie left, Jen could hardly wait to dig into the box that she brought over. "Dad, I just know that there is something in here that will point us in the right direction. Let's get started. When Tom gets here this afternoon, we are going to have something to show him, I just know it."

"Jenny, your enthusiasm is contagious. I agree with you though. Something may be in here that is important enough that both Grif and Jim kept it all of these years."

When they opened the box, they saw that it contained mostly old photos, but there were some notes too. Jake could see where Julie wouldn't be able to understand them. They were mostly scribbled notes about Grif's family life. You could tell that the man was getting more and more confused as time went on. Nothing made much sense really. Jake was frustrated. "Jen, I think these are nothing but the ramblings of an old man with some dementia. Nothing makes much sense. These photos are nothing but old family photographs that Grif had held onto."

Jen let out a frustrated breath. "I know, but we aren't done looking yet. Let's keep looking."

By the time they were at the bottom of the box, they were both frustrated and confused. Why on earth did Jim tell Julie to destroy this box of junk? There had to be something in it worth keeping, and worth getting rid of. What is it? There was a small book laying in the bottom of the box. It was the only thing left inside. Jake picked it up. He recognized the notebook as that of a police officer's pad. Every policeman carried with them a notebook that they kept track of ideas and names of people they were investigating and questioning. "This could be important." Jake held the notebook up so Jen could see it. "If I'm right, this belonged to Grif Grant. If it did, it could have some information in it about the accident. Something that didn't get told to anyone. This could be it Jen. Grif may be helping us from the grave. Even without talking to you about it. Wait a minute, do you think he could be who is coming to you now? It would make sense."

"Could be him I guess. I really don't know. I only hope whoever it is shows himself soon. This messing around is getting old. I want to know who it is so I can help them." Jen glanced at the book Jake was holding. "Let's go over these notes and see if Grif mentions any names, or some other information we need for this case."

Jake opened the book, starting at the beginning. "Grif kept very meticulous notes here. He has them all dated. I guess that goes to show how his mind was in the end. None of the other notes in the box make sense. I have a hunch. Let's get right to the day of the accident." Jake paged through the notebook to that day. "Here we go. Looks like Grif made a couple of routine traffic stops that morning. He keeps track of everything. Very interesting. Here we go. He does write that he was called to a hit and run on Pine Street. It comes as no surprise that he doesn't have anything in here on the identity of the victim, or the driver of the truck. We already know that he covered all of that up. Grif doesn't say much of anything other than the make and model of the victim's car."

Jake turned the page. "Wait a minute. This is dated a week after the accident. *I know that keeping this from my captain is wrong, but I have to protect my family. He is threatening to kill them if I don't cooperate. This goes against everything in me, but what can I do? The other boy that was in the car is the son of someone that I don't want to mess with. CS is the boy that was with JS in the car. There, I said it. No one can find this out. Especially the police. I will go to my grave with this secret. In the meantime, I will do whatever it takes to keep my family safe. That being said, I am going to try and figure out if there is anything I can do to get out of this predicament I have found myself in.*

Jake whistled, turning the page. "Wow! That's the last thing that Grif wrote in here. Jen, do you know what this means? Grif actually names the victim. And he says that there was someone else in the car with Jerod, who is JS, I'm sure. CS, what are the odds. This has to be the same CS in the name CS group. If it is, and I know that it is, Grif knew who it was. I'll bet that Jim knew too. This goes back a long ways, which we already knew. This is good, really good."

Jake's excitement was catchy. Jen could hardly wait to tell Tom about this. "Dad, what good is some initials going to do us. I know this is at least something, but really, how are we going to find out who CS is?"

"I'm not sure Jen, but we're going to try. I think we need to start at the beginning. Find out who was friends with Jerod and Jim at the time of the accident. Let's head back to the college. If we can find someone with the initials CS we have our man. We have to be back here this afternoon, so let's go now. Tom will be interested in this information too."

It was a disappointing trip to the college. There were several people listed with the initials CS, but none of them knew Jim or Jerod. This case was stalling again. Jake wasn't sure where to go from here.

When Tom arrived at the office, Jake and Jen showed him the notebook. Explaining to Tom what they had found at the college, he agreed that the boy probably didn't attend that college. They needed to dig further into Jerod and Jim's lives. Maybe they would come up with a name with the initials CS. It was all they had to go on for the time being. At least they were moving forward a little. Jake rubbed his eyes. He had been reading the notes over and over, hoping to find something he had missed earlier. "There's nothing else here. Nothing at all about a CS. Why didn't Grant just come out and say a name? It sounds like he was being blackmailed. He just didn't dare let anyone know a name. He should have told someone, or written it in his notes. That would be too easy I guess."

Tom leaned back in his chair and stretched. "I agree. This is more than we had yesterday though. I'm going to call it a night, and I think you should too." He patted Jake on the shoulder and gave Jen a quick hug. "You two watch your backs. It seems that people with any knowledge of this CS Group are mysteriously dying."

"We can take care of ourselves. You watch your back too. Can you tell us why you're undercover in the DEA? Do they have something to do with all of this?"

"You know I can't tell you that. I will say though, that you may have a point. This goes back a long ways, and through a lot of law enforcement agencies. That's all I'm saying. Good night you two."

When Tom left, Jake and Jen gathered up the evidence that was scattered all over the desk and put it in the safe. Making sure it was locked up tight, they headed home for the night. They were each in their own thoughts for the hour drive to the ranch. It had been a long day, and Jake just wanted to spend some time with the family, and maybe even do some barn chores. He needed the exercise, and it helped him burn off some energy before going to bed.

They pulled into the drive and Jake could see Sam in the corral. Abby was riding the new horse he had bought. She had grown into a great horsewoman. Sam had her training the horse, gentling him for the novice riders at the ranch. Jake headed that direction, while Jen went inside to help with supper.

Sam waved when Jake walked toward the corral. "Hey Jake. How did your day go? Any new information on the case?"

Jake shook his head. "Not really, just some more confusing evidence. I don't really want to talk about it right now. Can I saddle up a horse and go for a ride? I need to clear my head a little."

"Of course you can. You don't need to ask. This is your home too. Do you want some company?"

"No, I think I'd rather be alone. Sorry, I didn't mean it like that. You're welcome to come along if you want."

"No, that's okay. You go, have fun. Don't forget your cell phone though. I don't like the idea of you going out all alone. Remember, the sheriff thought something was going on out there."

"I'll be careful, and I do have my phone. Don't hold supper for me okay? I'll be fine."

Jake loved riding out on the ranch's vast expanse of land. It really did help him clear his head when he needed it. All that he could think about was the cases they were working on though. They still hadn't found out anything more on Phil Carson's death. They figured out that Grif Grant had killed himself. They still hadn't heard from Julie about Jim's funeral service. They were going to do a thorough autopsy before Jim was cremated. Jake was sure that Jim hadn't killed himself, though how someone got in and murdered him, he didn't know.

Before he knew it, the sun was setting. Jake turned his horse back towards the ranch. He let him run, loving the feel of the wind in his face. Jake knew supper would be waiting for him when he got back, and the horse knew that his would be too.

After giving his horse a thorough rub down after his run, Jake headed to the house. Sam was sitting in his usual spot, and Jen was with him. Jake sat next to his daughter. "Why are you two still out here? Were you worried about me?"

Jen laughed. "No, we weren't worried. Just wanted to say goodnight to my dad, that's all. Your supper is in the fridge. But since you started this conversation, are you okay?"

"I'm fine. Why wouldn't I be?"

"Well, you don't usually miss supper and go out on your own like that. What's up?"

"Nothing, really. I'm just a little frustrated with these deaths. How they occurred, the events leading up to them. Something just isn't adding up, that's all."

"Yeah, I know what you mean. It's frustrating how it seems that someone is holding us up at every turn. I have every confidence that we will figure it out though. Well, I'm tired, and tomorrow is going to be a busy day. I'm going to bed." She hugged her dad. "I love you Daddy. Good night."

"Good night Jen. Sleep tight."

Sam stood too. "I think I'll go too. Your supper is in the fridge. You know that Ann isn't going to let you go to bed hungry. Good night."

Jake nodded to his brother, and headed straight for the fridge. He suddenly was famished. Jen was right, they were going to figure this out, all of it. He wanted nothing more than to put this drug cartel out of business.

Jen washed her face and got ready for bed. She took her journal out of the bedside table and read what she had written. There weren't any entries past the one a week ago. She needed her mom's help in this. Nancy had told her that she really couldn't control when her mom and the others would come to her. She just needed to let them appear in their own time. She looked around her room. "Mom, or whoever you are. I really need your help here. I don't mind if you can't say who you are. If you know something, you need to tell me. As soon as possible." Silence greeted her. She shrugged, and shut off her light. Just like so many nights before this, no one came to her. Jen slept soundly, not waking up when the figure stared at her from the corner of her room.

*He couldn't tell Jen his true identity yet. He just didn't feel that she was ready. She and Jake were getting frustrated, he knew that. He has been watching them. Things would start falling into place soon. He did have one thing he could do to help them out though. He faded away, and reappeared in Abby's room. The little girl was sound asleep. He watched the little girl sleep. He needed to get Abby and Jenny to the old cabin they used to live in. The only way he knew how to do that, is to try and give Jen a hint somehow. Sara had tried to tell Jen earlier, but for some reason, Jen didn't listen. For some reason, he couldn't quite speak to her clearly yet. Should he wait until his power was stronger? Talk to her then? No, he needed to get them into that cabin, and let them know that there is something there. Something they needed to find. He went back into Jenny's room. Hovering above her, he tried to communicate the only way he could. Through Jenny's dreams. That was all he could do right now. He just kept saying the words, go to the cabin, and Phil. Hopefully, she would figure it out from there. He looked over to where Jenny's journal was sitting. He had to get her to look in there. He wasn't even sure that she had written down what Sara had told her. Did she even hear her tell her to go to the cabin? He didn't know, but all he could do is try.*

When Jenny woke up the next morning, she had a horrific headache. Rubbing her eyes, she dragged herself out of bed. Jen had a strange feeling come over her. "What is going on? I feel like I should be remembering something, but I just can't put my finger on it." Jen glanced over to her nightstand where her journal was sitting. She opened her journal, looking for some clue to what it was she should be remembering. There was nothing new written in there. She paged through it. When she got to the page where Sara, Phil, and Cara were appearing to her, she remembered something that her mom had said. It was something about the cabin that the Carson's lived in when they were at the ranch. "I just can't put my finger on it, but I really think it has something to do with Phil Carson. I need to take Abby to the cabin, and look around. Wait a minute, why did I just say that?" Rubbing her head, Jen finally realized what had happened. "Someone had to have come to me last night." These mind games were getting old. Jenny didn't understand why they couldn't just come out and say what they needed her to do. "I guess whoever it is, wanted me to go to that cabin. Now I remember. I sure wish that they would just come to me normally, like my mom does, instead of this mind thing."

Jen got out of bed and took some aspirin. "I need to be sharp today. We have too much going on to be distracted, but I am going to that cabin. Maybe there is something there we need. That's going to have to wait though."

# ••• 17 •••

THE PHONE WAS ringing in the office when Jen and Jake arrived the next morning. Jake rushed to answer it. "Long Agency. Jake Long here."

"Mr. Long, this is Julie Grant calling. The medical examiner's office just called me. They have some news on Jim's death. After examining his body closer, they found that he hadn't hung himself with the bedsheets. There was a pattern on his neck. Braided indentations were found on his neck. They missed it before because of all of the bruising. Jake, he was murdered. They are changing his manner of death. I knew that Jim wouldn't have done that to me. He wouldn't have killed himself. What do we do now?"

"That's very interesting. That definitely gives us something to go on. Let me get in touch with the ME. With your permission, I'd like to see the rope pattern on Jim's neck myself. If someone else was in that cell with Jim, the guard on duty should know who it was. People don't just go in and out as they choose. I'll be in touch. Thanks Julie."

Jake pumped his fist in the air after he hung up. "That was Julie Grant. She got a call from the ME. They are changing the manner of Jim's death from suicide to undetermined. That means they feel that they couldn't actually determine the manner of death, which is what exactly Jim was killed with. They know cause of death, but couldn't determine manner. I guess the ME found abrasions on Jim's neck that matched up to a rope being used in his strangulation. So, someone else was with him when he died. They covered up the rope abrasions by tying the sheet around his neck to fake a suicide. Julie was going to call the medical examiner and give us permission to see the body. I want to see it for myself. You don't have to come if you don't want to. It's not a pretty sight."

"No, I am going to be with you. I need to learn from the body also. I can handle it."

When they arrived at the coroner's office, Jake and Jen were shown into a cold, sterile room. Jen couldn't help but shiver. Jake put his arm around her. "It'll be okay. You can leave anytime you want to."

"I know. I'm okay Dad."

The coroner pulled back the white sheet from the body. Jake noted the bruising around Jim's neck. He put on the plastic gloves that the coroner gave him. Carefully touching his neck, Jake could see the abrasions. They weren't very clear, but he could definitely see the braided pattern of a rope. He nodded to the doctor, and he covered the body back up. Jake pulled off the gloves, and took Jen by the arm, leading her out of the room. The doctor followed.

"Doc, are there any defensive wounds on Jim's body? Anything to show that he fought his killer?"

"There were some abrasions on the back of his hands that could be from a struggle. It also could be from him trying to pull the noose off his neck at the last minute. Sometimes the person automatically tries to pull the noose off when he starts choking. It's a natural response. It's hard to tell from what we could see. That was the only other thing we found on the body. I'm sorry, we just can't say that it was murder."

After thanking the doctor, Jake and Jen left the morgue. Jen didn't know what to think. "So, was Jim murdered or what? Where did he get the rope? Where is the rope now? Someone was definitely in the cell with him when he died. If they didn't murder him themselves, they assisted him in the suicide. Then they covered up by replacing the rope with a bed sheet. Good grief, my head is spinning!"

"I know, mine is too, and I'm used to these puzzles. We need to get over to the jail where Jim died, and ask some questions."

They entered the police station where the prisoners were held while awaiting trial. Jake found the Sergeant in charge of the guards. "Hello, I'm Jake Long and this is my daughter Jenny. We are from the Long Agency. We're investigating the death of Jim Grant. Were you on duty at the time of his death?"

"No, I wasn't on duty. Let me check the log book. Let's see….it was officer Blake on duty that night."

"Great! Could we talk to him please?"

"Hmmm. Let me check where he is right now. Oh! I see he hasn't been back here since the night Jim Grant died. Says here that he called in sick the next day. No one has seen him since. I'm sorry, I can't help you any more than that."

Jake was flabbergasted. Another dead end. What was going to happen next in this case? "Do you have cameras back in the holding cells? Could we see them?"

"There aren't any cameras back there because of privacy issues. We have already looked at the cameras at the door. All they show are Blake going into the area, and coming out the door. That's nothing unusual. He wasn't carrying anything, nothing that we could see anyway."

"Okay, well, thanks for your help sergeant."

They left the station, not knowing much more than they did before. Jake was still excited over what they had learned. "If we can track down that guard, I think we'll have our killer of Jim Grant. Or at least he may know something about it. We need to find him. Let's get his address and start there."

After tracking down Blake's address, they headed over to his apartment. Not surprisingly, he wasn't there. Jake sweet talked the apartment manager into letting them in Blake's apartment. There wasn't much left in there. You could see that Blake had left in a hurry. He didn't leave much behind. This was a dead end. They left the apartment empty handed. "Okay, this hasn't been a very productive day so far, but at least we are getting somewhere. Let's go back to the office and start going over what we have so far."

• • •

The boss was livid. His face was red, and the veins were sticking out in his neck. Ted could tell that he didn't like what he had to say. "I'm just saying, I told you that we were jumping the gun on getting rid of Jim Grant. I had him talked into recanting his confession. He wasn't going to say anything to anyone. He was coming back into the fold. You shouldn't have had him killed yet. With these private dicks on our asses, we should have waited. I told you to let me handle it, but you insisted on doing it your way."

"You do as you're told, and don't question my motives on anything you hear! I know what I'm doing. Jim Grant was trying to blackmail me, and that wasn't going to happen. Listen, Long isn't going to get to us. Did you get rid of Blake?"

"Yes, he's out of the country. Now we need someone to replace him. Do you have any suggestions?"

"That's your job. You know better than to ask me who you can trust in your agency. Do you have anyone in mind?"

"I think so. There is a new guy. Just started in the company. He comes from an agency down in Los Angeles. From what I hear, he left there under some suspicious circumstances. I'm going to do a little more research on why he was sent to me. I'll let you know what I find out."

"Fine, just make sure we can trust him completely. I don't want any more weaklings like Jim Grant on my payroll. Now leave me alone."

"Sure thing boss." Ted scurried out of his office, a plan in mind to test the new guy's allegiance. He had a feeling that Dan Crowley would be perfect for the organization. From what he already knew of the man, he was definitely not a straight arrow. They needed to have another man on the inside, and Ted felt that Dan would fit in well. First, he had a little test for the man. If he passed, Ted could approach him on joining their group.

Ted planted the stash of drugs in Crowley's office. If he took the bait, Ted would know if they could trust him or not. All he had to do is wait.

Dan was beat. He was also frustrated. Nothing was coming of his undercover work with the DEA. Maybe the FBI was wrong. Maybe the DEA is clean. They were convinced that there was someone working in the DEA that was dirty. Dan hadn't seen any evidence of that yet. He knew that he needed to be patient, but people were dying around them. This needed to be resolved soon, before someone else died.

He plopped down on his chair and fired up his computer. Something caught his eye. Someone had been in his office. One of the drawers to his desk was left partially open. He always made sure that everything was closed up tight when he left his office. Dan grabbed a Kleenex and used it to open the drawer. He shuffled some papers around. There was a small package of what looked to be a white powder stuffed underneath. Dan knew that he didn't put it there. He took it out of the drawer, looking around for anyone who could have left it there. Dan quickly got up and closed the door, and curtains, so no one could see inside. He lifted the bag and cut a small hole in it. He took the knife, and placed a small amount of the substance on it. He tasted it with his tongue. Sure enough, it was cocaine. He let out a breath. "What the hell? What is this all about?" Had he finally caught the eye of whoever was in charge here? The FBI had made his background look shady enough to attract the attention of the bad guys, but not enough so anyone else would pay much attention. You had to be looking for it in order to find the information. A slow smile came over Dan's face. He knew just what he had to do. This wasn't his first rodeo.

Putting the drugs into his briefcase, he left his office. All he had to do was keep quiet about this. Whoever put the drugs in his desk, wanted to know if he was going to turn the drugs into his colleagues in the DEA. When that didn't happen, Dan was going to be in. He grinned. BINGO! This was just what he had been waiting for. Soon, very soon, he was going to be a member of this CS Group. He was more than ready.

Ted watched as Dan Crowley left his office. He knew that Dan had found the little package that he had hidden in his desk, but he had to find out for sure. Using the keys that he had to Dan's office, he let himself back in. Ted opened the drawer, and sure enough, the drugs were gone. Now all he had to do was wait and see if Crowley brought the drugs to him. After all, he was the director of the DEA. He was the one who handled this sort of thing. If Crowley didn't bring the drugs to him, he would go to Crowley, it was as simple as that. Blackmail always worked the best in these situations. When Dan finds out that his boss knows that he was stealing drugs, he would be like putty in their hands. He would do whatever they told him to do. Just like everyone else did.

Ted had to admit, he understood the rush of the feeling of power that the boss had. It was kind of like a huge burst of adrenaline running through your system when things started going according to plan. He had started out being blackmailed, just like the others. But now, he was the boss's right hand man, and he liked it. Someday soon, he planned on taking over the Cartel. The boss seemed to be unraveling. Ted couldn't figure out what he had against Jake Long, and he didn't care. As long as the boss was around, it was holding Ted back from his goal. All he had to do was wait it out. Ted knew that it was just a matter of time before the boss did himself in. If Ted got tired of waiting, there was other ways to get rid of him. In the meantime, he needed Dan Crowley to take the bait, which it looked like he already had.

Ted sat back in his chair. *If he would have listened to me in the first place, and trusted my judgement, Long wouldn't be an issue right now. The boss was losing his edge. The group needed to run like a well oiled machine. They couldn't afford a grudge to mess things up. Ted figured that he was going to have to clean things up after the boss was gone. He was more than ready.*

Dan arrived at the office the next day only to find the director at his door. "Sir? Good morning. Can I help you with something?"

Ted nodded. "Yes, as a matter of fact, you can. Can we talk privately?"

Dan opened his door, puzzled as to why the director himself was waiting for him to come into work. "Of course. Come on in."

Ted entered the office, looking around. "Crowley, I'm going to get right to the point here. I read your files and found out that the reason you left the office at Los Angeles was very suspicious. I think I know what happened, but I'm giving you a chance to come clean yourself."

"I-I don't know what you mean director." Dan purposely stammered a little. "Exactly what did you find out?"

"Don't beat around the bush with me Crowley. I know that you're not a straight arrow as you seem. It seems that some drugs went missing on one of your missions. Nothing could be proven, but I think that you took those drugs didn't you? What did you do with them Crowley? Are you a user yourself? Someone you care about perhaps?"

Dan started to sweat. He couldn't believe that the director himself was in on this. That was the last thing that the FBI figured out. They thought it was Gary Lawry that was the dirty cop, not the director. Dan hadn't been able to find anything that proved that Gary was anything other than a good agent. Now, things were becoming more clear. Tom, a.k.a Dan, was too experienced in undercover work to let the director know that he knew exactly what he was talking about. "I would prefer not to get into that director. There is nothing that proves that I stole any drugs."

Ted laughed. "Oh, I know that Crowley. But what about the little stash that I found in your desk drawer last night? Where did that come from? I know that you had it there. Is it gone now Crowley? Did you hide it better? It wasn't very bright of you to leave it in plain sight like that. Why, anyone could come around and find it."

Dan acted like he was a guilty man. Carefully averting his eyes. Looking anywhere but in the eyes of the director. "I don't know what you're talking about."

"Don't insult my intelligence Crowley! I know it was there, and I'm guessing it's gone now. Listen, I don't much care if you're a user or not. All I need to know, is if you want this to come out. It wouldn't do you much good in your chosen profession if anyone finds out you steal drugs, now would it? Do you want me to turn you in?"

Dan knew he had him now. "No, I promise it won't happen again. What can I do to prove it to you? I'll do anything!" He didn't want to go overboard on the acting. Just enough to make the director start to trust him. Dan knew that he would have to prove himself even more before they let him into the fold.

"I'll get back to you on that Crowley. Just remember, I know everything about you. I may need you to run an errand or two for me. When you do that, I may forget about this little indiscretion." Ted stood, looking very smug. "I'll be in touch."

When the director left, Dan let out a breath. This was even bigger than they thought. As soon as he was in the group, Dan was taking them down. He had been working on this for so many years. They had been setting up his cover for a long time. He was getting closer, he just knew it. If Ted was blackmailing him with the drugs, he was probably pretty high up in the CS Group. Dan felt that it was just a matter of time now before he was meeting the boss face to face. Dan was very good at his job. This guy was going down.

When Ted looked closer into Dan Crowley, and asked some questions, he found out a lot more about him. Crowley was suspected of stealing some drugs from a raid. Sometimes, when the drugs would get checked into the evidence locker, some of them would go missing. They could never prove who it was stealing the drugs in shipment to the police station, but they suspected it was Dan Crowley. The DEA in Los Angeles didn't have enough evidence to prosecute him, so they just shipped him off to the Portland office. "Gotta love bureaucracies! If you can't trust someone, dump them on someone else."

Ted picked up his phone and called the boss, letting him know of his progress with Crowley. He hated having to cower to the little weasel of a man, but it was a necessity…for now. Just a couple more tests and he would get Crowley into the group, then they could go on with their business. Ted wasn't going to take any chances on Crowley being a snitch, or worse yet, an undercover. He really doubted that was the case though. If Crowley was already stealing drugs, he was probably using too. Ted was sure that they could use him in the Group.

When Dan Crowley passed the rest of the tests that Ted had set up for him, he knew that he was going to be in. The tests were so easy he could have done them with a blindfold on. These guys thought they were so smart. Dan laughed to himself when Ted approached him with the details. Dan knew that he wouldn't be meeting the boss quite yet, but he planned on looking the man in the eye when he arrested him. It was just a matter of time. Dan only hoped that Jake and Jen stayed out of his way in this operation. He didn't want them mixed up in this.

Jake and Jen were going over the things that they had learned so far in their cases. When they gathered up all of the files, Jake thought that there definitely was a pattern going on. He showed it to Jen. "I really think that this all started with the hit and run. Jerod Sims was selling drugs, and Jim Grant was probably helping him. When Grif Grant found out, he tried to get his son out of it the only way he knew how. Tough love. Jim got upset, and ran into Sims with his truck, killing him. Grif covered for his son, probably feeling responsible in a way. Then, the guilt of it all got to him, and he killed himself. Case closed there. But what about Phil? Cara too, and Jim Grant himself." Jake rubbed his tired eyes. "We have to figure out the connection with all of these deaths. Figure out what was murder, and what was suicide."

The phone rang just then and startled Jenny. "Good grief! That scared me! I'll get it dad." She answered on the second ring. "Long Agency, Jenny Long here. Yes, Doctor, what can I do for you?" She listened for a minute. "Hang on, Doctor, could I put you on speaker phone so my dad can hear what you have to say?" She punched a couple of buttons. "Okay, go ahead Doctor."

Jake heard the coroner's voice come over the line. "Yes, well, to be perfectly honest, I probably shouldn't be calling you on this. But I feel that you have a right to know. The rest of the tests came back on Cara Carson. It turns out there was a lot of sleeping medication in her system. There was absolutely no way that she was going to wake up when that fire alarm went off. The problem is, there is no way of knowing if she took them herself, or if someone gave them to her. I am changing the manner of death to undetermined. She definitely died of smoke inhalation, but I can't say how the sleeping pills got in her system. Other than that, there isn't anything else new in her case. I just thought you should know the details of her death."

Jake let out a whistle. "We appreciate your telling us this Doctor. That definitely sheds some light on Cara's death. Thank you."

The doctor hung up, and Jake and Jen plopped down in their office chairs. They just looked at each other. Jen finally spoke. "Did you ever see Cara take any medication like that? I know I didn't. We are going to have to ask Abby about it I'm afraid. She should know if her mom was using sleeping pills. If she wasn't, then we were right. Cara was probably murdered too. Along with Phil, and Jim."

"Yes, I think you're right on that one Jen. We have at least three murders on our hands. The question is, why? What did Cara do to deserve to be murdered?"

Jen stood, and started gathering up all of the files scattered about on her desk. "I don't know. But I have a feeling that it involves this CS Group. If we find them, we'll find our killers."

Jake stood too. "I agree with you, but right now, I need to get going. Nancy and I are going out on the town." Jake threw his keys to his daughter. "You can take my truck home. This is getting to be a habit with us. It's one that I could get used to though."

"Dad, I'm so happy for you. Nancy is great. I really like her, and I think she likes you a lot."

Jake actually blushed. "I like her too, and I am happy. I'll see you later. Drive safe."

"I will Dad. Don't worry about me, you just go and have fun. We'll take up where we left off in our case tomorrow. I feel good about what we have learned so far. I'll say goodnight now." She reached out and hugged Jake. "I love you Dad."

Jake still got choked up a little when he heard his daughter say those words. "I love you too, Jenny. Good night."

The ranch was pretty quiet when Jen got home that night. She had eaten in town, so she went straight to bed. She was extra tired tonight. They had done a lot of paperwork, and it always taxed her brain. She had some homework to do before she went to bed. Jen yawned, and waited for her computer to boot up. When her schoolwork came up on the screen, Jenny shook off her weariness, and got to work. She was concentrating so hard that she almost missed the shadow forming behind her. She gasped, and turned quickly. "Who are you? What do you want?"

The figure formed more clearly now. Clearer that normal. Jenny could make out features this time. She didn't recognize the man. He was tall, with dark hair. That's about all she could see. Jenny asked again who it was. This time, Jen could hear him very clearly.

"Jenny, I think it's time that you learned my name. you may not know me, but your dad does. My name is Kurt Rommel. I don't want to go into too much detail right now. You can ask your dad about me. I know that he will not be happy that I am here, but I know things. A lot of things that you need to know. I can't go into detail yet, they won't allow it. Just suffice it to say, you will need to figure out a lot of things on your own. But, I can help you, and I will. You need to keep an open mind about me. Things weren't as they seemed. Just like things aren't as they seem right now. Phil and Cara's deaths were no accident, and not suicide either." He started to fade away, his voice getting weaker. Jenny stood.

"Wait, you can't just come here and say that and then leave. Your name seems familiar to me. Who are you exactly? Did you have something to do with my mom? With her death? Were you helping Billy? Tell me!"

Kurt faded away altogether then. Jenny was too excited to sleep now. She needed to find out who he was. "I know I've heard that name before. He has the same last name as Billy. He wasn't his dad though. My grandpa was killed by the man who thought he was Billy's dad. Wait a minute! That's it! Kurt was married to Liz Rommel, the mother of Billy." Jen grabbed her journal and started writing. "Kurt Rommel, Liz Rommel's husband. Liz had an affair with my grandfather which led to her husband Kurt killing grandma and grandpa. My mom and Ann escaped the fire. Kurt had shot himself after the murders. He even left a suicide note. What did he mean by saying things weren't as they seemed?" Jenny couldn't wait to tell Jake what she had learned from Kurt. Now she knew what her mom meant by keeping an open mind about who was going to be coming to help her. Jen didn't know if her dad would be able to get past this, but she could. They needed all the help they could get with these cases, and she, for one, was going to take it.

# • • • 18 • • •

JENNY WAS UP bright and early the next morning. She couldn't wait to tell her dad about everything that Kurt Rommel had said to her. She wasn't sure how to bring it up though. Jen decided that she was just going to come out with it and let her dad decide if he wanted to listen. She was sitting at the kitchen table when Jake came down for breakfast. Jake was surprised to see her there before anyone else even got downstairs.

"Wow, you're up early. What's going on? You look like the cat that ate the canary."

"Well, I couldn't wait to talk to you about what happened to me last night."

"Did you have another visit from your mom? Tell me! You have my full attention."

"Well, maybe you should sit down. This is interesting, but you may not like everything that I have to tell you."

Jake sat down, a puzzled expression on his face. "Okay, I'm sitting. Now what is going on? Jen, you can tell me anything, you know that, right?"

"I know dad. But this is complicated. Okay, I'm just going to say it. You can take it however you want, but it is what it is. Last night, the figure that has been trying to appear to me finally showed himself. He spoke very clearly now. He had a lot to say. First off, he told me that he was limited in what he could tell me. Someone is behind the scenes, so to speak, telling him what to do, and say. I know, weird huh? Anyway, he went on to say that you will know who he is, and he gave me a name. Kurt Rommel. I figured out who he is by the stories that my mom had told me about her parent's death. He killed Grandma and Grandpa, didn't he Dad?"

Jake was genuinely shocked. Kurt Rommel was a name he hadn't heard in a long time. It was a name that he never wanted to hear again. Especially involving his daughter. He stood, and started pacing the room. "Jenny, this is not good. That man was sick. He killed Joe and Ali when he found out about the affair Joe was having with his wife. Your mom and Ann would have been killed too, if not for Joe saving them. Rommel had no qualms about killing those children. He had a drug and alcohol problem, sure, but he still committed a murder. I don't want anything to do with him, alive or dead. And I don't want you to listen to him." He stopped his pacing, and stood in front of Jenny. Jake took her face in his hands. "Listen, Jen. Whatever he has to tell you, I don't believe any of it. Wait a minute! Is that why Sara isn't coming to you anymore? Did he do something to her again?"

"No, nothing like that. At least, I don't think so. I hope to see my mom again." Jen shook her head, trying to clear her mind. "Anyway, this Kurt Rommel told me that both Phil and Cara's deaths aren't as they seem. Dad, we have to figure out what happened to both of them. I always knew that something wasn't right about either of their deaths. Dad, I think that this goes way back. Even before the accident that killed Jerod Sims. We need to start connecting the dots here. I just don't know where to start."

"Hold on a minute. You got all of this from something that a known murderer told you? Jen, he could be just trying to lead us away from the real reason that Phil and Cara are dead. I don't trust him Jenny. You shouldn't either. Until we know for sure, I really don't want you to listen to much of what he has to say."

"I know all of that, but he seemed to know something. Kurt did say that he would tell me more when he could. Something is holding him back, just like it did Mom. This is just getting more and more confusing. Interesting, but confusing."

"Okay, if this is how you want to do this, we will go with it for now. But the minute that this Rommel character starts getting too close to you, we cut him off. I'm not sure how you would do that, though. Maybe Nancy could help you with that. I don't trust him. He could be just trying to go over Sara's head, and cause more confusion. Cover for someone else, I don't know. Let's just keep an open mind, that's all."

"I understand, and I will do that. I also will keep trying to communicate with my mom, and try to find out exactly what is going on. Where do we start Dad?"

"We start at the beginning. Let's go all the way back to Joe and Ali's death. Maybe something will come up there that will help us in our current situation. In the meantime, we need to get a hold of Tom, and see if anything has come up on his end."

Jake took out his cell phone and dialed Dan Crowley's number. There was no answer, so Jake left a message. He frowned when he hung up. "Well, no answer there. I asked him to call me when he gets my message. We'll see if he does or not. Something is going on with him. I think his undercover op is coming to a head. I suppose we had better not bother him right now. If we interfere with his undercover business, we could get him in trouble, and that's the last thing I want to do. His safety is paramount."

"I agree, let's just do this on our own. We need to leave Uncle Tom out of it for now. Let's head into the office and start with our research on Grandma and Grandpa's death. I can't believe that I am actually investigating my own grandparent's death."

Jake felt the same way. It was going to be weird investigating the Olsen's murders. Jake was going to go with this for now, but he just didn't know if he could listen to Kurt Rommel. He was the very person who killed them. Jake figured that whatever Rommel had to say, there must be a reason for his appearing to Jenny like that. All Jake knew, was that he was going to keep his daughter safe, at any cost. Even if it meant keeping Kurt Rommel away from her. How he was going to do that, he didn't know.

The drive into Portland was quiet. Jenny was thinking ahead on what they were going to find out about her grandparents deaths. Jake was *worrying* about what they were going to find out in the Olsen's deaths.

Jenny got the computers warming up when they got into the office. Jake sat down and typed in the names Joe and Ali Olsen. All he could do from here is google them and get the regular public information. They needed to get into the police database to get the in depth information. Jake knew just who to ask to get that information. He let Jenny take over what he was doing, and Jake called his old partner, Tony Scott. Since the murders happened in Los Angeles, Tony should be able to help him out. Jake knew that his partner would help. Tony didn't know anything about Jenny's abilities, so Jake had to approach this carefully. Tony answered his cell phone in the usual way.

"Hello, Tony Scott here. Can I help you?"

"Well, nothing changes does it? How are you doing Captain Scott?"

"Jake Long! I haven't heard your voice in so long, I thought maybe your wild lifestyle finally caught up to you. How are you doing old friend?"

Jake laughed. "I'm good Tony. How are you?"

"Great! Same old, same old stuff going on in good old Los Angeles. Are you ready to leave the boring life on that ranch and come back here? I could use another good detective around here."

"Actually, Jen and I are doing pretty good in our private detective firm. We already solved one case, and are working on another. That's why I'm calling you. Tony, I need your help."

Tony was serious now, all of the teasing put aside. "Well, this sounds serious. You know I will help you out if I can. Just what is it that you need Jake?"

"I need the police reports on the deaths of Joe and Ali Olsen. I need the coroner's report too. I also would like the reports on Kurt Rommel's death. Can you get them for me?"

Tony let out a whistle. "Wow, you're not asking for much, are you? I can try. That was a long time ago. The brass doesn't like it when we dig up old skeletons, but I will give it a try. Give me your email address, and I'll get them to you as soon as I can. Anything else?"

"No, and thank you Tony. I really appreciate your help on this. I can't go into detail, but something isn't right about the Olsen's deaths. Maybe even Rommel's. I need to learn all that I can about them."

"I understand. I hope that Jenny can handle dredging up the past like that. Are you sure you really want to do that?"

Jake had to agree with him on that, but he couldn't very well tell Tony that it was Kurt Rommel who started this ball rolling. "I know it's going to be tricky, but Jen will be fine. I'll make sure of that."

Jake rattled off his email address, and hung up the phone. He walked into Jenny's office, where she was pouring over the computer printouts. "I talked to Tony. He is going to help us as much as he can. I have him emailing the reports we need. Jenny, are you sure you want to do this? We are opening this can of worms all because a messed up killer told you to. I just don't know."

Jen looked up from the papers she was going over. "I'll be fine Dad. I really think that Kurt Rommel is trying to help us. He is going to tell me in his own time, but for now, this is all we can do."

Jake and Jenny didn't find anything more in the files they printed out. They were both pretty frustrated by the time their day was over. Jen blew out a breath and rubbed her eyes. "Dad, there just isn't anything here to show any wrongdoing other than by Kurt Rommel. I'm kind of surprised that the press didn't dig into this more. After all, the killing of a police officer is usually big news. They barely even mentioned it."

"Yeah, I see that. They probably weren't that interested being that it was pretty cut and dried that Kurt Rommel committed the crime. The papers do mention the fact that Joe was having an affair with Rommel's wife, Liz. We definitely know all about her. That brings up some bad memories. Jen, I'm sorry we have to rehash all of this. Are you okay?"

"I'm fine Dad. I know this is necessary. Kurt Rommel wanted us to go through all of this for some reason. It has to have some connection to Phil and Cara's deaths. We just have to figure out what it is."

"Well, nothing here is going to help us. I think we'll just have to wait until Tony gets me the police reports on Joe and Ali's deaths, or until Rommel gets a chance to tell you himself. I don't like the idea of him contacting you, I want you to be careful. You can't always believe the words of a murderer."

"I'll be careful, I promise."

They headed out the door just as Dan Crowley was coming to see them. Jake was surprised to see his brother. "Dan. What are you doing here?"

Dan looked around. "Can we talk? I have some information you might be interested in."

"Sure, come into the office. We can talk freely in there."

Dan followed them in and sat on the corner of Jake's desk. "Okay, this doesn't go any further than this room, understand?"

Jake and Jen both nodded, sitting in the two chairs around Dan.

"I just wanted to let you know that I am officially a dirty cop. My job was to get deep into the DEA so whoever is doing the dirty work there comes to me. Well, it happened.

I can't tell you right now who it is, but suffice it to say, it's someone pretty high up in the DEA. Anyway, I just wanted to let you know that I'll probably be out of commission for awhile. This drug cartel that you are investigating is the same one that I am investigating. The reason I'm telling you this, is because you need to know how dangerous they are. I haven't gotten in all the way yet, but when I do, I aim to bring them all down. I don't want you in the middle of it all. These guys are dangerous. They've been in business for a long time, and they plan on staying that way. They will shoot first, and ask questions later. I'm good at what I do, Jake. You need to trust me on this. Back off, and let me do my job, without having to worry about you two. I'm going to work my way to the top of the food chain in this organization. When I get to the top gun, I'm taking him in. The people in these cartels are killers and thieves. Promise me you won't dig into this anymore."

Jake sat back in his chair. His hackles were up now. "Listen, Tom. We are investigating this for our own reasons. We have no idea who this head honcho is, and we don't care. We just want to know who killed Phil and Cara. Then, and only then, are we going to back down. If this cartel has something to do with their murders, then so be it. We are already involved in this, and we aren't going to back off. All that I can tell you is this. We'll be very cautious, and we won't get in your way. Who knows? Maybe we can help you in some way. I have Tony looking into the deaths of Sara's parents. It's a long story, but Jen had a vision, and they told her that this is all connected with what is going on now. The drug ring, the murders, all of it. It all stems back to this hit and run that we were investigating in the first place. We solved that case, but there is more to it. When Tony gets me that information, I hope it helps, but I'm not going to hold my breath on that one. In a nutshell, we will be careful, but we are going to help figure this all out."

"Somehow I knew that you were going to say that. Listen, you aren't going to be able to call me, so you're on your own.

I'm going deep undercover in this cartel, and won't be able to answer your calls. You do what you have to do, and I'll do what I have to do." Tom stood and slapped his brother on the back. Hugging Jenny, he told them to be careful, and left the office.

Jake and Jenny locked up, and left for the school to pick up Abby. Jake was beat by the time they got to the ranch. He went straight to bed. He had a lot on his mind. Jake didn't think that Tony had time to get him the information he needed but he opened his email anyway, just in case. He was shocked to see the documents were there. Rubbing his eyes, he opened the email from Tony and started reading the reports on Joe and Ali's deaths. It was pretty much what he had figured. Nothing new really. What was interesting though, was the report on the death of Kurt Rommel. There was a suicide note. The autopsy report said he had drugs and alcohol in his system. That was nothing new. The coroner had written a side note on the report that no one had said anything about. Kurt Rommel was shot on the right side of his head. He shot himself with his police issued gun. The blood splatter was on the windshield of the driver's side and his driver's side window was rolled down. Now, if you were going to shoot yourself, why roll down the window?

Jake looked at the rest of the documents. There were some pictures of Kurt Rommel in his police uniform. Jake zoomed in on the picture of Kurt. He looked so proud, standing by his police car, grinning. What could happen to someone to make them go bad, just like that? I guess it wasn't that fast though, Rommel hadn't gone bad until he started with the DEA. Years after this picture was taken.

Jake looked closer, Something didn't look quite right. He frowned. "Wait a minute!"

Rommel's gun holster was on his left side. Jake looked over the other pictures. Every one showed him with his gun on his left side. Kurt Rommel was left handed. How could he shoot himself on the right side of the head if he was left handed? It could be done I guess, but normally you would use the dominant hand to pull the trigger. If this is true, Kurt may not have killed himself after all. This is big! Jake needed to call Tony right away in the morning and check in on this. If Kurt Rommel didn't kill himself, then who did, and why?

$$\bullet\bullet\bullet\ 19\ \bullet\bullet\bullet$$

KURT WATCHED AS Jenny slept. He felt bad about spying on her like this. He needed to get the girls to that cabin. No one liked to go there, he knew that. He had overheard Abby telling Jenny that it just brought back bad memories. There was something there that she had to find, and the only way he could think of to get her down there, was to try and tell her. It was hard to move objects, so he had to find a different way to tell Jenny to go there. For some reason, Sara was stronger than he was. He figured that could be why she came with him for help on this. One of the reasons anyway. She knew the truth about the night of her parents murders now. Soon, everyone would know the truth, he hoped.

Kurt and Sara teamed up on this effort. It was so important to help Jenny and Abby with this. Just a little push in the right direction, and their plan would come together. If they could get the girls to that cabin, and find the papers that Phil had hidden there, it would start the ball rolling. Just how they were going to do that, well…he wasn't quite sure. They would figure something out.

Of course, they could just tell Jenny to go to the cabin, but for some reason, they were only allowed to give her hints.

Besides, Kurt had already let her know, but Jen was too busy to take his hints seriously. Jenny was a smart girl, she would figure it out. Right now though, Sara and Kurt decided to not wake Jenny up. They could do their jobs without waking her. All they needed to do, was get her to think about that cabin again. Once she went down there, Jenny would find that trap door, they would make sure of it. Abby had to go with her there, and Sara knew that would be hard for the little girl. She had to do it though, she was the only one that knew about that trap door in the floor of that cabin. Her dad had shown her and Cara one time. He told them that he had something important there, but they weren't to look unless something happened to him. Cara had forgotten about it. Abby too, but if they could remind her, the girls would find those papers.

Kurt left Sara in charge of getting Jen to the cabin, he was in charge of what happened once they got there. After slipping through the wall of the cabin, Kurt looked around. *Well, that's just great! The cabin had been cleaned, but no one had seen it.* Kurt looked around and spotted the area in the floor that Phil Carson had told him about. It was just as he said it would be. There was a rug over the top of a trap door. Kurt couldn't believe that no one had found this opening in the floor. It was obvious that someone had been here since the Carson's. He hovered over the rug, manipulating it just enough so that it bunched up and moved just enough so that you couldn't miss the handle on the trap door. That's it. His work here was done.

Jenny woke up with a headache. That usually only happened when she was disturbed in the night by her mom or someone else trying to communicate with her. She rubbed her eyes. Jenny didn't wake up at all last night. Did someone try to wake her and she didn't hear them? She didn't think so. If that was the case, they didn't try very hard to wake her up. She sat on the side of her bed, looking around. Everything was in its place, as far as she could tell. Jenny stepped down from her bed, and immediately knew that something was off, though. She just couldn't put her finger on it. She took a closer look around her room, shaking her head. Why couldn't they just come out with it? Why all of the subtle hints? It would be so much simpler if she could just hear them better. Nancy was trying to help her with that, but there really wasn't much they could do. Jenny figured out that it was more on her mom's side that she couldn't talk to her outright. Jen could hear them, just not clearly. Something was holding them back from that. They were getting clearer though. Someday soon, Jenny hoped that would change for good, but for now, she had to use her sleuthing skills when they communicated with her. Jenny walked towards the bathroom, trying to figure out just what was off this morning. She tripped over something on the floor. It was the nursery rhyme book of her mother's.

"Not this book again!" It had been the catalyst that helped Jake solve the serial killer case. Could it help Jenny with her cases now? She doubted that it would. After all, the killer had used the book to murder all of those people. Jen didn't know why it would be laying out though, unless someone placed it there. She reached down to pick it up, and sure enough, it lay open to a certain page. Jenny picked it up carefully, looking at the page it was open to. The nursery rhyme on the page read:

"In a cabin, in a wood
Little man by the window stood
Saw a rabbit hopping by
Knocking at his door.....

Jenny frowned. What was this about? Was she suppose to know what they were talking about? She shook her head. "I haven't got a clue mom. You need to do better than this, sorry." Jenny laid the book on her bed and got ready for the day.

It was Saturday, so Abby didn't have school. Jen had promised her that they would go riding, and have a picnic, so Abby was excited. She ran down the stairs and looked for Jen in the kitchen. Ann was there, getting breakfast ready, as she always was.

"Ann, have you seen Jen? We are going riding today. Is she down at the barn?"

"No, sweetie, I haven't seen her yet this morning. I think she is still in her room. Why don't you go up and check there?"

Abby took the stairs two at a time. She skidded to a halt at Jenny's door, barely knocking once before flinging the door open. Jenny was just setting the book on her bed when Abby burst in. "Good morning Jenny. Are you ready to go?"

Jenny grinned. "Just about. Are you ready?"

Abby plopped down on Jenny's bed, grabbing the book. "I am ready." She glanced at the page the book was open to. "Were you reading the nursery rhymes last night? This one is about a cabin." She read the rhyme out loud. "In a cabin, in a wood… That reminds me, will you go with me to our old cabin? I need to see if my hat is there. Mom couldn't find it at the apartment. We were always going to check the cabin and see if we left it there, but we just couldn't bring ourselves to go back there. Will you go with me?"

"Of course I will." Jenny was beginning to think that the nursery rhyme book was opened to this page for a reason. She shook her head again. Evidently, someone wanted them to go to that cabin. Come to think of it, this cabin kept coming into her thoughts, but Jen pushed them aside. Maybe it was more important than she originally thought. When the thought had popped into her head to take Abby to the cabin, this could have been why. Someone had been trying to get her there all of this time, she just didn't listen close enough.

"I guess we are going to the cabin. Let's get our lunch ready, and then we can go there."

The two girls walked to the cabin that was Abby's home for a time. Abby was a little hesitant about going in. Jen put her arm around Abby's shoulders. "Abby, you don't have to do this if you don't want to. I can go in alone."

"No, it's okay. I think it's time to let go of the bad memories. I've been avoiding this long enough now. Let's go."

Jenny reached for the door, turning the knob. It was locked. "I forgot that Sam keeps these locked up. I tell you what, let's go for our ride, and I'll come down here later. Maybe my dad can go with me, and you won't have to."

Abby didn't realize that she was holding her breath. It came out in a whoosh. "That sounds good to me. Maybe I'm not as ready as I thought I was."

Jenny could see that. She knew better than anyone that you can't push the healing process when you lose a loved one. It was probably for the better anyway. Jenny had a feeling that Kurt was responsible for the book being left where it was. It was no coincidence that it was open to the page about the cabin. Kurt said that he could only do certain things right now, but moving a book? That was a pretty big accomplishment. It has to mean something. Jen couldn't wait to tell Jake about this.

Jenny forgot about the case, and the book, for awhile as they rode. She loved it out here, and she could tell that Abby loved it too. It was a beautiful area, and the crisp air felt good. The horses knew the path well, so Jenny let her mind wander a bit as they rode. Of course, it went straight back to the case. *I wonder what Kurt Rommel was trying to get at? Leaving that nursery rhyme book on that certain rhyme had to mean that he wanted us to go in the cabin. He had to have known that Jenny would figure that out.*

They stopped at their favorite spot, and had their lunch. It was great. Ann really knew how to feed them. The grapes and apples were crisp and sweet, and the ham sandwiches were made with fresh homemade bread. It was delicious. Abby chatted as they ate, and by the time they were done, it was late afternoon. "We had better get back Abby. This was a great idea. I'm so glad that we got to spend this time together. It doesn't happen that often anymore."

"Yes. I love it Jenny. I really miss our rides."

They mounted, and turned the horses for home. The sun was just getting low in the horizon when the girls got back to the barn. They unsaddled, and let their horses loose after pitching some hay for them. As they walked to the house, Jake met them half way.

"How was your ride?"

"It was great!" Abby's cheeks were flushed from the crisp winter air. "I loved it. I could ride every day."

Jake and Jen laughed together. "I believe it Abby. You head for the house okay? I have something to talk to my dad about, and I'll be right behind you."

Abby took off on a run, and Jake had to chuckle. "I wish I had that much energy. What do you want to talk to me about?"

Jen relayed the story of the nursery rhyme book, and told Jake her feeling that it was Kurt who moved the book to that page. "I really think that we need to go in there. I just have a feeling that he wanted us to. I don't know for sure, but it is just like him to be vague like that. What do you think?"

"I think that your feelings are usually spot on. It certainly wouldn't hurt to go in there and look around. I'll grab the key from Sam and meet you down there."

While Jen waited for her dad, she had some time to think. *If Rommel wanted me to look in this cabin, it definitely could have something to do with Phil and Cara's deaths. Maybe Phil had something in there that will give us a clue.*

Jake interrupted her thoughts. "I got the key, now let's go see what Kurt wanted us to find."

"You read my mind Dad. I was just thinking that there could be something in there that's important enough that Kurt thought we needed to see it."

"Well, maybe I'm getting clairvoyant too!" Jake put the key in the door, and it creaked open. There was a layer of dust on everything inside. Jenny sneezed. "Wow, no one has been in here for awhile. I guess it needs to be cleaned again." Jake reached over and flipped the light switch. The light illuminated the room. Nothing looked out of place. The cabin had been cleaned out, so there weren't any dishes or any personal items of the Carson's left.

"I don't know what Kurt would think we would find here. The place is empty."

Jake nodded, and started walking around the room. He tripped over a rug that was lying in the middle of the floor. Looking down, he spotted something. Jake took out his flashlight and pointed it to the object that had been uncovered by the rug being moved. "Jenny, come over here. You're not going to believe this. Look what I found."

Jenny trotted over to where Jake was standing. When she looked at what the flashlight was pointing too, she sucked in a breath. "Holy cow! Dad, what is that?"

"Looks like a trap door of some kind. This has to be what Rommel wanted us to find. Unbelievable! I still can't believe that he is helping us. If he didn't kill himself, like I am beginning to doubt, then this could explain just who did kill him."

Jake handed the flashlight to Jen, as he knelt down and pulled on the handle that was embedded in the floor. "Whoever made this space didn't want whatever is in here to be found by just anyone. If it was Phil, why didn't he tell us what he had hidden in here, and how did he do it? Cara had to have known about this. I wonder why she didn't tell us about it? Could have saved us a lot of time and energy. I guess in her grief, she just forgot about it. Phil was pretty secretive that's for sure." Jake tugged at the small, square door. It took a little bit, but he got it open. Jen handed him the flashlight, and Jake shone it in the small hole. Inside, there seemed to be a folder of some sort. Jake picked it up carefully, and blew the dust off of it. "Must be some important papers in here for Phil to have hidden it so well. Let's take them up to the house and look them over there. It's too dark in here with just one small light."

Jen could hardly contain her excitement. "Dad, this is big! I want to know what is on those papers. Could this mean that

Phil knew that someone was after him? I can hardly stand it. Hurry up! Let's go!"

Jake could hardly keep up with Jenny. She was running for the house, stopping every few minutes, waiting for her dad to catch up. "Dad, come on! You can go faster than that."

Jake trotted up to her. "I'm not as young as I used to be. I'm going as fast as I can."

She slowed down to his speed, and they walked to the house together. Jake laid the folder carefully onto the desk in Sam's office. He spread out the papers inside in the order in which they had been written. Jake could tell that the papers were written by Phil Carson. He knew his handwriting from the note he had written to Cara. Some of the papers were printed out and some were hand written. "Okay, let's start at the beginning. Phil seemed to be doing research on his shooting. It says here that his shooting was more than just a traffic stop gone wrong. He thought that the man who shot him was a member of the CS Group. We kind of figured that out. Wow, Phil was really doing his homework here. There are several pages mostly about the shooting that left him paralyzed."

Jenny frowned, and squinted at the pages they had lain out in front of them. "Dad, he seemed to think that this CS Group is stationed in Los Angeles, and has been for years. Did you ever hear of any of this when you were there?"

"Not really, there always has been a drug problem in LA, just like everywhere else, but nothing about a cartel working from there. The DEA and narcotics division are pretty tight lipped about that kind of stuff though." Jake turned to the next page. "Phil definitely was getting close to something here. That's probably what got him killed. Which I do think is what happened. He didn't kill himself. Wait a minute, Jenny, look at this."

Jenny looked where Jake was pointing on the page. Written in Phil Carson's own handwriting was the name Kurt Rommel, with a question mark behind it. She sucked in a breath. "Oh my God! Dad, how did he figure all of this out? What do you think Rommel has to do with this cartel?"

"Well, I know that Rommel worked for the DEA. If you bring it all together, we've got some puzzle pieces getting put in their place here. Think about it. Tom shows up, and is working undercover in the DEA. This cartel is killing people that get too close to figuring this out, and it has something to do with Los Angeles. I think the police are involved up to their necks. There has got to be some dirty cops in LA, and in Portland, helping to cover all of this up. I think that's why Jim Grant was killed too, and Cara. The fire that killed Cara was a statement. I think that was meant for us. Your mom was killed in a fire, and so was Cara. If I didn't know that Billy Rommel was dead, I would think that he was involved in this. Trying to scare us off. I think whoever is the head of this cartel, knew Billy, and Kurt. I think they were pawns in all of this. Jen, we need to go to LA."

"I agree. The rest of these papers all deal with something in Los Angeles, and Phil talks about the policemen that he thinks he can trust, and the ones that he can't. He has names and dates of all kinds of things in here. Dad, these papers can put a lot of bad cops away for good, but he doesn't say anything about who the boss of this cartel is. We definitely are going to Los Angeles. Do you think that we should try and get in touch with Tom and tell him what we have learned? I mean, he could be in great danger."

"We can try, but he knows that he is in danger every day. I think he can handle himself. I will try and call him though." Jake picked up his phone and dialed the number for Dan Crowley. Not surprisingly, he got his voicemail. Jake opted not to leave a message, Tom already told them not to contact him. He is probably deep undercover now. More than likely, Tom is in deep with the cartel by now. The very same cartel they were hunting.

••• *20* •••

DAN CROWLEY WAS trying to contain his excitement. The head of the DEA had come to him about helping with the next drug shipment. Dan figured he had passed all of the tests now. It was just a matter of time until he met this boss, and took them all down. He had been working on this case for so many years, he knew every detail of this organization. At least, he thought he did. He had to admit the head of the DEA being in on it set him back a bit. Dan knew that this was big, he just hadn't figured on it being that big. He knew that it went even beyond the head honcho of the DEA, though. Someone was calling the shots, and he had a huge organization helping him. It was going to take a lot to gather them all up and arrest them, but Dan was going to start at the top. This was a great beginning.

Just like clockwork, Ted came into Dan's office the next day. Dan had to hide his smile. Ted was all business, and looked to have something on his mind. Dan sat back in his chair, and waited for him to say whatever it was that was on his mind. Dan knew better than to push the target too far, just let them think that they were in charge. Piece of cake.

Ted looked Dan in the eye. *What an idiot! He really thinks that he is smarter than me. I am going to like knocking him down a few pegs.* He thought, as he grinned to himself. Ted plopped down on the chair opposite Dan. "Listen, Crowley, I've got a job for you. If you don't follow my instructions completely, I'm going to the authorities with what I know about you, and you're going to jail, understand?"

Dan nodded, staying silent. Ted continued. "There is going to be a huge drug bust next week. We need those drugs. These small time drug pushers think that they have it made, but they don't. Far from it. They're so stupid, they can't even figure out who is bringing them all down. Before long, there is only going to be one seller around, and it's going to be us. Now, this is what I want you to do. When the drugs come into the police station, you are going to be the one there to pick up the shipment. The drugs will be taken to the holding area in the police station. There are more drugs than just this in that holding area. When drugs are brought in, they need to make room for the other drugs. So, as you probably already know, the drugs are taken to an incinerator to be destroyed. This is where you come in. There are a couple of others in our organization that will be working with you on this. You are going to be in charge of taking the drugs to the incinerator. On the way there, someone will meet you half way. The drugs that are to be incinerated, will be exchanged with harmless powder. You will make the exchange, and the powder will be taken and incinerated. No one will be the wiser. No one will know that they are burning harmless powder, and the drugs will be on there way to their destination."

Ted was very pleased with himself. Dan had to admit, this was a brilliant scheme. He wanted to know how they had been getting by with this all of these years, but he kept his mouth shut. Ted was grinning now. "Well? Pretty smart huh? Do you think you can handle all of that Crowley?"

"I know I can. Who is my contact in the police department? Exactly how may cops do you have working for you?"

"All that you need to know, is the name of one cop. Don't worry about the rest of them. Listen, Crowley, if you screw this up, you're done. By that, I mean, no longer on this earth, understand? We keep a tight rein on our employees, one mistake could bring us all down. We run like a well oiled machine. You are just one cog in this machine, and can be replaced. Now, do you understand what your job is here? I'm putting you in a great position here Crowley. I trust that you can handle it, or I wouldn't have given you this job."

"I can handle it boss. No problem. Just point me in the right direction."

• • •

The job went smoothly, and Ted was happy with the way that Dan performed. He knew that he was right in hiring him. Everything was going along perfectly. Dan Crowley was going to be a huge asset to the firm in the future.

Ted was right, the boss was happy with Dan's job performance too. The drugs were flowing freely. There were no hitches in their process. It had been working well for them for a lot of years, nothing was going to stop them now. Especially a couple of newbie private eyes. For some reason, the boss was especially leery of these two. Ted had a feeling that he knew them somehow. He tucked that little bit of information aside, and planned to use it in the future. Ted planned on being the boss one day soon, and he was gathering intel wherever he could. If the boss got too careless with these Long's he could push them in the right direction. With everything Ted knew about this boss, he could bring him down. Then, Ted was at the top. He didn't care what it took, he was going to be at the top of this organization soon. He had worked too hard, and waited too long. This was going to happen.

• • •

Jake and Jen got to Los Angeles, and pulled up to the police station. Jake couldn't help but feel a bit of nostalgia when he looked at his old precinct building. Nothing much had changed. The same steps that he had bumped into Nancy, the same door that he had walked through so many times. Everything looked the same. He shook off the feeling that he got when he entered the building and walked passed his old desk. Someone else was sitting there now. Different pictures were sitting on the desk. He had to admit, he missed it a little. He was good at his job as a homicide detective. It was his life, his whole life, back then. Well, things had changed, and he had a job to do here. A different job, but one much the same, really. He was going to take down this cartel. He knew better than anyone what these drugs did to people, nothing but death and destruction followed the people who got messed up on drugs.

Tony stood as they entered his office. "Jake! It's really great to see you. I wish it was under different circumstances, but great nonetheless." He shook Jake's hand and put his hand over his heart when he looked over at Jen. "Tell me this isn't that little girl who took you off of my homicide division. She can't be this grown up already! Where is the little girt that I knew a few years ago?"

Jenny laughed. "It's me, Uncle Tony. It hasn't been that long has it? You look the same."

Jenny looked at the man whom she had known so well. Tony had insisted that she call him Uncle Tony. She didn't mind having one more uncle around, and she loved him like a member of the family. "You may be a little more gray haired, but you haven't changed."

Tony threw his head back and laughed. "I may have a little more gray hair, but I earned every one of them. How are you Jen?"

"I'm good Uncle Tony. I wish we were here for a different reason, but certain circumstances have brought us back here, and it's great to be back."

All business now, Jake brought out the papers that Phil Carson had written up, and showed them to Tony. "This is all we have so far. We know that there are some dirty cops around. As far as we have figured out, Phil had found out that the headquarters for this drug cartel is right here in Los Angeles. It sounds like the cartel works from here, and goes all the way to Portland. It looks as though Phil was getting close to figuring out how this cartel has been getting away with this all of these years. He was killed because of it. But Tony, look at this." Jake opened the files and took out the sheet of paper with Kurt Rommel's name on it. He pointed to the name and Tony let out a soft whistle.

"You've got to be kidding me! Jake, does this mean that Rommel was involved with this Cartel somehow? Just how far back do you think this goes?"

"We're not sure, but at least as far back as when Rommel was with the DEA. Tony, the DEA is in this pretty deep too. They seem to have a network of dirty cops working with them on this. We don't know who we can trust in the department. We can't bring this to just anyone. That's why I came to you, Tony. I know that I can trust you with this information. I wanted to work with you on this. I know you're in homicide, but you've been with the Los Angeles police department for a long time. I know that you know a lot of people in a lot of different divisions, including the DEA, and the narcotics division in Los Angeles. Do you have anyone that you know you can trust?"

Tony rubbed his chin. "Well, maybe, but I don't know if we should let anyone else know about this. Look what happened to Phil. Do you think there were any other deaths involving this cartel?"

"Yes, we do. Phil's wife Cara died mysteriously, by a fire no less. I think there is a connection there to Sara's death. I know, I'm probably grasping at straws, but I just have a feeling. Anyway, Grif Grant was a cop in Portland who went out to the hit and run that got this ball rolling. He died of a gunshot wound to the head. We got a lead on him by searching the police files. That's where this all started. Julie Grant, Grif's daughter, came to us wanting us to investigate her father's death. Things snowballed from there, really. We learned of Jim Grant, Julie's brother, who was the one in the hit and run. To make a long story short, Grif covered up for his son, and he did kill himself. He couldn't take the guilt anymore. Jim was arrested for manslaughter, and ended up dying in jail. We tracked down the guard that was working that night, thinking that he probably had something to do with Jim's death, but he is in the wind. Then, we find these papers that Phil Carson had been writing up. We think that he died because of what he was finding out. It led us all the way back to here. Phil left a note to Cara saying he would never kill himself, and I believe he was murdered. Cara too, and Jim Grant. This cartel has an in with the police everywhere from LA to Portland. That's how they have been covering their tracks all of these years. I haven't figured out yet how they are getting these drugs, but I think the police have something to do with it. These cops are expendable. I think that if we dig deeper, we are going to find some more so called suicides that end up being murders. This goes pretty deep Tony. We have to stop them, before any one else dies. We have got to get these drugs off the streets. I know there are a lot more of these cartels around, but this one is big, and has been around a while. This will be a good start anyway."

"I agree, Jake. I'll look into it on my end, and gather together some people I know that I can trust, and you do the same. Jake, if this guy feels threatened, heads are gonna roll. We need to be very cautious, and ready for anything. I don't want you or Jenny getting hurt. If this has something to do with Kurt Rommel, and Sara's deaths, this person probably knows you. He, or she, probably has it out for you. You just watch your backs."

"We will Tony. Let's get this ball rolling."

• • •

The boss swiped his arms over his desk. The papers went fly-ing. "Damn it! I told you to get all of those papers that Phil Carson had. I thought we had them all. What happened?"

Ted cringed. "Boss, I thought we had them all too. Evidently Carson was smart enough to hide copies of his work. How was I to know that Long would find them? I still can't figure out what made him go look for those papers. I thought getting rid of Carson's wife would be the end of it. I knew we should have gotten more info out of her first. We rushed the job. That's on you. Your vendetta is getting the better of you. Maybe you should back off a little and let me handle this." Ted knew that he was pushing his luck, but the boss's vendetta was going to bring the organization down, and he wasn't having it. He had worked too hard for too long to have it all come tumbling down now. The boss was losing it. It all started with him witnessing that car accident. Then his dad dying, and him taking over the family business at such a young age. He got cocky when he used his own initials to name the organization. Ted had a bad feeling that this was going to be the end of it, and he wasn't going down with the ship. It was time to clean things up around here, beginning at the top. He just needed a plan, that's all. He was good at that. He just needed a plan.

## ••• 21 •••

JAKE AND JEN got a room at a local hotel, and checked in shortly after talking to Tony. Jen plopped down on the bed in her room, and grabbed her cell phone. She just had a feeling that she needed to call her Uncle Tom. She didn't know if he would answer, but somehow she needed to get word to him on what they had learned so far. First, she called her dad and told him what she was doing. Jake came right over to her room and they discussed it at length before deciding to try and call Tom.

Jake dialed the number that Tom had left for them, and waited, while it rang and rang. Before long, the answering machine picked up. Jake didn't leave a message, he didn't want to take the chance of someone else hearing it. Jake sighed when he hung up. "Well, at least we tried. I guess we are on our own here. Tom can take care of himself, we go ahead as planned."

Jenny agreed. "Yes, we do. Where do we start?"

"We start with trying to figure out who in this area has the power to run such a huge organization. He would need a headquarters, and an area that would hide what they are doing there. It would have to be big, and very well hidden."

"Yes, and there are a lot of buildings that fit that criteria. It gives me a headache even thinking about all of the research we are going to have to do."

"Well, I think Tony can help us there. There has to be some record of gang activities going on in a certain area. That's where we are going to start."

"Let's get to it then." Jenny stood, ready to get after it.

"Okay, but we need to let Tony do his investigating first, so we have a little time to kill. Jen, don't you want to go to the cemetery and visit your mom? We haven't been here for a while. Let's take the rest of the day off, and visit the cemetery. We could do some sightseeing, visit some old haunts, things like that. Then we can get after it tomorrow."

Jen looked at her dad with a surprised look on her face. "Oh my gosh! I can't believe that I didn't think of that. That goes to show how much this case has consumed me. Wow, now I know how you must have felt when you got immersed in a case." Jen nodded. "Yes, we definitely need to do that. Let me get cleaned up, and I'll meet you downstairs in the lobby."

Jake chuckled, and went to the door, turning as he grabbed the knob. "Jen, I don't want you foregoing a life because of this job. You need to find a happy medium between your job and your personal life. It would be good to start now, before you get in a rut." He turned to walk out the door. "I'll meet you downstairs in an hour."

Jen knew he was right. She didn't want her job to run her life. But, first things first. This cartel was getting broken up and the bad guys put in jail. Then she could worry about her personal life. She needed to finish her online courses, then maybe she could meet someone nice, and tough. She shook her head and headed for the shower. No problem, right? Someone who would work by her side maybe? Right! No problem!

Jen felt better after her shower. She walked down to the lobby, where Jake was already waiting. She smiled, and walked over to where he was sitting. "Hey Dad. I'm ready for our visit with Mom. Can we stop by a store and buy some flowers to put on her grave first?"

"Sure thing. Let's grab our rental car and get started."

After stopping to get flowers, Jake drove to the cemetery and pulled up to the parking area. They got out and looked around at the beautiful cemetery where Sara lay. Jake breathed deeply, enjoying the many flowers on the various graves. "It really is beautiful here. I'm so glad that we decided to lay Sara to rest in this area. Everything is very well kept. Just look at the freshly mowed grass, and the flowers that people have brought to their loved ones. You can see that people care about how this cemetery looks."

"I agree. Let's go find Mom's grave. I'm sure that the flowers that I brought the last time I was here are brown and shriveled up by now. The caretaker probably removed them. I feel bad that Mom doesn't have someone visiting her daily. Well, we're here now."

They walked silently towards the area of Sara's grave, Jenny gripping the bouquet of flowers tightly with one hand, while she gripped her dad's hand with the other. When they got closer to Sara's grave, they were shocked at what they saw. Laying on the mound of dirt where Sara lay, were several yellow roses. Jake and Jen stopped when they got to the headstone that had Sara's name engraved on it. Jenny looked around, confused. "What the heck? Dad, who would be coming here and putting flowers on Mom's grave like that? Has Tony, or one of your brothers, been here?"

"Not that I know of. It could be Tony, or maybe even just some passer by who felt bad that her grave was bare. Whoever it is, they certainly like yellow roses. There has to be two or three dozen here. They're beautiful."

Jen carefully laid the flowers they had bought down on the mound of dirt that was covered with the roses. "They are beautiful, but I have a feeling that this is more than just some stranger that happened to be walking by. Whoever this is, they obviously cared about Mom. Does anyone come to mind?"

"No, you forget, your mom and I didn't talk much towards the end. She could have met someone. You would know better than me about that." Jake couldn't help but feel a twang of jealousy, even now, after all of the years that they were apart. He always loved Sara. Never stopped loving her, and he thought she felt the same.

Jenny broke into his thoughts. "She never had anyone that she was close to. All she ever did was work, and take care of me, and Ann, of course. No men in her life, if that's what you're thinking. I think that she always loved you Dad. No one else. But, obviously someone cared about her deeply. Let's go find the caretaker here and see if he knows anything."

"Good idea. He may be able to tell us who has been visiting Sara."

It took them awhile to track down the caretaker. When they caught up with him, they introduced themselves. Jake held out his hand. The man shook it, and introduced himself as Cal.

Jake asked Cal about the flowers, and the man rubbed his grizzled beard. "Oh yes. I know the grave you're talking about. Not too many people come around every day like that. This guy never misses a day. In fact, you just missed him."

Jake was shocked. "What can you tell me about this guy? Did he give you a name? Anything like that? It's just that we only know a handful of people who would go to this much trouble, and they don't live around Los Angeles anymore."

"Hmmm…Well, he didn't give me a name. He never wanted to be bothered at all. The guy got downright nasty when I tried to talk to him. So I just left him to his business. I never really approached him after that one time. Always saw him from a distance though. He is a small guy, looked to be in his sixties maybe? That's about all I can tell you. Maybe she had a secret admirer."

"Maybe so. Well, thank you for your time Cal."

After talking to Cal, Jen and Jake walked back to Sara's grave. They sat silently for awhile, each of them thinking about Sara. When Jen stood, Jake did the same. "Well, it looks like Mom is in good hands here. We don't have to worry about her grave being taken care of at least. I am curious though, who this secret admirer is. Oh well, I guess it isn't a big deal, as long as he doesn't bother anyone."

Jen walked to the beautiful marble tombstone that they had made for her mom. She started cleaning off some of the dirt and dust, when she noticed something lying on the ground by the tombstone. It was glittering in the sunlight, and Jen reached down to pick it up. She sucked in a breath. "Dad, this is Mom's ring. She never took it off. Not even to shower or bathe. She told me that you gave it to her when you were in high school. It meant a lot to her. How did it get here? I thought it was buried with her."

Jake grabbed the ring out of Jen's hand. "This is the ring I gave to her before we were actually engaged. It was a promise ring. I told your mom that this would tie us together until we were actually married. I promised my love to her that day." Jake's voice faltered a little at the end of his sentence. "I honestly don't know if it was buried with her. I think it was though. I know that I saw it on her finger at the funeral home when we had her service. Whether it was actually buried with her though, I couldn't say for sure." Jake palmed the ring, turning it over and over. Looking closely at it. "This is the ring alright. It's very odd that it would be here. It's not like it's worth a lot of money, just sentimental value. But, how did it get here when it should have been with her? This is strange Jenny. Something isn't right here."

"I agree. I think that whoever has been putting flowers on Mom's grave is the same person who put this ring here. I want to know who it is, and how he got this ring off her finger. That will have to wait though. We have to put an end to this cartel first. Then, I'm sticking around LA until I figure this mystery out."

"I'm with you on this one. We need to find out why someone felt the need to take this ring, and then leave it here like that. Seems odd to me. Well, now what should we do for the rest of the day?"

"Well, Uncle Tony invited us to supper. We'll do that, and I want to ask him if he happened to come here and put flowers on the grave. I know it wasn't him, but maybe he has an idea." Jen laid her hand on the tombstone. "Bye Mom. I love you."

When they asked Tony about the flowers later on that night, he said that it wasn't him. He did notice the flowers though, when he visited the grave. "I didn't think much of it really. I guess I just figured that it was a stranger that felt bad about the bare gravesite. But this ring is interesting. Why would someone do that?" Tony shivered a little. "Do you think that they nabbed it from the body at the funeral? I ask it again. Who would do that?"

"I don't know, but I am going to find out. After this case with the cartel is over, I want to meet this secret admirer."

Jake agreed with Jen. "Yes, we will find out, but first things first. Tony, I know it hasn't been more than a couple hours, but, have you found anything out that will help us with our case?"

"Not yet. I put out a few feelers though. I think I'll hear something soon. In the meantime, I want you to come into the precinct tomorrow, I have something else to show you. I found some suspicious deaths that may be connected to your case. Cop suicides, or so they say. I think you're right, these so called suicides were probably murders. I think that this cartel just got rid of people after they were done with them. Whoever this is that's running the show is ruthless. Maybe even a little crazy. We need to put a stop to it, and fast."

The rest of the meal was spent catching up with each other's lives. No more shop talk, just an enjoyable meal between friends. Jake was glad to see Tony. He hadn't realized how long it had been since he had seen him. He decided then and there, that he was going to try and keep in touch with Tony from here on out. He missed his old friend.

They parted ways, and Jake and Jen headed back to the hotel. Jen was surprised at how tired she was after the long day. She said goodnight to Jake, and headed to bed. Jen had many thoughts going through her head as she lay there. Thoughts of her mom, the secret admirer, and most of all, the connection with this cartel with Los Angeles. *Could my Mom's death be connected somehow with all of this? After all, she died in a very similar way to Cara. That couldn't be though. Billy was killed, she saw it with her own eyes. He was the one who killed her mom. Billy was jealous of her life with their father, so he targeted her, killing the others along the way to appease his mother.* Jen suddenly sat straight up in bed. "Wait a minute! I almost spaced out the fact that Kurt Rommel is the one who has been helping us along the way. He was married to Liz Rommel, who was the driving force behind her son Billy killing those people. Could that be the connection? What are we missing?"

Jen laid back down on the bed, all kinds of things running through her head. She fell into a restless sleep. Many dreams plagued her during the night. She woke to a very vivid dream about the time that Ann and her had spent in that old house when Billy kidnapped them. She could still feel the fear. Jen could see them huddled in the middle of the floor, waiting for Billy's next move. Jen was drenched in sweat when the sun began to rise. She tried to get back to sleep, but the dreams just kept coming, one after the other. *Could this be a sign from Kurt? Or from Sara herself? What does this mean?* She dragged herself out of bed. She wasn't going to get any more sleep now. "Might as well get up. Kurt, if you're around, I just want to say one thing. If you want to tell me something, just say it. This messing with my mind has got to stop. I don't know what you're trying to tell me." She shook her head. "Now I'm talking to myself. Maybe I'm going crazy."

Jen took a shower, thinking about what she had dreamt. She couldn't shake the feeling that she was dreaming about this for a reason. Did something happen during that time that she had spaced out? She hated to involve Ann in this, but it may be necessary. She needed to remember everything that happened during that time. With Ann's help, she would remember, and it may give them the push they need to solve this case. Jen got out of the shower and dressed. She had a very positive feeling about all of this. But, before she called Ann, she needed to tell Jake about her dreams.

"Dad, I really think that I am forgetting something that happened during our captivity that is important. I don't know why, but I just do. What do you think? Is it worth dredging up all of that with Ann? I hate to do that. I know what she went through, I was there. Well? What do you think?"

Jake listened to Jen carefully, and felt her excitement about this dream. He held her hands in his and looked her in the eye when he replied. "Jen, these dreams you had may be just something brought about by being back here, visiting your mom, and all of the mystery surrounding this case. It may be nothing, but if you think there is something to it, then go for it. Call Ann, and try and figure out what it's all about. I think she can handle it. She has Sam with her now. Let's call her right now, and figure out if we need to run with it, or forget about it."

Jen knew that Ann would be cleaning up after breakfast, but she needed to talk to her, and she called her cell phone. Ann answered right away, she always did. "Jenny! How is LA? Have you found anything out? I miss you guys."

Jen filled Ann in on the flowers at the cemetery, and told her about finding the ring. Ann was shocked. "How could that ring be there? I know that I put it on Sara's finger myself. Who would have taken it?"

"I don't know, but there's something else. Ann, I had a dream last night about the time that we spent in that old house when we were kidnapped by Billy. I hate to even bring this up, but I need your help. Can you remember anything at all that would be important to this case? It would be impossible for Billy or Liz Rommel to be involved in this case. I can't remember anything that happened during that time that involved a cartel. Billy was alone whenever we saw him. I don't know, maybe it's nothing."

Ann sat down at the kitchen table, sighing. "Oh man. I haven't thought about that in a while. I'm trying to forget about all of that. Okay, let's start at the beginning. We went shopping, got in the car, and then all hell broke loose. He had us drugged most of the time, until we figured out what he was doing, and stopped eating, as I recall. All I remember, is huddling together in that room, praying for Jake and Sam to find us. We could hear Billy talking to himself off and on, but other than that, I don't think anything that happened there connects to a drug ring."

Jen huffed out a breath. "That's what I thought too. I have been racking my brain since I woke up this morning. I hated to bring back all of the bad memories.....wait a minute. Did you just say that you remember Billy talking to himself? I had forgotten all about that. Ann, remember the first time we heard him doing that? We actually thought that someone else was there with him, but we never saw anyone. Do you think that someone else was actually there?" Jen looked up at Jake, who was listening to their conversation. He shrugged, but was very interested in the way this was going.

"You know what? There very well could have been someone else there. We always thought that we heard Billy talking to someone else. Listen, I have to go. You two be careful. If there was someone else involved in our kidnapping, he, or she, may still be out there."

Jen hung up her phone and grinned at Jake. "Dad, we're on to something here, I just know it! Dad, we have to go back to that house." She jumped up, grabbing Jake by the hand.

"Wait a minute Jen. Are you sure that you want to go back out there? Maybe it's not even there anymore."

"If someone else was in on the kidnapping with Billy, there may be a sign of it out there. Maybe even a fingerprint, or some DNA or something. We need to go out there."

"Okay, but let me call Tony and let him know what we're doing. If something happens, I want someone to know where we are at. You know, that house and grounds would make for a good headquarters for this drug ring. You may be on to something here Jen. We need to be cautious, but I'm with you, we need to go out there."

After calling Tony, Jake and Jen got in their rental car and drove the lonely isolated road out to the house where Jen and Ann were held. Jen couldn't help but shiver, as they drove the same road that Ann had been forced to drive not that long ago. The winding, lonely, road hadn't changed any. It didn't look like anyone had driven on it lately, but that didn't mean that no one had been out here. There were alternative routes that an ATV could take to get to the property.

Jen found herself slouching down in her seat as they approached the gate to the property. She sat up straighter in her seat, not wanting to let the oppression envelop her. Too many horrible memories were coming to her as they got closer to the house. She was having a harder time than she thought she would. Jen shook it off, as they drove closer. The house was still there. It didn't look much different than it did then. What was left of the crime scene tape was fluttering in the wind. Jake looked at Jen before opening his door.

"Are you sure that you want to do this? I can get Tony to come out here with me. You don't have to go in there."

"Yes I do, Dad. This has been coming for awhile now. I need to put this to rest. I didn't realize that I had been holding so much inside, I need to let it go. Come on, let's go inside."

Jake grabbed Jen by the arm as they walked to the house. The door creaked when they opened it, the same way it did before. When they stepped into the house, Jen almost went to her knees, when she looked at the basement door, standing open. They walked around, looking for any signs of occupancy.

Of course, nothing was there. No one had been there since Billy died. The mice had taken over the house. They could here them shuffling around in the walls and cupboards. Jenny shivered again. "Dad, let's go upstairs, I know someone was here with Billy. Maybe something was left there to give us a clue."

They were disappointed when they left the old house. There was nothing there that showed anyone else had been there. Definitely not a headquarters for a drug ring. Jake knew that it was a long shot anyway. No drug lord in his right mind would stay out here. It was too old and isolated. They needed to be in the center of things. Hiding in plain sight, so to speak. Jen was a little pale when they started back to the city. Jake was worried about her.

"Are you okay?"

"Yeah, I'm fine, just bummed out. I know that someone else was with Billy. Well, I didn't actually see anyone, but Billy was talking to someone. And, wouldn't he have needed some help in taking Ann and I down the stairs when he drugged us? I really am convinced that someone else was there. I don't know if it has anything to do with this case we are working, but I have a feeling it all connects somehow."

"Well, it definitely could be related to Billy. After all, Liz Rommel was the instigator in the murders he committed, and Kurt was her husband after all. I wish that we could get ahold of Tom. I think that he could shed some light on all of this. Let's head on back to the hotel for some lunch, and go over what we have."

Jake looked in his rear view mirror as he turned onto the street. A black sedan was behind them. Nothing unusual there, but Jake was always on the lookout for cars like this. After all, they had been followed before. "Jen, don't turn around, but there is a black car behind us. Keep watching behind us, and see if they keep following. I may just be paranoid, but let's call it being cautious."

Jake turned on his blinker and turned again. The car followed about two car lengths behind. Jake turned again. So did the black car. They were definitely being followed. "Hang on. I'm going to lose this bastard."

• • •

His phone rang just as he was leaving the office. He thought about not answering it. He wasn't in the mood to talk to anyone. It kept ringing. He answered abruptly. "What is it!"

"Boss, we have a situation. I need to talk to you about it."

"Well, go ahead and talk! I want to know right now. What kind of a screw up have you done now?"

"We didn't screw up. I had someone following the Long's all day. Anyway, I wanted to let you know that Long and his daughter were out at the house today. Don't ask me why, there is nothing there. I made sure of it. I think they may be getting a little too close. What do you want me to do?"

The boss plopped down on his chair, anger overwhelming him. He was angrier than he had ever been. "I want Long dead! That's what I want you to do about this. Do not harm the girl, I have other plans for her. If I couldn't have her mother, then I will have her, do you understand?"

He reached over and pulled the yellow rose from the vase on his desk. "Billy screwed me over by killing Sara, I won't have it happen again. I want Long dead, and I want the girl brought to me. Get it done, and make sure you find someone you can absolutely trust to do it. I don't want anymore screw ups." He slammed his phone down on the desk, a look of pure evil on his face.

• • •

<h1 style="text-align:center">••• 22 •••</h1>

TED HUNG UP from the dreaded phone call to his boss. He turned to his partner. "This guy is out of control. He's losing it completely. He wants us to get rid of Jake Long. His obsession with Sara Long almost brought us down once before, now he is obsessing over the daughter. Good grief, he is old enough to be her grandfather."

The man sitting next to him tried to hold in his shock at this revelation. Dan Crowley had to think fast. He was good at that. "Listen, if he wants Long dead, then that's what we'll do. I have done a lot of hits before, and I can take care of one dumb Private Eye. Let me take care of Long, and I'll nab the daughter later on. It will satisfy the boss, and maybe he will start taking care of business instead of focusing on the Longs. I can handle this, let me prove my loyalty."

Ted sat back in his seat and thought long and hard about what Crowley was saying. "Perhaps it is time for you to do just that. Okay, listen, make this go away. If you screw this up, it's all on you. I won't stand behind you on this if you get caught. You will be on your own, understand?"

"I understand. Don't worry, I won't mess it up. I know what I'm doing. When do you want this done?"

"The sooner the better. I don't want to hear from you until this is done, and I'm going to need proof of death to show the boss."

"No problem." Dan opened the car door and stepped out into the warm California air. He had the perfect plan for this.

Jake's phone rang when he got up to his room. It was Dan Crowley, aka Tom. "It's about time you called me back. Can you talk freely?"

"For the time being. Listen, Jake, we need to meet. Where is a good spot that we could meet where no one will see us together? It's imperative that no one sees us."

"We could meet at the docks at Downtown Harbor. It's busy enough that no one will care if we're there or not. I was being followed earlier, but I will make sure no one follows me there. We'll meet you at ten o'clock tonight."

"I'll be there."

Jake hung up and quickly dialed Jenny's number. He was short and to the point. "Jen, Tom just called. We are meeting him at the docks at ten." He looked at his watch. "That's two hours away. I'm going to go down there and do some surveillance. I don't want anyone to recognize us down there. I'll be back in a couple of hours."

"Do you know what he wants to meet us about?"

"No, but it must be important for him to break protocol like this. I'll see you later."

"I'll be ready."

Nothing looked out of place at the docks. Jake slowly walked around, looking every bit the tourist. He fit right in. His light green T-shirt blended in with the other brightly colored shirts on the people around him. The camera around his neck was an added plus. Even if someone followed him here, they wouldn't think anything of it, but Jake was sure that he hadn't been followed. This place was a perfect meeting place. No one knew them here, he was sure of it.

By the time Jake got back to the hotel, Jen was ready to go. It was nine-thirty. Just enough time to get back to the docks.

They pulled into the parking lot and slid in beside a compact car. Jake and Jen got out of their car and started browsing around. Looking up now and then to make sure there was no one interested in what they were doing. There were still a few people roaming around the area, even at this hour, which was a good thing.

Jake looked over at a bench by the water, and noticed a man sitting there. He thought it could be Tom, but wasn't sure. He looked a little different than when they met Dan Crowley at the DEA offices, but Jake was pretty sure that it was the same man.

Jake and Jen moseyed over and sat down on the bench. The man looked up at them, and Jake knew it was his brother. "Are we alone?"

Tom looked around. "Yes, but I don't want to risk being overheard. Let's go to your car, we can talk there."

The three of them walked to the parking lot, and Jenny got in the back seat, letting the two men sit up front. Jake started the conversion. "Okay, why all the subterfuge? Everyone knows that we know each other from our meeting at the DEA offices. What's going on Tom?"

"It's a long story, but I had to think fast today, and I got a brainstorm."

"Oh boy. We all know what happens when you get your brainstorms. What is it this time?"

Tom had to laugh. "This one is a matter of life and death, literally. YOUR life and death, specifically."

Okay, Jake hadn't seen that one coming. "What are you talking about? Who would want me dead? Strike that, I guess there are a few people who would want me dead. What's your plan?"

Jen drew in a breath from the back seat, and the men turned to see her face turning white.

"Someone wants to kill Dad? Who?"

"It's the boss of this cartel. I'm deep undercover and managed to gain the trust of the second in command. I don't know what you two have been up to, but you've angered the man in charge. He wants Jake taken care of, and he wants Jen kidnapped later on. That's all I know for now. Lucky for you, I was the one that was with him at the time of the order to kill you. I managed to convince him that I could do it. Kill you and not leave a trace, then nab Jen and deliver her to the boss. I'm not sure what's up with him, but it seems he has some issues with you Jake. The second in command didn't give me any details, but it sounded like the boss wants Jen for himself, and he wants you out of the way."

Jake sat up straighter. "Okay, this boss is pissing me off now. No one is taking Jenny. I tried to call you before, but you didn't answer your phone. Jen and I have been digging into these so called cop suicides, and found a few that weren't suicides at all. We also found some papers that Phil had hidden away in the cabin at the ranch. It's a long story, but basically, he had been doing some work on his own and it led us back to Los Angeles. I think the base of operations is here in LA. Now, after seeing that you're here, I'm sure of it. Tom, I think that this goes all the way back to Joe and Ali Olsen's death. I can't get into it right now, but suffice it to say, a little birdie told Jen as much. If that's the case, and if this boss wants me dead, we must be getting close. Too close. Tell me you have a plan."

Tom grinned. "I do. This is what's going to happen. You are going to go back out to that old house alone, without Jen. Let's just say that you needed to check something out on your own. I'm going to be there waiting for you. Let me put it this way. You won't be coming back to your daughter. The boss wants proof of death, so I will take a picture of you laying in the hole I am going to dig out in the forest for your body. Far enough away that no one will find you. After the boss is satisfied that you're dead, I'm hoping he settles down a little, and I won't actually have to kidnap Jenny. But we'll cross that bridge when we come to it. If things go as planned, I can take this cartel down. Starting right at the top. I'm sure he will be pleased with my job performance, and I'll be in like Flynn. What do you think?"

"Well, it's a good plan, but what am I suppose to do after I'm dead? I want in on taking this guy down. I'm not going to just sit back and let you handle all of this. Not that I don't trust you. Besides that, who is going to take care of Jen?"

"I have a safe house set up for you to reside in while I figure out what to do next. When it's time, I'll call you, and we can take this jerk down together. It's not the best plan, but it's the best I could come up with on such short notice. You need to get Tony in on this. He can take care of Jen."

"Okay, I'm in. It sounds like this could all be coming to a head soon. I had better go and get prepared to die, and call Tony. Call me when you get this all set up."

Tom grabbed the door handle. He looked back at Jen. "You need to trust me okay. I won't let anything happen to you or your dad. You need to act like the grieving daughter okay? Make it look realistic. I hate to do this to Sam and Ann but we have no choice. Sam is going to be pissed, but he'll get over it. The fewer people that are in on our plan the better. I'll be in touch." With that, he was gone.

Jake and Jen just sat there for a minute, taking in all of these new developments. Jake looked back at his daughter. "Listen, I'm sure that Tom knows what he's doing. This will all go like clockwork, and then we can put an exclamation point on all of this. I think that we are going to answer a lot of questions by the time we're done."

Jen just nodded, and opened her car door, getting back in the front seat. She was overly quiet on the way back to the hotel, and Jake just let her be. She needed to absorb all of this. It was something that she had never had to deal with. All of the subterfuge, the acting she'll have to do, dealing with Sam and Ann. Jake didn't blame her for being doubtful, hell, he was too. Even the best laid plans can go awry. He knew that better than anyone.

Jake wanted to get her mind off of it for tonight, and he knew just what to do. "How would you like to go grab some ice cream, and then visit your mom's grave? The cemetery is on the way to the ice cream parlor that we used to go to when we lived here. What do you say?"

"That sounds good. It may be the last time we do anything together." Her wry comment wasn't lost on Jake.

"Maybe, for awhile, but we have a lot of things we are going to accomplish after this. It's going to be fine, I promise."

Jen just nodded, and looked straight ahead. Jake knew that she was uncomfortable with all of this, but she would get over that when the time came. She would nail the grieving daughter thing, he knew that.

Jen felt better after ice cream. This place brought back a few memories, good memories. It helped her cope with this elaborate scam that they were going to attempt. She was more herself when they pulled up to the cemetery. It was very dark, and somewhat creepy, here at night. "Um, maybe we should come back during the day Dad. This is kind of creepy."

Jake threw his head back and laughed. "This coming from the girl who talks to ghosts! You can hold my hand if you're scared." He knew that comment would get Jen's hackles up.

"I can walk on my own, thank you very much."

She opened her door and started marching towards Sara's grave. Jen slowed a little when Sara's gravesite came into view. She turned to her dad, who was trotting to catch up to her. Putting her fingers to her lips, she motioned to him to stop. Jake came to an abrupt halt, and looked to where Jen was pointing. There, standing at Sara's grave, was a lone figure of a man. His shoulders were hunched, and he was laying something on the ground. A yellow rose. It was the stranger that had been visiting Sara's grave all of this time. Jake and Jen crept closer, trying to get a closer look at the man. As they approached, all they could make out was a silhouette. The man had his face covered with the collar on his jacket, and was wearing a derby hat, all black. He blended in quite well. Jake could tell that he didn't want to be seen.

As they approached, Jake made a rookie mistake. He wasn't watching where he was walking, and stepped on a branch. It cracked loudly. The man suddenly looked up. His face was in shadows, so Jake couldn't make out who it was. The man turned and started running for the nearby trees. Jake and Jen took chase, trying to make up for the head start he had. By the time they got to the edge of the trees, the man was nowhere to be seen.

Breathing heavily, Jake and Jen gave up the chase. "I'm not going to run after someone who can hide in there with a weapon. Let's go back to the gravesite and see what he left there."

Jen agreed, and took one last look at where the man had run to. "We almost had him Dad. We were so close."

"I know, but I think we have him running scared now that he has been seen. We'll see what happens next."

When they got back to the grave, the only thing that they saw were the yellow roses. Evidently, the man had placed another rose on the grave. There was no way of knowing which one, they just blended together.

Jen sighed. "Well, so much for that. I wonder who he is Dad? Why would he run from us like that if he has nothing to hide?"

"Obviously he doesn't want his identity known. Little does he know, that's what we do. I think we should stake out the cemetery and find out who this is. It bothers me that someone would be so mysterious about this. If Sara met someone after we split up, it's all water under the bridge now. It wouldn't bother me a bit. Well, scratch that, I still loved Sara, but why wouldn't he just talk to us?"

● ● ●

The man was breathing heavily. That was too close. He was being careless, going to the cemetery like that. He should have known that the Longs may show up there. But he couldn't help himself. He just had to visit her. He couldn't help it. He needed to be close to Sara, and that was the only way he could. He was so tired. He wasn't sure that he could go on like this. Was it all worth it in the end? Maybe he should just join his love in the afterlife. Then, they would be together forever, just like he wanted. He shook off the feelings of doom. He was too smart for that. The boss stood up straighter now, a plan forming in his mind. Jake Long had to die, and die he would…soon.

● ● ●

Jen fell into a fitful sleep that night. She knew that usually meant that someone was going to visit her. It was like her brain was willing these spirits to come to her at certain times. Well, they needed all the help they could get on this one. Jenny hoped that they could solve this case before something bad happened. She didn't feel comfortable about Tom's idea to *kill* Jake, but her dad and uncle seemed to know what they were doing.

Just like clockwork, as soon as she started to fall into a deep sleep, Jen felt a presence. It was Kurt Rommel. Jenny knew it was him. Rommel was growing stronger too, his shape was more pronounced now, and Jenny could hear him better. He was alone, no sign of her mother.

"What is it? What do you have to tell me?"

*Jenny, you are getting very close now. Soon, everything is going to come to a head. The person that you are looking for is starting to feel the end coming too. Keep pushing, don't stop. Let your dad do what he thinks is right. I promise if you stay in Los Angeles, and keep digging into the deaths of these police officers, you are going to put this to bed for good. I wish I could just tell you who this person is, but they won't allow it. Even in the afterlife, there are people in charge that we have to answer to. I can only give you hints now and then, and you have to figure it out from there. One thing that I can say is this. Your dad knows this person, he only met him briefly, but he will know him when he sees him. That's all I can say for now.*

Jen could hear him a lot better now. Rommel must be getting stronger. He faded away then. Jenny frowned, grabbing her notebook, and writing down everything he said. "Dad knows this guy? How could he know him and not figure out who it is? Things just got even more interesting."

••• *23* •••

THE NEXT MORNING, as Jenny was sharing with Jake what had transpired the night before with Kurt Rommel, Jake's phone rang. Jake looked at the caller ID. "It's Tom." He answered the same way he always did. "Yeah, Long here."

"Jake, this is Dan Crowley. I was wondering if you could meet me out at the old farmstead where Jenny and Ann were kept. Something has come up, and I need to show you something. And Jake, come alone. I don't think Jenny needs to see this."

He hung up, looking at Jen. "It's time. I'm afraid our staking out the cemetery, and looking into more deaths of cops, will have to wait. I have a date with death."

"Dad, don't say it like that. I don't like this at all. What if something goes wrong? What if someone decides to come along with Tom? I really think that I should go with you."

Jake reached out and grabbed Jenny's hands. "No, we have to make this look real. When the time is right, I will 'come back to life,' but until then you need to take care of a few things. You heard Rommel, we are getting close. This boss is losing it. If he is going to the trouble of getting rid of me, he is planning to kidnap you next. You need to watch your back, and don't worry about me. I will be working behind the scenes. Hopefully not for too long."

"Fine, I'll go along with this for now. But the moment I think something is going sideways, I'm stepping in."

"Fair enough. Now, let's get this show on the road."

Jake got prepared to *die*. He had to admit, it felt weird. Not too many people get to say that. He kissed Jenny good-bye, and started his journey towards death.

Pulling up to the old house, Jake had to shake off the feeling of dread that was threatening to overtake him. *Stop it Long, this isn't for real. Tom has thought this all through. His plan is fool proof.* He walked towards the house, looking around to make sure no one was following him. He was alone, as far as he could tell. Jake couldn't even tell if Tom was there yet.

Taking a deep breath, he entered the old house. He was kind of startled by the sight of a man standing in the shadows. He breathed a sigh of relief when Tom emerged, grinning. "Did I have you worried Jake? Were you scared?"

"Knock it off Tom! It's not every day a man walks into a house knowing he is going to die. Now shut up and tell me what your plan is from here."

"Okay, but I couldn't help but give you a little grief." All business now, Tom laid out his carefully laid plan. "First off, you need to cover yourself with this fake blood. I'm going to shoot you in the head, so there will be a lot of blood. I'm going to take a picture of you lying in a pool of blood on the floor. Then, we are going to go on out to the stand of trees behind the house, where I have a grave already dug. You are going to lie down in it, and I'll take another picture of that. That's all the proof of death this crazy man needs. Listen, I haven't met him yet, so I don't have a name, but I can tell you one thing. The second in command is none other than the head of the DEA."

Jake sucked in a breath. "No way! Holy cow, if this guy has enough power over the head of the DEA to get him to do his dirty work, who knows how deep this goes."

"Yes, but greed definitely is a factor. They are making a lot of money with this gig. With money, brings power. It also brings more greed, and more enemies. We need to be careful here. If they catch even the slightest wind that this is a scam, we're done for. I brought a disguise for you to wear when you have to leave the safe house, but I want you to stay in the house if you can. I brought some supplies too, so you're good to go. Alright, let's get this party started."

Everything went exactly as planned. Tom took the necessary steps to make sure his boss thought that Jake was dead. He didn't like it. It felt weird, *killing* his brother, even though it wasn't real. Everything looked good when he met with Ted that night.

Ted looked at the photos, nodding with satisfaction. "This is good Crowley, real good. The boss will be happy. You did good."

"I told you I was thorough, and I was careful. No one will find the body, I made sure of it. That daughter of his will be distraught when she finds out her dad is missing. You know she'll call in the cavalry. The other brother will come running. Are you sure that's wise? Maybe we should have let them find the body, so they know that he is dead."

"No, this is just how the boss wanted it done. He has a plan for the girl. It makes me shiver thinking about it, but that's none of my business, nor is it yours. You just keep doing your job, and you'll keep rising in the ranks. That's what you want, right Crowley?"

"Definitely. I can be an asset to this organization. I think I've proven myself enough already. When do I get to meet the boss?"

"Slow down Crowley. He doesn't show himself to many people. That's part of his strategy. The fewer people that see him the better. He's like a ghost." Ted threw his head back and laughed. "Like anyone actually believes in ghosts. Anyway, you lay low for awhile now. I'll show the boss these pictures, and then we'll go on with business as usual."

Tom let out the breath he had been holding. *So far, so good. If things go as planned, this boss was going to go down soon. I only hope that Jake does as he was told and stays out of sight for awhile.*

Ted was right. The boss was ecstatic. When he saw the pictures of Jake Long lying in a grave, he couldn't stop staring at it. It even gave Ted the heebie jeebies, the way he kept looking at it. "You don't know how long I've waited for this moment. That damn Billy took Sara away from me, and Long took Ann and Jenny. But now, it's all coming together. I can finish what I started. It's so close now, I can taste it. Nothing is going to stop me now. I need you to report back to me in the days to come, with poor Jenny's reaction to her father going missing. Then I can step in and console the poor girl. I am sure that she will need a lot of consoling. She doesn't know me now, but she will. I have the perfect plan for running into her." He laughed hysterically at his comment. Ted couldn't see the humor, but he tried to laugh with him.

"Well, if you don't need me anymore, I will get the second part of the plan going."

The boss dismissed him with a wave, picking up the photo, looking at it again. He walked over to his safe, and put the pictures in. "Everything is going perfectly. I'm too smart for all of these people. They can't even figure out who I am. Well, I know the only one I want to get to know me is Jenny. She'll learn to love me, just like I loved her mother." He smiled, thinking to himself just what he was going to do.

When Tom came back to the hotel the next day and broke the news to Jenny, she acted appropriately. Worried about her dad when he hadn't come back to the motel the night before, Jenny looked like she had been up all night. She was beside herself with worry, and she had already called Sam, telling him what was going on. Surprisingly, Sam didn't seem that worried yet. "Listen, Jen, I'm sure your dad is fine. He probably got some lead on the case, and is so busy following it up, he forgot to call. Let's give it a couple more days before we really start to worry. I'll call Tony, just to make him aware of what is going on, if it will make you feel better."

"Yes, that would make me feel better. In the meantime, I am going to look for him. I know that we were going to stake out the cemetery, so maybe he is doing that. I will head out there, you call Tony."

Jen hung up, feeling bad for deceiving Sam this way. She knew it was necessary, but she didn't like it. She was telling him the truth though, she was going to the cemetery. If nothing else, she could talk to her mom. That always made her feel better.

The next few days were fairly quiet. Jen called Sam several times, and she also talked to Tony. Neither one of them was that worried about Jake gong missing. Jenny didn't know where he actually was, so this felt a little too real to her. She was getting antsy. Jen wanted this to come to an end, so they could stop this cartel for good. Maybe even figure out the connection with her mom and grandparents. Kurt Rommel was involved somehow, and maybe even Liz and Billy. She just couldn't quite put her finger on it.

Finally, after a week of waiting and worrying, Sam decided it was time to go to Los Angeles. Jake had never gone this long without talking to anyone before. Something was up, and he wanted to be with Jenny. She needed someone to take care of her. She was getting more frantic by the day. Ann understood, and she knew that he wanted her to stay at the ranch. Sam didn't need to have to worry about her too, and LA brought back too many bad memories for her. Sam started preparing the ranch, and the hands, for his absence, not knowing how long he would be gone. He wasn't coming home until he found his brother.

Jen was happy that Sam was coming to Los Angeles, but she knew that he, more than anyone, could read her like a book. Sam may figure out that she was hiding something. She had to be on her toes at all times.

$\bullet\ \bullet\ \bullet$

There really wasn't much going on with the case right now. It seemed that this cartel boss was laying low. Jake didn't know what he was waiting for. If he wanted to kidnap Jen, why not just do it? He had been hiding in the shadows, watching over his daughter. Nothing was going to happen to her. Jake knew that she was tough, but a person can only take so much in one lifetime. He knew that he was taking a risk, but the disguise he was wearing was good. Not even Jen recognized him. They had to figure out who this was before he made good on his promise to take Jen. Jake shook his head as he watched his daughter head into the police station. Obviously, she was going on with the investigation into the suspicious police deaths. "Good girl. Keep it up, Jen." Jake turned, and headed back to the safe house, Jen was safe for now. She could take care of herself.

$\bullet\ \bullet\ \bullet$

Jen was growing more frustrated by the day. *What is this guy waiting for? Let's get this show on the road!* She was sick of being cooped up in this hotel room every night. *I need some air, and I know just where to get it.* Jen put on a light jacket, and headed for the cemetery.

It was just getting dark when she pulled into the parking lot at the cemetery. She pulled her jacket around her, and started walking toward Sara's gravesite. As she approached, she could see a figure standing in the same spot as before. She slowed her footsteps. *This time this guy is not getting away.* She thought to herself, as she walked stealthily along. Quietly, she approached. The man raised his head, as if hearing something, then went back to what he was doing. When Jen got up to him, she could see him more clearly. She was surprised when he spoke first. "Well, it's about time that we met, Jenny." As he turned, Jen was even more surprised. She had no idea who he was. After all of this, she thought for sure that she would know him.

"You don't know me, but I know you." His voice brought chills to her.

"Why don't you just tell me who you are then?"

"All in good time, dear girl. I can tell you this though. Your dad knows me, and I knew your mother very well. We were good friends, as a matter of fact. I loved her, and she loved me."

"It's funny, she never mentioned meeting anyone to me. She told me everything."

"I met her in Portland, but we met each other briefly here in LA too. I was a customer at the diners she worked at, both here, and Portland. I was her favorite customer, and we grew very close. Would you like to go somewhere and talk? I can tell you all about it."

Jen was wary, but her curiosity got the better of her. She was hungry for the company, and the information about her mom. Besides, this guy looked fairly innocent. He wasn't very big, and his glasses made him look like he was just some friendly guy. She could see why her mom would have liked him, Sara was a friendly person. Jenny doubted that Sara would have shown him any affection though.

As they walked, Jen questioned the man some more. "So, tell me. Why the subterfuge about the flowers on her grave? Why did you run from us? If you know my dad, why run?"

"I don't know what you're talking about. This is the first time I have seen you. I certainly would have stayed and talked to Jake. That wasn't me."

Jen doubted that this guy was telling the truth, but she went along with it. "Okay, well, tell me more about how you know my mom and dad."

"All in due time Jenny, all in due time."

As they neared the cars, Jenny suddenly felt a foreboding coming over her. This didn't seem right. Just as she had that thought, the man took out a gun, and stuck it in her side.

"Now, now Jen. I don't want to hurt you, but you really must come with me now. Get in the car."

Jen froze. This was just the same as before. Except this time, she was alone. But, she was a stronger person now. She couldn't believe she let this happen. How stupid could she be? She had let her guard down for just a moment, and look what happened. Her only hope was that Jake would find out somehow that she was gone, and come looking for her again. In the meantime, she needed to keep this guy calm, and rely on her training. She could do this, she knew it, but when she saw where they were driving to, Jen froze. "Why are you taking me here? How did you know about this place?"

The man laughed. "Oh, my dear. I know more than you think I do. I will tell you everything, but for now, just relax, and you'll be okay. I won't hurt you, unlike that other lunatic who held you here."

"You knew Billy Rommel? How did you know him? Please, just tell me the truth. I promise I wont try to run. Don't do this. Don't put me in that room again."

He got a strange look on his face as he spoke. As if he wasn't even talking to her. "Now, now, I'll do what I want. I'm in control here, and you don't have anyone that will come and save you this time, I made sure of that. It's just you and me now, Jenny."

She shivered, as she heard the creak of the old door, the same sound that she had in her nightmares. Jen took a deep breath, trying to calm herself. *Think Jen. You have to get away from here! Don't let him win!* Jen tried to keep him talking, biding her time until she could make her move. "Okay, just tell me who you are. Maybe my mom talked about you. Don't you want to know about that? If she really loved you, she would have told me."

"Well, I actually knew her killer better than I knew her. That boy just wouldn't listen to me. After all I did for him. All of those murders, taking care of his mother. He was so unappreciative. I didn't realize until it was too late, that Billy was Sara's brother. Or that his mother and him wanted her dead. Believe me, that's the last thing I wanted, Sara dying. We were supposed to be together forever. Alas, we will be together again. Now, no more talking!" He grabbed Jen by the arm, and shoved her through the door of the same bedroom Ann and her had been kept in. Nothing had changed in here. Jen was feeling very alone and scared when he left her there. Jenny's only hope was Jake, Sam and Tom. Tony was aware of what they were doing, but none of them had any idea where she was. She knew her mom was watching out for her too. That's about all that kept her going over the days that followed. Jen knew that he was drugging her, but she also knew that she had to keep up her strength. She ate and drank just enough to keep going.

Jake was furious. He glared at his brother. "How could this have happened? You promised me that Jen would be safe. She's gone Tom! What happened?"

"I don't know Jake. She slipped away from the guy I had following her. She's damn good, I'll give her that. All I know is that she was going to the cemetery. Then, she just disappeared. Her car is still parked in the lot there. Nothing looks amiss, except that she is not there. I'm sorry Jake, but we will find her."

They both turned as someone knocked on the door to the safe house. Tom took out his gun, and peeked out the door. He smiled, and holstered his gun. "Oh, I forgot to tell you, I brought in the cavalry." Tom opened the door, and Sam stepped in.

"Well, look who we have here. This is what happens when I leave you two alone. Where do we start?"

Jake glared at him, and then at Tom. "Well, you know I can't do much right now, so it's up to you two. There has to be someone who knows where he took Jen. Tom, you have to try and get it out of Ted. I think he knows more about this than he is letting on."

"I agree, but I can't just start questioning him. We have to have a plan."

It just so happened that Ted inadvertently helped them out on that score. When Tom got to work the next day, Ted called him into his office. "Listen, Dan, the boss wants to meet with you. I don't really know why. He never wants to meet with the people who work for him. I think it has something to do with Jake Long, but I'm not sure. Anyway, you and I are going over there right now. I hope you're ready for this."

Tom nodded, and followed Ted out the door. His mind was working overtime now. *What on earth could the boss want? We haven't had time to formulate a plan yet.* He was really going to be tested this time. Tom hoped that his acting skills would be up to par.

Ted drove them up to a big brick building. Tom made a mental note of the roads they took. It was pretty plain where they parked. No names, no nothing on the outside of the building, except for a big steel door. There was a speaker mounted outside the door. Ted pushed a button and waited for someone from the inside to answer. It finally crackled to life. "Yes? Can I help you?"

"Tell the boss we're here." That was all that needed to be said.

Tom could hear the lock turning, and the door creaked open. A huge man stood in the doorway. "He is waiting for you."

Tom looked around the room they were in. There was nothing there. It was probably the most stark place he had ever seen. He shivered. He didn't like the looks of this place. The big man led them to another area of the building. This was totally different from the rest of the place. There was a hallway that led to offices on both sides. They stepped into an office that was decorated with some expensive looking artwork. A bespectacled man sat in an oversized office chair, looking every bit the businessman. *Wait a minute, this can't be him. This scrawny little guy is the head of a cartel that had been avoiding the law for all of these years?* Tom held back his surprised look, hoping no one noticed. They stepped into the office, and an overwhelming scent of roses overcame them. Tom had to hold back a sneeze. Looking around, Tom noticed that there were yellow roses everywhere. This guy had to be obsessed with them.

Ted cleared his throat, and nodded at Tom to sit. So far, the boss hadn't said a word. Just stared at them. Tom had to admit, he was a bit intimidating, even though he wasn't very big. Tom tried not to breathe in the smell of the roses too much. He stared back at the man in charge, waiting for him to talk. He didn't have to wait long.

"So, you're the new recruit. Ted here, tells me that he has enough on you to keep you in line. I'm counting on his being right. This isn't the norm around here. I usually like to remain more of a figurehead than my people actually seeing me in person. But, this is an exception. I understand that you took care of Jake Long?"

"Yes sir. He is no longer going to be a problem."

"Yes, I know that. You did a good job. Well, I'll get right to the point then." He scooted forward in his chair. "It's not that I don't trust Ted's judgement here, but I want to see that body for myself. I need to know for sure that Long is dead before I move on with my other plans. There can be no mistakes. Where did you bury him?"

"I took him out in the trees by the old house where I killed him. Believe me, he isn't going anywhere, and no one will find him out there. I made sure of that. You don't need to worry about anything. Did you see the pictures I took of the body?"

"Yes, I have looked at them again and again. But I want to see him in person. There will be no argument here. You will take me to the body tomorrow. That will be all." He waved his hands at them, dismissing the two men.

The big man that took him in, appeared at the doorway as if by magic. "Chester, will you please show these two out?"

Tom and Ted stood and followed the big man out of the offices, and down the hall. Tom got a glimpse of a plaque in the wall. Oakdale Psychiatric Hospital. Now why did that sound so familiar to him? He made a mental note to ask Jake about it later. A plan was forming in his mind, and if it worked, this would all be over by tomorrow.

Tom stepped through the door to the safe house. Jake was pacing back and forth, and Sam was slouched on the sofa. Jake ran towards Tom when he came in. Tom put his hands in front of him. "Whoa, hold on there. Would you settle down?"

"Settle down! How do you expect me to do that, when my daughter is missing again? I'm not going to sit around here any longer! I'm going out to find my daughter. I did it once, I can do it again."

"Okay, listen. I know it's been tough, but I think an end is in sight. Let me fill you in on what transpired today. I think you'll find it very interesting."

After Tom got Jake settled down, he told them about Ted telling him that the boss wanted to meet him.

Jake was shocked. "So you met the guy? Tell us who it is."

"I didn't get his name, but I did get a few clues I wanted to share with you. We drove up to a brick building, there wasn't any words anywhere that I could see. Just a door with a speaker on the outside of it. We walked up to it and Ted pushed a button to gain entrance. A big, burly guy came to the door. He was huge! Anyway, he took us back to some offices, where we met with the man. He was just this skinny, small guy with glasses. I never would have picked him out to be a drug lord. But he had a vibe about him. He really gave me the creeps. And his office was full of yellow roses. I found that odd too."

Jake interrupted him. "Did you say yellow roses?"

"Yes, yellow roses, why?"

"Okay, this may be nothing, but when Jenny and I went to Sara's grave, it was covered in yellow roses. The caretaker said that someone brought one out every day while visiting the grave. I don't believe it's a coincidence that this guy loves yellow roses and there were yellow roses on Sara's grave. This is really getting interesting. Go on, is there anything else you noticed?"

"If you would let me finish, I'll tell you. This is where it gets interesting, and I wanted to ask you about it. I saw a plaque on the wall that said Oakdale Psychiatric Hospital. This guy is using a hospital for his cover. Do you believe that?"

Jake sucked in a breath. "Are you sure? That's where you were at?" He looked from Sam to Tom, a completely incredulous look on his face. "Tell me more about this place. Did you see any names?"

"The only name I heard was Chester, that's the guard that accompanied us to the office. I never got a name of the boss. He did all of the talking."

"Oh my God! Do you realize where you were at? That was the scene of one of the murders that Billy committed. Liz Rommel was living in that hospital. This is all coming together now. I think I know who this guy is, and when I tell you his name, you will get it. Corbin Sims is the director of that hospital."

There was a dramatic pause, before Jake saw the looks of disbelief coming over his brother's faces. Sam looked at Tom, and they said in unison. "Corbin Sims?"

"Yes, as in CS. The CS Group. How could we have missed that? I never in a million years thought that someone would name a cartel from his own initials. Now I know why Rommel was telling Jen that this was all related to Sara and her family. I don't have all of the puzzle put together yet, but I think Sims had something to do with all of these deaths. But he is too young for Joe and Ali's murders. He had to have taken over the cartel from a family member, maybe his dad or something. I also think that I know where Jenny is. That same old house that Billy had kept her and Ann." Jake grabbed his gun and jacket. "Come on. We are going to get Jenny right now."

Tom grabbed his arm to stop him from going out the door. "Hold on Jake. We need a plan here. If we go barging in there, we are going to lose Sims for good. He'll go underground for sure. We have to take him down, and save Jenny, and I have a plan."

Jake reluctantly agreed, and the three men sat with their heads together all night, formulating a plan. It was a good one, Jake only hoped that Jenny could hold on until they got her out of there.

"One more night Jen. The cavalry is coming to the rescue tomorrow."

• • •

Jenny couldn't sleep. The drugs that he had been giving her were making her so tired, but she was fighting sleep. She looked out of the window that was covered with bars. The moon was bright in the sky. "Mommy, if you can hear me. Would you please come to me now? I don't want to be alone right now. I need you okay? I need you." For the first time since this madman took her, Jenny broke down and cried. Her mom never showed up, and neither did anyone else. She was all alone.

• • •

The next morning, Jake was up at the crack of dawn, preparing for the plan. His brothers came out of their rooms looking like they were all business. Jake didn't waste any time. "Okay, what time is all of this going down? Have you heard from Ted?"

Tom grabbed his cell and looked at it. "No texts yet. I'm sure it will be later this morning. Sims didn't look like a morning guy."

"From what I remember of him, it didn't look like he ever left the office. I still can't believe it. All these years, and right under our noses, he has been running this cartel. How could I have missed the signs? I guess I was too caught up in the murders to think of anything else. I aim to get some much needed answers to my questions from this guy before I blow him away."

Tom was taken aback by Jake's comment. "Wait a minute. You are not going into this with that attitude. Jake, for your daughter's sake, you need to get your head together. If you can't, then this plan is out the door. I can take care of it myself."

Jake took a deep breath, running his hands through his hair. "I know, and I won't shoot him unless I have to. I guess I'm just a little frustrated."

Tom's phone rang. "Yes, Crowley here. Ted. Okay, what time? I'll be there." Tom hung up and looked at his brothers. "It's show time. Jake you head out there first, and listen, no going into the house. I know our main plan is to get Jenny to safety, but I want this guy too. Go out to where I told you. You'll be able to see where the dirt was disturbed. Wait for my cue to show yourself. Sam, you wait on the other side of the clearing, come out only when Jake does. Now let's roll!"

They waited fifteen minutes for Jake to get into position first. Then Sam. Then, and only then, did Tom go and pick up Ted. He knew that they were meeting Sims at the house. Tom hoped that Sims didn't bring anyone else with him. He didn't think he would though. He didn't want anyone knowing what was going on out there. Tom felt the familiar butterflies that he often felt when a case was coming to a head.

They drove in silence. Tom didn't mind, he didn't want to talk anyway. He was done talking. The only talking that was going to be done now would be from Sims. They followed the winding road to the old house. There was a car sitting in the driveway, that Tom assumed was Sims. He came out of the house as they approached. "No need to come in here, take me to the body."

Tom turned toward the stand of trees to their left. The other two men followed him, as he led them to the small clearing where he had dug the grave. Sims was getting more and more excited now, a grin coming over his face. Tom was disgusted. This guy was pure evil. Tom turned and waved to a small mound of dirt. "It's right here." Then he spoke a little louder. "This is where Long is buried."

With that cue being said, both Jake and Sam walked out of the forest. You could have heard a pin drop when Sims saw Jake. Ted reached for his gun, and Tom put a fist into his face, while knocking the gun out of his hand. Ted was out cold. Sims started backing away from the men. "What's going on here? Long, you're alive? You're suppose to be dead! You're dead!" As Sims backed up, he ran into Tom. "Who are you?"

"Just call me Tom." He said as he grabbed Sims by the arms.

Corbin started to fight him, trying to wiggle out of his grasp. The small man was no match for Tom. He was in handcuffs before he even knew what was happening. Jake approached him, a look of determination on his face.

"I can't believe that you are the cause of all of this anguish Sims. You are a nobody, you always have been, and you always will be. You are going to tell me where Jenny is right now. While you're at it your going to tell me what you had to do with Sara and her death. But first, I want my daughter."

Corbin sneered at Jake. He couldn't help but glance back at the old house. "You're too late Long. Jenny is dead. I cleaned up after that idiot Billy. Did what he couldn't do."

Jake took off at a dead run towards the house. He could hear Sims laughing. "You're too late! She is already dead!"

Jake got to the house, and ran up to the door. The first place he went was the basement where he had killed Billy Rommel. She had to be there! She had to be okay! He yelled her name as he went down the stairs. Only silence greeted him. She wasn't there. He ran back up the stairs and took the stairs to the rooms two at a time. Jake was screaming Jenny's name as he ran. Still nothing. Noticing a door with a padlock on it, Jake ran straight to it. He yanked at the lock, listening for any sounds inside the room. He heard a faint voice through the thick door. "Daddy? Is that you?"

Jake hit the door hard, trying to break into the room. "Jenny! It's me, Dad. Are you okay?"

"Dad, I knew you would come. I'm fine, but get me out of here. Please!"

"I will, hang on Jen."

He ran back down the stairs and outside, where Tom and Sam were bringing the two handcuffed men to the cars. They gave Jake a puzzled look.

"Did you find her?"

Jake wanted to rub the smirk off of Corbin Sims' face with his fist. Instead, he reached into his pockets, searching for a key. There it was, in Sims' jeans pocket. Jake grabbed it without saying a word, and turned back for the house.

The key fit into the padlock, and Jake ran through the door. Jenny ran for him, and they hugged tightly. He didn't want to let her go, but he had to know if she was alright. He held Jen at arms length, and looked her up and down. "Are you okay?"

"I'm fine, just a little woozy from the drugs. Please, just get me out of here. I want to know the whole story of this guy. How did he know Mom? How did he know you?"

"I will tell you all that I know, but most of it he has to tell us. I don't know if he will or not. Some of the pieces to this puzzle have come together though. Let's get out of here, and I'll fill you in."

When Jenny and Jake got outside, Sims was just getting into the car. He looked at Jen with his expression softening. "My darling! Please know that I would never hurt you. I never hurt your mother either. That was all Billy's fault! I loved Sara! I loved her!" There was spittle coming out of Sims' mouth as he spoke. Jake took Jenny by the hand and led her to his car as Tom took the other two men into custody. The other members of this cartel were being arrested by the FBI even as they spoke. It was over, but Jake still wanted to know the rest of the story. He wondered if they ever would.

# EPILOGUE

Jenny was nervous, she didn't know if she could do this. She knew that she had to, she was the only one that Corbin Sims would talk to. He insisted on telling only her the whole story of his life, and what had led him to commit all of these crimes. She had to hear it for herself anyway.

Jake didn't like it. "I don't want you going anywhere near him Jen. He's a bad man. You're just a kid. You don't have to do this."

"I'm not a kid anymore Dad. I can handle this. I need to know why he was so obsessed with Mom. He was older than her. I need to know what led up to all of this. I know that I'll be safe. He can't hurt me anymore. I'll be okay. Besides, I know that you will be right on the other side of that glass. You will be there all the way."

"That's right, and don't you forget it." Jake paused, holding the door for her. "Well, here goes nothing."

"No Dad. Here goes everything."

Corbin Sims was squirming in his chair. "How long until she gets here? I'm not saying a word to anyone but her, do you hear me? I know you're watching Long! Do you really think that you can keep her from hearing what I have to say? I will tell her everything, only her."

Sam and Tom cringed a little, and looked up as Jake entered the room. He walked in just as Sims was spouting off. "I am going to kill him if he upsets Jenny. I swear, I will get to him somehow."

"If he tries anything, we will all be in there in a second. She's tough, Jake. She can handle herself."

They all turned as Jen walked into the room with Sims. They were silent, listening as Sims started talking softly. "Jenny, my dear. I knew that you would come. I missed you so. Have I told you that you look just like your mother? Beautiful, just beautiful."

Jenny cringed, and sat down across from him. "Thank you. Now, will you tell me what I need to know?"

"Of course. I said I would didn't I? Where do you want me to start?"

"At the beginning. How far back does this story go?"

"Oh my dear, it goes all the way back to your grandparents. You see, my father was a very powerful man. He could frighten you with one look. He did it to me many times. I was scared of him, and so was everyone else."

Jenny swallowed. "Let's get back to the story, here. How did my grandparents fit into this? Did Kurt Rommel have anything to do with it?"

"Now that's a name that I haven't heard in a while. Yes, he was one of my father's minions. Along with his wife, Liz. I'm afraid they all had to die when Joe Olsen got a little too close to figuring out who my father was. Daddy dearest was grooming my little brother to take over the business. He was the golden boy you know. He could do no wrong. Little did my father know, he was testing the product, so to speak. My brother met Jim Grant in college. They hung out a lot. Are you getting all of this Long?" Sims shouted to the two way glass. He turned back to Jen, laughing. "Anyway, my brother died in that hit and run accident. That's right, there was someone else in the car that Grant hit. It was me, I was there. I hated Jim for that. Then his dad covers for him! Do you believe that?

My father was livid! He knew that Grant covered for his son, and used that to blackmail him into doing his bidding. The drugs were coming in every day to the police station. Father had a lot of police under his command. Most of them were just greedy. Some he blackmailed into working for him. It was so easy. The drugs would come in from a bust, and the police who were trusted to take the shipment to the disposal, traded it off for bags of common sugar. No one bothered to check before the drugs were incinerated. It was all too easy really. Right under their noses. Anyway, Joe Olsen came along and tried to ruin the whole thing. Rommel was on the payroll, so he killed Olsen. He was killing two birds with one stone, so to speak. You see, Olsen was banging Rommel's wife too. My father made me go along with Rommel that night. Said I might learn something." Sims laughed at his little quip. "The two little Olsen girls were just collateral damage. After Rommel started the house on fire, he sat in his car for awhile. Surveying his handiwork I suppose. He was drinking heavily and doing drugs. My father decided that Rommel was a loose cannon so he sent someone to take care of him. They made it look like a suicide. My father was good at that. He always got away with it. His hands were clean. He did that more than once I'm afraid. Anytime anyone got the least bit carried away with the product, or too greedy, Father had them taken care of. I learned from the best you see. I took over where he left off. I always knew that I was second best in his eyes. When my brother died in that car accident, Father lost it a little bit. I had to work hard to live up to his expectations. Anyway, when I saw little Sara taking her sister's hand and leading her from that fire, I knew that I had to have her. She was so young. I knew I had to wait for her to grow up. Then she was taken from me by that idiot Jake Long. I couldn't believe it when they actually got married. How dare he! Sara was younger than me, but I knew we belonged together. I never forgave Long for that. I watched from afar for awhile. Then Billy Rommel came along. Liz ended up in my hospital. That was very convenient you see. I could manipulate Billy through her. She thought I loved her. Oh my, she was a crazy one, but it worked to my advantage. She thought that she was doing me a favor, getting Billy to kill all of those people. I just thought it was fun, getting to Long like that. It even split him and Sara up. That was even more than I could have hoped for. But then, Billy killed Sara. I must admit, I never saw that one coming. I was infuriated with them. I took care of Liz, and Billy lost it, kidnapping you and Ann. He was definitely a loose cannon. I was glad when Jake took care of him. Did my light work for me. I was devastated h n he killed Sara. I lost the love of my life. I had been befriending Sara at the restaurant where she worked. I know I could have won her love. I know I did. Have I told you that you look like her? We could have been so good together. Jake Long didn't deserve her. Billy deserved what he got."

Jenny tried to hold back her surprise at his confession. She was trying to make sense of his ramblings. It was all too much. It was almost more than she could take, but she had to get the whole story. "What about Phil and Cara Carson? Jim Grant? How come they had to die? I'm assuming you did that."

Corbin Sims got a pensive look on his face. "Ah yes. The beautiful Cara and that husband of hers. Phil was getting too close to figuring out what was going on, so I sent his ex partner to take care of him. I told him to make it look like a suicide, but he bungled that didn't he? His wife, Cara had to die because she had gone through all of that paperwork that Carson had accumulated. Even if she didn't understand what she was see- ing, I couldn't let her live. I thought the fire was a nice touch. I was growing fond of fire." His mind wandered for a moment before he got back on track. "Then Jim Grant. I wanted to kill him myself, but I don't dirty my own hands. I bribed a guard to take care of him. I'm afraid that's all I can tell you. I have already said too much to the police. But if I have to go down, so is everyone else. No one is running the show without me there. There will be a lot of heads rolling in the days to come."

Jenny couldn't believe her ears. "I have just one more question. The ring we found on my mom's grave. How did you get it off her finger? I know it was in her casket."

"That was easy. I knew that Billy was going to the funeral, so I had him bring me back a little keepsake. He said it was a piece of cake. Now Jenny dear, please say that you will come and visit me in prison. I have to see you. Oh, and please continue to take yellow roses to your mother's grave for me. She loves them so much." Corbin reached out and tried to grab Jenny's hands, but the shackles held him back. "Please, Jenny. Promise me you'll come back."

Jenny cringed, and jumped back when he tried to touch her. "I will never see you again after this, you monster. May you rot in hell!" With that, she pushed her chair back, and walked out the door with her head held high. She collapsed into her father's arms when she got outside the room. Jake held her tight, and the group of Longs walked out of the jail, relieved that it was finally over.

• • •

Jake and Jen rode high up on the hills overlooking the ranch. It was their favorite spot. Dismounting, they let the horses graze, as they stood arm in arm. Jenny lay her head on her dad's chest. She looked up at the sky, the sun brightly shining. Just a few clouds trying to cover up the blue sky.

"Dad, I hope that Mom doesn't leave me for good. It has helped me cope with everything that has happened. Knowing that she is watching over me has kept me sane."

"I know that if she has any say in it she will be talking to you. But if she is done with what she came back to do, she will never be gone Jen. Sara will always be with you, right here in your heart."

• • •

www.ingramcontent.com/pod-product-compliance
Lightning Source LLC
Chambersburg PA
CBHW061018120726
47910CB00006B/2000